# That Last Carolina Summer

# *That Last Carolina Summer*

## A NOVEL

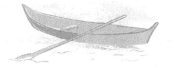

# KAREN WHITE

PARK
ROW
BOOKS

PARK
ROW
BOOKS™

ISBN-13: 978-0-7783-1069-3

That Last Carolina Summer

Park Row Books
22 Adelaide St. West, 41st Floor
Toronto, Ontario M5H 4E3, Canada

**Printed in U.S.A.**

To my mother.

*Hope is the thing with feathers*
*That perches in the soul,*
*And sings the tune without the words,*
*And never stops at all.*

−EMILY DICKINSON

# Prologue

~

## *Phoebe*

*2001*

MEMORY IS A disloyal friend, an unreliable narrator whose motivations are not always benign. There are some things about that summer I remember with absolute clarity: the scalp-scorching heat; my dog, Bailey, getting hit by a car; getting my ears pierced. Yet other events are charred around the edges, obscuring my view when I peer through the lens of hindsight and with the longing for a life that was never meant to be mine.

That summer seemed to linger longer than most, with stories of cars overheating and people dropping from heatstroke the subject of front porch and grocery store conversations. Dogs didn't venture past the shady boundaries made from giant magnolias and river birch trees, and the scalded leaves on our azaleas turned brown. Mother and Daddy stopped talking about how hot it was, as if naming it would summon the devil.

I spent most of August out on the water hoping for a reprieve in the form of a good breeze, wishing some temporary, but nonetheless debilitating, disease would befall me while I dreaded the waning days of freedom until the first day of school.

Which is how I found myself squatting at the end of our dock on that scorching hot August afternoon mentally flipping through the list of possible afflictions I'd accumulated while reading the library's collection of *World Book Encyclopedia*. My preoccupation with weird diseases would explain why I wasn't paying as much attention to the weather that afternoon as I should have been. And why I ignored Mother's often repeated warning to be careful what I wished for.

My bare feet on the dock were impervious to the uneven planks and loose splinters as I checked my crab pots and thought about lunch. I was always thinking about food. Mother had put me on another diet, something none of my nine-year-old peers knew anything about.

Mother was a former Miss South Carolina, with Standards and Rules that my older sister, Adeline, and I forgot to our peril. Not that Addie ever needed a reminder. But I found crabbing and fishing a better use of my time than practicing how to walk in high heels.

I'd been left to my own devices while they went for another fitting for Addie's Peach Queen pageant dress, leaving me under the loose supervision of my aunt Sassy. As a single woman with no kids of her own, my aunt understood better than most the importance of letting children be children. She was also profoundly deaf, which made things easier for a growing girl who loved the wild freedom that existed outside her back door.

A blue heron perched on its long, skinny legs at the edge of the water, waiting for an unlucky snack to swim by, its cold yellow eyes pretending not to see me. I wasn't offended, having grown used to being ignored, and had long since discovered that I thrived under the lack of attention. Otherwise, I'd be at

Gwyn's department store getting squeezed into a satin and tulle nightmare and being forced to suck in my tummy.

The wind blew the bird's straggly white plume on top of its head, ruffling the feathers on its S-shaped neck. The light blue painted bird feeder I'd made in Bible camp for Aunt Sassy swung in the strong breeze, thunking against the oak tree's trunk. It was only one of about a dozen feeders filled daily by my bird-loving aunt but now unusually abandoned by the chatter of finches and other songbirds.

I dropped an empty pot back into the water and looked up at a quarreling flock of royal terns with their bright orange beaks and forked tails skimming low over the water instead of their usual hunting position high in the sky. I straightened, for the first time noticing the opaque wall-like cloud with the flat bottom hovering over us like a spaceship.

Birds were better forecasters than the weather people on television, and it was my own fault for not paying attention. According to Aunt Sassy, birds didn't need mathematical calculations to predict the weather, and they were always right. Which is why I never took offense when Addie called me a birdbrain.

The first growl of thunder made me think of lunch again. I pulled up the second crab pot, frowning at the untouched raw chicken necks I'd used as bait, aware again of the statuesque bird. It twisted its long and slender neck to turn its head in the direction of the disappearing terns. With a great swoop of blue-tinged feathers, the heron lifted into the air and raced inland. I watched it disappear as I became aware of the peculiar hush around me. Behind the rustling grass and moving water the deafening absence of bird sounds roared in my ears.

I turned at the squeak of the back screen door's hinges. Aunt Sassy stood in the doorway, her face scrunched in worry as she glanced up at the darkening sky. She signaled with urgent hand gestures that I needed to come inside quickly.

I signed to her to let her know I'd understood, realizing she must have felt the rumble of thunder. A jagged bolt of lightning pierced the marsh in the near distance. I began counting the seconds—*one Mississippi, two Mississippi, three Mississippi*—just like Aunt Sassy had taught me, walking sideways to keep an eye on the sky and the wooden boards at the same time so I wouldn't slip off.

My toes brushed the edge of the dock where it met the prickly Spartina grass of the yard as I struggled with recently learned third-grade math. *Count the number of seconds between the lightning flash and the sound of the thunder and then divide by five to get the distance to the lightning.*

"One Mississippi . . ."

The humid air crackled and snapped like thousands of ghost crabs, lifting my hair from root to end and shooting a tingling sensation tumbling up my bones. The sky burst open, and I started to run. A powerful punch struck me in the middle of my back, stealing my breath and knocking me onto my stomach.

Everything went dark, and I knew that meant I must be dead. Except I was aware of the spiky grass under my cheek, and the pelting of chilly rain on my bare arms and legs, and the briny smell of the marsh. But the familiar pulse of blood in my ears had disappeared. I was like a bug caught under a china cup. A vague sense of disappointment washed over me as I figured that this must be all there was to know about death, regardless of what Reverend Bostwick told us every Sunday.

A shout, a boy's voice, came from somewhere. Far away at first and then up close. My elbows smacked the ground as hands flipped me over like a beached dolphin. I tried to open my eyes, but they only fluttered, revealing a rotating screen of solid gray and white.

Then the boy's voice again, shouting for someone to call 9-1-1. Rain splattered my body but not my face, as if something was blocking me from the deluge. I heard a sound of rustling like fabric against wet wood next to my ear, and what felt like a rock began pounding rhythmically against my chest again and again, my body ignoring all my commands to get up and run.

Cold, wet fingers pinched my nose closed then tilted my head back, my hair tugging my scalp as my ponytail rubbed against the ground. I wanted the boy to stop, to go away, because a gray-and-white world was better than this unprovoked beating.

Then a warm breath was blown into my mouth once. Twice. My eyes flickered open, and a face appeared above me, the angry sky behind it forming an imperfect halo. My gray-and-white vision burst into full color. Startling green eyes the same shade as the marsh in August peered down at me, and I wondered if Reverend Bostwick had been right after all.

The boy sat back, and my eyes focused on the shark's tooth he wore on a leather cord around his neck. My chest expanded with an involuntary intake of air then shrank again as a piercing pain cut through my consciousness. I gasped for breath, my skin and bones aching as the reassuring beat of my heart again rumbled within my head. An approaching siren melded into the noise of the rain and the wind and the sound of Sassy's bird feeders crashing into each other as my eyes followed the boy.

"She's going to be okay," he said to someone I couldn't see. His words cracked from exertion or because he was at that age when boys and their voices got stuck between childhood and manhood. I didn't recognize him, most likely on account of me attending a private girls' school in Charleston and not being around boys in general.

Soft hands cupped my face. I gazed up at Aunt Sassy, at her mute agony as she knelt beside me, stroking my face again and again like I was Lazarus raised from the dead. The boy stood as the sound of shouting men neared. He turned toward the house, his shirtless arms and torso bronzed by the sun, his wild bleached-blond hair longer than Mother or Daddy would approve of.

Aunt Sassy bowed her head over mine to kiss my forehead, and when she lifted it again, the boy was gone. I only learned his first name much later, but I remembered his eyes and the way the color matched the summer marsh. That day became the line of demarcation where the before of my life intersected with the after, and his appearance in it an unwelcome reminder of all I had lost.

They say that lightning never strikes twice. Which is understandable considering the odds are one in about fifteen thousand of being struck once in a lifetime. They also say that if you survive a lightning strike, you will have no memory of it.

But, as I've learned from experience, both are just the lies we tell ourselves. Like the platitudes a mother might use to soothe a scared child, we cling to myths and other assurances so we can sleep at night.

That doesn't make them the truth.

# 1

*~*

"The homing instinct in birds and animals is one of their most remarkable traits: their strong local attachments and their skill in finding their way back when removed to a distance. It seems at times as if they possessed some extra sense—the home sense—which operates unerringly."

**—John Burroughs**
**From the blog *The Thing with Feathers***

# *Phoebe*

*2025*

MY PHONE RANG at five fifteen in the morning. I'd fallen asleep on the couch, having convinced myself the night before that I would just close my eyes for a moment before getting up to get ready for bed.

I blinked, waiting for the phone to ring again so I could locate it in the cushions of the couch, gradually becoming aware of the soft voices on the television that I'd forgotten to turn off. Bette Davis's black-and-white face was saying something to Henry Fonda in a passable Southern accent.

I recognized a scene from the movie *Jezebel*, a favorite classic I watched countless times with Aunt Sassy during my adolescence and her battle with pancreatic cancer. At the time, both afflictions had made everything seem untenable except for the Turner Classic Movies channel and benne wafers from Olde Colony Bakery. I had managed to outgrow my adolescence, but Sassy's cancer remained intractable no matter what the doctors did or how many times I promised God I'd be the daughter my mother wanted me to be if He would only make my aunt better.

My phone rang again as I patted the cushions around me. The random thought struck me that Sassy and I had never watched *Jezebel* or any other movie with the captions turned on. Maybe Sassy's lipreading abilities were better than she'd let on, or maybe she believed it wasn't always necessary to hear what people were saying to understand everything you needed to know.

I stood, the movement revealing my phone's hiding place by shifting it from my lap onto the floor. My sister's name and number appeared on the screen, momentarily paralyzing me. Addie and I hadn't had a real conversation since our father's funeral nearly ten years before, and never on the phone. Even now we only interacted once a year during the awkward Christmases at the house in Mount Pleasant, South Carolina, where we'd grown up.

It hadn't always been that way between us. Despite having enough bedrooms in our family home, we'd insisted on sharing a room. She was my ally against our mother's constant attempts to civilize me, and I was Addie's alibi on the occasions when she escaped our parents' supervision.

But like all things of childhood, we'd slipped off those skins like outgrown clothes. I don't remember exactly when it happened, but by the time I reached high school, Addie had moved to her own room, and my sister became a stranger to me. I had lost my ally, but I remained loyal, hiding her increasingly wild escapades from our parents in the futile hope that she would remove her mask and become my sister again.

I continued to stare at the screen, waiting for it to go to voice mail. Instead, it rang again. I picked up the phone without answering and carried it to the kitchen, knowing that I would need coffee first before dealing with whatever Addie had to say.

The coffee canister sat in the middle of the counter, its lid hinged to the open position to remind me that I was out of coffee and that I needed to go to the grocery store. *Damn.* I took a deep breath. "Hello?"

My sister exhaled loudly, every ounce of her breath weighted with anger, annoyance, and the superiority only older siblings can manage. "It's about time, Phoebe. Why can't you just answer your phone like a normal person?"

I let the barb vibrate in its target before mentally dislodging it. "Wow. That was quick, even by your standards. I'm doing well. Thanks for asking. What about you?"

She didn't bother responding, her usual form of dismissal. Instead, she said, "Have you spoken with Mother?"

A surprising and unwelcome scattershot of varying emotions peppered my insides. "No. Should I have?"

I heard our mother's voice in the background, calling Adeline's name with growing agitation. "I'll be right there, Mother," Addie called, her muffled voice followed by the sound of a door quietly clicking shut.

"Addie?" I asked.

"I'm here, I'm here. You need to come home, Phoebe. Right now."

A heavy mixture of dread and worry congealed in my stomach. "Why? What's wrong?"

"It's Mother. She got lost driving to Home Depot for Christmas lights, and the police called me at work to come get her."

I thought for a moment, letting that sink in. "But it's only May. Why was she buying Christmas lights?"

"That's my point, Phoebe." Her voice sounded even more agitated than before, and I wondered what I was missing.

"Okay," I said slowly. My eyes drifted to the clock on the microwave. If I didn't hurry, I'd be late for work, and I hated to be a bad example for the eighth-grade students I taught at the science academy. "Maybe there was a Christmas in July sale. Was it at night? You know how she's never had a good sense of direction and can't see at night. I'm guessing the police overreacted when one of them told her she shouldn't be driving." I walked toward the bathroom, shedding my clothes along the way.

"It's more than that. Last week, she forgot to pick up my daughter after school."

"Maybe she thought you were supposed to do it?"

"No, Phoebe. Mother always picks up Ophelia. Always. It's her job."

I felt the first stab of worry but pushed it aside. It seemed like the unfolding of one of Addie's many minidramas she seemed to enjoy inflicting on the rest of us and nothing at all to do with our mother. I expected Mother to take the phone from Addie at any moment and tell her to act like a lady and stop being so dramatic.

"I'm sure she was out shopping and forgot the time. She was always late for school pickup, remember?"

"You need to come home. Now." She screamed the last word, which solidified my opinion that she was being dramatic and that it was most likely all about an argument she'd had with our mother.

I turned on the shower, knowing she could hear the water hitting the tile. "Look, I've got to go or I'll be late for work." I wanted to tell her that today was the first day of the science fair and as the lead teacher I was in charge, but I didn't bother.

"You have no idea what my life is like." I heard the studied control in her voice, the steadied breathing. She was angry. I was an expert on reading people, but especially my only sibling. I'd grown used to living in her shadow, allowing me ample opportunity to study and observe, to learn where to find her vulnerable spots.

Maybe that was the thing between sisters: knowing exactly where to aim the arrow. We rarely missed. When I was seven and Addie nine, she'd convinced me that the reason I looked so different from the rest of the family was because I'd been found in an osprey's nest as a baby and our parents adopted me out of pity.

I was a teenager when I realized that being adopted wouldn't be so bad if it meant that maybe my real family was out there looking for me. That was the faint hope I'd carried with me through my twenties until in a stupid moment fueled by too much New Years' Eve champagne, I'd confessed my dream to Addie. Her expression of ridicule had extinguished that small glimmer of possibility that maybe somewhere, I belonged to anyone else.

Addie inhaled sharply. "I took her to her doctor, and after, when she was putting her clothes back on, she put her dress on backward with the open zipper in front. Fortunately, she wore a slip, but still. She should have been mortified—I certainly was. Anyway, he wants her to see a neurologist."

"A neurologist," I repeated. I sat down on the edge of the tub, suddenly feeling ill. "Oh, no." I kept the water running, billowing steam now filling the room and obscuring my reflection in the cracked mirror over the sink.

I'd last seen my mother two Christmases ago. While selecting wineglasses to place on the dining table, I'd noticed my mother's prized Waterford crystal barware covered in a heavy layer of dust. It was more than just a single week of the housekeeper's forgetfulness. It looked like the shelves and glasses hadn't been touched for months. In the past, Mother always gave a thorough inspection after our housekeeper, Patricia, had cleaned and would let her know if something wasn't up to Mother's standards.

Those dusty glasses were the equivalent of Mother leaving her slip exposed in a public place. I'd been eager to head back to the West Coast and didn't want to find a reason to extend my visit and so had brushed my thoughts aside, thinking of dozens of reasons to explain the lapse.

"Yes," Addie continued. "The neurologist will need to run some tests."

"When is the appointment?" I asked, the feelings of animosity toward my sister subsiding.

"I didn't make one," she snapped. "You get the whole summer off, so it would make sense if you could spend it here."

I thought of my summer plans of learning to cook. Of hiking in the Cascades with some of my fellow teachers. Of finally starting a blog containing all the bird wisdom I'd learned from Aunt Sassy. Returning to the place I'd worked so hard to get away from was not anywhere on the list. "Look," I said. "Mother will be seventy this year. It seems to me that small memory lapses are a normal part of aging and—"

"Those aren't *small memory lapses*, Phoebe. And seventy isn't even considered old anymore. I need you to do this. I'm working a lot of night shifts now. Plus, I have Ophelia." She added her daughter almost as an afterthought.

I stared in the mirror, my eyes round dark smudges staring back at me like some nameless monster. I pictured my beautiful mother, her hair and makeup always perfect, even first thing in the morning. Addie looked just like her. I was as different in coloring as I was in temperament from our mother. I'd been happy to relinquish all maternal affections to my older sister.

"It can't be as bad as it seems." I wasn't certain if I was trying to reassure Addie or myself. "You know she's always dieting—that can affect her cognitive abilities. After school ends, I can come home for a week or so to help out. But I already have plans for the summer. And I've been asked to cover one of the summer classes, which I agreed to because I could use the money. Someone has to pay my mortgage."

The dig had been intentional. After a brief foray into broadcast journalism following college, Addie had returned to our parents' house unemployed, pregnant, and single for what was supposed to be a temporary arrangement. Ten years later, she was still there. Addie had never remained employed for long, which meant I was pretty sure she didn't pay for rent or food, and she definitely didn't pay for Ophelia's tuition.

Addie's voice rose a notch. "She's your mother, too."

The words came out before I could hold them back. "But you're her favorite."

She sucked in her breath, meaning I had hit my mark. "Don't be childish, Phoebe. I'm asking for your help with *our* mother. You're acting like your stupid job is more important than she is. You've always been that way, acting like Mother is an afterthought. No wonder I'm her favorite. I at least give her love and attention, two things you don't seem capable of."

I felt chastised and angry. Everything she'd said had a grain of truth embedded inside vague inaccuracies that I didn't have the time to unearth right then. "Look, Addie," I said with a conciliatory tone. "School's out in a couple of weeks—"

"Adeline!" Mother's voice came through the phone, accompanied by pounding. "Open this door right this minute or I'm going to get your father." She never raised her voice, even when Addie had failed so spectacularly or when my dog, Bailey, had eaten her prized heirloom roses. She didn't need to. The threat of our father was enough to make us repent. Except he'd been dead for years.

I squeezed my phone, the edges digging into my palm, and listened to my sister's tight, shallow breaths.

"I. Can't. Handle. This." Addie's voice rose to a shrill scream.

I held the phone away from my ear and clenched my eyes shut, trying to block out the unwelcome reminder of my childhood, the feeling of helplessness and resentment knotted together and impossible to untangle. Ever since I could remember, checking out had been Adeline's method of handling all negative emotions and events. It focused all the attention on her as people stumbled over themselves trying to figure out how to fix whatever might be bothering her.

I'd grown to believe that this was a flaw of beautiful people: they didn't need to be clever or funny or emotionally grounded to survive. The rest of us had to forage for what genetic scraps had been left behind, and sometimes we found what we needed to survive and sometimes even to flourish.

The call ended. I waited for Addie to call back, to tell me she was sorry she'd overreacted, that of course she'd take care of things and we could discuss when I visited after school ended. And then I could feel that she had everything under control and didn't need my help. My extraneous existence as the younger sister had been one of the reasons why I'd fled across the country to Oregon. Just not the biggest reason.

But she didn't call back, and a growing unease about my mother and what might be going on with her took up residence in my head. I quickly showered and dressed before returning to the kitchen. Despite not being hungry, I grabbed a granola bar to sustain me through first period with a classroom full of students. I stood at the sink to eat, looking out the large picture window, the one selling point to the 1970s duplex. It framed a view of the distant Cascade Mountains surrounding my adopted home of Bend, Oregon, where I'd escaped as soon as I had my masters. Teaching eighth-grade science had been my first job offer, and I took it for the main reason that it was far enough away from South Carolina. Away from where I was known as the girl who'd been struck by lightning and left with scars I couldn't hide.

The Deschutes River that flowed through Bend bore no resemblance to the waterways of the Lowcountry, the sights and scents of the high desert as foreign to me as the moon. I'd hoped in time I'd forget the fragrant wax myrtles or the call of the night herons over the marsh and the smell of the pluff mud at low tide.

Nine years later, I was still pretending that I was better here, that the shapes of mountains nudging the gray skies were an adequate substitute for the flat horizon of watery savannas, that I didn't miss the wraithlike arms of Spanish moss that was as cold-intolerant as I seemed to be. I'd hoped to grow to love the smell of snow before it fell. And I had. But all my new experiences were like a borrowed coat: offering warmth but with pockets empty of the small treasures from past seasons.

A goldfinch landed on the feeder hanging on the high branch of a western juniper. It was the same feeder I'd made for Aunt Sassy, the wooden sides and roof faded and warped from too many South Carolina summers. I'd replaced parts and repainted it over the years, and it had come with me to college and grad school, and then across the country. I always forgot to fill it, and then felt bad when a bird landed on it and regarded me with judgment like the goldfinch was doing now.

I squinted, recalling what Sassy had told me about gold-finches. They mated for life, shared nesting duties, and migrated together, side by side. They were happy, chatty birds and usually congregated in what was called a *charm*. But this bird was by itself, watching me through the window.

I pulled out the bag of seed from a cabinet and took it outside. The yellow bird flew to a higher branch but continued to keep a watchful eye while I poured out the remaining contents from the bag.

Wild birds always reminded me of the remarkable woman who loved nature even though she couldn't hear the croaking frogs or singing birds or anything else the rest of us took for granted. I don't know what it was Aunt Sassy heard when we stood in the backyard near sunset and watched the wrens and sparrows sweeping down from the dusky sky to feed, but from the rapt look on her face, I imagined it was a full symphony orchestra playing Mozart or Rachmaninoff or the soundtrack from some huge blockbuster film. She knew how to make the smallest things important and beautiful.

I still felt guilt at the memory of pretending to be bored listening to Sassy's bird stories, careful not to be noticed showing an interest by my sister or her friends. It didn't help that I'd been named after a bird. Unlike the name Adeline, Phoebe appears nowhere on our family tree. My father told me that an eastern phoebe had perched on a tree branch outside Mother's hospital window after I was born, and she loved its bright, two-pitched song.

But Adeline said the name was given to me because of Mother's disappointment at having another girl, so she had named me after the little bird of unremarkable coloring with its plump body and large head because it reminded her of me. I never asked my mother which was true, mostly because I was afraid of her answer.

I crumpled up the empty seed bag and waited for the little yellow bird to return to the feeder, recalling something my aunt had told me about how the appearance of a goldfinch is meant as an encouragement to travel to new places, to let people see your beauty and the true you.

An unexpected wave of grief blew through me, and I found myself wishing, just for a moment, that I could believe it was my aunt's soul sending me a message that my mother would be okay and that I would know what to do if she wasn't. But the goldfinch remained on his perch out of my reach until he fluttered his wings and flew away.

# 2

"The male goldfinch's bright vibrant yellow fades to a muted
olive brown in the fall just as the female's brightens. My mother
used to say that to force a cheerful mood, wear a bright
sweater. Not quite the same as a bird's feathers changing for
the season, but it's a worthy effort on our part for effecting
something that Mother Nature omitted from our survival skills."

**Excerpt from the blog *The Thing with Feathers***

## Phoebe

THE OLD DREAM returned to me the night before I left for
Charleston. It's always the same. A lone car on a two-lane bridge
straddles the double lines, moving quickly toward the other side.
The sun has already set, but the sky still glows with the memory
of light. Heavy clouds block the moon, and the asphalt shines
with fallen rain collecting in the dips and hollows of the road.
I don't know this bridge, but the uneven pavement and broken
wooden side rails could be any bridge over any creek in this
corner of South Carolina. It's too dark to see the water, but the
briny scent and the scream of a night heron tell me I'm not far
from home.

Two people sit in the front. I can't make out their faces or
anything about them except I know that something's not right.
My chest constricts as the car swings too close to the side of the
bridge, scraping along the side rails with a demonic squeal, and
then overcorrects with the screech of tires. The passenger grabs

the steering wheel, but I can see it's too late. That what has been put in motion can't be reversed.

The side of the bridge collapses from the impact, offering little resistance as the vehicle crashes through the opening and plummets into the water. I don't see it go in, but I hear the splash, so I know what's happened. I wait, suspended in the dream world where I'm a passive witness despite how loud I scream. But it's useless. What's happened is already past. I can't stop it. All I can do is wait and see.

A dark shiny head emerges, the hair color masked by the twilight sky and the soaking water. I wait for the second head to appear, mutely observing the single head duck back under the surface. I hold my breath, listening as my heartbeat grows louder in my ears with each passing second until the single head reappears and dives beneath two more times before breaking the surface one last time. I feel their weariness as they continue to tread water, sensing the fear of unseen creatures that lurk in the waterways of the Lowcountry.

I taste sediment and salt in my mouth as the head involuntarily dips in the water, feeling my own muscles go slack, each limb a leaden weight. With a final burst of energy, the person flips onto their back with their face turned toward the sky and begins slowly paddling with flattened palms toward the bank where rocks glow like skulls.

Pale hands climb the incline, fingers and feet slipping on the rain-soaked rocks before the person collapses at the place where the grass meets the road. I feel the nauseating combination of fear and grief bubbling in my own stomach as the survivor vomits into the grass. The rain has stopped, leaving behind the crying of a million insects and the haunting scream of a nightjar.

Slowly then, crawling then standing, they stagger to the road. They glance back at the inky-black water with a stab of loss and regret that I feel down to my bones. Then they walk across the bridge, avoiding the open maw of the railing, until the night swallows the person, and the road and creek are now silent with a secret kept.

The lightning strike I'd sustained when I was nine years old scarred me with a purple vinelike mark that crept up my spine before curving over my left shoulder like a snake. This was the scar others could see. The reoccurring dream was the other scar, the one I couldn't hide with makeup or cover with a shawl. Its presence hovered on the other side of my consciousness, a relic from when I was brought back to life by a boy with marsh-green eyes. I kept this vision to myself, pretending that it would go away if I didn't talk about it, always afraid that if I stared too long at the unknown survivor, I might see my own face.

Ever since my near-death experience, my dreams were often interrupted with premonitions, but none as terrifying as the recurring nightmare, and always containing faces I recognized. I'd seen a classmate in a cast with crutches before she'd had a skiing accident, and I saw my sister wearing a crown before she won Peach Queen. My ability to see into the future became my special power at an age when I was too young to know that being different was worse than being invisible.

I became Addie's show-and-tell for her friends, an endless party trick she never grew tired of. I welcomed my newfound celebrity status and relished being showered with Addie's attention again, at least until I overheard my mother telling a friend that my notoriety had become her greatest embarrassment and she hoped that it was just a phase that would go away, like a cold or a case of chicken pox.

I eventually learned to keep my visions to myself. Addie stopped asking me to join her and her friends, and I was once again left alone. But the dream of the car and the bridge never left me, appearing sporadically enough that at times I thought it had stopped. It hadn't. It was only once I'd moved across the country that I believed I'd finally escaped it and the other premonition dreams that had interrupted my sleep since the day I'd almost died. Which was one of the reasons why I resisted returning home to the place where I knew the bridge existed and where my dream at any moment could become real.

Yet no matter how many times I've seen the accident, I still can't see the faces of the two passengers. Nor do I know if the accident is in the past or still to happen. And I'm not sure which scenario scares me more.

The night before I left for Charleston, I'd slept on my couch, having anticipated the dream, yet been delusional enough to believe I might avoid it by not sleeping in my bed. But the certainty of my return to South Carolina overrode my safeguard, and the dream seized me with startling clarity as if I'd just experienced it for the first time.

My friend and school nurse Holly McCormick drove me to the airport, promising to keep birdseed in my feeder during my absence. She and her husband were having their kitchen and bathrooms renovated and would be staying in my house and paying rent, which eased some of my financial worries.

I pressed my forehead against the airplane window as we approached the Charleston airport, watching as the watery landscape beneath me separated into landmasses embraced by tidal creeks and rivers of home.

I'd told Addie that I'd arrive Monday around five o'clock but not any specific flight information. I didn't want to set myself up for disappointment if she didn't show up. I made my way to baggage claim, suddenly aware of my rumpled appearance. In the casual atmosphere of the Pacific Northwest, I'd long since forgotten where my clothes steamer and iron were. My mother had always kept one or the other in the front hall cabinet just in case we needed touch-ups before heading out the door. They were as foreign to me now as hairspray and Spanx.


"Hello, Birdbrain."

I looked up to see my sister. She was a head taller than me and still as slender as a blade of sweetgrass. She wore a Lilly Pulitzer sundress that showed off her tanned legs, the pale green color of the cotton material the same shade as her eyes. Her arms were covered with a long-sleeved cardigan, something I'd never seen her wear in the summertime. Wavy strawberry-blond hair was piled on top of her head in a perfect messy bun, and around her neck lay a fine gold chain with a black pearl pendant from Croghan's Jewel Box.

Our parents had given the necklace to Addie for her sixteenth birthday. She'd lost it sometime during her senior year, but it had been quickly replaced because Mother claimed it was Addie's lucky charm whenever she wore it in pageants. The new pendant was missing the small diamond that perched at the top of the pearl like the original, but it still looked stunning on Addie's long, elegant neck.

"Hey, Addie," I said, aware of the attention focused on us. Addie had always attracted attention just by breathing. I'd long ago realized that my nonchalance about what I looked like annoyed her almost as much as my lack of the adulation she was used to from everyone else.

We stared at each other as if daring the other to make the first move. Our family had never been big on shows of physical affection, so I wasn't expecting a hug. She kept her arms crossed as she examined me. Before I could say anything else, she moved aside to reveal my niece, Ophelia, who'd been standing behind her mother. In the year and a half since my last visit, she hadn't grown much taller, and she still wore her baby fat in her face that made her look much younger than her nine years. Large round glasses sat perched on her nose, lending her face a cute owlish look.

Addie gently pushed her toward me. "Say hello to your aunt Phoebe."

"Hello," she said, keeping her gaze down.

I wanted to crouch down to look in her face but had to remind myself that she was nine and wouldn't want to be treated like a little kid. "Hello, Ophelia. Thanks for coming to welcome me back. Did you drive?" When she was younger, she'd enjoyed the ludicrous alongside me, both of us laughing at the same silly books and television shows. I was relieved when she smiled and met my eyes.

"No," she said softly. "Mama did."

Her light brown hair had been pulled back into a sloppy ponytail, leading me to believe she'd done it herself. It needed a wash and had lumps throughout as if it hadn't been brushed. But I could see the golden highlights of sun-lightened strands, making me imagine how pretty it must look when it was clean. She wore a matching Lilly Pulitzer sundress and white Tory Burch sandals, but that's where the resemblance to her mother ended. Her eyes were brown with a touch of green and flanked by thick black lashes and highlighted by her smooth olive skin. Freckles dotted her nose and cheekbones, and when she smiled, I saw that a front tooth was chipped on a corner. That bit of imperfection probably drove my mother insane.

A necklace hung on her neck, too, the gold-colored chain tarnished and the blue enamel paint of the little bird flaking. She saw me looking at it and reached up to clasp it. "It's the bluebird of happiness," she said.

"I know. My aunt Sassy gave it to me when I was about your age. But don't worry, you can keep it. I haven't thought about it for years." I felt a small pang at the memory, the loss of the necklace reminding me of the absence of my aunt.

"You left it in your jewelry box in your dresser when you left," Addie said. "We didn't change out the furniture or anything else when we moved Ophelia into your old room last year."

I met Addie's eyes. "I didn't know."

She shrugged. "You made it clear this isn't your home anymore, and Ophelia's old room was too small, so it made sense."

I felt a surge of anger, not at Addie or Ophelia but for all the reasons why I'd had to exile myself from everything I'd known and loved.

"Sure," I said, relieved to see my small suitcase appearing on the baggage belt.

"Is that all you brought?" Addie asked.

"It's all I need. I'm only here for a couple of months. I'm assuming we still have a washing machine."

"Of course we do. We also kept all your clothes in your closet." She gave me a critical look. "Are you the same size?"

"I have no idea. I don't shop, and I don't own a scale."

She grinned, and she looked so much like the sister I'd once known that I couldn't help but smile back. "That's not natural, Phoebe." Turning to lead the way outside toward the parking lot, she said, "I knew you were from outer space."

I hoisted my bag, and Ophelia and I ran to keep up, following Addie to the parking garage. She hit a button on a key fob, and the back trunk lid of a Lincoln sedan raised for me to put my suitcase inside. "This might have to go in the back seat," I said, staring at the multiple packages of toilet paper and four plastic grocery bags containing milk, browned lettuce, plastic-covered packages of gray meat, and a gallon of ice cream with its contents spilling down the sides. The smell of rotting food rolled out toward us and Ophelia and I stepped back.

Addie just stared inside the trunk, her lips pressed together. "I wondered what that smell was." Then she hit a button and closed the trunk before heading to the driver's door.

I stayed by the back of the car. "Shouldn't we throw out the food? There's probably a garbage can somewhere."

"I've got to get to work. You can throw it out once we get home."

"Sure," I said, opening up one of the back doors and tossing in my bag.

The lingering smell of tobacco smoke mixed with the faint stench of rotting food greeted me as we piled into the navy blue Lincoln. Addie briefly lowered all four windows and blasted the AC. Despite the car being in covered parking, it was broiling inside, making my scalp sweat as I sat down in the passenger seat.

Mother got a new car every other year—always the same make and model and always navy blue because she considered it an elegant and understated color. Addie and I had tried to get her to try a lighter color, but our mother was as intractable as a dog with a bone. As I'd grown older, I realized her refusal to budge had less to do with color and more to do with admitting that she might be wrong.

I pointed to a box of Virginia Slims on the dashboard. "Those yours?"

Addie gave me a side glance then put the car in Reverse without saying anything. I'd known before asking that they were hers. Our mother considered cigarettes tacky and unladylike and said they caused wrinkles around the lips, which is why Addie had hidden her nasty habit since she was a teenager.

"I quit for a while, but . . ." She glanced in the rearview mirror at Ophelia.

I turned and saw Ophelia reading *Pride and Prejudice*, the same dog-eared copy that I'd left on my bookshelf when I'd fled to the West Coast.

Addie redirected her attention to the road ahead then reached for the pack. "I quit for a while, started again when Mother started acting strangely. You have no idea what I've been going through." She tapped one out then stuck a cigarette between her lips before lighting it. She inhaled deeply before tilting back her head and exhaling.

"You've got a kid in the car, Addie. Have you never heard of secondhand smoke?" I waved my hand in front of my face then stopped when I realized how passive-aggressive that sounded.

In response, she lowered her car window and took another drag then turned on the car stereo to a rap station, raising the volume enough to discourage conversation. I took a quick look into the back seat where Ophelia appeared not to have noticed, her attention still on the book.

Lowering the volume, I attempted to make peace with my sister. "You look good, Addie. Life must be treating you well. Are you dating anyone?"

She blew smoke out of the corner of her mouth in the direction of her window and grinned. "Depends on how you define *dating*." She glanced in the rearview mirror again. "Let's just say I like to keep my options open."

"Never mind," I said then leaned forward and raised the radio volume.

We headed out onto I-26 for the short drive, just long enough for me to prepare myself and get my bearings. As we climbed the Ravenel Bridge, with Charleston's church spires behind us and the sprawling town of Mount Pleasant in front, I felt something like heartbreak, like I'd lost something valuable and didn't know where to find it.

"What's wrong?" Addie shouted over the roar of the wind from her window.

"Nothing. Why?"

"You're crying."

"No, I'm not." I rubbed my eyes with the backs of my hands, feeling the telltale wetness against my skin. "It's your cigarette smoke. It stings my eyes."

She stabbed her cigarette into the ashtray then flicked it out the open window before closing it.

We rode the rest of the way in silence, exiting the bridge and heading into the heart of the Old Village of Mount Pleasant. Even though the windows were up, I imagined I could smell the nearby Atlantic Ocean and the saltwater marshes that surrounded this corner of the world. My new home in Oregon was less than two hundred miles from the Pacific, but I'd only seen it once in the hope that it would remind me of home. It hadn't. The only similarities between the two coastlines were that they each abutted an ocean and were filled with sand. I'd stood on the beach, feeling the shifting sand beneath my feet and felt a longing like grief. I hadn't gone back.

The Old Village had been laid out in an irregular grid pattern to allow for the eccentricities of the surrounding water that borrowed and returned parts of the coastline at the whim of the tides. Scraggly lawns were dotted with sparse tufts of grass, victims to the generous shades of old-growth trees. As a girl I'd ridden my bicycle up and down each street, grateful for the shady respite from the scorching summer sun. Every road, dock, and sunset vista was as familiar to me as the childhood scars on my arms and legs.

Addie and I had been born and raised in the same house as had our mother and our maternal grandparents and great-grandparents. Like all great Southern ladies, the Old Village had aged well, her wrinkles subtly adding to her grandeur and almost imperceptible to all except those who knew her best.

The car crunched over the broken shell driveway, the sound like a familiar friend welcoming me home. Even the heat that sucked the air out of my lungs felt more like a hug than a slap as I pushed my door open and stood facing the red-roofed house.

Our house was easily distinguishable in aerial photos of Mount Pleasant due to the distinctive hue of the hip roof and the long dock on Jeannette Creek that resembled a finger pointing toward Sullivan's Island.

Addie rolled down her window. "Hurry up, Phoebe. Grab your suitcase and close the door. I can't be late for work."

Ophelia slowly pushed open her door and slid from the seat, her head still buried in her book.

"What about the groceries? Shouldn't we take them out?"

Addie shifted the car into Reverse. "Not now. If it's slow at the restaurant, I can use one of their dumpsters."

I quickly grabbed the handle of my suitcase and had barely shut the car door before Addie backed out of her parking spot, the tires spinning on the broken shells before speeding away.

I turned to Ophelia. "Does she still work at that restaurant-bar place in Shem Creek?"

The little girl shrugged. "I don't know. Mimi says it's tacky, so we don't go there."

"I see." My stomach grumbled as I realized how long it had been since I'd eaten. I hoisted my bag and headed toward the brick walkway, noticing the peeling paint on the white picket fence that mimicked the railing on the second-floor balcony. I stopped to look up at the house, pausing just in case my mother decided to come out and greet me.

The house had been built in 1902 by a ship captain before passing it to my family shortly afterward. I'd always wanted to know the story behind the quick turnover, since as far as I knew we weren't related to the sea captain. I couldn't help but wonder if there might be something unsavory to the story.

"Come on, Ophelia," I said, climbing the porch steps. The bottom one was wider than the top giving the deep front porch a regal feel and looked like the palace steps in a Cinderella movie. When we were little girls, Addie used to pretend she was a princess walking up and down the steps while I played photographer, making her swing her hair and show off her dress.

But now the steps appeared sun-blistered and in need of sealing, the white round columns across the front in the same sad shape. Somehow the neglect didn't detract from the beauty of the house, with its pretty gabled window over the front door and the white clapboard siding that blushed in the fading light.

The color of the sky had started to shift, casting the walkway and porch into shadows. It had always been a point of pride to my mother to make her house appear welcoming to friends and strangers alike by keeping it lit at night. Yet as the supper hour approached, the outdoor lights were dark, and the ginger jar lamp in one of the front windows had not been turned on.

"I'm hungry," Ophelia said.

"Me, too," I said, forcing a smile to hide my unease. We stepped up onto the porch. "Maybe we can go out to eat."

"We don't have a car," Ophelia said quietly.

"Doesn't your mama have one?"

She shook her head. "Mama wrecked it, and it couldn't be fixed."

"Oh." I put down my suitcase and opened the screen door then turned the tarnished brass knob of the front door. I exhaled loudly when the door swung open, letting out the peculiarly comforting scent of wood polish, my mother's rose potpourri, and mothballs. Sometimes, when I'd dream of this place, I could smell the scent of home, and it always made me cry.

"Hello? Mother? It's me, Phoebe."

"What are you doing here?"

I jerked back, startled by the shrill voice that had come from the staircase. As my eyes became accustomed to the darkened foyer, I made out the form of my mother standing on the bottom step and regarding me with narrowed eyes. She wore a white nightgown, which meant she was already dressed for bed or had never put clothes on that morning.

I reached for the overhead light switch and flipped it on. "It's me," I said again. "Phoebe."

At the continued look of confusion on her face, I added, "Your daughter."

She straightened her back. "My daughter is Adeline. Who are you?"

I considered calling an Uber to take me back to the airport. There was something so lost and empty in my mother's face, and it scared me. But I couldn't turn my back on her no matter how tempting the idea. As if reading my thoughts, Ophelia moved to stand next to me.

"It's your other daughter, Mimi. You gave me her bedroom, remember?"

My mother continued to watch me through narrowed eyes, confusion now replacing suspicion. She took a step down, and I saw that her feet were bare, chipped pink polish clinging to too-long toenails. Her usual smooth blunt cut was straggly and uneven, the unwashed blond strands dulled with gray.

This person was an impostor. My mother didn't come down to breakfast without a full face of makeup and wearing heels. She had standing appointments at both her hair and nail salon so that she never appeared less than perfect. Elizabeth Manigault had always been someone to be admired and feared and in whose presence I never felt anything more than inadequate. But she was still my mother, and this impostor was not an acceptable substitution.

"Mother," I said, trying again, "it's Phoebe. Your second daughter."

Her face softened, her lips twitching before settling into a half grin. "You were supposed to be a boy."

The familiar flare of old anger shot through me, and I welcomed it. I could handle the anger. I just had no idea how to handle someone who resembled my mother but who inspired pity.

"Yes," I said. "But you got me instead."

She pursed her lips, moving them back and forth as if checking her teeth. "I think I'm hungry," she announced before stepping down into the foyer and walking toward the kitchen.

Ophelia widened her eyes and asked me, "Can you cook?"

I tugged on her hand and began following my mother. "Let's just say I know how to use a microwave."

"It's not working."

I stopped and took a deep breath. "No problem. I've got a cell phone. Do you like pizza?"

She gave me an enthusiastic nod. "Mimi doesn't let me have it because she says it will make me fat." She looked down at her feet. "But sometimes I eat it at my friend's house."

I pressed my lips together so I wouldn't say anything I'd regret and pulled my phone out of my pocket before handing it to my niece. "Please call your friend and ask her where her mom orders their pizzas. I'm going to step outside for a minute."

I walked into the kitchen where my mother sat at the small table under the window with the golden glow of the lingering summer sun settling over her. Surprise bloomed on her face as she spotted me heading toward the back door. "Phoebe! What are you doing here?"

"I'll be right back," I said. I walked past her and pushed open the screen door before running down the porch steps to the dock. I stood there sucking in the salt-tinged air and watched the sun drift farther past the horizon as I fought a rising panic. I had finally come home. Except this was a home I no longer recognized.

# 3

"The black eagle mother is known for being one of the worst parents in the animal kingdom. The eldest and strongest of her offspring will be favored over the weakest, which are often neglected. She will allow her children to fight for food and will also let the eldest bully or sometimes even kill their younger siblings before throwing them out of the nest. This instinct is necessary for the breed to survive by allowing only the strongest to survive, but it also begs the question of what other qualities are being excluded with each expulsion from the nest."

**Excerpt from the blog *The Thing with Feathers***

## *Phoebe*

I WAITED ON the front porch for my sister to come home, listening to bugs ping against the outdoor lights while drinking the last two bottles of beer I'd found in the fridge. The sweet scent of the wax myrtles that hung in the humid night air had a calming effect on me.

Ophelia pushed open the screen door, then stood in the doorway still wearing the sundress she'd worn to the airport.

"It's almost midnight, Ophelia. Shouldn't you be in bed?"

She shrugged. "I don't have a bedtime. I just go to bed when I'm tired."

I wasn't surprised that Addie would be unaware of the importance of schedules for children, but my mother would never have allowed this. At least the mother who had raised me.

I'd already fed my mother—which included cutting up her pizza into bite-size portions—and then got her into bed. This was after a struggle to change her dirty nightgown and brush her teeth. Yet I'd felt only heartache when I'd pulled back the sheets on her unmade bed and smelled the acrid scent of stale urine and had to change her bed linens. The mother I'd known would have been horrified and embarrassed, and a small part of me was almost glad that she wasn't aware of this humiliation. I'd searched her bathroom for a bag of adult diapers while she'd followed me insisting with growing anger that she didn't wear them because she didn't need them.

I was so exhausted by the time I'd drained the last beer that I didn't have the energy to put myself to bed, presumably in the guest room since Ophelia had taken over my room. If my brain had been less fried, I would have had the presence of mind to wait until morning to have a conversation with Addie, but I also knew that I wouldn't sleep anyway. The threat of having the nightmare again loomed over me, and as eager as I was to lie down and sink into oblivion, I knew that the respite would be temporary.

"Then have a seat," I said, indicating the rocking chair next to mine.

Ophelia perched on the edge of the chair like a bird prepared for flight. Her feet were bare, something my mother had never allowed when Addie and I were girls. I wondered if that's why Ophelia did it now, when there was no one around to notice.

I waited for her to say something, but she remained silent as she stared out into the yard toward the two-hundred-year-old oak tree with limbs that bore the weight of years as if they needed the ground to hold them up. My sister and I had played house on that tree, pretending the limbs were the beds and sofas of our make-believe castle where Addie was always the princess and I was either her maidservant or mistress of the hounds using my sweet dog, Bailey, who was always a willing participant. I smiled at the memory and wondered when those two girls had become strangers to me.

"What's so funny?" Ophelia asked, her face turned toward me.

"I was just thinking of your mother and me when we were little girls climbing that old oak tree and pretending it was our castle. I'm sure you and your friends probably do the same thing."

She peered out into the darkness again where the night was filled with a familiar chorus of katydids and tree frogs. "I'm not allowed to climb trees," she said softly.

I started to say "We weren't either" but stopped, once again remembering my role as visiting aunt and not willing to defend the arbitrary edicts of my mother. We both turned at the sound of an approaching car and saw headlights pulling into the drive. I waited for Ophelia to run inside before her mother caught her still awake, but she didn't move.

Addie didn't appear surprised to find Ophelia and me on the porch as she slowly climbed each step, fatigue dragging on each leg. Despite the heat, she still wore the sweater with the sleeves pulled down to her wrists.

"You should have prepared me," I said, not bothering to hide the anger in my voice.

"Can this wait until tomorrow? I'm exhausted."

"Me, too, but I won't be able to sleep. And no, it can't wait. It looks like things have gone on too long as it is."

She let out an exaggerated sigh. "Fine. Then I'm going to need a beer."

"They're all gone. I drank the last one. And there's no food in the fridge or pantry, either."

Addie sat down hard on the top step. "You have no idea what it's been like the last six months. If you were here more often, you'd know."

"I'm sorry. But you could have called me earlier. She needs help, Addie."

She jumped up. "I will not send her to one of those awful old people's nursing homes. She would rather die, and I would rather see her dead than to end up there."

I stopped rocking. "I didn't say that. What I started to say is that there are meds available now that can help her and at least buy time to figure out what's next. That's why she needs to see a neurologist, to get some kind of diagnosis and game plan. Have you made the appointment yet?"

Addie leaned against one of the columns, her gaze on me. "I told you. I'm busy. But now that you're here, you can take care of it."

"Fine. But you need to come with me. I'm only here for a couple of months, so you'll have to be a part of the conversation. This won't be a quick fix."

"How do you know? It could be a quick fix, Pheebs. There's definitely something wrong, but it could just be a hormonal imbalance or something. I mean, she was playing bridge up until a few months ago. A person doesn't lose it that quick, right?" The porch light shone in her face, her perfect features still as impossibly beautiful as I remembered.

Her fear vibrated in the air, and I knew that her reluctance to call the doctor had nothing to do with a lack of time. "I have no idea. I hope so. But I think we should prepare for the worst just in case and plan accordingly. All I know is that we need to get this figured out before I go back to Oregon."

A panicked expression contorted her face. "You can't just leave, Phoebe. She needs help."

"You live here, Addie, by choice." The alcohol loosened the pent-up anger I'd been carrying around like a steel anchor for decades. "I'm sorry it's been hard on you for the last few months. But you both made my life miserable for eighteen years. I've worked too hard to get where I am, and yes, she's my mother and I love her, but I cannot stay here. She wouldn't even want me to stay, and neither would you. You finally have exactly what you wanted." I stood, swaying on my feet from the combination of the beer, my lack of sleep, and jet lag.

She took two shuddering breaths before speaking. "Mother used to say you were the nice sister. I guess she was wrong." Addie threw open the screened door and let it close behind her with a loud slap.

I stared at it, wondering at her last words. I'd never heard our mother say anything nice about me at all. I felt sick as I tasted beer and pizza in the back of my throat, and I wondered if that's what regret tasted like. "I'm sorry," I said quietly to the blackness behind the screen.

I made my way slowly to the door, leaving the beer bottles on the porch floor.

"You can sleep with me tonight, if you like. It's queen-size so you won't be squished." The quiet voice came from behind me, and I turned to see Ophelia standing at my elbow, looking up at me with wide, troubled eyes. I'd forgotten she was still there and felt even worse realizing that she'd heard every word.

Feeling as if she needed the companionship almost as much as I did, I nodded. "Thanks, Ophelia. That's very nice of you. I'll try not to snore too loud."

She smiled her chipped-tooth grin, and I felt immediately better. I'd apologize to her and Addie in the morning. Right then, I was way too tired to string together more than two words. I grabbed my bag that was right inside the door and headed up the stairs, instinctively avoiding stepping on the spots I remembered from childhood that would squeak. It was beginning to feel as if my past had swallowed my present and nothing had changed at all.

I awoke to the sound of the air-conditioning clicking on and bright orange light shining in my face from the slats in the closed shutters. I glanced at the Cinderella digital clock that had once been mine and saw it was after eleven o'clock. I rolled over onto my back, grateful that I'd slept through the night without a re-currence of the old nightmare.

Ophelia was gone, her nightgown and sundress from the day before left in a heap on the floor next to my open suitcase. No sounds came from the TV or outside, and no note had been left to let me know where my niece had gone. It was clear somebody needed to keep an eye on my mother and Ophelia when Addie was at work. Granted, I'd been left to my own devices when I was nine, but that had been a different time. And I'd had my aunt Sassy. I hadn't been back for a full day yet, but I could tell that Ophelia had been set adrift for the summer. I tried not to think how she'd clung to me in her sleep or how Addie hadn't kissed her good-night.

I slid out of bed and stretched, feeling the tightness in all my muscles. A long swim would take care of it, but I had more press-ing issues I needed to deal with first. I quickly showered and put on a clean T-shirt and the same jeans I'd worn the day before.

My stomach rumbled as I stuck my head inside Addie's room and then my mother's to find both beds empty. The downstairs remained quiet, and there were no lingering scents of breakfast cooking. Slowly, I descended the stairs while checking my phone for messages and found two. One was from my friend Holly let-ting me know that the house was fine and that she'd hung up a hummingbird feeder outside the kitchen window. The other was from Addie. It was short and to the point, omitting punc-tuation and complete words, but the gist was that she'd gone to the grocery store with our mother and that she'd left the card for the neurologist on the hall table. My phone buzzed with an incoming text. It was another message from Addie telling me to make sure I'd removed the card before she got back so our mother wouldn't see it.

This might have been a typical exchange between sisters, but with Addie I knew she was offering a quid pro quo: she was sacrificing her own time to get groceries, so I needed to do my part by calling the neurologist. I bristled, knowing that Addie had been sitting on that card for over a month and could have already had the appointment by now.

I took another step down, then stopped as I noticed the faded spot on the wood of a single stair halfway up the flight. It had been Bailey's favorite place to nap, and she'd worn away the stain over the twelve years we'd had her. My mother hadn't wanted a dog at all, and when I'd brought home a stray, she'd made it clear it would be my responsibility, but she didn't make me give it up. Which made me wonder why this stair had been excluded from the remodeling and staining that had happened nearly a decade before and years after Bailey had died.

I heard a soft humming from the back porch and hurried down the rest of the steps, snatching up the business card on the foyer table as I passed it. I glanced at it long enough to read the name: L. M. Fitch, MD, with an office address on Coleman Boulevard in Mount Pleasant. I shoved the card into my pocket before opening the back door. I found Ophelia lying faceup with her head tilted backward over the top step, her bare feet facing me and tapping against each other to the beat of a silent tune.

"I didn't know you were here," I said. "I thought you'd gone to the store with your mother and Mimi."

"They didn't ask me."

I paused then crossed the porch to sit down on the step beside her. I followed her gaze up to the blue sky that promised another heat-soaked afternoon. "What are you looking at?"

"Nothing. I'm waiting for interesting clouds."

"Yeah? What kinds of clouds are interesting?"

She shrugged. "Ones that don't look like clouds. Sometimes I see cats and dogs and birds and sometimes people. I like to make up stories about them."

"That sounds fun. What else do you like to do?"

Ophelia shrugged again. "I like to play with my friend, Emily, but she's at camp this month, so I mostly read and look at clouds."

I felt an unreasonable anger rise, and I had to remind myself that Ophelia wasn't me. "What about riding your bike? Do you like to do that?"

She nodded vigorously. "Yeah, but my tire has a flat. Mimi said she'd get it fixed, but I think she forgot. We used to go for walks, too, but she doesn't like to do that anymore."

I frowned as I watched the lazy glide of a snowy egret, its yellow feet dangling beneath its white body.

My stomach rumbled loud enough that Ophelia heard it. "Are you hungry?"

"Yeah. I haven't had anything since our pizza last night."

"Me, either. We don't have any cereal in the pantry, and the milk smells bad." She said this matter-of-factly, like she was used to it.

I stood. "Then come with me. We're going to walk downtown and get something to eat."

We exited through the front door, leaving it unlocked because I didn't have a key and I didn't know if I'd be back before Addie. Ophelia stopped at the top of the porch steps, her eyes wide with worry. "Just don't tell Mama or Mimi. I'm not supposed to leave the house when they're not here."

I felt relief that there was at least one rule. "But you're with me, and I'm the next best thing to a mother and grandmother."

"That's not what they say."

I tried to keep my voice neutral. "Really? And what do they say?"

She frowned as if trying to remember. "That you've picked up bad habits since you've been living so far away and that they don't want any of them to rub off on me."

"Really," I said, wanting to ask more questions but unwilling to put Ophelia in the position of an informer. "Well, then. I won't tell if you don't. It will be our little secret."

She laughed, showing me her chipped tooth, and I smiled back at her, happy to have someone with whom I could celebrate the uniqueness of imperfection.

# 4

## Phoebe

OPHELIA AND I walked the short distance to Pitt Street and to the quaint cottage that housed the Gala Café and Bakery. We entered the brightly lit shop through a porch with a blue painted ceiling, and I let Ophelia select a pastry for each of us. I added avocado toast along with yogurt and granola to share.

A mint-green iron table with two matching chairs became available on the porch, and we made our way outside. I watched as my niece placed her napkin on her lap before taking a bite out of her cannoli.

Between bites, she said, "If we walk back really fast, we can burn all the calories from our pastries so we don't get fat."

I stopped chewing, then swallowed. "Ophelia, you're only nine years old. You shouldn't even know what a calorie is. For the rest of the summer while I'm here, let's play a game to see how long we can go without thinking about calories and instead think about fun ways we can be active, okay? Like riding your bike."

"But—"

"I know. Your tire's flat. I can get that fixed, and while I'm at it, I can take a look at my own bike and see what it needs to make it functional. Then we can go for bike rides together. How does that sound?"

She took another bite of her cannoli and nodded, her mouth closed over a wide grin.

A dog barked, and Ophelia peered through the porch railing to the sidewalk. Sliding back her chair, she jumped up and ran down the steps. "Miss Celeste! Miss Celeste!"

I turned to see a tall and slender older woman wearing a wide-brimmed hat and holding the leash of a medium-size fluffy brown-and-white dog. Both the woman and the dog recognized Ophelia, who dropped down on her knees in the middle of the sidewalk to scratch the little dog behind her floppy ears and to allow wet licks all over her face.

Before I could say anything, a man crossed the street and stopped next to the woman. Holding out a set of keys, he said, "I almost forgot to give these back. And yes, I locked the front door. If Will leaves his stuff at your house again, he's going naked."

The woman took the keys and smiled. "Thanks again for lunch."

He waved and began crossing the street, turning his head to watch for traffic before heading toward a line of vehicles parked at the curb. I stared at him, and not just because he was attractive. There was something else about him, something familiar. Something that stirred in me a jumble of emotions I couldn't unravel or understand. I watched him until he'd climbed into a pickup truck and drove away.

Unwilling to abandon our food to the flies, I stood and leaned over the railing. "Hello," I said. "I'm Phoebe Manigault, Ophelia's aunt."

The woman's smile dipped briefly as she greeted me. "Phoebe. How nice to see you. I'm Celeste Fitch, and this," she said, indicating the little dog, "is my Annie, who, as you can see, adores your niece."

"My aunt's visiting from Oregon," Phoebe announced. To me, she said, "Miss Celeste teaches art at my school sometimes." She was now sitting cross-legged in the middle of the sidewalk with the dog in her lap. Realizing that Celeste needed to be rescued, I wrapped up in napkins what food I could and shoved them in my old high school satchel I'd found buried in the back of the closet.

"I'm a substitute," Celeste explained as we both tried to corral the girl and dog to the side of the sidewalk. "The art teacher was away on maternity leave for the last part of the term, so students considered me a permanent fixture. I was occasionally allowed to bring Annie, and she developed quite the fan following."

"Ah, that explains it," I said, looking into the woman's face for the first time. White hair mixed with blond strands curled around her face where they'd escaped from her hat. A thin web of wrinkles radiated from her mouth and eyes, but her skin was otherwise remarkably smooth. She wore pale pink lipstick and a small gold earring in the shape of an egret dangled from each ear.

But it was her dark green eyes that caught my attention. "Have we met?" I asked. I was sure we hadn't, but there was something vaguely familiar about her so I had to ask.

"No," she said without pause. "Although I've met your parents. Years ago. We have a house on Shem Creek, so not exactly neighbors."

"Do you live in the Old Village now?" I asked curiously.

She shook her head. "No. Same house I've always lived in. I did move away for a short time but came back because I missed it too much. I retained ownership of my cottage and allowed my grandson to put it in a rental program so I was able to move right back in when I returned and the last tenant moved. I come to the Old Village to run errands and walk Annie for a change of scenery."

"Was that your grandson I just saw? He looked familiar, but I can't think of why."

"Yes, that was him." She stopped speaking, as if waiting for me to say more.

"Can I walk Annie now?" Ophelia asked, her voice close to pleading.

"I don't think—" I began.

Celeste interrupted. "It's fine with me if it's all right with your aunt. I'm done with my errands, and I'd enjoy the company. I know Annie would love it."

I thought about the business card in my pocket and the appointment I needed to make but figured it could wait a little longer. "Sure. We don't have any pressing plans."

We guided Ophelia off busy Pitt Street and onto Venning Street where there were fewer pedestrians and cars and more tree shade. We walked slowly while Ophelia patiently waited for Annie to take her time sniffing blades of grass and mailbox posts, allowing for Celeste and me to talk. I kept stealing glances at Celeste, wondering what it was about her that seemed so familiar.

"How long are you here visiting?" she asked.

"Only until the end of summer. I'm an eighth-grade science teacher in Oregon, so I'll need to go back for the start of school."

"That's so far away. I'm sure your family misses you."

It took me a moment to prepare my response. "I miss home." I thought for a moment to come up with a way to verbalize the one thing that made me feel the absence of home the most. "I miss the light after a storm and the way the marsh smells. I never thought it was possible to grieve for a place so much."

I felt her green eyes assessing me, as if she'd heard everything I'd said as well as all that I hadn't. "You talk like an artist. Are you?" I shook my head. "I didn't move beyond stick figures and a round, smiling sun, I'm afraid. But I am a good *noticer*, for lack of a better word. I notice the things in nature that most take for granted, which is why I'm a science teacher. I have my aunt Sassy to thank for that. She was deaf, so her other senses were a lot more attuned to what was going on around her."

"Does she still live here?"

I shook my head. "She died of pancreatic cancer when I was in high school. She was obsessed with birds, which is where I acquired my interest, I guess."

"No doubt. I've always been a painter. My dream since I was a little girl was to go to art school. But then . . ." she gave an elegant shrug beneath her white linen blouse ". . . things changed. I married young and had my daughter nine months later. Then my husband died of a heart attack when Lucy was still in diapers."

"I'm sorry," I said. "I can't imagine how hard that must have been."

"Thank you," she said. "At the time I thought it was the worst thing that could possibly happen to me. It was a struggle to keep a roof over our heads and food on the table. I gave up my dreams of becoming a painter and went to night school to become a nurse instead."

I felt for Celeste. I understood the cost of having to push dreams aside, the depths of loss that I could never adequately express in that single, stupid word.

Celeste reached down to untangle Annie's leash from an elderberry shrub then continued. "Nursing was never part of the future I imagined for myself. I was only interested in obtaining my nursing degree as a means to provide for my daughter and me. Which meant that I was resentful for many years because I could only focus on what I'd lost. But eventually, I found my calling working as a nurse at a retirement community where I also incorporated art therapy. It brought me a joy I'd never expected."

"Your daughter must be so proud of you."

She turned to look at me, but the sun shone in her face hiding her expression. Instead of answering, she said, "What about you? Did you always want to be a teacher?"

I shook my head. "No. Never. I'm still kind of amazed when I realize I'm a science teacher in Bend, Oregon. It seems like it's someone else's life."

We stopped to allow Annie to sniff a small patch of grass, and I felt Celeste's assessing gaze on me. "What did you envision your life to look like?"

"Don't laugh, but I wanted to be the weather girl on TV." I felt myself flushing, embarrassed at having admitted it. Feeling the need to explain, I said, "I survived being hit by lightning when I was nine and ever since became a little obsessed with the weather. I never missed the morning news because I wanted to hear the forecast. I even kept a chart of the accuracy of the meteorologists on each of the local stations. I thought being hit by lightning was a sign that the weather was my calling."

"Mama was a weather girl," Ophelia announced. "Before I was born. Mimi showed me pictures."

Celeste raised her eyebrows to allow me to continue or not.

"Right after college my sister received several job offers from local stations. She got a lot of fan mail, so she must have been good."

I felt the older woman watching me, but I didn't turn. Nor did I tell her that our mother thought that Addie looked like she should be on television and I didn't. I'd never stopped to think that she might be wrong.

"I'm trying to think if I've ever seen her," she said. "What's her name?"

"Adeline Manigault. She only worked as a meteorologist for a year and then decided to stay home to raise her baby as a single mom. Addie and Ophelia still live with my mother."

"I see," Celeste said. "And you became a science teacher and moved across the country instead?"

"I did."

She continued to walk without speaking as if waiting for me to add something.

"My aunt Sassy—my father's sister, who lived with us since I was a baby—was fascinated by the natural world and got me interested in birds. It's amazing how much bird behavior mimics that of humans. They've taught me a lot. I've just started dabbling with writing a blog on birding."

"Ah," she said. "So you're a twitcher."

I laughed. "Guilty. Although most people aren't familiar with the word UK birders used to describe themselves except for fellow twitchers."

"True, and proud of it. I have to be a close observer of birds so I can paint them."

We had already gone around the block and were now back on Pitt Street. "We should go," I said. "My sister took my mother to the grocery store and might need my help putting the groceries away."

"Of course." Looking at Ophelia, she said, "Thank you for doing such a good job walking Annie. I can see that she loved it. I hope we can do it again soon."

Ophelia reluctantly gave back the leash then bent down to hug the little dog. "Can we, Aunt Phoebe?"

"I, uh . . ."

"I don't have a cell phone," Celeste said, "but if you tell me your number I can remember it, and the next time I'm running errands or can't walk Annie, I can give you a call. I think Annie would appreciate a little more energy than I can give her when it's this hot out. She loves to play fetch. Maybe sometime we can take her to Alhambra Park."

"That sounds fun." I gave her my number and said, "I'm so sorry—my memory is apparently not anywhere near as good as yours. What did you say your last name was?"

"Fitch. Celeste Fitch." She said it with a pointed emphasis on the last name as if I should recognize it.

"It's nice to meet you, Celeste. I hope to see you again soon."

I watched her walk away, wondering what it was about the older woman that seemed so familiar.

"Come on," I said to Ophelia as I began walking in the opposite direction. The jangling of the dog's collar tags ceased, and I wondered if they'd stopped and were looking at us. I didn't turn around to see.

As we headed back toward home, Ophelia said, "I wish I had a dog."

I wasn't going to get involved in this conversation knowing what my mother would say. Yet I couldn't forget that faded spot on the stairwell that had been allowed to stay as a memorial to my childhood dog.

We were almost home when I remembered the business card in my pocket and pulled it out to call the number so I could at least tell Addie I'd made the appointment. I'd started dialing the number for the neurology practice when I read again the name of the doctor. *L. M. Fitch, MD.*

"Didn't Miss Celeste say her last name was Fitch?" I asked Ophelia.

My niece nodded emphatically. "There was a boy at my summer camp last year whose last name was Fitch, but he doesn't live here all the time."

"Do you know if they're related?"

Ophelia shrugged. It wasn't that it mattered. I was just searching for a reason why Celeste seemed to expect me to recognize her last name.

When the receptionist answered, I made the appointment for my mother even though I was unable to answer questions about insurance or other medical information. I'd have to make sure I got everything I needed from Addie beforehand.

I had just finished typing the appointment into my phone calendar when we reached our house. My mother's car sat in the driveway, the trunk's lid open to reveal grocery bags. The spoiled food was gone, presumably disposed of by Addie.

"Mother!"

Addie stood inside the open front door. When she spotted me, she ran down the steps, panic on her face. "Have you seen Mother? She was supposed to be helping me bring in the groceries, but when I turned around she was gone."

Being a teacher had taught me how to remain calm and clearheaded in emergencies. "Go walk down the street and look in every yard. I'll go search behind our house." At Addie's uncertain expression, I said, "Go," then gently pushed on her back.

I turned to Ophelia and said, "Go inside and check in every room—even closets and bathrooms, all right? Shout if you find her." She nodded then ran inside, taking the porch steps two at a time.

I walked quickly around the house, passing my mother's hundred-and-fifty-year-old prized camellia bushes at the side of the screened porch. I peered past the screens, but the porch was empty, as was the chair set in the shade of a cedar tree that had been planted before my mother was born. I was almost at the base of the long dock when I spotted her standing near the end, staring out over the marsh at high tide.

My mother had never liked the water. She said the salt ruined her hair and made her skin itch. We could never coerce her into a boat of any kind, and I doubted she'd owned a bathing suit since her beauty pageant days. I was certain that she didn't want to get in the water, but I approached her carefully, making enough noise so that I wouldn't startle her. She wore a pale blue silk shirtdress with empty belt loops and her bedroom slippers. Assuming she hadn't gone inside to change, this meant she would have worn this ensemble to the grocery store.

I stopped behind her. "Mother? It's me. Phoebe. Are you okay?" She didn't turn. "This is my favorite view, I think. It's where your father proposed."

I felt relief at the normalcy of her voice, and at the accuracy of her memory. Maybe things weren't as bad as Addie thought. "It is beautiful," I said. "Aunt Sassy and I used to stand here with our binoculars to watch the migrating birds in the spring and fall."

She was smiling when she turned to look at me, and she was the good mother, which is what I called her when things were going the way she wanted them and I hadn't disappointed her.

The sound of trickling liquid brought our attention to the wood planks of the dock between her feet where a growing puddle was slowly forming. My mother watched the expanding dark spot with a confused expression. When she glanced back at me, her face tightened.

"What are you doing here?"

"I've been here since yesterday, remember? I ordered pizza last night, and we had it for dinner."

She pressed her lips together, highlighting the fine lines that sprouted around her mouth. "You are a liar. I have never eaten pizza in my life."

I turned to see if Addie had discovered us yet, unsure as to what I was supposed to do. I was all alone with my mother who'd just peed on the dock and couldn't remember yesterday.

"We had pizza yesterday," I said again, as if repeating it would make her remember. "You ate three slices and wanted a fourth, but there wasn't enough to go around. You got some sauce on your nightgown, and I had to help you change into a clean one before you went to bed."

"Liar," she hissed. "I did no such thing."

"Fine," I said, my voice shaking. I felt like Alice in Wonderland where everything in my world had suddenly turned upside down. "Let's go inside where it's cooler, all right?"

She looked at me again as if she didn't know who I was, then brushed past me and marched to the end of the dock where it met the backyard. She paused as if unsure of which direction to go, so I gently touched her shoulder to show her.

With an uncharacteristic grunt, she pushed away my hand and headed toward the house. As we neared the screened porch, my mother stopped, and I spotted Addie trying hard to blend into the glossy camellia bushes. I paused to speak to my sister. "She's wet herself. I'll finish bringing in the groceries if you'll go take her inside to change."

I didn't know a slap was coming until I felt the sharp sting of my mother's ring on the side of my face. "You're a liar!"

I pressed my hand against my cheek, my eyes smarting from the blow and from a deeper pain.

Addie avoided looking at me as she wrapped her arm around our mother's shoulders and began leading her toward the front steps.

I leaned against the side of the house and sucked in the hot, humid air, holding my breath until I saw spots before my eyes. It was something I'd done as a child to hide from circumstances I didn't like. *Two months, two months, two months.* But I knew I was ignoring the permanence of what was happening and that pretending everything was fine wasn't going to make the problem go away.

# 5

~

"Many birds like starlings sing in notes too high for the human ear to hear. This means there are bird conversations all around us that we are deaf to. I think there are a lot of people like this, too, existing in a different frequency so that they can hear what others choose not to."

**Excerpt from the blog *The Thing with Feathers***

## Celeste

TIME IS A slippery thing, escaping from our fingers no matter how tightly we grasp it. I am seventy-five years old, and I have only recently reconciled myself to this unalterable fact. My grandson, Liam, tells me that I'm trying to freeze time by displaying photographs of Julie around my house where she never ages beyond eighteen years. That the constant reminders prevent me from accepting that she is gone.

Like I can forget. My granddaughter left the house one day and never came back, leaving no trace of where she went. It's been almost two decades and neither the police nor the private detectives I've hired have turned up a single clue. People are convinced she ran away, which I might be tempted to believe if I didn't understand Julie as well as I do. I raised her, after all. Which is how I know that she would never have left me or her brother without saying goodbye.

I've been locked in a stalemate between reality and make-believe ever since. I know that there is a ninety-nine percent chance that Julie is no longer alive. But until I have proof, I'm pretending that she's somewhere else, living a life she chooses not to share with us. It's the lie I have to tell myself to help get me out of bed each morning.

"Gran!" My great-grandson, Will, crashed through the kitchen door at a fast run, followed by his father, who caught hold of the door before it could slam against the wall. I'd always loved Will's exuberance and was secretly glad that at age ten it hadn't diminished. He was a vexation to his teachers while still managing to be their favorite student, no doubt owing to his mischievous smile that never outshone his innate kindness. This winning combination seemed to run in the male members of the Simmonds family—on my husband's side—passed down from a long line of seamen who captivated women as surely as they commanded the sea.

Will planted a loud kiss on my cheek, something I treasured since I knew those days of outward shows of affection were numbered. I'd already noticed that he didn't hug or kiss me when his friends were around, which I understood. I'd gone through this while raising his father, so at least I knew the hiatus would be temporary.

"What did you catch for dinner?" I asked, resisting the urge to ruffle his tawny hair like I'd done when he was smaller. Now he was quickly catching up, and soon I'd have to reach up, which didn't seem right at all.

"Trout," Will said. "They're all huge, and I caught two out of three. The smallest one Dad caught."

"You sure about that, son?" Liam asked as he dropped a line of three fish into the sink. To me, he said, "I'll clean them if you'll fry them."

"How about I do both so the two of you can go get cleaned up?" As much as I loved my grandson and great-grandson, the smell of the trout mixed with sweat and what I liked to call *eau de boy* threatened to ruin my appetite.

Liam slid off his Gamecocks baseball hat and swiped his forehead with his arm. "Good plan. I'll make the salad. Need green stuff to offset the fried stuff."

"Spoken like a true doctor," I said as I took his place at the sink and turned on the faucet.

"Eww," Will moaned. "How about macaroni and cheese instead? That's a vegetable, right?"

"Not quite," Liam said as he gently steered Will out of the kitchen. "But nice try."

After supper, Will gravitated to the living room to play on the Xbox he kept at my house when he visited. The dishes had been washed and dried, and Liam and I sat on the porch swing on the screened back deck of my small cottage.

The growing popularity of the Lowcountry was one of the reasons we never had trouble finding tenants for my cottage. I'd moved away after Liam went to college, leaving behind empty rooms and the unresolved disappearance of his sister. But just like others with saltwater running through their veins, I couldn't stay away for long. Despite the new construction and condos now surrounding me, I planned to live here until I died, the scent of the saltwater marsh my last conscious memory.

"Was it a productive day?" he asked, indicating my folded easel and large sketch pad leaning against the wall by the kitchen door.

"Not in the way you're thinking," I said. "But I did run into somebody interesting while running errands."

"Interesting how?"

"Annie and I were walking past Gala Bakery when we were recognized by a girl from one of the art classes where I volunteer." At the mention of her name, Annie lifted her head from where she was napping on the swing between Liam and me.

"Anyone I should know?"

"I shouldn't think so. But you'll remember her aunt, I'm sure. Phoebe Manigault."

Liam stopped moving the swing with a jerk. "Really. Now, that's a name I haven't thought about in a while."

"She lives in Oregon and teaches eighth-grade science. From what I could tell, she doesn't visit often."

He nodded slowly, his foot bracing the swing so it couldn't move. A sticky breeze blew through the screen, cooling the perspiration on my face. The name Phoebe Manigault alone had brought back a flood of bad memories I wanted to leave behind in the past where they belonged.

"Did she recognize your last name?"

I shook my head. "No. She wouldn't have. I changed our last name from your father's name to my maiden name after we first met the Manigaults when she was too young to remember. It wouldn't surprise me if she'd never heard of us."

"But surely she remembers the lawsuit."

"I don't think so. Her father dropped the lawsuit against you, and he didn't seem the type to share the sordid details of his job with his family, especially a nine-year-old daughter. Phoebe and I walked and talked for a long while and not once did it appear she knew of my connection to you."

"Her sister might. She and Julie were the same age. We were definitely not in the same social group—Phoebe and her sister went to Ashley Hall, I think—but we all knew each other just from hanging out with the same people during our summers."

I nodded slowly, my clasped hands suddenly cold and clammy. "I wanted to ask her if she still has her premonitions."

"Please tell me you didn't."

"I didn't."

"Thank goodness."

"But I'd be lying if I said I didn't think about asking."

He rubbed his hands over his face. "No good can come from dredging up the past, Gran. Julie's gone. I thought you'd accepted it and moved on."

"I have. It's just that . . ." I measured my words. "I'm planning to be here for a long time, but before I leave this earth, I need to know where she is. There's always the chance, no matter how small, that she's still alive."

Liam leaned forward, planting his elbows on his legs, his face bowed beneath steepled fingers. This was an argument that was as endless as the rivers and creeks that surrounded us.

"Please, Gran. Let it go. You're only going to get hurt again."

I turned to him, his eyes the same shade as mine. "What if Will went missing? Wouldn't you comb the ends of the earth looking for him? Julie is my granddaughter. I raised the two of you since you were small. I've been the only parent either one of you remembers, your only advocate. If I give up, who is left to keep hoping?"

Will threw open the back door. "Can I have dessert now?" His pleading eyes were impossible to resist. His mother, living in Nevada with her new husband and his two kids, didn't allow sugar in her house. Which meant I made sure Will had his fill while spending summers with us. He'd reached that sweet spot where he was still mostly little boy with none of the prepubescent attitude, his limbs long and bony and his appetite endless. I took my job as grandmother seriously, and I tried my best to fatten him up before returning him to his mother.

Eager to end my conversation with Liam, I stood. "Absolutely. I made your favorite, coconut cake. And I'll wrap some up for you and your daddy to take home for later."

"Yay," he said, before heading back into the kitchen. He held open the door for me, just like his father had taught him.

I felt Liam watching me as I entered the kitchen but didn't turn around. I didn't want him to ask another question just as much as I didn't want to answer.

The following day, I sat on a bench with Annie at my feet near the end of the Pitt Street pedestrian bridge an hour before sunset, waiting for Phoebe and Ophelia. I'd waited until after noon before calling Phoebe, half hoping that she would be doing something else or wouldn't answer the phone at all. She picked up on the second ring, almost as if she'd been waiting for me to call.

Ophelia spotted us first and began running toward us, her eyes on Annie, whose tail wagged in recognition. Ophelia was easier to read than her aunt, her expression and her beautiful brown eyes behind her too-large glasses broadcasting her emotions. This was in direct contrast to Phoebe, whose face remained closed to the casual observer, like a person who'd grown used to her feelings being disregarded. During our walk the previous day, I noticed that she rarely let down her defenses. I'd seen it twice: when she mentioned her job as a teacher, and when she spoke to her niece. I doubted she was aware of how much of herself she gave away to those of us who were interested in getting to know her better.

"Annie!" Ophelia dropped down to her knees to hug my dog, who reciprocated with wet kisses.

I watched as Phoebe approached. Her clothing and ponytail were simple, yet she managed to stand out in a crowd. She was of average height with a slim build easily hidden beneath baggy jeans and a T-shirt. She smiled as she approached, clearly not aware of just how beautiful she was.

"Hello again," I said.

"Hi." Phoebe looked down at my open sketch book. "Wow. You told me you were an artist, but—wow. That's incredible."

"Thank you." I turned the sketch pad so she could see the drawing better. "I think I'll use this for the new piece I'm starting to work on. I just need to study the great blue heron a bit more to get the personality of the bird." I grinned. "I don't think I need to explain what I mean to a twitcher."

She smiled back at me. "No, you don't. They're fascinating birds. They're also quite clever. I love how they wade through water stirring up silt and mud to find food. Much easier than perching for hours or flying overhead in the hopes of catching their dinner."

"We humans could learn a lot from watching birds."

"True. I've heard that if you spot a blue heron it could be an omen that if you're searching for something, you'll have to stir up some dirt to get information to rise. Sounds about right to me. I might include that in my next blog." She tented her hands across her forehead to shield her eyes as she gazed across the harbor through the alley of palmetto trees toward the Charleston skyline. "I haven't been here in years. My aunt Sassy and I used to come here to walk my dog, Bailey. It's a great place to bird-watch—even better than the dock behind my house." She slapped at her arm. "It seems the midges and mosquitoes are the same."

I dug into my bag and handed her a bottle of bug spray.

"Thank you." Phoebe took the bottle and began spraying her exposed skin. "I grew up here. You'd think I'd remember."

"Can I walk Annie to the end and come right back?" Ophelia bounced on her toes with excitement in dirty white Keds.

I handed her Annie's leash, and she headed toward the end of the walkway where pilings from the old vehicle bridge jutted out from the water like ghostly arms. Annie barked at a large brown pelican flying low over the pedestrians before perching on one of the pilings, its long bill tucked against its chest in silent perusal of a teenaged boy fishing off the edge of the pier.

"Maybe in your head you're still in Oregon," I said. "It takes a while to reacclimate. I was gone for five years but never felt like I'd left. There's something about the scent of the marsh at low tide that I could never leave behind. It's like a magnet, isn't it? This place. It pulls us back no matter how far we wander."

Phoebe joined me on the bench, keeping her gaze across the harbor at the majestic spires of the Ravenel Bridge, her face still, her beautiful skin glowing in the late afternoon sun. "I try not to think about it."

She brought her ragged thumbnail to her mouth, and I wanted to touch her arm, tell her to stop. "I always wonder if there's a rogue bird or two who flies to South America for the winter and then decides to stay there full-time. It can't just be humans who sometimes decide to move for a change of pace."

Phoebe gave me a lopsided grin. "I think that's a wholly human prerogative. Birds migrate by instinct for survival, but who knows?"

We both smiled, but her posture remained tense. I wondered if she was thinking about her own flight across the country and why she'd deemed it necessary for her survival. There were so many questions I wanted to ask, some to which I already knew the answers. I should have told her then that I knew who she was. That I knew at least part of why she'd left and let her decide if she wanted to get up and walk away from me right then. But I couldn't. She was my last hope.

I drew a deep breath. "Do you plan to stay on the West Coast forever? It must be hard with your family all here."

She laughed. "Actually, that makes it easier." When I didn't say anything, she added, "There's always been a lot of drama that surrounds my sister, Ophelia's mom. It gets magnified when I'm under the same roof mostly because my mother sees the need to pick sides regardless of who's in the wrong, and apparently that's always me. There's a lot of storming away and door-slamming. I think that's why Ophelia prefers to stay under the radar, her nose deep in a book. I did the same thing when I was her age, so I can relate. But this visit is a little different." She pressed her lips together. "I'm sorry. I don't know why I'm telling you all this. I usually don't talk about any of this with anyone."

"I'm easy to talk to." I gave her an encouraging smile. "I think it's the white hair. Gives me an air of wisdom."

She smiled, gave a small shrug. "Must be. You're a good listener."

"Thank you. I learned how to listen without judging while raising my daughter and two grandchildren and then working in a nursing home. It's certainly an acquired skill."

Phoebe nodded, then focused her attention on her hands.

"You were saying something about this visit being different?" I prompted.

"My mother . . . isn't well. It's why I'm here. Addie—my sister—asked me to come home to help her manage."

"I'm sorry."

She looked down at her hands again, flattening them against her thighs so I could see the rough edges of the nails and cuticles of a habitual nail-biter. "Me, too. I've only been home for two days, and there's a lot to absorb, but mostly it's like I'm seeing Ophelia for the first time. My mother was responsible for most of Ophelia's care, but that's changed now. And without the constant supervision, she seems . . . adrift. With my sister working nights and my mom not able to care for Ophelia like she used to, my niece is basically left alone all day to fend for herself. Taking my mother to a doctor's appointment seems a lot more manageable than fixing what's wrong with my sister's mothering skills."

"I can imagine it's a lot for you to handle. What about your father? Can he help?"

"No. He's been gone a long time. He had a heart attack at his law office on Broad Street downtown when he was only fifty-nine."

"Your poor mother. That must have been hard to lose him so early."

She stared at me as if the thought hadn't occurred to her before. "Yeah, you're probably right. They'd been married since their sophomore year at Clemson. People were terrified of him, but Mother had him wrapped around her finger. They adored each other."

Phoebe shifted on the bench, her hands gingerly touching her ribs. "Remember how I told you I was struck by lightning?"

I nodded, holding my breath.

"A local boy—the son of a shrimper, I think—saved my life by giving me CPR. He'd been in his jonboat fishing when he saw the storm roll in and was pulling his boat to the neighbor's dock and saw it happen. That's how he got there so fast. Anyway, he broke some of my ribs while saving my life. So my dad sued his family."

"That's terrible," I said through stiff lips.

"I know. The worst part is that I didn't know any of that until my sister let it slip at my father's funeral. I never even knew the boy's name, even though I'd asked my dad to find out so we could thank him. Maybe invite him over for dinner. Daddy must have found that hilarious. I know Addie did."

"Were you close with your father?" I asked.

Phoebe shook her head. "Not really. I can't say I even knew him that well. He was always working. And when not working as a lawyer, he was throwing his weight as a longtime town council member. He was always proud of my report cards and would announce to friends and family that I'd inherited his brains and Addie had inherited Mother's looks. It took me years to realize that he was basically calling Addie *dumb* and me *ugly*."

"Well," I said, my voice bristling with anger, "he must have had terrible eyesight."

"Not really," she said matter-of-factly. "You haven't seen my sister." Phoebe turned to me. "So why did you leave?"

Now, I thought. I can tell her now. "My granddaughter—"

"Aunt Phoebe, help!"

We both turned to see Ophelia laughing in the middle of the boardwalk trapped by Annie's leash and that of an angry and yipping dachshund. The dachshund's owner, a teenaged girl, was trying ineffectively to talk her dog into unwrapping itself from Ophelia's legs.

"Hang on," I said placing my bag on top of my sketch pad before rushing over to pick up Annie and unlatch her leash. Ophelia sat down on the walkway, still laughing as the dachshund jumped in her lap and began licking her face.

I helped the teenager gather her dog and leash then returned to the bench where Phoebe waited, her eyes on the blushing horizon. I wished I'd brought my paints and canvas. Not just to recreate the brilliance of the sky and the setting sun, but to paint this scarred, lonely woman and show her how the world saw her.

I sat down with Annie on my lap to watch as the sun melted into Charleston Harbor. Phoebe and Ophelia remained standing, and I watched as Ophelia leaned her head against Phoebe's side. After a brief hesitation, Phoebe's arm came around the girl's shoulder.

A hush descended on the bridge as pedestrians paused to watch the sun set, the silence broken only by the percussive chatter of insects and the occasional whisper. No one moved until the orange ball had been absorbed by the water, leaving a glowing stripe of pink along the horizon as if to remind us that just because we couldn't see it didn't mean it wasn't there.

As the other spectators began to gather their things and leave the boardwalk, Phoebe and Ophelia remained where they were.

Phoebe was saying something to her niece, her teacher's voice quiet yet clearly audible.

"This phase of twilight right after the sun dips below the horizon is called civil twilight. It's when the brightest stars are visible, and if you're outside, you don't need any other light to see. I've always loved the name of it because it sounds so polite, which it should be since it's the bridge between day and night. And sometimes, if the timing is right, you can see the sun set on one side of this boardwalk, and the full moon, in all of its beauty, rise on the other. It's a glorious thing to see."

Ophelia pushed her glasses up the bridge of her nose. "Do you know all of that because you're a teacher?"

Phoebe smiled. "No. My aunt taught me that when I was about your age. And now I'm passing it on to you." She dropped her arm from Ophelia's shoulders and turned to me. "We should all get going before it's too dark to see where we're stepping."

I put Annie down and stood. "I enjoyed our conversation. I hope we have the opportunity to chat again soon."

"Me, too," Phoebe said.

"You have my number," I said. "Call anytime. I turn off the ringer when I'm painting, but I have an old-fashioned answering machine, so leave a message and I'll call you back."

We said our goodbyes, and Annie sniffed the area around the bench while I watched them walk away. I recalled what Phoebe had said about the moon, and how she'd called it *glorious*. I wanted to go after her and remind her that the moon had scars, too, but people only saw its beauty.

But I stayed where I was, watching them disappear from view as the sky deepened into night.

# 6

~

"The arctic tern is a small bird that flies from the North
to the South Pole each year, logging thirty thousand
miles. These incredible birds live as long as thirty years,
but what is even more remarkable is the reason known
only to them that they leave one pole for the other. Is the
North Pole really so different from the South Pole that
this tiny bird can't decide where it wants to call home?"

**Excerpt from the blog *The Thing with Feathers***

## Phoebe

THAT NIGHT I had the dream again, catching me by surprise. It
had stayed away on my first night home, so I'd convinced myself it wouldn't come back at all.

Nothing had changed. The lone car. The rain-soaked bridge.
The single survivor walking away into the night. The stillness
of the water over where the car had vanished. I awoke with my
heart pounding and my body soaked in sweat as a tiny memory
skirted across my brain, too faint for me to retrieve. Bright
moonlight illuminated my childhood bedroom as shadowed
shapes of familiar furniture stared back at me like ghosts from my
past. I shivered, knowing that I wouldn't be going back to sleep.

I sat up carefully, not wanting to awake Ophelia, who was
pressed closely against me. She sighed then rolled over, and I
waited until I heard the gentle pattern of her breathing before
sliding from the bed. I had planned to move to the guest room
the previous night, but when I'd checked to see if there were

sheets on the bed, I'd discovered it and most of the floor had been covered with packages from various online retailers, many of them unopened. I'd closed the door so I could ignore—at least temporarily—one more sign that things were not all right in my childhood home.

Standing in the quiet upstairs hall, I took a deep breath, grateful for the silence. After Ophelia and I had returned from the bridge earlier that evening, we'd found my mother in the front yard wearing only her nightgown. Addie and the car were gone.

I'd spent the next two hours coaxing my mother into bed with the clean set of sheets I'd washed that morning. I'd searched again for adult diapers, knowing I'd told Addie to get some at the store, but gave up after looking in all the most obvious places.

Finding something for us to eat for dinner had been a similarly frustrating experience. Addie had restocked the fridge with beer and bottled water. There was also a package of individually wrapped processed sliced cheese, two large bottles of Diet Coke, hot dogs, and cheese in a can. The freezer remained empty except for three frozen cans of margarita mix.

I'd had Ophelia order pizza again, and by the time it arrived I'd already downed one beer and was considering a second when I'd seen Ophelia watching me. It had been enough to remind me that someone needed to be the adult. I'd put the beer back in the fridge and closed the door.

Now I tiptoed to my mother's bedroom and cracked open the door to peek inside, feeling reassured when I spotted her still form under the sheets, her breathing slow and rhythmic. As I moved toward the steps, I saw Addie's door was still wide open, her window blinds allowing the moonlight to highlight the piles of clothes on her floor. The unmade bed was empty, the sheets wadded against the footboard.

The height of the moon told me that we were nowhere near dawn, but late enough that my sister would have finished her shift and come home. A twitch of worry made me reach for my phone, but I was wearing only my long sleep shirt without pockets and had left my phone charging on the bedside table.

As I walked toward the top of the steps, I told myself that I would call Addie from the landline in the kitchen. Hopefully she'd answer so I wouldn't have to call the police, a familiar scenario from Addie's teen years.

I made my way downstairs in the dark, avoiding the squeakiest floorboards. Buttery light spilled through the windows as no one had thought to draw the curtains. That had once been my mother's ritual, just one more thing she didn't seem to be doing anymore. An unfamiliar sensation tightened my throat. I leaned against the banister and rubbed my neck as I stared through the front window at the tangled outlines of the old oak tree's branches, trying to identify the feeling and wondering why I suddenly felt so bereft.

I continued into the foyer and stopped at the round hall table. A decaying bouquet of flowers bent over the edge of the porcelain vase, the old water reeking. I reached for the vase to take it into the kitchen to throw out the flowers and empty the rancid water. Instead I picked up a small oval frame next to the dead flowers.

I didn't need to look at it. I knew the frame contained a photo of my brother, Charlie, at the age of four with Addie, twenty-one months younger, sitting in a child-size electric jeep. Addie is wearing a large bow in her hair and a prescream pout. A blue cowboy hat is perched on Charlie's head, and he's grinning with all the joys of childhood illuminating his face.

I'd never met my brother. He'd died of a bacterial infection shortly after that photograph was taken. Mother kept pictures of him everywhere, his round blue eyes and golden curls decorating the tops of book stacks, shelves of knickknacks, and various tables. Even though he was older than me, I'd always thought of him as my baby brother, the perfect little boy and my father's namesake: the child I was meant to replace.

Except things rarely work out the way they're supposed to. Charlie and Addie were cherubs, worthy of Pampers commercials and Gerber baby food labels. I was the brown pelican in a nest of snowy egrets.

Addie enjoyed repeating the story of how I'd come to be. How Mother and Daddy had expected another boy, to restore the matching pair they'd lost. Mother didn't look during her sonograms, calling it amoral to know a baby's gender before birth. Which meant I was a double surprise. I was female, and one of those rare ugly babies, two things Mother hadn't prepared for. I'd spent most of my childhood trying to make it up to her until the day I'd been hit by lightning and discovered there were worse things than not measuring up to my mother's expectations.

The grandfather clock in the front room chimed twice just as a pair of headlights turned into the driveway. I peered out the sidelights by the front door and saw the lean figure of my sister stumble out of our mother's Lincoln then lean on the car door for a moment before closing it.

I listened as uneven steps climbed up to the front porch and waited as Addie fumbled with her keys, dropping them once before guiding the correct key into the lock. I didn't move until she'd opened the door, surprising her when she spotted me, making her drop the keys again. She squatted to pick them up, spending longer than necessary returning to a stand before closing the door and leaning against it.

"You could have helped me." Her slurred words slid into each other making them nearly unintelligible.

"You're drunk," I said.

"Thank you, Captain Obvious." She tried to move past me, but I blocked her.

"And you got behind the wheel of a car."

"I can handle it." She pulled away again and headed toward the stairs.

"You can handle it?" I couldn't believe I was having this conversation with a thirty-five-year-old woman. "You can barely walk. If you don't care about your own safety, fine. But what about the innocent drivers out there you might kill, not to mention, in case you forgot, you have a nine-year-old daughter who just might care if you don't come home?"

She stopped on the first step and turned to face me, holding tightly to the banister, and I noticed again the long-sleeved sweater she wore pulled down to her wrists. "Don't you dare tell me how to live my life." She swayed as she paused to catch her breath, her words bumping against each other like a train wreck. "I'm the one who's been holding it all together while you escaped to Oregon."

My breath shook, but I refused to engage because I knew that Addie was spoiling for a fight, and if I didn't respond the way she expected, I'd take away her power. A therapist had told me this was classic passive-aggressive behavior, most likely learned from our mother. But I'd learned early on that it was my only defense against my sibling who had an arsenal of weapons to wield if I opened that gate. If we were younger, we might have resorted to hair-pulling and scratching, but I liked to think that we were too old for that, regardless of how good it would probably make me feel.

I struggled to keep my voice low, aware of Ophelia and our mother sleeping upstairs. "I am not having this conversation now because you're too drunk to remember any of it. So go to bed and sleep it off, and make sure you set your alarm so we have time to talk before you go to work tomorrow."

She stepped down into the foyer, clinging to the newel post as she swayed. "You think you're so smart and know everything."

She stopped in front of me, reeking of beer and men's cologne. "Well, you're not. You might have all the book brains, but you don't know anything about being responsible for another human. You. Have. No. Idea."

Those last four words were delivered with an index finger jabbing me in the chest. I didn't step back.

She dropped her hand. "I'm going to bed. Some of us have to go to work tomorrow."

My plan to not engage disintegrated. "You forgot to get diapers for Mother."

The shadows of the room played on her face, showing me, just for an instant, what she'd look like as an old woman. "I didn't forget. She said she didn't need them."

I stared at her in disbelief. "Are you kidding me? You asked her? Would you ask a baby if they wanted to wear diapers?"

"Would *you* want to wear diapers? I know you don't care what you look like, but Mother has standards."

"Right. And leaving a wet stain on her dress or a puddle in her chair at the club is so much more elegant."

She opened her mouth, then closed it, pressing her lips together as she abruptly sat down on the bottom step and began to retch.

I ran to the half bath off the foyer and grabbed the small wastebasket. It was overflowing with used tissues, and I dumped it out on the floor before bringing it back to Addie. This was a familiar ritual, done quietly in the dark so as not to awaken our parents.

She grabbed the wastebasket, and I turned my head while she vomited. When she was done, I stared at her in the dim light and saw a weariness she kept hidden, and for the first time in my life I felt sorry for her.

"Here," she said, handing me the wastebasket, a weak smile on her lips.

"Nice try." I stepped back, unable to stop my own smile. I sat down on the step next to her, feeling my own exhaustion. "We need to get the cleaning lady back. The house is a disaster. Ophelia told me Mother fired her, but maybe we can work around that."

"Mother won't remember." The words were spoken too quietly, as if this one disloyalty needed to be kept secret.

"Okay. If you give me her number, I'll call. You'll just need to get Mother to write the check."

Addie let her head fall into her hands. "Except I don't know where the checkbook is. Her purse is missing. I only have her one credit card because I took it out of her wallet a while back." She lifted her head to look at me. "To cover my expenses. Mother always let me use it, so it was okay."

I sat up straighter. "So did you cancel her other cards? Or at least call the bank or go online to check her statements to see if anyone is writing checks?"

Addie leaned her head against the base of the newel post. "I don't have a clue what cards she had or even where to start with her bank info."

"What about the statements that get mailed to the house? Where are those?"

She closed her eyes and for a moment I thought she might throw up again. "Probably in the desk drawer in Daddy's study. I've just been putting Mother's mail in there until she's better and can deal with it."

My stomach hollowed out, and for a moment I thought I might need the wastebasket. I tried to keep my voice calm, knowing that Addie would close up and get defensive if I sounded the least bit critical. "How long have you been doing that?"

She straightened, her hand gripping a spindle to keep her steady. "I don't remember. It's been a while. I might have shoved the overflow in a basket on the bookshelf."

I stood, and I had to grip the railing because my body was shaking, my temples throbbing. "Go to bed, Addie. We'll talk about this in the morning." Her eyes were in the shadows so I couldn't read them, but I held out my hand anyway.

She brushed my hand away, but after several attempts at trying to stand on her own I grabbed her elbow and hauled her up. Addie stood still, her head lowered. When she lifted it again, her eyes met mine. "Do you still see the future in your dreams?"

I sucked in my breath. I hadn't been asked this in so long I was no longer prepared with an answer. I thought of the car and the bridge and the lone survivor, the scent of the rain on the asphalt still fresh in my mind. But I'd never told anyone about that dream, still not knowing if it was in the past or in the future, or the identity of the person emerging from the dark water. I shook my head. "No. Not since I left home."

She sighed. "That's too bad."

"Why?"

"Because I'd like to know where I'm going."

I didn't help her climb the stairs or get her into bed. I waited until I heard her door shut then made my way to our father's wood-paneled study, my stomach tightening the way it would before a final exam or an oral report. I stood in the threshold, watching the shadows slip over the large desk that was as much of my childhood memory of him as his piercing blue eyes and towering build.

Our father's study had been forbidden territory when Addie and I were children. I had once been spanked for borrowing a pencil from the cup on top of his desk, and I'd never ventured inside again, but Addie would go in whenever an adult wasn't present and would freely riffle through the drawers in search of money or anything else she thought she might need.

Feeling something between nausea and fear, I flipped on the light. Very little had changed in the years since my father's passing. Thick law books lined the built-in bookshelves on two sides of the room, the heavy mahogany partners desk dominating the center. My father had spent most of his evenings and weekends in here. Even our mother had respected that boundary, only intruding to bring him a cup of coffee and the morning paper or a glass of bourbon in the evening. She'd kiss him and then retreat to her sitting room off their bedroom where her antique secretaire sat in front of the window facing the side yard with the stone koi pond that had been installed in 1939.

Her desk was what she referred to as her command central, where she orchestrated calendars for the family, bridge club, the garden society, and the Old Village Historic District Commission. Its position at the window was so she could keep an eye on the pond for any sneaky herons who thought to prey on her exotic fish. Her desk contained a single photo of Charlie standing in front of my father and my mother holding Addie in her christening gown. My father's desk and office were devoid of photographs.

Part of me now wanted to back out of the room and close the door. But what Addie had said about unread mail forced me forward.

The heavy leather chair had been pulled back to allow the top drawer to protrude, its opening like a mouth spewing unopened envelopes. Some had fallen onto the chair and floor and my mother's beloved seagrass basket on one of the bookshelves.

I flipped on the desk lamp and the bulb popped, startling me, then I gathered up the envelopes preventing the drawer from closing and placed them on top of the desk. The drawer still didn't close, so I crouched in the kneehole to look from underneath and see if something might be stuck. A yellowed manila folder was wedged against the back of the drawer, as if it had slipped from the top of an overstuffed drawer.

Standing again, I pulled out the drawer and retrieved the folder. Although it appeared worn and creased, the edge on the bottom rounded as if it had once contained thick documents, the folder was now empty. The only indication that it had ever been used was the typed label affixed to it that read SIMMONDS. The name was only vaguely familiar, and since the folder was empty, I placed it on the floor to start my throwaway pile.

I replaced the drawer and sat down in my father's chair. Fighting the urge to look behind me to see if anyone might be watching I pulled out the ivory-handled letter opener from the pencil box then picked up the first envelope from the stack, noticing the words FINAL NOTICE stamped in red on the front.

With a shaking hand, I sliced open the first envelope and felt glad in a perverse way that I had an excuse to stay awake all night. The faint memory from my dream had expanded in my subconscious and now exploded in my mind with full-blown clarity. I'd seen something I thought I'd recognized, a small shiny object floating on the surface at the spot where the lone survivor had emerged. It bobbed up and down before being upended by a small ripple and then swallowed by the dark, silent water.

# 7

"Pelicans are thought to symbolize the love and self-sacrifice of a parent because they store the food they've hunted in their large gular pouches before returning to the nest and regurgitating the chewed-up fish to feed their chicks. I am once again left to wonder if the children have a choice to eat at home or how far they might get trying to survive on their own in a hostile world. I'm sure at least one will manage it, knowing that starvation might be preferable to living on leftover scraps."

**Excerpt from the blog The Thing with Feathers**

## Celeste

I AWOKE TO birdsong piercing the early morning stillness. I took a minute to stretch my tight back and limbs before standing, telling myself that it wasn't too late to start training for another marathon, even if it meant just power walking for most of it. I'd injured my knee six months before while jogging, and despite physical therapy it didn't seem to want to heal completely. Growing older had its challenges. But, as I frequently reminded myself and friends of the same age, it beat the alternative.

I pushed aside the lace curtains, still hearing Julie's voice in my head telling me they were *old-lady curtains*. She'd probably been right twenty years ago, but I still liked them even if I didn't consider myself an old lady.

I spotted the brown-and-white songbird right away. It sat on my windowsill, its tail wagging side to side as it sang and chirped its sweet and distinctive tweet. *Fee-bee. Fee-bee.*

I pressed my forehead against the glass to see it better. It tilted its head toward me so I knew it was watching me, too.

Maybe it was my artist's eye that saw the varying shades of taupe, gray, and ivory in its feathers. Its face wore a sweet expression, reminding me of a dolphin's, and when it opened its beak to chirp out another *fee-bee, fee-bee*, the sound high and melodic, I saw much more than an ordinary bird.

The sound of feet running down the stairs reminded me that Will had stayed over the night before because Liam was seeing patients this morning. I let the curtain fall then grabbed my bathrobe from the foot of the bed and slid it on along with my slippers.

Annie roused herself from her own bed next to mine and gave a big stretch before slowly trotting to the bedroom door. She was almost ten in people years and thankfully still mobile and sharp, despite losing some of her hearing. We were two women of a certain age living together for companionship.

I heard the sound of Will's Xbox as I entered the kitchen. I stuck my head into the living room. "You could be reading a book instead."

He didn't turn away from the screen, but I could see the side of his mouth turn up in a smile. "I could."

"Let's stop by the library later today so you don't waste away with your hands frozen on those controls. Your mother would never forgive me."

He laughed, his hands and eyes still focused on the game. "No, thanks."

"Excuse me?"

Will sighed. "All right. But I get to pick the books myself."

"Of course," I said. "Just don't pick any with covers I might be embarrassed to see."

"Whatever," he said as I turned back to the kitchen to let Annie outside and to make breakfast.

★ ★ ★

An hour later we left the house for Annie's morning walk to the park, Will holding her leash. He hadn't complained when I'd pulled him away from his Xbox mostly because I'd promised that we'd stop at the Pitt Street Pharmacy's soda fountain to get a thick chocolate milkshake but also because he loved Annie and seemed to enjoy spending time with his grandmother.

When I continued straight on Pitt Street, Will said, "You just passed the pharmacy. Shouldn't we stop for a bit? Annie's getting old, and I think she needs a break."

"Nice try, Will. You'll get your milkshake later. Let's keep going. Unless you can't handle it."

He scoffed. "If you get tired, jump on my back, and I'll carry you the rest of the way."

"What about Annie?"

"I can hold her, too." He smiled that beautiful smile that was just like his father's and grandfather's, and my heart melted like ice cream on a summer's day.

"Well, let's hope it doesn't come to that. You'd probably pass out from heat prostration."

"If I do, we can always call Dad to give me CPR. He knows how to do it."

I slid a glance toward my great-grandson. "Are you sure?"

Will looked at me with surprise. "He's a doctor, Gran. All doctors need to know CPR. Isn't that sort of what they do all day?"

"Sort of," I said. "I know your dad saved someone's life once when he was a little older than you are now. Did he ever tell you the story?"

"No, he didn't! So what happened?"

I wasn't surprised that Liam hadn't shared his moment of heroism with his son. Most likely because he didn't consider himself a hero for doing what he said anybody else would have done given the same circumstances.

"He saved a nine-year-old girl after she'd been hit by lightning. Which is a good reminder to seek shelter when you see storm clouds, and not under a tree." I gave him a stern look. More than once I'd caught him standing out in the yard during a storm, and after I'd dragged him inside, he'd said that he wanted to watch the lightning to see if it was true that lightning never struck in the same place twice.

"That's so cool," he said. He reached down and plucked a small stick from the sidewalk to toss to Annie when we reached the park.

As we continued straight on Pitt Street, Will turned to me. "I thought the park was that way," he said, pointing to the right.

"It is, but I wanted to go this way. I'm hoping to run into a new friend."

"Why didn't you call her?"

"That's a very good question. I think because I just saw her last night."

"And you don't want her to think you're a stalker?"

"No." I paused. "Maybe a little. I like her, and I think she could use a friend. But the thing is I need her help with something, but I don't want her to think that's the reason I'm her friend."

We stopped to allow Annie to sniff a patch of grass. Will looked up at me and scrunched his eyes. "Aren't you old enough to have figured all that out by now?"

"It's never too late to figure out new things. Let's just go knock on her door and ask her to come walk with us. She has a niece about your age, Ophelia. Maybe the two of you can hook up this summer."

Will made a strangled sound in his throat. "I think you mean *hang out. Hook up* means something I'm not supposed to know about, but my older stepbrother uses it a lot."

I sighed. "Ophelia is a nice young lady. I'm sure you'll get along just fine."

"Does she like playing Xbox?"

"I know she likes to read, but you can ask her yourself about the Xbox."

We'd made it to the Manigaults' street. I'd only ever driven by their house and had never been invited inside. Until the lawsuit, I'd never had a reason to be on a familiar basis with either Charles or Elizabeth, my awareness of them confined to the *Moultrie News* where their names made frequent appearances due to his involvement in local politics and hers in reference to the Garden Club. And then the lawsuit had made front-page news and I'd stopped reading it for a time, unable to bear the biased reporting about my grandson being raised in a broken home by a grandmother who worked full-time, leaving her two grandchildren home alone to fend for themselves.

There'd been little mention of Liam and Julie's father's accidental drowning, focusing instead on his mother's suicide shortly afterward, leaving the two children orphaned. The unfairness had driven me to find the Manigaults' house at the far end of the Village, perched in an ideal spot facing the marsh, to see where the kind of people who would sue a young boy for saving their daughter might live.

"Look at that car!" Will said, pointing toward the white house with the unmistakable red roof.

I had to get a little closer to see where he was pointing. A dark blue sedan had been left in the front yard with one flat back tire on the drive. The front tire on the same side was also flat, the rubber appearing to be melting into the sparse grass. The car's front door had been left open and a plastic cup still partially filled with an amber liquid lay on its side on the ground next to the car. As I approached, I noticed a tan leather purse on the passenger seat, a half-eaten burger partially wrapped in a napkin rested next to it. Annie began pulling on her leash, undoubtedly smelling the burger or my sudden nervousness. Something wasn't right with this whole scene.

"Will, I need you to wait here. Please hold tight to Annie's leash. I just need to make sure everybody is okay."

"Sure, but shouldn't I come with you? You might need my help."

I grimaced, not sure if he thought I was too old or if he considered himself more intimidating than he was. "It's all right. I'll let you know if I need assistance."

He gave me a serious nod as I turned toward the porch steps. I rang the doorbell, hearing the soft chime from somewhere inside. I listened for the sound of approaching footsteps, my worry growing at the silence. A grandfather clock chimed once, marking the quarter hour, and I waited for another minute before ringing the doorbell again.

My worry had begun to dip into dangerous territory, making me wish I had a cell phone, when the doorknob turned and the door slowly opened. Ophelia gazed up at me through smudged glasses and smiled in recognition.

"Miss Celeste," she said, her voice sounding more relieved than surprised.

"Is everything all right?" I asked, deciding to save the lecture about opening doors before determining who was on the other side.

She pushed her glasses up on her nose then opened the door wider. "Mama is still sleeping, and I don't know where Aunt Phoebe is. But Mimi is awake." She closed her mouth, pressing her lips together, but I could see them beginning to quiver. "She says she has to get to her bridge club meeting but can't find her car keys. She keeps yelling at me, but I don't know where they are, and Mama says I'm not supposed to wake her up." The sound of something heavy being dropped came from the back of the house along with a string of curse words no child should hear.

I wrapped her in my arms, noticing her dress was on inside

out and had a large grass stain on the back. Her stringy hair was matted on one side, and she'd pulled it back with a pink bow hair tie. I patted her back and murmured soothing words, a drop in the bucket to what this child needed.

When Ophelia had stopped crying, I held her by the shoulders. "My great-grandson, Will, is here in the yard with Annie. Why don't you go say hello to both of them, and I'll go inside to see if I can help. Just stay in the yard, all right?"

Ophelia nodded, then wiped her eyes and nose with the backs of her hands. Another crashing sound came from the back of the house, and Ophelia looked up at me with worried eyes. "That's Mimi looking for her keys."

"It's all right. I'll take care of it." I gave her a smile of encouragement, then waited until she'd reached the bottom of the porch steps before I stepped inside.

Leaving the door open, I followed the sounds toward the back of the house, vaguely aware of the elegance of the furniture and the graceful turn on the mahogany banister as I passed the stairs toward the back hallway.

I found my way to the kitchen, narrowly avoiding being hit by a rubber spatula that clattered on the floor behind me. I turned to see a woman grab the handle of a kitchen drawer and pull it all the way out before upending the contents on the floor. She dropped down to her hands and knees and began rummaging through the pile.

"Elizabeth?" I said softly.

Her limp hair fell over her face as she stared at me with vacant eyes. Her eyes were a stunning light blue, but they lacked focus as if all her memories were locked inside, her vision turned inward. "I can't find my keys."

I knelt on the floor beside her. "We can look together. Let's put everything back in the drawer first, okay? It will help us find them."

She sat on the floor watching me while I replaced the items in the drawer, stealing glances at her while I worked. She was still a beautiful woman, although her clothes hung on her as if she'd lost weight and her makeup had been applied with a heavy hand.

"Who are you?" Her brow furrowed. "Does Charles know you're here? He doesn't like it when strangers show up at the door."

"I'm Celeste," I said. "I'm a friend of Phoebe's."

"Phoebe?"

"Your youngest daughter."

She smiled softly. "My baby." Her bright pink lips tilted up. "She was such a sweet thing. Such a good baby—always so happy. Not like the other one." Elizabeth gave me a conspiratorial smile.

"Addie," I said. "Your oldest daughter."

"Addie," she repeated. "She was so needy. But not my Phoebe." She paused, looked down at her chipped fingernail polish. "She didn't need me at all."

"Hello?" Phoebe's voice rang out from the front of the house. "Is someone here?"

"We're in the kitchen, Phoebe." I pulled myself up then reached out a hand to help Elizabeth.

She tucked her hands into her lap. "Who are you?"

"I'm Celeste. I'm a friend of Phoebe's." I smiled, trying to be as nonthreatening as possible.

Phoebe entered the room looking as if she'd slept in her clothes. Her face was crisscrossed with pressure marks from whatever she'd fallen asleep on top of. She stopped short when she saw me. "Celeste. I didn't know you were here." Her gaze fell past me to her mother on the floor. "Is everything all right?"

"Yes. Everything is fine," I said calmly. "Your mother and I were just looking for the car keys."

"Are they lost?" She quickly crossed the room and helped her mother stand. A panicked expression crossed her face. "I'm taking Mother to her doctor's appointment this morning before Addie needs the car for work." She ran her hands through her tangled hair. "I don't know what happened—I fell asleep in my dad's office going through the mail." She squeezed her head between her palms. "Mother, I need you to get your checkbook."

"Now might not be—" I started to say.

But Phoebe's eyes were tightly closed, and I knew she was only listening to the panic sirens inside her head. "I found a lot of overdue bills, and if we don't pay them now, the gas, electricity, and water will all be shut off. We also need to find your health insurance card."

Elizabeth's lips pressed together as if she'd just tasted something bitter. I wanted to step between them, to tell Phoebe to wait, and to stop the words percolating in Elizabeth's mouth like bile, words like darts that couldn't be recalled once they'd been thrown.

"Where's Addie?" Her eyes narrowed as she regarded Phoebe. "Why are you here?" Elizabeth said, growing agitated.

"To take you to your doctor's appointment, remember? I told you last night before you went to bed."

"Liar!" Elizabeth began twisting her hands, drawing her attention to her fingers. "My rings! Where are my rings? Did you take them?"

Phoebe pulled back. "Of course not. I don't remember you having them on yesterday, so they're probably upstairs in your room."

Elizabeth's hands clenched with rage. "You lying bitch!"

Phoebe sucked in her breath. I doubted that Elizabeth Manigault was in the habit of using that word. I put my hand on Phoebe's arm to encourage restraint, knowing from experience that anything she said would be like pouring oil on a fire.

She straightened, pulling her shoulders back to regain her composure. With a controlled voice, Phoebe said, "Mother, let's go upstairs and get you dressed, and then I'll drive you to your doctor's appointment." She reached out and took hold of her mother's elbow.

Elizabeth yanked back her arm, her enraged face nearly unrecognizable. "I wish I'd miscarried you!"

Phoebe froze. Tears pooled in her eyes, her expression revolving around hurt and anger. My own heart felt the blow, and it ached for both of these women. This battle was only just beginning, and neither one of them would emerge unscathed.

Stepping in between them, I turned to Phoebe. "Your car has two flat tires. My own car keys are in my purse I left in the foyer. My car's sitting in my driveway. It's a bit of a jog, but my car's not being used, and you're welcome to borrow it. I'll get your mother dressed and watch the children until you return."

Phoebe nodded then gave her face a swipe with the backs of her hands as if embarrassed to have anyone see her cry. I gave her my address, and she took off without a backward glance.

Elizabeth sat down at the kitchen table, her agitation gone. She folded her hands in her lap, and she sat with a straightened back and her ankles crossed beneath her nightgown.

"Are you hungry?" I asked.

"Yes." She smiled up at me. "I'll have the chicken pot pie, please. And make sure it's hot. Last week it was served to me ice-cold."

"Of course." I opened the door to what I assumed was the pantry, scanning the pitiful contents for something resembling real food, and pulled out a box of Lucky Charms. I opened the correct cabinet containing china plates and bowls on my first attempt. After pouring the cereal, I found a quart of milk that hadn't expired and added some to the bowl.

I placed it and a spoon I'd found in a drawer in front of her. "Thank you," she said before meeting my gaze. "Who are you?"

"I'm Celeste. A friend of Phoebe's."

She smiled serenely at the mention of her daughter's name, and I wished Phoebe was still there to see it and to help her understand that her mother's words and emotions had been taken over by an illness that was as hard to understand as it was to find a cure. "Phoebe is a teacher," she said. "A very good one. Probably the best."

"Probably."

I joined her at the table, watching as she picked up her spoon and began to eat, moving the spoon away from her just like they taught at etiquette school. After three bites, she put down her spoon and scowled at her bowl. "This is taking too long." She picked up the bowl and held it to her mouth, drinking it like a young child might before they'd learned how to hold a utensil.

I let her finish, then used a napkin to gently wipe up the drops of milk on her mouth and chin. "Let's go upstairs and get you dressed."

"Where am I going?"

"To play bridge."

She nodded slowly, her eyes on my face. "Who are you?"

"I'm Celeste. I'm here to help Phoebe."

"Phoebe?"

"Your youngest daughter."

She scowled. "I know my daughter's name. But Phoebe doesn't need any help. She's too . . ." She struggled to find the word.

"Self-sufficient?" I prompted.

"Yes. Something like that." Her eyes focused on me again. "She almost died once. When she was a little girl."

"Yet she survived."

Her face softened. "Because she's fierce." She stopped, her gaze turned inward. "I named her after a bird."

"Mother?"

We both turned toward the doorway where a young woman stood. She was stunning despite no makeup, her blond hair rumpled by sleep and dark circles under her eyes. Her T-shirt barely hid her long, lean body or her voluptuous chest. Her self-assurance that she was the most beautiful woman in the room reminded me of Liam's ex-wife. I tried not to hold it against her.

"Addie," Elizabeth said, "are we late?"

"For what?" Addie walked into the kitchen and planted a kiss on her mother's cheek.

Elizabeth turned to me for an answer.

"Your mother has an appointment this morning," I explained. "Your car has two flat tires so Phoebe has gone to my house to retrieve my car."

"Oh, crap. How am I supposed to get to work?"

"Watch your language, Adeline," Elizabeth admonished.

"I'm sure there's a bicycle somewhere you can use," I suggested.

Addie regarded me for longer than necessary, as if waiting for me to offer her the use of my car. "I guess I will," she said, heading toward the coffee maker, the scent of stale beer following her. As an afterthought, she turned to look at me. "And who are you?"

"Celeste Fitch. I know Ophelia from volunteering at her school. My grandson and I were walking my dog this morning and—"

She cut me off. "How do you know Phoebe?"

"We ran into each other two days ago while she and your daughter were having lunch at the Gala Bakery, and then we decided to take a walk so Ophelia could spend time with my dog."

"Hm." She regarded me closely. "I feel as if I should know you for some reason. Maybe Ophelia has mentioned you." She grabbed a dirty mug from the sink and rinsed it under the tap then let out a heavy sigh when she saw that the coffeepot was empty.

"We've never met." I stood then helped Elizabeth from her chair. "I'm going to get your mother dressed for her appointment.

I used to be a nurse and I worked in a retirement community, so I think I can handle it, but I would welcome any help." I looked at her expectantly.

Addie turned toward the coffee maker, avoiding my eyes. "I'll come up in a bit to do her hair and help her with her makeup. But first I need coffee." She leaned against the counter, the sun coming through the window spinning her hair into gold. A blue jay squawked, and Addie lifted her head to peer outside, her perfect profile visible. "Then I'm going to call a friend of mine at the local garage. He owes me a favor." She grimaced.

I began leading Elizabeth away, not wanting to speculate as to what kind of favors Addie Manigault used to barter or how Addie and Phoebe could have come from the same family. We passed the round table in the foyer, its surface filled with photographs of a little boy.

"What's your name? I think you forgot to tell me," Elizabeth said as we began to climb the steps.

"Celeste."

We continued to climb and had made it to the upstairs hallway when she turned to me. "I knew a Celeste once. A long time ago."

"It was. Now, let's get you dressed so Phoebe can take you to your appointment."

She nodded then led me to her bedroom. "Phoebe. I named her after a bird, you know. My husband named our first two, but I insisted on naming our last."

"It's very pretty." The closet door stood open. I walked in and flipped on the light. Grabbing two summer dresses near the front, I held them up. "Which one would you like to wear today?"

She pointed toward one, and when I went to return the other to the rack, I spotted an opened purse, its strap dangling on the adjacent hanger, a wallet visible inside. I closed the purse and placed it on a shelf. I'd tell Phoebe where to look, hoping the errant health insurance card was somewhere inside. I thought about looking for it myself but was worried I'd already crossed too many boundaries.

I was helping Elizabeth into her slip when Addie appeared in the doorway, holding a steaming cup of coffee. She hadn't brought another for either her mother or for me.

She leaned her head against the doorframe. "I figured out how I know you."

"Did you?" I asked, adjusting the thin shoulder straps of the slip.

"Yeah. Your married name was Simmonds, wasn't it? And then you and your grandchildren began using your maiden name after the lawsuit."

"Yes. But—"

She held up her free hand, palms out. "I'm not accusing you of anything. I would have done the same thing."

"Arms up," I said to Elizabeth. She complied, and I slid the dress over her head.

"Does Phoebe know?" Addie asked.

I shook my head and began to fasten the buttons on the front of the dress. "Not yet. But I need to tell her. I don't want her to think that I've been withholding information from her."

"But isn't that exactly what you've been doing? You could have told her when you met her."

I looked up sharply, but she was taking a sip from her cup, her eyes focused demurely on its contents.

"No. I fully intend to tell her."

"I'm sure." She pushed off from the doorframe. "You ready for your hair and makeup, Mother?"

Elizabeth smiled. "That would be lovely, dear. Thank you."

I turned to leave as Addie picked up a silver-backed hairbrush.

"Celeste?"

I stopped.

"Even though it's been years, I'm sure you remember that after the accident, Phoebe became known as *the girl with the peculiar talent*."

"It's a hard thing to forget," I said, keeping my voice even. "And I wouldn't call it *peculiar*, either. I'd call it *a gift*."

Addie shrugged. "Yeah, well. It was a long time ago, and it was the main reason why my sister moved away. My mother and I would like to see Phoebe come back home because this is where she belongs. But that's not going to happen if you bring up that psychic business."

"I'm sure you have her best interests at heart." A car pulled up in front of the house, and I moved to the window to peer outside. "That's Phoebe now. I'll let her know that your mother is almost ready to go."

I'd made it to the door before Addie spoke. "Thank you, Celeste."

"You're welcome. I'm glad I could help."

When I'd reached the top of the stairs, I heard Elizabeth ask, "Who is that? Is that a friend of yours?"

I didn't stop until I'd reached the front porch. I watched as Ophelia, Will, and Annie greeted Phoebe while I filled my lungs with the thick, humid air. Swollen clouds rolled in over the marsh, chasing a flock of screaming black skimmers. Phoebe focused on the sky, her features tightening with something that went beyond fear. Like a wide-winged stork gathering its young, she flapped her hands and herded the children inside.

A storm was coming. I could only hope that we might all find a shelter that would protect us from the deluge.

# 8

*~*

"Mammals can taste capsaicin, the active component of chili peppers that gives them that spicy kick, but birds don't have the receptors and therefore aren't affected by the pungency. If only humans could adopt this ability to not be susceptible to situations and people that we find unpleasant. But that's assuming we would have a choice to turn it on or off instead of being born without them. I often wonder if the northern cardinal might crave a spicy treat every once in a while, finding itself longing for something it never knew, even if it meant risking getting burned."

**Excerpt from the blog *The Thing with Feathers***

# *Phoebe*

THE RUMBLING SKY made me flinch as it always did. I quickly led the children and dog up to the porch where Celeste waited then into the house as Addie and my mother were walking down the stairs. Mother's hair and makeup were done to perfection, and she wore an Hermès scarf with a silk shirtdress and a pair of Ferragamo low-heeled pumps. She and Addie walked with linked arms, their heads held high as if walking across a pageant stage.

I smiled at the familiarity of this scene of my elegant mother looking the way I remembered her, clinging to it like a child wishing the sun wouldn't set on a long summer's day. Mother smiled back when she saw me then leaned in to kiss my cheek, leaving the scent of Shalimar wafting in the air. "Phoebe. You should have told me you were going to be here. I would have prepared something special for supper."

Addie and I shared a rare grin at her comment about preparing a meal since our mother didn't cook. I knew if I looked at the inside door of the pantry I'd find handwritten notes thumbtacked to the wood in Aunt Sassy's spidery cursive with instructions on how to hard-boil an egg and at what temperature to set the oven to reheat a casserole. We'd always had delicious meals and family dinners in the dining room with fresh flower arrangements in the center of the table and sterling silver flatware, but not a single dish had ever been prepared by our mother.

This was undoubtedly the reason Addie and I didn't know how to cook, although in a pinch I could create a passable meal from a repertoire of five dishes I'd been taught by Aunt Sassy.

"Are you ready to go?" I asked.

Her powdered eyebrows rose. "Go? I'm not going anywhere."

I glanced at Addie for help, but she kept her gaze focused on her feet, our brief flash of camaraderie gone. "I'm taking you to your appointment, remember?" I wondered if I should have said the club or bridge, but even in my growing panic, I knew it wouldn't matter.

My mother drew back her head. "I don't have an appointment. It's Sunday. Addie's taking me to church. You might consider joining us." Her critical gaze took in my rumpled appearance, and I didn't have the time to explain that I hadn't had the chance to get dressed yet.

With growing desperation, the sound of the ticking grandfather clock seemed absurdly loud. "Right. Addie, could you please help Mother into the car so I can wash my face and change my clothes?"

Mother stiffened. "I don't need help, and I am perfectly capable of driving myself." She looked down at her empty hands. "Where is my purse? And my rings are gone!" The panic on her face must have matched my own. I turned again to my sister for help.

Instead, she said, "It's all right, Mother. Why don't we stay here and look for your purse and rings?"

My rage clouded the edges of my vision. I clenched my hands to keep them at my side and fought the urge to scream or cry or turn around and walk out the door. I wasn't surprised but still disappointed that even now Addie was still trying to play the nice sister. I failed to keep my voice calm. "What the hell are you doing, Addie?"

"Mother doesn't want to go anywhere. We'll just wait until she's feeling up to it."

I took two deep breaths. "This isn't a choice, Addie, and you damn well know it."

Mother put her arm around Addie's shoulder. "There is no need to get vulgar, Phoebe. Don't make me wash your mouth out with soap."

I shut my mouth, trying to repress a scream. Celeste touched my arm, reminding me that she was still there. "When I was helping your mother get dressed, I found her pocketbook in the closet and put it on a shelf. Why don't you go get it? I can help Addie walk your mother outside to the car while you do that and get changed."

I sent her a grateful glance then bolted up the stairs and ran into my mother's closet. I shut the door then curled up on the floor under her long evening dresses just like I'd done as a child, the scent of Shalimar haunting the small space like a lost spirit, and buried my face in her out-of-season sweaters and screamed until I couldn't.

I didn't know how long I stayed there before I heard a brief knock on the closet door. The overhead light flickered on, revealing Celeste's concerned face. "Phoebe? Are you all right?"

I blinked at the sudden light. "Not really." I placed my arm over my eyes. "I'm so sorry you had to see that."

"Oh, sweetie," she said dropping to her knees next to me with a small wince. "You don't need to apologize. Families are hard."

It was such an understatement that I almost smiled.

"I convinced Addie to get in the car with your mother with the air-conditioning on and they're waiting for you. I won't need my car for the rest of the day, so I'll stay here with the children and wait for Addie's friend from the garage."

I met Celeste's eyes, seeing in them a breadth of understanding that was out of proportion to the short time I'd known her. It went beyond the wisdom expected from someone her age. "Thank you," I said through a tight voice. The words didn't completely express my gratitude, but it was all I could allow without opening the floodgate of tears her sympathy threatened to unleash.

"There's something I've been meaning to . . ." she began.

I rocked up to a sitting position at the same time, unintentionally cutting her off. "I don't think I can do this," I blurted in a burst of my familiar self-loathing and inadequacy. I wasn't sure if *this* meant finding the energy to stand or joining my mother and sister in the car. Or simply facing all that had changed when I wasn't looking and the vast unknown looming in front of me.

"Yes, you can." Celeste leaned forward and gently lifted my chin. "Your mother and that sweet little girl need you. And even though I don't think she would admit it, your sister does, too."

"I didn't sign up for this." I was embarrassed by how pathetic I sounded.

"We never do, Phoebe. But the strong do it anyway."

I shook my head. "I'm not strong. I ran away, remember?" I kept my eyes on Celeste's, searching for rejection.

Instead, she smiled. "When birds migrate, are they running away? Or are they just temporarily going somewhere else out of a need for survival? It takes a lot more strength to leave than to stay."

I wondered if she was talking about herself, of how she'd left for a while. But we'd both returned, compelled by some inexplicable force.

Celeste continued. "And survival is why the birds return to the place they started, isn't it?"

"Unless they hit a window." I attempted humor to deflect the heaviness of the truth, that I would die in this place if I didn't leave as soon as I could, that the family ties that bound me here were the same ones that would smother me. That I might have had the strength to leave once, but I doubted I could do it again if I didn't do it soon.

"You are so much stronger than you know, Phoebe. And if you don't think you are, then imagine you're strong for just one day. You can renegotiate with yourself tomorrow."

Before I could argue, we both turned toward the sound of running feet approaching the closet.

"Aunt Phoebe? Mama wants to know if you're coming. She says she's getting a headache from smelling the exhaust from the running car."

I met Celeste's eyes. "Just one day," she said. "Right now, you only need to make it through this day."

I slowly pulled myself up. The only thing I was sure of was that I could pretend to be strong for one day, stringing together enough days to get me through the next two months.

"Phoebe, can I ask you something?"

I looked down to where Celeste still knelt on the carpeted floor of my mother's closet. "Of course."

She held out her hand. "Could you please help me stand?"


I felt like a chauffeur driving my mother and sister who sat in the back seat. My mother's purse sat on the passenger seat. I hadn't had a chance to go through it, but I'd seen her wallet inside and could only hope that I'd find her insurance and credit cards and maybe even a checkbook.

"Where are we going?" Mother looked out the window at the strip shopping malls and palm trees crowding Coleman Boulevard. The avenue was the main artery through Mount Pleasant and one that she'd traversed thousands of times, but her frown told me that she didn't recognize it. Her sense of displacement matched my own, a feeling that added to the surreal state of my life since my return to South Carolina.

I glanced in the rearview mirror to see if Addie would answer, but she was looking down at her phone, her fingers rapidly tapping on her screen.

"You have a doctor's appointment."

"No, I don't. I'm not sick. I haven't been sick a day in my life. Where are you taking me?"

My stomach tightened at the growing agitation in her voice. I glanced again at Addie, whose attention was still focused on her phone.

"This is just a wellness visit." I groaned inwardly as the approaching traffic light turned red. It was a short trip to the doctor's office, but having this conversation with my mother would make it seem interminable. I forced a light tone. "We want to make sure your mind is sharp so you can continue winning at bridge."

"My mind is sharp as a tack," she bit out. I heard the unmistakable click of her seat belt being unlatched. "Let me out of this car this minute."

I glanced at the GPS screen on the dash. We had less than three miles to go. I just needed to keep my mother inside the car. "Addie!" I shouted. "Get off your damned phone and help me."

"Watch your language!" Mother said. "I know I raised you much better than that. Just you wait until I tell your father. You're not too old for a spanking." She settled back into her seat, her arms crossed and wearing an expression of the aggrieved and disappointed mother.

"Where are we going?" Mother asked again as I pulled into the parking lot of the office complex.

"It's a surprise," I said. "Addie will help you out of the car." I slammed the car into Park, grabbed the purse, and exited. Leaning against my closed door, I took a few deep breaths.

Addie slowly got out and glowered at me. "What's your problem, Phoebe? Is it your time of the month?"

Blood rushed to my head while I tried not to allow Addie's dig to affect me. If I'd had more than an hour of sleep the night before, I might have even succeeded. "I'm sorry to pull you away from your OnlyFans site, but in case you didn't notice, our mother is confused and needs assurance. I'm doing the best I can, but I can't do this alone."

"Well, I've been doing it alone for months, and now it's your turn."

I wanted to shake her. "This isn't about taking turns," I said, not willing to admit that I'd had that exact thought during my meltdown in the closet. "This is about *our mother*. I'm sorry that the burden of her care has fallen on you, but you didn't tell me what was happening. And this was your choice, remember? You wanted someone to raise your daughter and pay your bills while you refused to grow up. It seems to me that the bill has come due."

"You think raising a daughter as a single mom is easy?"

"It doesn't seem that you've been doing much raising at all."

She took a step toward me. "So much for this being about *our mother*. I should have known you'd find an opportunity to make me feel bad. You've always been jealous of me and my relationship with Mother, and now you're just trying to punish me."

"I'm here, aren't I?" I threw my arms wide to emphasize my point and to stop my hands from causing harm to my sister. "I want the best for her just as much as you do. Stop making this all about you!" I was shouting now. I glanced around to see if anyone was watching.

That's when I spotted our mother making her way across the parking lot toward the street. "I'll get her," I said, already sprinting toward her, but not before I saw that Addie was crying.

By the time I'd corralled our mother into the building, Addie had dried her eyes and was avoiding engaging with me at all. She slid her arm through Mother's and led her to a seat in the waiting room. I usually don't notice office artwork, but the framed watercolors of various birds caught my attention. I found myself smiling at a small painting of a bluebird, the attention to detail so lifelike I swore it would move.

"Where's my pocketbook?" Mother began looking around her chair with short, agitated movements.

I grabbed the wallet from the purse and tucked it into the waistband of my jeans before handing her the pocketbook, mentally crossing my fingers that she wouldn't look inside.

After signing in at the front desk, a middle-aged receptionist sitting behind a small nameplate identifying her as Stephanie Ray greeted me with a warm smile and handed me a clipboard full of forms. I took it to a seat out of view from Mother so she wouldn't see me with her wallet. I sighed with relief when I spotted her credit cards and her checkbook, and began filling out the forms.

I'd reached the final page before encountering a question I couldn't answer. I took the clipboard back to the receptionist and asked, "What does it mean by health care power of attorney?"

Stephanie looked behind me to where Addie and Mother were looking through an issue of *Vogue*. "Is that your mother?"

"Yes. And my sister."

"Are either one of you her power of attorney or legal guardian?"

I stared at her blankly. "I have no idea."

A flash of sympathy crossed the receptionist's face. "Most of our patients will usually have one or the other who brings them to their appointments. Most of the time it's a spouse or child who is selected to help make decisions on the patient's behalf if the patient is unable to make them herself. There's a health care power of attorney and also a financial one, but we deal mostly with healthcare POAs."

I turned to get Addie's attention, but she'd left to use the restroom on the other side of the waiting room, leaving our mother eating candy from a dish on the coffee table, a dozen wrappers surrounding her chair.

I faced the receptionist again. "I'm sorry—I don't really know the answer to that question. Can I call the office later once I figure it out?"

"Of course." Her eyes showed understanding. "Does your mother have a computer?"

I thought of the clunky ancient laptop on my mother's desk. "Yes, she does, but—"

"Great," the receptionist said. She slid over a business card and underlined a web address on the bottom. "Have her create an account on the portal so she can access her medical records and medications. There's also a place to upload forms. Make sure she clicks the box that will allow us to share her care plan with you or your sister. That way we can discuss her care while we wait for you to locate the paperwork."

I stared down at the business card, recognizing it as the one I'd used to call for the appointment. L. M. Fitch. I'd forgotten to ask Celeste if she and the doctor were related. Not that it would have changed anything, but it might have given me a point of reference.

Looking up at the receptionist, I said, "I'll have to help my mother navigate the website . . ." I let my voice fade away.

I thanked the receptionist and walked back to my mother as Addie returned from the bathroom and resumed looking through the fashion magazine. I knelt on the floor and began picking up the wrappers, blocking the view of the candy dish so Mother would stop eating the chocolates. I counted twelve as I crumpled each one in my hand, feeling disheartened since Mother was a habitual calorie counter.

"Addie?" I said.

My sister looked up from the magazine.

"Are you Mother's power of attorney?"

She screwed up her face. "I don't have a clue."

My stomach turned. Every time I thought I'd cleared a hurdle, a brick wall appeared. "Never mind."

"Where are we?" My mother twisted in her seat to see the space around her. She spotted a woman sitting next to an elderly man, presumably the woman's father. "Who are you?" Mother demanded, her tone agitated.

"I'm sorry," I mouthed to the woman then reached behind me and grabbed the candy dish before thrusting it at my mother. "Would you like a piece?"

"I don't eat empty calories, Phoebe. It's a good habit, and one which you might want to consider."

Addie snickered, her attention still focused on the magazine.

"I need to use the ladies' room." Mother stood and began marching toward a door marked *PRIVATE*.

"Hang on," I said, gently pulling her back. "That's not the bathroom. Addie knows where it is."

Addie slammed down the magazine. "Come on, Mother. This way." They headed toward a short hallway while I sat down and put my head in my hands. I felt as if I were experiencing a waking nightmare where I show up for class to find out I'm late for an exam I hadn't studied for.

"Miss Manigault? The doctor is ready to see your mother now."

I lifted my head to see the door marked PRIVATE standing open, a man in a white lab coat holding an iPad in the threshold. I stood. "She'll be right back. She . . ." I pointed toward the hallway where Addie and our mother had disappeared then stopped midsentence.

The doctor was looking at me with an odd expression that might have mirrored my own. I took in his tieless shirt, his light brown hair bleached by the sun, its bright tips touching the top of his collar. These details didn't register right away because I was focused on his eyes. They were an earthy green, the hue made more vibrant by the contrast of his bronzed skin. I'd seen them before. Only once, but they were hard to forget. They were still the color of the marsh in summer. My gaze flickered down to his neck, and I wondered if he still wore the shark's tooth on a leather strap. As if feeling the weight of my gaze, he reached up and scratched his chest.

"I'm Phoebe Manigault. I think we've met before." The words were ridiculously inadequate, but I couldn't think of anything else to say.

"We've definitely met before." He glanced down at his iPad. "So my new patient Elizabeth Manigault . . ." He glanced at the receptionist, who was pretending not to be listening.

"Is my mother," I finished for him.

"Of course. And I'm sorry, I usually go over my list of new patients, but I didn't get a chance this morning." His eyes narrowed slightly. "Did my grandmother send you?"

"Your grandmother?" I stared back at him for a long moment until I realized who he was talking about. "Celeste Fitch," I said slowly as I put the pieces together. "No. My mother's GP referred her." I shook my head. "I saw your grandmother just an hour ago, and she never mentioned that her grandson was a neurologist."

I waited for him to offer an explanation, but he was staring at me with the kind of expression a person might use when finding an unwanted visitor on their doorstep.

Blood rushed to my cheeks. I couldn't stop staring at his eyes and remembering the last and only time we'd met. To fill the awkward silence, I said, "Why would you think she might have sent me here? Because our families have a history?"

His mouth twisted as if I'd said something amusing. "*A history?* That's one way to put it."

Addie and our mother returned from the restroom, sparing me from responding. Addie smiled her pageant smile, her radar no doubt sensing an attractive male within pouncing distance, and offered her hand to shake. "I'm Adeline Manigault, but you can call me Addie."

Dr. Fitch took her hand and shook it. "Nice to meet you," he said without smiling. "Liam Fitch. Although you might remember me as Liam Simmonds."

I remembered the name I'd seen on the empty folder in my father's desk. *"Simmonds?"* I repeated.

Addie froze, her expression shifting from flirtatious to suspicious. She pulled her hand away.

"You're Celeste's grandson," I said, even though I was now as confused as Addie appeared to be.

"We need to go," she said, drawing our mother's arm through hers.

"Addie. Stop. What are you doing?"

"We need to find another doctor. He's not the right doctor to give our mother the care she needs."

I stared at her with a mixture of surprise and anger. "No," I said a little too loudly as the woman and her elderly father both looked at me, but I didn't care. The lack of sleep compounded by the stress of the morning's events numbed me.

"No," I said again, even more loudly. "I made the appointment just like you asked, and I'll be damned if you change your mind now."

"Phoebe, watch your language." I turned my attention to my mother, and it was only then that I noticed that the bodice of her dress was incorrectly buttoned.

"Sorry, Mother."

"It's all right. We all make mistakes."

Her smile deflated my anger. This woman was still my strong, opinionated, and elegant mother. The mother who hadn't wanted a dog but left the faded spot on the stairs as a reminder of the pet I'd loved with all my heart. The mother who called me every birthday first thing in the morning and always said "I love you" before hanging up. Despite the mixed feelings I harbored for her, she was still my mother.

I turned to Addie. "Feel free to leave or stay. But Mother needs to see the doctor now, and she and I are staying for her appointment."

"You can't be serious, Phoebe. We know his family."

The emphasis on the word *family* brought back the memory of me telling Celeste about how my father had sued the boy who'd saved my life for breaking my ribs and how she hadn't said anything. Nor had she mentioned that her grandson was a neurologist in Mount Pleasant. It was almost as if she didn't want me to make the inevitable connection between her and Liam. The connection certainly explained why there'd be a folder with their name on it in my father's desk. But not why it had been emptied.

"May I say something?"

The three of us turned toward the doctor, my mother the only one with a benign smile. She'd been raised to never question authority, especially that in a white coat.

"I'm not going to take offense that you might question my professionalism or judgment in treating your mother because of a past history. As distasteful as it was, it has nothing at all to do with why you're here. I'm experienced and qualified to be your mother's neurologist, but if you would rather I refer you to another practice—"

"No," I said, almost without thought. Years of contradicting my sister made it my go-to response, but it was more than that. As a boy, this man had run into a thunderstorm to save a girl who was stupid enough to be caught outside in a storm. He had breathed his own breath into my lungs and restarted my heart. I didn't doubt that this was the doctor with whom I could trust my mother's care. "We're staying here."

"Mother, let's go." Addie began walking away, tugging on Mother's arm as if she were a toddler.

Elizabeth Manigault dug in her heels and pulled her arm away. "I don't want to go with you."

I was as shocked as Addie, but I didn't feel like gloating over my win. This wasn't a competition.

"Fine," Addie spat. "It's your funeral." She headed toward the exit, the soft close of the door robbing her of a final slam.

I fought the urge to run after her to make sure she remembered that I had the car keys and that she could call an Uber. She'd always been the one with the big dreams, but I'd always been the practical sister who took care of the planning and details. This should have meant that we would fit together like yin and yang and that we could form a partnership to help care for our mother. But life was never that easy.

Turning his attention to my mother, the doctor said, "I'm Dr. Fitch. Shall we?" He indicated his office where I could see a watercolor of a ruby-throated hummingbird hung between two large windows, and I knew without asking that his grandmother, Celeste, was the artist. It had been painted against a dark, cloudy background making the iridescent green feathers almost glow on the canvas. The painting made me think about how hummingbirds are the only birds in the animal kingdom that can fly backward, and I wondered at the painting's prominence inside Liam's office and if he also sometimes found himself wishing he could fly back in time and do things differently.

Mother gave him a gracious smile as if she were doing him a favor, and I followed her inside the office just as the sky lit up with a flash of light followed by a roll of thunder that shook my bones.

# 9

"To be better adapted to flying, many of the bones in a bird's body are hollow, and their feathers help to balance and steer in flight. In contrast, we humans are forced to learn what tools we need to survive. We might struggle for years before we learn what we really need, and some of us never do. It's funny to think that humans are considered the smartest of all the beasts on earth. I've met sparrows with a keener sense of survival than most people I know."

**Excerpt from the blog _The Thing with Feathers_**

## Celeste

THE SKY SHOOK with thunder, the rain pelting the metal roof with fury. I peeked into the dining room where Ophelia and Will were playing gin rummy at the table. Annie slept peacefully on the floor between them, her growing deafness a blessing during a storm. I'd taught Will how to play gin rummy, and he was now a bit of a card shark and rarely lost. When he got a little older, I'd teach him blackjack, mostly because his mother wouldn't approve.

While waiting for the women to return from the doctor's appointment, I made myself useful by tidying up without being intrusive. In the kitchen I returned the scattered contents of the drawers to their proper place and then ran a vacuum and dust rag over the entire downstairs.

My motives were not wholly altruistic, although I was glad I could help where it was so badly needed. Helping others was one of the reasons I'd become a nurse. But the truth was that I was apprehensive about seeing Phoebe after the appointment, after she learned that I hadn't been completely straightforward with her. I hoped that Phoebe's appreciation might soften any anger over my omission.

A car door slammed outside. Instead of seeing the tow truck I'd been told was on its way an hour before, I saw a small white sedan backing down the driveway and Addie running through the rain toward the front porch.

I met her at the front door. "Is everything all right? Where are your mother and sister?"

She brushed past me without a word before spinning around to glare at me. "Why are you still here? And why are you here at all?"

"I was passing by this morning—"

"Passing by? By accident? Like you weren't hoping to run into my sister?"

I closed the door behind me. "Partly," I said, guessing that being straightforward with Addie might be the only way to defuse her anger. "I did want to see Phoebe, and when I saw your mother's car parked erratically on the front yard, I came up to the porch and knocked on the door to make sure everyone was all right."

"We're all fine. So you can leave now."

I thought of how Ophelia had opened the door to a stranger that morning while Addie slept and Elizabeth ransacked the kitchen looking for her car keys, and I felt my own ire stir. "I can't," I said, keeping my voice calm. "They have my car, and it's storming outside so I can't walk. I'm sorry that I withheld my connection to your family. I will apologize to Phoebe when I see her and explain—"

"No. I want you out of here before they return." She began marching toward the stairs.

"I will wait until I speak with Phoebe before I leave. Because someone needs to be here for Ophelia."

She turned on me with fury. "Ophelia is *not* your responsibility, and we do not need you interfering where you're neither wanted nor needed."

I knew better than to argue with her, her fury so out of proportion to my crime that I knew there was something else fueling her anger, something that had nothing to do with her assumptions of why I'd befriended her sister.

The grandfather clock chimed. "Shit! I need to get to work. What am I supposed to do now?" She pressed her hands against the sides of her head. "Why is this happening to me?"

I restrained myself from answering what I was sure was a rhetorical question. "Why don't you take an Uber?"

She shook her head, her wet hair flinging around and splattering my face. "I can't. My credit card is maxed out because Mother hasn't paid the bill, and I just gave the last of my cash to the taxi to get me home. So now what am I supposed to do?"

There were so many things I wanted to suggest, the first being to lower her voice so that Ophelia and Will couldn't overhear her. Instead I said, "I would be happy to drop you off at work on my way home after I get my car back if Phoebe gets home soon. And I have some cash you can borrow if you want to call another taxi."

She glared at me again, her running mascara and wet hair giving her a wild beauty. "I know what you're doing. You're being nice so I won't insist that Phoebe stay away from you. Because you and I know why you want to be her friend, don't we? But I won't allow my sister to be taken advantage of by you or anybody else. Besides, just in case you haven't already asked, she doesn't have her dreams anymore, so she can't help you. So why don't you go ahead and leave? A little rain isn't going to kill you. I'll tell Phoebe you had to go, and then she doesn't have to hear from you again. You can pick up your car tomorrow."

I took a deep breath. "To be clear, I like your sister. Her curiosity of the natural world and her eagerness to make others happy, despite how she might be treated, reminds me a lot of my granddaughter, which is probably why I enjoy being with her. I also think she could use a friend right now, and I'm happy to oblige. If you object to my presence, maybe you could try to be more of a sister to her so Phoebe won't need me as much. It seems as if the two of you might need each other now more than ever."

She narrowed her eyes. If I hadn't felt so sorry for her, I might have felt alarm. But I'd seen a glimmer of fear that I found more confusing than alarming. Maybe she really was afraid that I was trying to take advantage of Phoebe's strange gift, but I doubted Addie had matured past being concerned only about herself. Maybe she was afraid that I understood her family's dynamics better than she did. Either way, nothing justified her antagonism toward me. I was determined to kill her with kindness until she understood that I wasn't a threat.

"Just wait until I tell my mother who you are. Over the years I know she's tried to forget that stupid lawsuit ever happened, and I know your presence—or that of your grandson—will not be welcome. Speaking of which, I'm going to find another neurologist for my mother. Because I'm sure you would have no problem using your grandson to further interfere in my family's business."

She turned on her heel and headed for the stairs. I didn't have the heart to remind her that my family had been the victim of the lawsuit or that her mother wouldn't recall it or, if she did, wouldn't remember to be offended that I had reinserted myself into her life.

I called out to her. "Addie, I was about to ask the children if they'd like a snack, and I'd be happy to fix something for you, too, if you're hungry."

She continued up the stairs, her response the slamming of her door.

* * *

By the time Phoebe and her mother returned, Elizabeth's car had been towed, and Addie had left in a taxi. I didn't want to make her ask for money, so I'd left cash tucked in between the framed photographs on the hallway table. When I'd emerged from the kitchen after preparing a shopping list for easy-to-prepare meals and other essentials I thought Elizabeth might need, the cash and Addie were gone.

The rain had stopped by the time I heard their footsteps slowly climbing up to the porch, and when I opened the door, they both looked exhausted.

Elizabeth glowered at me. "Who are you?"

"Mother," Phoebe began, her voice vibrating with her last nerve.

"I'm Celeste. Welcome home," I said cheerfully, throwing the door wide. "Elizabeth, I can't think of anybody else better to show me the correct way to set a table, and I know you'd like to eat in the dining room tonight with Phoebe and Ophelia."

Mollified, Elizabeth allowed herself to be ushered inside as Phoebe raised her eyebrows in question.

Turning to Phoebe, I said, "Will showed me how to use an app on his phone to order a nice dinner for the three of you, and it should be here in about half an hour."

She looked like she might cry, so I continued, "Go ahead and get a beer from the fridge and put your feet up. The children can help your mother set the table to give you a few minutes to gather yourself."

By the time I had the children and Elizabeth situated in the dining room practicing various napkin folds with antique Belgian lace squares, Phoebe had already polished off a bottle of beer, the nearly empty bottle sitting on the kitchen table in front of her. "Can I get you another?" I asked.

She stared at me with eyes bleary from exhaustion. "Why didn't you tell me who you were? Or mention that the chances of the neurologist I was taking my mother to just might be your grandson? There aren't many in Mount Pleasant, so the odds were pretty high that it would be him."

I pulled up a chair and sat down. "You're absolutely right. I should have said something the moment I realized who you were. Although a part of me was confident that your knowledge of the legal wrangling was most likely secondhand and that you wouldn't recognize our last name since it had been changed. That doesn't excuse me, of course."

"No, it doesn't. So why didn't you just tell me? Your silence makes it seem like you've been harboring this grudge all these years and finally found an opportunity to seek revenge on my family."

We stared at each other in silence, and then before I could stop myself, I began laughing, not just at the ridiculous thing she'd just said but at her earnestness while saying it.

Her eyes narrowed with anger, her expression gradually softening as a reluctant grin crossed her face. "That sounded weird, didn't it? Sorry. I watch a lot of film noir, so my mind gravitates toward plot twists." She became serious again. "So please give me a better answer because I'm confused."

"I'm sorry. I truly am. If it makes you feel any better, I hadn't even realized Ophelia might be related to you until I saw you together. Meaning I didn't really have time to come up with a long-simmering revenge plot." She didn't return my smile.

I continued. "I harbor no ill-feelings toward you or your family. The only person against whom I might hold a grudge is your father, and he's been gone a long time. If I felt any ill-will against your mother—which I don't—it would have disappeared as soon as I saw her. I remember your father was a lot like a bull in a china shop, charging at anything he considered a threat to his family. I imagine your mother, as strong as she might have once been, chose other avenues in which to exert her influence and left the nasty business of defending your family up to him."

Phoebe looked down in her lap as a smile softened her face. "Yeah. That would be about right."

"It wasn't a surprise to me or anyone who knew his reputation that he would sue my family because my grandson had broken your ribs while saving your life. I had to hire my own lawyer, which nearly bankrupted me, but Liam and I survived. What almost broke me was the disappearance of my granddaughter. Liam's sister, Julie."

"Julie Fitch? That's your granddaughter?"

I nodded.

"I only vaguely remember the story, which is probably why I didn't get the connection when I learned your last name. I'm so sorry. It was all anybody could talk about for a while—except for us. Mother and Daddy forbade us from discussing it at home because they said it would be too upsetting. They threw away the newspapers, too, so all my knowledge is from what my best friend, Mary-Simms McSwain, told me at school. Which didn't really amount to a lot. She lived in Charleston, so she and her family were a little removed from us here in Mount Pleasant. Even Addie wouldn't talk about it with me. So all I can recall is that Julie stayed after school for something and never came home. Did you ever find out what happened to her?"

"That's the million dollar question, isn't it? We still don't know. She was in her final semester her senior year at Wando. She'd stayed late one night after choir practice to go over a song on one of the practice pianos—we didn't have one—and that's the last time she or her car was ever seen. The police and the private detectives I hired couldn't find any trace of her. Once in a while there will be renewed interest in the case, but it's been almost seventeen years. If there are clues out there, they've either long disappeared or are too well-hidden to ever be found." I sighed. "I know it's not likely the case, but I like to tell myself that she decided to run away and start a new life elsewhere. Liam, however . . ." I shrugged. "He's more practical and has been urging me to have her officially declared dead. I won't stop hoping until she's found."

"I'm not going to say *I'm sorry* because it's so inadequate. I can't imagine what you and Liam have been going through all these years. It's unfathomable to me."

"Thank you. And that's why I needed to leave for a bit. I found a wonderful job as the lead nurse at a retirement community in the mountains of North Carolina—far enough from here, but close enough that I could see Liam during his college breaks."

"And then you came back."

"I did. As you grow older, you'll begin examining the parts of your earlier life that you once believed were detrimental to your well-being. That's when you find that the wounds that hurt you the most were what you needed to survive."

Phoebe began chewing on the nub of her fingertip. "I just don't understand why everything has to be such a struggle. I survived my childhood. I'd like to think that was enough trauma for one lifetime. And you lost your husband and daughter way too soon, and your granddaughter is missing."

"That's the thing, isn't it? We can't see the bottom of our bags of trouble, so we have no idea if we're nearing the end of them or still near the top or even somewhere in the middle. I believe the trick is to stop counting and look for something else to occupy your time."

Phoebe forced her hand into her lap, tucking her finger into her closed fist. "Why didn't you come right out and tell me about our connection when Ophelia and I saw you at the Gala Bakery?"

I placed my hands flat on the table, studying the knobby knuckles and ropy veins, the scratched gold wedding band that I never took off. I was proud of these hands. They'd rocked babies and held the hands of the dying. They had cooked countless meals and comforted the inconsolable. I didn't wear nail polish or jewelry to disguise the fact that they'd been around for a while because their age spots and purple scars made them beautiful.

I met her eyes. "Because I knew from that first moment that you were lonely and might be in need of a friend, and I'm one of those annoying people who offers friendship to every lonely soul I encounter. It drives Liam crazy when I invite strangers to dinner. When I met you, you appeared to have been ripped from your element, like a baby owl finding herself in an osprey nest."

Phoebe nodded, digesting everything I'd just said.

I continued. "I didn't want to bring up that nasty business and have you suspicious about any ulterior motives because, I promise you, I don't have any."

She nodded slowly then stood and opened the fridge. "Can I get you something to drink?"

I declined, and she returned to the table with a bottle of water. She took a long swig then swallowed. "I'm guessing you know that the lightning strike gave me more than a bad burn. It also sometimes gave me premonitions in my dreams."

"Yes. It would have been impossible not to have known about it. It's a small town. But your brush with celebrity has nothing to do with me befriending you."

The doorbell rang. "I'll get it," I said. "That must be the food."

I'd made it to the doorway when she spoke again.

"So you were never intending to ask me about my dreams."

I stopped and faced her again. "I didn't say that."

"Save your breath. They're unpredictable and not something I can turn on or off. Besides, I don't have them anymore."

The doorbell rang again, and I hurried out of the kitchen. Phoebe was lying. It was her secret to keep, but it gave me hope. I entered the foyer at the same time as Elizabeth.

"Are our guests here already?" she asked.

"No, just the caterer," I responded.

I reached the handle just as the lights flicked off and the air-conditioning stopped humming. I threw the door open allowing the sticky rain-soaked air to sweep inside uninvited.

# 10
~

"Australian brush turkeys emerge from their eggs entombed
by their nesting mound and spend up to two days on their
backs clawing their way out. With no guidance or protection
by their parents, it's not surprising that the survival rate of the
brush turkey chicks in the first week is less than three percent.
Yet somehow, the breed survives—and even flourishes—most
likely because only the toughest chicks survive then pass
along their genetic will of steel to their own offspring."

**Excerpt from the blog *The Thing with Feathers***

## *Phoebe*

I AWOKE BATHED in sweat as the remnants of a dream nudged me fully awake. It was a new dream, and it took me a moment to recall the details and the person at the center of it. A woman was riding her bike down what seemed to be a neighborhood street, black asphalt and no painted lines. I wasn't the cyclist, but my leg muscles felt the strain of pedaling, my face and hair slapped by the wind.

I felt all of this, but my vantage point was that of a spectator on the side of the road, watching the bike approach while also aware of a gaping pothole in her path. I began shouting for her to watch out, my throat growing raw from the effort, but she didn't hear me as she barreled toward the deep dip in the road. My teeth felt the jarring motion as her front wheel fell into the hole and she was catapulted over the handlebars, her bare arms and legs sliding over loose gravel until coming to a stop, the bicycle landing on top of her.

I watched in mute horror as she lay still, my muscles softening with relief when she moved and began to extricate herself
from the mangled bike. I could feel the bleeding scratch on her
right cheek and the raw patch on her chin that still had small
stones embedded in it. She lifted her head so I could see her face.
I knew this woman. Although I couldn't think of how I did or
what her name was.

I lay in the silence listening to Ophelia's breathing, trying to
place who the woman was. In the past, my premonitions had
always involved someone with whom I'd had recent contact,
which is why Addie had started inviting me out with her friends.
I hadn't been lying when I'd told Addie and Celeste that I didn't
have them anymore. Other than the one of the car going over
a bridge, this latest was the only one I'd had in a long time, not
since I'd moved across the country.

I squirmed, my back aching from sleeping on the hard floor
of my old bedroom, erroneously believing it might be cooler
there than in the bed with Ophelia's body pressed against mine
and her hot breath on my back. I lay there wallowing in my
misery as my anger at Addie grew. The electricity had been
shut off, and we were stuck with the heat of a South Carolina
summer until the electric company's office reopened on Monday. We just needed to suffer through the weekend, assuming I
didn't murder my sister and end up in prison where at least I'd
have air-conditioning.

The windows had been opened upstairs allowing in an in-
effectual breeze from the water. A buzzing insect, whose size
could only be determined by the loud thwapping sound it made
against the window in its desperate throes to free itself, had found
its way through a hole in the screen.

My main concern was for my mother, whose heat intoler-
ance was as well-known as it was surprising for a South Carolina native. She'd insisted on sleeping in her bed and wearing

her long-sleeved nightgown. At least she had windows that allowed a cross breeze, but every time I opened one, she shut it and then asked me to turn on her fans. Thankfully full dark had descended so that after she fell asleep I opened her windows and pulled down her covers.

I carefully extricated myself from the heap of blankets we'd used as a makeshift mattress and went into the hallway. Addie's bedroom door was open, and I used my phone to turn on the flashlight to see if she might be sleeping on the floor. I kicked at the piles of clothing on the floor, not caring if my foot made contact with my sister's sleeping body. It didn't.

I made my way into my mother's room. It was much cooler in here, a soft breeze riffling her hair as she slept curled onto her side in the fetal position. She seemed so frail and helpless, two adjectives I would have never used to describe her and which would have undoubtedly made her angry. As I watched her sleep, I wondered at the irony that would have put me in the position of her caretaker. She had never tried to hide the fact that I wasn't her favorite child or that I was the source of her biggest disappointment.

With hindsight and distance, it had occurred to me that my mother had probably loved me in her own way if only because I was her daughter. I'd accepted her terms and stopped trying so hard to win her approval. I had always hoped that at some point we might find a way to meet in the middle, to find the thing in each other that completed us and made us whole.

As I listened to her breathe, a darkness consumed me, swallowing my heart and tightening my stomach. That one day I'd always dreamed of would never happen. Because time passed and people got older and the hope of *one day* that we'd relied on fell by the wayside. I wanted to kneel by her bedside and shake her awake and tell her I was sorry for all the ways I'd fallen short. To finally have the conversation I'd been planning to have and that was more than a decade overdue. But like so many of the things we put off in life, it was too late. I gently pulled up the sheet and let it fall softly on her shoulders.

Outside, the choking squawk of a night heron disturbed the night, the hollow echo in tandem with my thoughts. I had the sudden and irrational need to talk with Addie. She was the only person in the world with whom I shared a mother. It was our only connection, but it might be the bridge we needed to find our way back to the hushed middle-of-the-night conversations and confidences we'd shared before the burdens of growing up had separated us into two seemingly opposing camps.

A bead of sweat dripped down my back between my shoulder blades, a reminder of our current predicament and how the entire situation was Addie's fault. If she'd paid attention to the *Past Due* messages stamped on the envelopes before she'd shoved them into piles in our father's library, I'd be sound asleep in my air-conditioned bedroom instead of wandering the darkened house in the middle of the night.

I turned to leave, but the hulking shadow of my mother's desk and ancient laptop computer made me pause. I recalled what the receptionist at Liam Fitch's office had said about setting up an account to access my mother's medical records.

After slowly easing myself into the desk chair, I opened the lid and hit the power button. I doubted my mother had used the laptop in a while, but she always kept it plugged in, which meant that the battery should be fully charged even if the vintage processor chugged along at a snail's pace.

When the screen lit up, I glanced behind me to make sure she was still sleeping. Aunt Sassy used to say that Mother could sleep through a hurricane, which was one of the reasons Addie never got caught sneaking out at night. Daddy was deaf in one ear due to a rifle mishap during a hunting trip, and he always slept with his good ear down. The only thing that had prevented Addie from throwing a full-scale party after our parents had gone to bed had been me and my growing role as the rain on Addie's parade.

I set the laptop's Wi-Fi to my phone's hot spot and recalled the website I'd seen on the doctor's business card, typing it into the struggling browser, trying to be patient while the page opened. I set up a username and password for my mother and then assigned myself and Addie to be our mother's personal representatives. Once I figured out the power of attorney, I'd upload those forms, but this was enough for now.

I was about to shut down the computer when it occurred to me that I could probably set up online accounts for all the utilities and schedule automatic payments, too. I felt a surge of hope as I searched for the electric company's website to pay the bill, my hope deflating at the message alerting me that the website was down until Monday morning for maintenance.

My mother sighed in her sleep, and I froze, feeling as if I'd been caught committing grand larceny. A half laugh emerged from my mouth as I considered the legality of what I was doing. But my priority was making sure my mother was taken care of and could live in her house with running water and electricity.

I shut down the laptop and closed the lid. In the morning, I'd find a coffee shop where I could plug in my phone and the computer so I could sit down with the stack of bills and pay the overdue accounts and set them up for automatic payments. Assuming there was money in the checking account.

I had always believed that my father had left my mother with enough funds to pay her bills and live comfortably for the rest of her life. I wasn't sure if he'd also planned on paying for Ophelia's education and room and board for both Addie and her daughter. I had the horrifying thought that he hadn't and that the money my mother had been living off was slowly trickling down the drain.

I quietly left my mother's room and made my way to the top of the stairs, peering down into the darkness with the stray thought that Addie might have decided to sleep down there. I was halfway down the steps when the woman's face from my dream drifted from my subconscious. It was Liam Fitch's receptionist, Stephanie. Our interaction had been brief yet memorable. At one time, I would have warned her of what would happen. Now I was more wary of the attention and was reluctant to make myself vulnerable again. I also couldn't think of a scenario that made sense for me to call her and let her know that she would fall off her bike at some undetermined day and time. Besides, I told myself, people fell off their bikes every day, and she hadn't been—or wouldn't be—seriously hurt. I continued justifying my inaction as I went down the stairs.

I threw open the front door and stepped out onto the porch. Our house was the only residence shrouded in darkness, but the neighbor's outdoor lights illuminated our empty driveway. I hadn't expected to see my mother's car, but I was hoping to find some indication that Addie had made it home.

I turned on my phone's screen and checked for messages to see if Addie had thought to let me know that she wasn't coming home. I wasn't surprised to see that she hadn't. Just in case, I sent her a text, listening inside the quiet house for a responding ping. But the only sounds were the dripping of the day's rain from the eaves and the incessant ticking of the grandfather clock.

It was much cooler outside, so I closed the door behind me and sat down on one of the front porch rocking chairs to wait for her. I wasn't going back to sleep anyway. A spark of worry for my sister flickered briefly then just as quickly diminished. Addie not coming home wasn't unexpected. She knew lots of people who would be happy to offer her a couch or bed for the night. She was like a cat who always ended up on her feet no matter how far she fell.

My rocking was frantic at first then slipped into a more relaxed pace. I remembered sitting in these exact chairs with Aunt Sassy, watching her hands sign. *Worrying is a lot like sitting in a rocking chair: it gives you something to do but won't get you anywhere.* I smiled at the memory and closed my eyes as I listened to the sounds of millions of crying insects rubbing their gossamer wings together in a vain attempt to be heard over the din.

Hot sun struck my face, popping my eyes open as I found myself slumped over the arm of my chair, telling me that I had somehow fallen asleep. I winced as I sat up and attempted to straighten my neck. A car-door slam brought my attention to the foot of the driveway in time to see an old rust-colored Camaro pulling away and my sister approaching the house. She absently tugged on the ends of her sleeves as she walked, her shoulders rounded. She appeared defeated, which was a strange word to attach to Addie.

I stood, needing to hold on to the railing while the blood returned to my extremities, and waited for my sister to notice me.

When she spotted me, she straightened, pulling her shoulders back. "You're up early," she said, as she walked past me and opened the front door. She stepped back quickly. "Why is it so hot inside?"

I grabbed the door and pushed on it, slamming it in her face. "Because we don't have any air-conditioning, Addie. It got shut off because the bill hadn't been paid despite repeated attempts to let us know that we were late."

My voice shook as I brought my face closer to hers. "Our mother and your daughter are upstairs sleeping in their own sweat because you couldn't be bothered to open an envelope. Do you have any idea how pathetic that is?"

Her face blanched, but she tried to hide behind it with a familiar smirk. "Take a chill pill. All you need to do is pay the bill."

She reached for the door handle, but I knocked her arm away, hitting it harder than I needed to.

"Ouch." She rubbed her forearm. "That hurt."

"Good. You deserved it. But one more oblivious comment from you, and I swear I will not be able to restrain myself."

Addie crossed her arms. "Fine. So, what do you want me to do?"

I sat in the rocking chair. "Sit down. We need to talk."

"Just do it quickly. Joe's coming back at nine to take me to the garage to pick up my car."

"Is Joe your new boyfriend?"

Her shudder was almost indiscernible, so slight that I might have imagined it. "I guess you can call him that."

"I was going to say that you haven't grown up at all, but I changed my mind. At least you know the guy's name now."

She half stood, but I held her back. "We need to talk about Mother's finances."

She sat back in her chair as if trying to distance herself from something distasteful. "You were the one with straight As in math and science. I don't have a clue."

"This isn't about math or science, Addie. And I don't have a clue, either. I was hoping that maybe the two of us could figure this out together."

"But you actually like that stuff. I don't. It's one of the reasons I asked you to come home."

I tried to force a smile, but I was certain it looked more like a grimace. "This isn't about being good at math, Addie. It's about responsibility. It's about putting systems in place so that bills are paid and Mother takes her new medications. I need her insurance card, too, if you can get that for me, so I can fill her prescriptions from Dr. Fitch. I searched in her wallet, but it wasn't there."

Her face hardened. "If you're trying to make me feel bad, it's working. Mother never asked for my help with any of that, so of course I have no clue where she keeps it."

My fingernails dug into the palms of my hands. I somehow managed to keep my voice level. "But what about recently when you noticed she wasn't acting like herself? Didn't it occur to you then to start asking questions?"

"I've been busy. I've got a life. Besides, you know how Mother gets when someone tries to interfere with her way of doing things."

"Yeah. I know." I studied my sister with her defensive posture and complete lack of understanding. I wanted to hate her, to blame her for being oblivious about pretty much everything. But I couldn't. Our mother had made Addie believe that she was the child who could do no wrong simply because she looked like an angel and had the charm needed to get away with questionable behavior. Even her atrocious grades in everything except music and drama got overlooked and excused.

She tucked her hair behind an ear, and I saw crusted blood surrounding the empty hole where she usually wore an earring. "You're bleeding," I said.

She reached up to feel her lobe and winced. "Yeah, I accidentally pulled out my earring while I was brushing my hair." She shook her head, covering her ear with her hair again.

I took a deep breath. "Let's work together to figure this all out, all right? I'm going back to Oregon at the end of the summer, so it's important that everything is in place for you before I leave. I'll set up online accounts to help manage bills, and I can do that from Oregon. But I need you to do something first."

Her mouth tightened. "What?"

"Remember Dale Prioleau at Daddy's law firm? He had such a crush on you." Dale had joined the firm as a young associate when we were in high school, and even then I remembered the way he hung on to every word Addie said. "Actually, didn't you two go out a few times when you were working for the TV station?"

A pink flush blossomed on her cheeks. "Yeah. I remember. He's a nice guy. Just too nice for me." She pulled nervously on the sleeves of her sweater, then crossed her arms.

"Is *too nice* not a good thing?"

Instead of answering, she said, "Why are you mentioning Dale?"

"Because I need you to set up an appointment with him to see if the firm has records of a power of attorney for Mother for both financial and health matters. Daddy was a good lawyer, and that's one thing he wouldn't have left to chance. We also need to know where the monthly deposits into her account are coming from. I'm assuming it's a trust Daddy set up, but I need to know for sure so I can budget her expenses. I'm sure it will be easy to get Dale to help you."

She rounded her shoulders again as if trying to disappear into her sweater. I noticed sweat beads forming at her hairline.

"Why don't you take off your sweater, Addie. It's a hundred degrees out here and even hotter inside." I reached for a sleeve to help her, but she yanked her arm away.

"Stop. I want it on."

I sat back. "Fine. So will you call Dale, please?"

"I guess I can do it Monday since that's my day off."

"Great. And once it's light out, I'll find a place to plug in Mother's computer and set up online checking and autopay for her monthly bills."

"See?" Addie said. "You're the smart one. That's why you can figure this stuff out."

I turned to her. "You're just as smart, you know. You could have figured it out on your own."

"Hardly."

A mockingbird alighted on the sagging branch of the old oak and began singing its morning song, its bright and chipper voice at odds with my current mood.

Keeping her gaze on the bird, she asked, "What did Dr. Fitch say yesterday after I left?"

"Not a lot. He gave her several cognitive tests for which Mother was surprisingly cooperative—probably because the doctor was young and male. He'll write up his notes and post them on her patient portal so that we can read it, but he said that it does appear that Mother has significant short-term memory loss along with dementia-related mood swings. He gave me a couple of prescriptions to help with both of those issues." I pressed my hands against my head at one more hurdle I'd have to jump. "If you have any idea where her health care ID cards might be, please let me know. I really need to get those meds."

I'd expected another shoulder shrug and was surprised when Addie answered. "Mother sent me to the CVS on Ben Sawyer Boulevard to pick up prescriptions for her. All they needed was her date of birth and address."

"That's very helpful. Thank you."

She seemed uncomfortable with my thanks and focused on rocking the chair back and forth. "Will the meds make her better?"

She sounded so much like a little child that I considered lying to her. But she was my adult sister, and we were both too old to pretend. I recalled a sailing trick our father had taught us, to keep our gaze focused on the horizon if we felt seasick to fool our brains into thinking we weren't moving. But we were no longer children, and there was no turning the boat back toward the sanctuary of home.

"No. They won't. The medications available right now can only alleviate symptoms. There's no cure."

"But how do we know that she's been diagnosed correctly? That's only one doctor's opinion, right? We need to take her to another doctor who knows how to make her better."

I reached for her hand and squeezed it. It was the first time I'd touched her without any feelings of animosity since my return, and it felt like finding a favorite yet forgotten sweater hidden in the back of the closet. I was reminded of when I'd crawl into Addie's bed during thunderstorms, while we each pretended to be the strong one. "I'm scared, too."

She stilled her chair, and then, without saying anything, she pulled her hand away and stood. "I told you Liam Fitch was the wrong doctor for Mother. He doesn't know what he's talking about, or he's deliberately making it sound worse than it is."

"Do what you want, Addie. But it's not going to change anything. Liam gave me a few information booklets to read as well as recommendations for further reading so we can educate ourselves on the progression—"

"See? He's already talking about progression as if there's no chance of getting better. He's given up."

I was torn between sympathy and anger, but in the end my exhaustion won out, and I could only sit there, staring back at her.

She yanked open the door to go inside.

"Are you still planning to call Dale?"

In response, she slammed the door shut, leaving me alone again on the porch with the cheerful mockingbird, contently oblivious to the turmoil brewing under our roof.

# 11

"Siblicide is characteristic among pelicans, ospreys, egrets, and other birds that lay two eggs. If you see a baby bird that's fallen from the nest, it may be an intentional propulsion from a sibling. This behavior may seem cruel to us, especially since neither bird parent will intervene during a sibling squabble, but such actions ensure the highest probability of passing the parents' genes on to the next generation."

**Excerpt from the blog *The Thing with Feathers***

## Celeste

WILL AND ANNIE walked at a brisk pace in front of me while I tried to keep up. I had a blister on my heel from power walking the previous day in new sneakers, and the bandage I'd applied that morning had already fallen off. It was barely nine o'clock in the morning and the blanket of hot and humid air felt like someone had left the oven door open. "Where's the fire?" I called out.

"It's not me, it's Annie. I think she already knows the way to Ophelia's house."

He wasn't wrong, but I also knew that he was just as excited about visiting the Manigault home. He and Ophelia had bonded over gin rummy, and he was as eager to return as I was for him to be doing something besides spending his summer playing video games.

"Could you please try Phoebe's phone again? I'm worried because she hasn't called us back."

He pulled his iPhone from his back pocket. "You really need to get your own cell phone, Gran. Not having one makes you look old."

"Believe me, Will. My lack of a cell phone has nothing to do with me looking old."

He redialed the number I'd been asking him to try since we left my house. After a moment, he shrugged. "Still no answer. Maybe she forgot to charge her phone and it ran out of battery."

"Probably," I said, although I sounded as unconvinced as I felt.

When we reached the Manigault house, everything appeared the same as when I'd last seen it, including the empty driveway. Yet the whirring of the cicadas and buzzing insects seemed much louder. It took me a moment to realize that the air-conditioning wasn't running.

Holding on to Annie's leash, Will raced up onto the front porch and rang the doorbell. "I don't hear it," he called out before pressing it two more times.

For the second time in as many days, I felt that there was something not right at the Manigault house. The morning temperature hovered in the blistering nineties and there wasn't a house in South Carolina with access to air-conditioning that didn't have it on full-blast for the entire summer.

"Maybe they're in the back." Will ran down the steps, Annie faithfully keeping up as they ran past an enormous camellia bush and disappeared around the corner of the house. By the time I'd made it to the screened porch, my heel throbbed, but I felt relief at the sound of Ophelia's voice.

I stood still as Phoebe approached. Her T-shirt and athletic shorts were drenched with sweat, her hair pulled behind her head in a high ponytail. A bright blue slash of paint bisected one of her cheeks.

"Celeste, hi. Is everything all right?"

I nodded, fanning myself with my hand in a feeble attempt to cool off. "I was about to ask you the same thing. Will has been calling you from his phone, but it keeps going straight to voice mail."

"Yeah. Sorry about that. The electricity was shut off—long story—and we can't get it turned back on until Monday. Same with the landline. I'm saving my phone battery since I can't charge it. I'd planned to go to a coffee shop with air-conditioning and outlets so I can charge and get some work done, but Addie's not here and I didn't want to leave my mother."

I looked behind her toward the foot of the dock where Elizabeth sat beneath a wide-brimmed straw hat, tucked under the shade of a tall cedar. An empty chair was placed next to her. She was watching Ophelia paint a small piece of wood that had been placed on top of newspaper in front of the chairs, but splotches of blue on the grass showed where she'd overshot the wood. Will squatted next to her, holding a squirming Annie who seemed desperate to decorate the dock with blue paw prints.

"What is Ophelia making?" I asked.

"A bird feeder. My aunt Sassy taught me when I was a little girl, and I thought Ophelia could use a project." She narrowed her eyes as she regarded me. "So, you decided to stop by because I wasn't answering my phone?"

"I promise I'm not stalking you." I shrugged. "I'm sorry. I'm overprotective of Liam and Will as well. Ever since Julie disappeared, I can't help but imagine the worst-case scenario. I suppose because of Ophelia, my protectiveness has netted in the two of you."

Phoebe kept looking at me, making me uncomfortable.

"I'm sorry," I said again. "I'll pretend to be more aloof where you're concerned if that might help, but I don't think I can completely turn it off."

A half smile lit her face. "No, that's not necessary. It's just . . . ."

When she didn't finish, I said, "It's just that you're not used to having anyone check in on you?"

Phoebe shrugged. "Pretty much. Not since Aunt Sassy, anyway. It's not like I was a wild child or anything. Not like my sister, although our parents didn't have a clue to most of her exploits. The wildest thing I ever did was skip school one day to read *Gone with the Wind*."

"You wicked girl," I said with a laugh.

"Not quite. I do wish I'd messed around more. Been a little more like Addie."

"Speaking of which, where's your sister?" I asked. "Camped out in front of the electric company to be there when they open?"

"Ha. I wish. A *friend*," she said using air quotes, "took her to the garage to collect our mother's car, and then she picked up an earlier shift at the restaurant because it's air-conditioned. Can't say I blame her." Phoebe wiped the inside of her elbow across her forehead. "It's hotter than Hades out here. I tried to pay the bill online, but their site is down for maintenance until Monday morning." Forcing a smile, she said, "Why don't you go take a seat next to Mother? It's in the shade and a little cooler by the water—*cooler* being relative. Sort of like comparing Death Valley to hell, but whatever."

"I'd love to. Would you mind getting us some water? We ladies of a certain age get dehydrated easily."

"Sure. How about some lemonade? It's the fake low-calorie stuff my mother likes, but it'll do in a pinch. Unless you'd like plain water. Just as a warning, neither one will be cold."

I took Annie's leash from Will. "Whatever is easiest for you, Phoebe."

She turned to her niece. "Ophelia, could you please grab one of those folding tray tables and a chair from the screen porch and set them under the tree next to Mimi?"

"I'll do it," Will said, jumping to his feet.

Phoebe and Will walked away together as I took Annie to sit in the shade next to Elizabeth. A great white egret glided down from the sky to the shallow edge of the marsh, posing like a model on stick-thin legs.

"Who are you?" Elizabeth asked.

"I'm Celeste. And this is Annie."

She smiled at the little dog. "Bailey?"

"Annie," I corrected.

Elizabeth frowned. "Bailey is Phoebe's dog, but I give her treats when no one is looking."

"Really? And why don't you want anyone to see you doing that?"

She blinked, her eyes showing a clarity I hadn't seen before. "Because I said I don't want a dog. Bailey lets me spoil her. Charles says it's because our other daughter doesn't let me spoil her."

"Phoebe?"

"She's never had much use for me." She frowned then reached down to pat Annie's head. When she looked back at me, a cloud had moved over the surface of her eyes. "Who are you?"

"I'm Celeste. Are you the wonderful gardener who tends the camellia bush on the side yard? I bet it's stunning when it blooms in winter."

Her eyebrows knitted together over her nose. "I think I am." She turned toward the camellias. "They're so beautiful, aren't they? They should have a fragrance to match." A weary grin pinched her face. "Such a disappointment, really. You can't see beauty when you close your eyes." Her gaze focused on Ophelia, who was painting a bluebird on the roof of the feeder. The bird was a whimsical rendition, with oversize eyes and what appeared to be a smiling beak. But the proportions were all correct, the bird immediately identifiable.

"That's wonderful, Ophelia," I said. "Do you need orange paint for the breast? I've got some in my studio I can bring next time I see you."

Ophelia nodded vigorously, her glasses slipping down to the middle of her nose. "Yes, please."

She tried to slide them up with the back of her wrists since her fingers were coated with wet paint, but she couldn't get them high enough to stay. I was about to hoist myself out of my chair when Elizabeth stood. Bending over her granddaughter, she gently placed the glasses on the bridge of Ophelia's nose before smoothing the girl's hair behind her ears.

Elizabeth straightened. "You remind me so much of a little girl I once knew. So smart and talented."

"What happened to her?" Ophelia asked.

Elizabeth studied her hands and spread the fingers wide before reaching forward and dipping her thumb into the blue paint. She brought it to her face, examining it as if she wasn't sure what it was, and then brought it down to the skirt of her dress and smeared it across the fabric. "She went away." The grin of a naughty child settled on her face. Elizabeth pointed at the smear of blue. "She did that."

Ophelia looked at Elizabeth in confusion. "You did, Mimi."

Elizabeth's grin faded, her gaze focused on the blue streak. "I yelled at her, and she went away. Sassy told me to apologize, but I didn't." Her lips twisted. "I think I forgot how."

The sound of a banging door turned our attention toward the back deck.

"I think we have everything," Phoebe said, emerging from the screen porch, Will waving a bag of Cheetos behind her.

"I found these, too," he shouted, jumping from the middle step down to the ground.

I watched as Elizabeth took an unsteady step. "Ophelia, sweetie, could you please help your grandmother back to her chair?"

She took Elizabeth's hand and led her back, her grandmother shuffling next to her.

Phoebe approached with a tray table and folding chair, noticing the bright blue slash on Elizabeth's dress as she set them up in front of us. "Oh, no. What happened?"

Elizabeth looked at her with confusion and then smiled softly. "You came back."

"Of course I came back. I only went inside for a moment to get us something to drink."

"The paint will come out," I said. "I've got something at my house, and I'll bring it with the orange paint for Ophelia."

I took a plastic cup of lemonade from the tray Will had set on the table and handed it to Elizabeth. She studied it as if wondering why it was in her hand, and I helped her bring it to her mouth. When she was done, I replaced the cup on the table between us.

Phoebe sat down on the edge of her seat, watching me closely. "My mother is a very take-charge person. She usually doesn't need help to do anything."

"I understand. You must have learned that from her."

"I don't . . ." She stopped, reconsidering her words. "That's not true," she said.

"She needs help now but doesn't know how to ask."

"But if she could, she'd ask Addie."

"The child who could do no wrong."

Phoebe frowned. "How would you know that?"

"I've been around for a long time. I raised a daughter and two grandchildren and spent years with the elderly. I feel as if I've earned a degree in family dynamics by now. It's just not that unusual for one sibling to be so bright and shiny that their parents are blinded to their child's faults."

"Look at the . . ." Elizabeth struggled to find the word. Her attention was focused on a ruby-throated hummingbird circling the blooms of a midnight marvel red hibiscus.

"Hummingbird," Phoebe offered. She turned to her mother, eager to redirect the conversation. "You always said that they're one of the reasons to love summer. They're amazing little creatures. So tiny, but they manage to fly five hundred miles across the Gulf of Mexico during migration."

Elizabeth scowled. "I know that." She looked down at her hands. "Where are my rings? I put them on this morning, and now they're gone." She turned to Phoebe. "Did you steal them?"

Phoebe's nose flared. "No, Mother. I didn't. And you didn't put them on this—"

"You are a liar!" Elizabeth shouted, making Will and Ophelia turn to look.

"Elizabeth," I said softly. "I think I saw them on your dressing table. After you finish your lemonade, we can go find them together."

Elizabeth's lips twitched with her next words then stopped as soon as they were forgotten. She returned to watching the frenetic movements of the hummingbird as he flew over Ophelia in her red shirt before heading back to the flowers.

"That doesn't mean she doesn't love you," I said softly.

Phoebe frowned and turned away.

"Ophelia," Phoebe said, "why don't you take Will to the shed and help him choose some wood scraps so he can make another feeder? You can show him how."

"I don't need a girl—"

I gave Will my warning glance.

"Whatever. Come on, Ophelia."

When the children had gone, Phoebe glanced at her mother, whose head beneath her straw hat was now lowered toward her chest as she snored softly. Phoebe took a deep breath and sank back into her chair.

I handed her a glass of lemonade.

"Thank you," she said. "I only wish it was something stronger. It's already been a long day, and it's still morning."

Will's phone began to vibrate on the ground where he'd left it. It stopped and then started again.

"Should I answer it?" Phoebe asked.

"No. He's a ten-year-old boy so it's not an emergency. He'll be back shortly and can return the call then. It's probably a friend in the neighborhood who wants to play Xbox, and I'd much rather he make a bird feeder."

Phoebe smiled and closed her eyes as she sat back in her chair, her fingers clinging tightly to the arms as if expecting to fall. "Please don't let me go to sleep. I'm afraid you wouldn't be able to wake me for a week."

"You poor thing. You've had to deal with a lot since you've been home. Have you thought about what you'll do with your mother once you go back to Oregon?"

She attempted a laugh. "I haven't figured out what I'm going to do with her tomorrow. My priority is figuring out how to pay the electricity bill and what kind of medical insurance she has. Then I can move on to the next thing."

"Can your sister help?"

This time she did laugh. "I've asked Addie to do one thing on Monday. If she follows through, I'll give her a new assignment. I don't want to overwhelm her."

I grinned, although I was fairly certain she hadn't meant to be funny. "Have you had a chance to do anything fun since you've been home?"

She tilted her head back as the shadow of a pelican crossed her face. "I haven't had a chance to do anything but put out fires, it seems. Not that I can think of any fun things, anyway. Even as a kid, I didn't really go out and do things. Everything I wanted was right here in my backyard." She indicated the sea of Spartina grass without opening her eyes. "Or if the weather was bad,

Aunt Sassy and I would watch old movies together. That was as much fun as I could handle."

She scrunched her nose. "I was such a nerd. Even in the summers when all the neighborhood kids would hang out together at the Pitt Street Pharmacy soda fountain or on the beach at Isle of Palms, or head out on the water on boats, I stayed here while Addie went out and had fun. I was probably waiting for my mother to notice that I was the good daughter."

I wanted to let her know that self-pity didn't look good on her regardless of how warranted, but my focus was instead on something she'd said. "I'm just realizing that Julie and Addie might be about the same age."

"Despite acting like a sixteen-year-old, she's actually thirty-five."

"Julie would be the same age. They might have known each other."

"Addie knew everybody, but I can't say she was friends with everyone. I hung out with her group sometimes, and there wasn't a Julie that I can recall. You can ask her, though. Even if she didn't know her, I'm sure she and her friend group would have talked about Julie's disappearance since they were the same age. But she never mentioned anything to me, and my over-protective parents kept me in the dark. I wasn't even allowed to have anyone spend the night except for my best friend, Mary-Simms McSwain, and that's only because my mother and her mother were friends. We'd stay up all night and watch old movies. Wild and crazy, I know."

"If it makes you feel any better, I always kept Liam on a tight rein because I thought that, of my two grandchildren, he would be the one to give me the most trouble. Which meant I was more lenient with Julie. I let her go to parties, and I gave her a later curfew because she was older but really it was because I never expected her to get into any trouble."

I noticed Phoebe watching me, a sympathetic look in her eyes. "I'm so sorry."

"Me, too. My point is that parenting isn't black-and-white. You can read a million how-to books and still have no idea what you're doing. Your mother had her reasons for raising you and Addie how she did. I promise that it wasn't to torture you."

"I never said that."

"You didn't have to."

I watched the hummingbird return to a feast of red petals, restlessly pumping its tiny wings so fast that they seemed invisible. "After fights with my own mother, my grandmother would tell me that I only had myself to blame. She believed that before we are born, the angels allow us to select our parents. That's how we end up with the parents we need. Even though it seems we spend most of our lives rethinking our choice."

Will's phone began to vibrate again. Phoebe stood and retrieved it. "I can't listen to that anymore—it's making me anxious. I'll take it to him so at least he can tell his friend he's unavailable."

As she headed toward the shed, we both heard the sound of tires crunching on the driveway. Changing directions, she said, "Could be Addie. Let me go see."

She disappeared around the side of the house, returning a few moments later followed by a familiar face.

"Liam," I said. "What are you doing here?"

"Looking for you. Is Will with you? I've been calling his phone for over an hour, and he's not picking up."

Phoebe held up the phone, her cheeks reddened from more than the day's heat. "Sorry. I was just bringing it to him. We didn't think it was an emergency."

"It's not your fault, Phoebe," I said. "I told her to ignore it. I couldn't imagine what could be so urgent in a boy's life during summer vacation."

Liam was dressed for work in a long-sleeved shirt and began unbuttoning the cuffs to roll them up. "Damn, it's hot. Apologies, ladies," he said as an afterthought. "I was looking for you, Gran."

"For me? What's wrong?"

"I was hoping you could manage the front desk at the office for the rest of the day. Stephanie was riding her bike to work this morning and hit a pothole. She didn't break anything, but she's a bit battered, so I sent her home. It's Saturday, so I'll only need you for a few hours."

We both turned at the sound of something crashing onto the dock. Phoebe was already bending down to pick up the plastic pitcher and cups along with the tray that she had knocked over. Elizabeth was still sitting, awakened now by the commotion.

"Are you all right?" Liam rushed toward Phoebe and straightened the table.

"Fine. Just . . . clumsy." She grabbed a handful of napkins and began wiping lemonade off her mother's legs, apologizing the whole time. Someone needed to tell her that everything wasn't always her fault.

"Stop that!" Elizabeth shouted. "Stop touching me!"

"It's okay," Liam said softly, stilling Phoebe's hand and taking the napkins. "I've got it."

Phoebe stood, hugging her arms over her chest as Liam smiled up at Elizabeth. "Hello, Mrs. Manigault. I'm Dr. Fitch. Can I help clean you up? It's just a little lemonade."

Elizabeth smiled back. "Thank you, Doctor. You're very kind. Have you met my beautiful daughter?"

Liam straightened. "Phoebe? Yes, actually."

Elizabeth shook her head. "No. My Addie. She needs a man in her life."

Phoebe looked mortified. "I'm glad Stephanie's all right. She was very kind to me yesterday, and I . . . ." She grabbed another clean napkin and began dabbing at the chair she'd been sitting in. "I'm glad she's all right."

"You should sit down," Liam said. "You're looking over-heated. Do you feel faint?"

Phoebe shook her head. "No. I think I'm just tired, and I'm still getting used to the heat."

Before he could press his point, Ophelia and Will came from around the house, each carrying an armful of wood scraps. Sitting on top of Ophelia's pile was a dusty red hummingbird feeder. "Look what we found!" she announced. They marched past us and dumped their treasures on the grass.

"Sorry to ruin your fun," Liam said to Will, "but I need Gran in the office this afternoon, so you're stuck coming with us."

Will's face fell. "But that's so boring. Can't I stay here with Ophelia?"

Liam shook his head. "Will, you shouldn't be inviting yourself—"

"It's fine," Phoebe interrupted. "I really don't mind. He can keep Ophelia company and help keep an eye on my mother if I have to run inside for a minute."

"Please, Dad?" Will asked. "I promise to listen, and I won't climb any trees."

"Really, it's fine," Phoebe said. "We'd love to have Will stay."

I stood then turned to Phoebe. "When we return to pick up Will, why don't you all come back to my house until you have your air-conditioning back on?"

"Please, Aunt Phoebe?" It was Ophelia's turn to start jumping up and down.

"That's very kind," Phoebe said. "Maybe just Ophelia? I know without even asking that Mother will want to stay here, and we'll both sleep in her room where it's cooler."

After we all came to an agreement that included my offer of bringing back takeout when we returned, Liam, Annie, and I left.

As we drove away, Liam asked, "Why were you here?"

"I was worried when Phoebe didn't answer her phone, and Will and Annie wanted to see Ophelia, so we decided to stop by." I shook my head. "I think it's a toss-up between you and Phoebe as to who is more suspicious of my motivations. It's starting to hurt my feelings."

"You can't blame me, Gran. I know how your mind works. But why would Phoebe not want you here?"

"She thought I might have ulterior motives because of the lawsuit." I sat back against the leather car seat, adjusting the cool air from the vent to hit my face. "If only I had the kind of energy to hold grudges."

We had reached the next traffic light when he turned to me. "Go ahead and ask the question that's been burning your tongue since I first showed up."

He'd always been able to read me just as easily as I could read him. Julie used to say it was as if Liam and I were the siblings and she were the stray.

"Fine. How did you know where we were? And how did you find the house? As far as I know, you'd only been there once before."

The light turned green, and we began to move forward. "Since Will was with you, I assumed he was looking for Ophelia. And I guess you're not the only one who thought it would make it easier to understand their motivations by seeing where they lived. I'm surprised they never arrested me for stalking back when I would come here and park my car across the street. I completely deserved it, too, but I was just so angry over what they were doing to you."

"They never saw you?"

"The parents and the sisters didn't. But there was another woman living with them at the time. She was a lot more observant than the other four. She saw me lots of times, but I guess she never told anyone. I always wondered why. I thought that Addie spotted me a couple of times, but she never said anything, either. Now that I've met her, I'm going to guess that she had lots of admirers and enjoyed being watched. If it makes you feel any better, I never used binoculars to see inside the house. I just paid attention to their comings and goings. And telling you this definitely makes me feel like a creeper."

He pulled into the parking lot as I pondered over what he'd said. "So, did you ever figure out by watching them why we were put through that mess?"

He put the car in Park and leaned back against the headrest. "Of course not. But I did learn something."

"Yes?"

"Addie spent more time out of her bedroom at night than in it. I think she was the same age as Julie, but they were polar opposites."

Memories of Julie sideswiped me, stealing my breath and tugging at my heart. Even after all this time, I missed her just as much as I had the day she'd walked away.

Liam squeezed my hand. "I miss her, too. Every day."

"Then why don't you want me to talk to Phoebe?"

He grimaced. "Because none of that is real. No one can predict the future. She had a few lucky guesses—that's all. I don't want her to give you false hope."

He let go of my hand and exited the car then came around to my side to open my door. We walked to the office in silence, my heart having already decided that false hope was better than no hope at all.

# 12

~

"A bird flying into the house and dying supposedly
foretells death. When I was a teenager, a bluebird flew
into my house, but it died despite our attempts to guide
it out. Nobody I knew died that year or the next, but
that didn't stop me from trying to decipher the meaning.
Probably because we all have a part of us that wants a
peek at the last page of a book or some kind of guide
for this life's journey, so we can avoid the potholes."

**Excerpt from the blog *The Thing with Feathers***

## Phoebe

I SAT IN my mother's darkened bedroom, the glow from the laptop screen highlighting her sleeping form in the bed. I hadn't
had a chance to go anywhere to get my phone battery charged
because I'd been with her all day, and I was using it to power
the Wi-Fi again and hoping it would last.

The scratches and whirs of the marsh night's busy orchestra
drifted through the screen along with the pungent scent of the
pluff mud, taking me back to a time before the nightmares
started, when my father and Aunt Sassy were still alive, Addie
was my part-time ally, and my mother wasn't a stranger.

On nights when I'd heard Addie sneak out, I'd sit up waiting
for her to come home, unable to sleep unless we were all under
one roof. Being back home was like opening a time capsule, the
memories stored behind the wallpaper and between the heart-
of-pine floorboards.

I stared at the screen as I waited for the slow browser to load, fighting a rising gnaw of anger at my sister for putting us in this situation. As I'd predicted, no coercion, begging, or bribing could get Mother to leave the house for the night, even to escape the oppressive heat at Celeste's. My father had once said that he'd known brick walls that were more pliable than my mother once she'd made up her mind. I'd found it funny until he'd added that I was just like her.

I'd helped Ophelia pack her overnight things in a small grocery bag since she didn't have her own suitcase and then sent Addie a text to let her know that I'd given permission for Ophelia to spend the night at Celeste's house. She hadn't responded, which alleviated any guilt I might have had about making decisions about her daughter without prior approval. Then my mother and I shared the takeout dinner Celeste had ordered, eating it in the candlelit dining room.

Staring at the computer screen now, I unbuttoned two more buttons on my sleeveless blouse in an attempt to cool off but brushed aside the temptation to take off my blouse and bra and sit there in my shorts and underwear. My mother would have a heart attack if she woke up and found me that way, and she'd never let me hear the end of it from either side of the grave, assuming she remembered it at all.

The upside to having absolutely nothing else to do was that I'd been on the laptop since Mother had fallen asleep and I still had thirty percent battery life left. I'd continue to use my hot spot until I got down to five percent of battery life, planning to use my car charger as soon as Addie got back.

I worked fast, setting up more online accounts and trying to hack into Mother's AOL email. I didn't feel right using my personal email for her banking and utilities, but if I was going to keep track of everything, I'd need to have access to hers. Her screen name self-populated, but the password wouldn't.

I only had one more guess at the password before I got thrown out and was feeling desperate. She had once kept all her passwords on her phone in her contacts, but when I'd found her phone at the bottom of her purse, the battery was dead.

My gaze settled on a silver frame on the desk holding another photo of Charlie as a baby, lying on his stomach with a blanket draped over his head. There was an identical one of Addie at about the same age. If there'd been one of me, I'd never seen it. I liked to tell myself that my mother had come to her senses by the time I came along and saw how ridiculous and clichéd the pose was.

I sat up, staring at the blinking cursor, the answer suddenly obvious. Being careful to type it in correctly, I entered Charlie's birthday and was immediately greeted by the AOL welcome screen. I mentally patted myself on the back for the single win of the day.

I scrolled down the long list of unread emails. Not surprisingly, most emails were from her various clubs or sale notices from her favorite boutiques or just spam, but nothing that resembled an invoice.

I was about to close it out when I spotted an email from eight months prior. It was from the Charleston County public library system, and it caught my attention because it had an attachment. The email was brief, stating only that the information from the archives that my mother had requested regarding the last published article concerning the referenced subject matter was attached.

I quickly clicked on the link, my mouth drying when I read the headline.

## POLICE CALL OFF SEARCH FOR
## LOCAL MISSING GIRL

The article was only a single paragraph, telling me nothing that I didn't already know about the disappearance of Julie Fitch. But the one thing it couldn't tell me was why my mother had requested the article in what seemed to be her last lucid months.

I scrolled up and down the list of emails looking for anything that might explain her seemingly random interest so late after the actual incident. Maybe that's how a deteriorating mind worked, bringing forward events as if they were recent. Maybe she'd simply wanted confirmation that a suddenly remembered event wasn't current. I glanced at the sleeping form of my mother and felt a fresh heartbreak at the knowledge that I'd never be able to ask her.

I closed down AOL, wanting to keep working on setting up online accounts, but it was almost too hot to think. After making sure everything was turned off to save precious battery life, I checked on my mother to make sure her skin felt cool to the touch. A three-quarter moon had risen in the sky, allowing enough light to see her face, the bluish glow softening her features so that I could see Ophelia's face. It unnerved me. Ophelia looked like me, and I didn't resemble my mother at all.

Needing fresh air, I headed downstairs to the front porch, using the light from the moon to guide me. I sat down on one of the rockers but kept it still, not wanting to exert any energy or make myself sweat even more. I'd have to burn the memory of this heat onto my brain to revisit every time I felt the magnetic pull of the tides drawing me back.

I was contemplating taking another ice-cold shower before trying to sleep on my mother's floor when a car turned into the street, the two headlamps like spotlights on the drooping oak tree, reflecting its shiny leaves.

Thinking it might be Addie, I prepared to run inside and hide in my room. I was too tired and hot to deal with her, my anger over her obliviousness regarding our mother and Ophelia like a huge stain I couldn't rub out. Neither of us wanted an explosive argument right now.

I was halfway to the door when I realized it was a pickup truck and not a sedan. I watched it pull into the driveway, recognizing the truck from earlier that afternoon when Liam had arrived to pick up Celeste.

A tall, familiar form climbed out of the pickup. I rushed to the bottom step, worst-case scenarios involving Ophelia racing through my mind. "Liam? Is everything all right?"

He held up his hand. "Yes. Sorry, didn't mean to alarm you by just showing up. I texted, but I think your phone is off. I tried calling the landline, but it's been disconnected."

"Of course." We stood awkwardly facing each other in the darkness, and I realized this was the first time we'd been alone together since that stormy afternoon twenty-four years ago. He'd changed into a T-shirt and shorts, so he looked more like the boy I'd remembered and less like the doctor. Moonlight reflected off something around his neck, and I thought again of the shark's tooth, another reminder of our brief encounter that had become a bruise that wouldn't completely go away.

"I brought you some supplies to get through the rest of the weekend." He opened the back door of his double cab and pulled a large cooler from the seat. He brought it over to the porch, setting it down with a clunk and the sound of shifting ice. He returned to the truck and retrieved something from the floor of the back seat, the clinking of glass making me thirsty and reminding me of how hot I was.

Shutting the door with his hip, he approached with a six-pack of beer. "Celeste told me what brand you like and thought you might need something cold."

He popped off the top and handed me the bottle. "Thanks." I held the cold bottle against my neck, feeling his gaze, then took a long, slow drink.

"Mind if I join you?"

I wanted to say no. The pointed edges of the dream pressed against my consciousness. Whether it was his presence or the memory of the part he'd inadvertently played in its conception made me want to step back inside the house and close the door.

Sensing my hesitation, he said, "I should bring the cooler into the kitchen. I brought more ice and water, as well as watermelon and oranges to help you and your mother stay hydrated. Also . . ." he reached into his front pocket ". . . a battery pack for your phone and . . ." reaching into his other pocket, he pulled out a flashlight ". . . this. You can still use your candles, but I wouldn't recommend those in any room where your mother might find herself alone." He placed the items on the table next to my rocking chair.

"And one more thing." He returned to the passenger side of the truck and pulled out a laundry basket filled with folded clothes, which he placed on top of the cooler. "Celeste thought your mother might appreciate clean clothes."

"That was nice of her. Thank you for bringing them." He was still holding his beer bottle, clearly waiting for an invitation to join me. Not wanting to appear any ruder, I said, "Why don't you join me for a beer? And then I can help you bring everything inside."

Lifting the bottom of his T-shirt, he twisted off the cap and took a swig. "Mind if I sit? Unless you have other plans."

"Sure." I sat down next to him. "I'd planned to take my mother clubbing, but since you're here I guess we'll stay put."

He smiled, and I found myself wishing I could see his eyes up close like I had that first time, to see if they were as beautiful as I remembered. I turned away and took a long drink from my bottle, feeling the old dream inching closer.

I held the cold bottle against my cheek. "I'm so exhausted and I should be in bed, but I can't find the energy to go upstairs. My mother keeps asking if my father has called to let us know when he'll be home for supper or accusing me of taking her rings. My head hurts from trying to reason with her."

"Then don't." His voice was soft and low, and I wondered if he used that as his bedside manner voice or just when he was alone at night with a woman. Both thoughts made me flush with embarrassment to be thinking of my mother's doctor like that.

"Just tell her what she wants to hear," he continued.

"That feels a lot like lying."

"You're not alone in that mindset. Most, if not all, caretakers struggle with that one. My rule of thumb is in choosing your words or actions to seek to reduce distress and promote well-being or happiness. Just be prepared to experience a lot of trial and error."

I drained the rest of my beer. "My sister needs to hear this. I'm scared to leave her alone with our mother when I go back to Oregon."

He stood and grabbed two more bottles and opened them both. "Have you thought about hiring someone for your mother?"

"I have, but I have no idea where to start looking or if my mother wouldn't flip out at having a stranger in her house. Not to mention the pushback I'd get from Addie, who I think actually believes that Mother will get better."

"That's rough," he said.

"Yep. It is."

I turned to look at him. "You were really great with my mother and Addie at your office, by the way. Have you always been good with understanding family relationships, or did you learn how to navigate dysfunction in medical school?"

He grunted. "I think I learned most about relationships from my grandmother, but I wouldn't say I'm good at it. I'm divorced, remember."

"Whose fault was it?" My directness surprised me. Maybe it was the confessional quality of the darkness that emboldened me.

"Both, in equal measure. At least at first. I was working too hard and never home, assuming my wife understood what was needed to establish a private practice and that I was doing it for our family."

"She didn't?"

He lifted his beer to his mouth and took a long drink. "Apparently not. On the day she asked me for a divorce, she informed me that she and Will would be moving in with her personal trainer. I was too stunned to fight back. And I felt guilty, too, for letting it happen. The fact that I have visitation with Will is because of my grandmother shaking some sense into me."

"I'm sorry," I said.

"Me, too."

We sat in silence, nursing our beers and watching the neighbor's porch lights flip off one by one. Somewhere in the shadows of the marsh, the melancholy whistle of a chuck-will's-widow called out into the darkness.

Liam turned toward the sound. "I've been hearing that every summer since I was a boy, but I have no idea what it is. My dad used to tell me it was the ghost of a fisherman's wife who haunted the docks at night looking for boys to drown. I think that was his way to keep me out of the water at night."

I smiled. "Did it work?"

"For a while. Until I discovered girls and I decided it was worth taking the chance."

The bird's plaintive call came again, this time closer. "I hate to be the one to call your father a liar, but that's a chuck-will's-widow, a member of the nightjar family and related to the whippoorwill and just as ugly."

"Is that why it only comes out at night?"

I laughed out loud. "Probably. They're colored to blend in to the dirt and leaves so they're basically shades of brown, with short necks and flat heads. They've also got enormous mouths, which they use to eat the occasional songbird whole."

"I think I like the idea of the bloodthirsty ghost better."

"At least the nightjars only kill for survival instead of killing for vengeance like your ghost. The bird world is a strange one, although one that makes a lot more sense than ours, hence my fascination. Remind me sometime to tell you about bird siblicide."

"Can't wait," he said, then tilted back his bottle. "That would be a good subject for your blog."

"You've read my blog?"

"Celeste told me about it, so I had to check it out. I'm a devoted reader now. I've learned a lot and not just about birds. So, thank you."

I smiled to myself. "You're welcome." I found myself sinking back into my chair and relaxing for the first time in days. I wanted him to stay almost as much as I needed him to leave. I reached for another beer, not because I wanted another, but because if I got drunk enough, I'd have the courage to tell him to leave. Or be oblivious enough not to dream when I finally fell asleep.

I turned toward him, his profile barely visible against the night sky. "This is too little and too late, but thank you. For saving my life. I never got the chance to say thank you before. My parents shipped me off to my grandparents in Spartanburg for the rest of that summer, so I had no idea what my father was doing—not that I would have anyway, since I was only nine, but I was a pretty good eavesdropper back then. I'm sure I would have picked up on something." I pressed the dripping bottle against my cheek, my skin heated with embarrassment and shame. "You'll find this hard to believe, but I wanted to invite you and your family over for dinner one night to properly thank you, but my father said no. He wouldn't even tell me your name, saying that you were a summer visitor and had gone home."

"I know," he said softly. "I didn't see you leave your house for a while." He drained his bottle. "And that's also another story to save for later."

The reflection of the moon winked from something hanging around his neck. I pointed at it with my bottle. "You still wear it."

"I haven't taken it off since my sister gave it to me. After she left, I told myself that if I kept wearing it she'd come back. I don't believe that anymore, but old habits are hard to break."

Too tired to form words, I just nodded then closed my eyes. The darkness swallowed me, and I imagined I could hear the sound of tires on wet asphalt. The loud splash of a car entering the water. My eyes shot open. "You should go now."

"All right." He didn't sound offended or ask for an explanation. "Let me carry the cooler inside for you first. It's really heavy."

I wanted to argue and tell him that I was more than capable, but all I could do was nod.

I held the door open for him then followed him into the house, deciding to wait for him in the foyer. A new sound crept through the darkness, behind the ticktock of the grandfather clock. The chuck-will's-widow cried again, sending a cold shiver over my body despite the oppressive heat inside the house. Taking a step toward the staircase, I listened again, disoriented. I imagined I heard the flapping of wings and wondered if the nightjar had found its way inside the house. I took a cautious step onto the first stair tread, closing my eyes to hear better. I heard it again, a mixture of babbling undecipherable words mixed with sobs, then started to run.

I found my mother standing in the middle of her darkened bedroom and clutching something to her chest. I flipped the light switch, forgetting that we didn't have electricity.

"Mother?"

She turned toward me, and I recognized the silver frame of my father's photograph that she kept on her nightstand next to her side of the bed. She'd been a widow for over a decade but still only slept on her side of the bed as if she believed he might return to her.

"I miss him." Big, choking sobs shook her body, and I went to her, holding her tightly as if my small embrace might fill the enormous space my father had left behind.

"I know. We all do."

"Addie?" she whispered.

"No, Mother. It's me, Phoebe."

"I've missed you, baby. You've been gone too long."

I patted her back. "I know. But I'm here now."

She pulled away abruptly. "It's so hot. Why is it so hot in here?" She took a step toward the doorway, the forgotten frame slipping from her grasp. Shards of broken glass exploded as it hit the wood floor, peppering our legs.

Her piercing scream shattered the night. I grabbed my mother and pulled her away so she wouldn't step in the broken glass with her bare feet. I half dragged, half walked her to the other side of the room.

"What are you doing? Let go of me! Wait until your father gets home!" She escaped my hold and rushed to the door, where she collided with Liam.

He'd brought the flashlight with him, and he trained the beam on us and then the floor. "Mrs. Manigault, it's Dr. Fitch. Are you hurt?"

His voice managed to cut through her hysteria. "She broke it." She pointed her finger in my direction. "She broke it," she said again, louder.

Blood dripped down my calves, the open cuts stinging. "No, Mother, I didn't. You dropped it, but it was an accident." I knew from one of the booklets that I'd picked up at Liam's office that this was not the right way to speak to someone with dementia, but I was way past the point of reason.

"Liar!" she screamed. "You are lying! Just wait until I tell your father."

"My father is dead!" I roared, and the room fell silent except for my mother's muffled sobs and the lonely calls of the nightjar outside the window. My anger evaporated, replaced with shame. "I'm so sorry . . ."

"You should go," Liam said quietly. "I'll stay here with your mother and get her cleaned up and ready for bed. I'll let you know when I leave."

I ran from the room, my feet sticky with my own blood as I fled to the front porch to grab the remaining beer bottles before retreating to the dock. The moon glared down on me as the somnolent sounds of the night marsh closed around me and I tried to forget, if just for a little while, that I had screamed at my mother. Or that she wouldn't remember it in the morning. But I would.

# 13

~

"There's a wonderful quote by C. S. Lewis that I have printed on large poster paper at the front of my classroom. He talks about the difficulty a bird has hatching out of an egg but how much harder it would be to remain an egg while learning to fly. He compares us all to the egg and challenges us to change. To grow. To not remain that ordinary egg no matter how comfortable it might be in there. We must be like the birds: break the shells that surround us or go bad."

**Excerpt from the blog *The Thing with Feathers***

## Celeste

I STOOD IN the doorway of the living room watching Will and Ophelia playing Xbox. Or rather Will was playing while Ophelia sat next to him with a controller in her lap and her nose in a book.

"Aren't you done with that chapter yet?" Will asked, not taking his eyes from the screen.

Ophelia didn't look up. "Almost. I'm getting to the good part."

Will groaned. "That's what you said last time. Hurry. I want to teach you how to play this game."

Ophelia peered over the top of her book and sighed. "Oh, I know how to play. I just like reading better."

He scrunched up his face in disbelief and continued to play.

"You two are like an old married couple," I said.

Will gagged while Ophelia simply looked horrified.

I quickly changed the subject. To Ophelia, I said, "Would you like eggs, cheese grits, pancakes, or made-to-order omelets?"

"Yes, please," Ophelia said.

Will laughed. "You have to pick one. You can't eat all of that."

"That's not for you to say, young man. Ophelia is entitled to her own opinions. Now, sweetheart, would you like all of that?"

She shook her head, her tangled ponytail slapping each side of her face. "No, ma'am. It all sounds so good that I couldn't pick just one. When Patricia used to come, she'd make me eggs and toast and sometimes French toast, but she doesn't come anymore because Mimi yelled at her and told her to go away. Now Mimi usually just gives me a waffle from the toaster without butter or syrup because they're fattening."

I bit back the words I really wanted to say. "In this house we love our butter and syrup, within reason of course. You'll find that when I cook, you don't want to smother the taste. So how about a short stack of buttermilk pancakes, with butter and syrup, and an omelet with all sorts of fresh veggies?"

She nodded excitedly.

"What about you, Will?"

"I'll have the same thing. And orange juice, please."

"Me, too, please," Ophelia said, her nose already back in her book.

"All right. I'll let you know when it's ready."

I was just pulling out the eggs and butter from the refrigerator when the doorbell rang. When I didn't hear Will getting up to get it, I called out a warning shot. "Will—remember what your daddy said. I'm sure you don't want to lose any privileges."

He responded with a heavy sigh followed by the sound of bare feet running down the hallway toward the door.

I recognized Phoebe's voice as she greeted Will. She'd barely made it into the kitchen before Ophelia ran to throw her arms around her aunt in a tight squeeze. Phoebe's hands floated over her niece for a moment, like a bird unsure where to land, and then returned the hug.

"Did you have fun?" Phoebe asked, looking directly at Ophelia, indicating that she really wanted to know. I imagined she was a favorite teacher because of this, although I could tell she was probably a little strict, too, which her students most likely grumbled about but liked her even more because of it.

Ophelia nodded enthusiastically. "I did. Miss Celeste let us stay up late to watch a movie. I beat Will at gin rummy so I got to pick the movie. And then we made popcorn and ate it in front of the TV."

Phoebe gave her a genuine smile, the fatigue and stress she wore on her face softening slightly. "Wow. That does sound fun. What movie?"

"*Beethoven*. He's a Saint Bernard dog."

"I love that movie! It's an oldie but goodie. As soon as the electricity is back on, we can watch the sequel. I'm glad you had a good time. Did you thank Miss Celeste?"

Ophelia nodded, her glasses slipping down her nose. Phoebe slid them back up and then bent to kiss the top of the girl's head, the action seeming to surprise them both. Ophelia left to join Will in the living room as the electronic bings of the game resumed.

"She was very polite—the perfect guest," I said. "She and Will are already good friends. And I'm sorry if I misunderstood, but I thought I was supposed to bring Ophelia back after breakfast."

"Yes, well, that was the plan but I was desperate to get out of the house so I thought a walk across town to pick up Ophelia would feed two birds with one seed, and I needed the exercise to clear my head. Right now, Addie's with Mother, and I told her she couldn't leave until I got back. She wasn't happy since she just came home after sleeping who-knows-where, but I honestly couldn't care less." She moved to stand in front of the wall-unit air conditioner and stuck her face near the vent. "I don't think I'll ever cool off."

"Can I offer you some coffee?" I took in the dark circles under her eyes and the faint smell of beer mixed with that of mint toothpaste and sweat. My phone conversation with Liam that morning had given me a hint as to what had happened the night before without breaking any confidentiality rules, and my instinct to fix things had been kicked into overdrive.

"Yes, thank you. Just black. I don't know if I miss the AC or the coffee maker more. I guess I could buy a jar of instant, but that would mean that I've hit rock bottom. Not that I'm far away, but I'd like to think that I still have my standards."

I laughed and pulled a mug from the cabinet and poured her a cup. "There's no shame in rock bottom as long as you're looking up and not down. That way you can see the stars."

"I need to remember that." She took a sip from her mug. "Can I set the table or help you in any way? I'm good at taking direction. Just don't ask me to cook."

"I don't need you to do a thing. Go ahead and take your coffee to the screen porch while I get breakfast ready. Have you eaten? I can bring something out to you."

"I'm too tired to be hungry. I wouldn't mind just sitting outside and sipping my coffee until the caffeine kicks in." She took the mug and wandered out onto the screened porch where my easel was set up with my work in progress.

I followed her to flip on the ceiling fans while she stood in front of the easel sipping her mug and studying the unfinished painting.

"It's a phoebe," I said. "But of course you already know that. I was inspired by the sudden appearance of one on my windowsill." I studied her as closely as she examined my half-finished painting, seeing the beauty behind her exhaustion, and the way the morning sun gave her skin a golden glow that matched the downy underfeathers of the bird. But it was the light in her eyes that I wished I could translate onto canvas. It showed all the hope and strength she seemed afraid to admit to herself, let alone allow others to see. "I keep meaning to look up what they symbolize. Not that I believe in any of that, but I like to keep an open mind."

Her mouth twisted. "According to the so-called experts, the phoebe bird symbolizes resilience and overcoming adversity. The Phoebe woman, not so much."

"Don't be so hard on yourself."

Her smile wobbled. "I yelled something awful at my mother last night."

"If it were a crime to say something awful to those we love, we'd all be in jail." I drew a deep breath and continued. "The last thing I said to Julie as she headed out the door was that I hoped she'd catch her death because it was cold outside and she wouldn't wear a sweater." I shrugged. "If time travel were real, I'd go back and delete every single word. But that's not how life works, is it? We all make mistakes. That means that at least we're trying. Anyway, I'm sure you had your reasons, just as I'm sure that, if your mother were able, she'd forgive you."

"I'm not so sure. My relationship with my mother has always been . . . complicated."

"Because you believe she wished you were more like your sister?"

She turned back to the painting.

"As an outsider who is only just getting to know you and your family, I'd say that it's not that simple. Love is complicated. A mother will love each child differently depending on what that child needs. Maybe your mother thought that Addie needed her more than you did. But that doesn't mean she loved you any less."

"It's not just my mother's situation that's keeping me on edge. I'm worried about Ophelia, too. Addie is ignoring our mother's new limitations and still acts as if she is capable of supervising Ophelia. I don't know how to make Addie accept the truth, and I'm running out of time." She ran her hands over her face, briefly covering her eyes. "Have you ever gone out in the marsh, followed a break in the sawgrass, and gotten lost? That's how I feel right now. Everywhere I look the tall grass obstructs my view, and I can't find my way."

"Keep paddling. You'll eventually find firmer ground." I indicated the deep wicker armchair I liked to nap in. "Why don't you relax for a bit while I feed the children?"

She stifled a yawn. "Thank you. I think I will."

After breakfast, I sent the children outside to refill the bird feeders then went to check on Phoebe. As expected, her half-empty mug of coffee sat on the side table, and she was fast asleep in the chair, which had been my plan all along. I didn't want to wake her since I knew she needed the sleep, but I also knew that her sister was waiting for her.

"Phoebe?" I spoke gently so as not to startle her.

She jerked awake then began to scream. I put my arms around her, but she continued to struggle as if she were still in whatever nightmare she'd been having. I held her tight and repeated her name until she calmed down. I didn't let go until I felt her muscles relax.

"Phoebe . . . are you all right?"

Her eyes darted around the porch and then back to me as if trying to get her bearings.

"It's all right, Phoebe. You're safe. You're with me, Celeste, on my back porch. You fell asleep and had a bad dream."

Her breathing had slowed even though her chest continued to heave. Finally, she nodded. "I'll be fine."

I sat down on the ottoman, the wicker creaking as it stretched beneath me. "Do you want to tell me about it?"

"No." The word was almost shouted. "Because then I'd have to relive it."

I looked at her with concern, her unease evident. "Have you had it before?"

Her eyes snapped up to meet mine. "I don't want to talk about it."

"Okay. That's fine. But I'm here if you change your mind."

"Thank you."

I sat up. "Can I get you some ice water or more coffee?"

Phoebe shook her head. "No. I'm good. And Ophelia and I need to go." She rested her elbows on her thighs and put her head in her hands.

"So, I've been thinking," I began.

She lifted her head.

"I think I might be able to help you."

"Thank you, but I don't need any help from anyone but Addie. I'll figure it out."

"I have no doubt. You've done brilliantly so far, even though I know you can't see it. But I'm talking about filling in where you need it. I can help you communicate with your mom. She seems to like me even if she doesn't remember my name, and I used to be a nurse and have experience working with the elderly."

When she didn't immediately dismiss me, I continued. "I know I'm not a spring chicken, but I'm relatively fit. I also have a car and can drive to the pharmacist or beauty salon or wherever she needs to go. I can offer you not only time to think and get things done, but also a bit of mind space to handle the stress of your situation."

She put her head in her hands again. "You must think I'm the biggest whiner in the world. Caring for my own mother shouldn't be this hard. Other people do it all the time without complaint."

"Well, speaking from experience, you're wrong on both counts. Eldercare is never easy, even for those with perfectly sound minds. And everyone complains at some point. It's hard work, both physically and mentally. Also, your situation is more complicated than most, seeing as how you live across the country and your sister still acts like a teenager without any responsibilities. It says a lot about you that you even care."

"Don't make me into a martyr, all right? I'm counting the minutes until I can go back and resume my life."

"As you should. But for the next two months, I'm offering to make things easier for you while you get everyone situated with the new reality."

"Did Liam ask you to say all that?"

"He didn't have to. From what I've seen, it's clear that you and your sister need a bit of help right now, and I have the time and the experience to do that. And if Addie chooses to keep me on after you've left, that would be even better since when Will goes back home at the end of the summer, I'll need a distraction."

I could see hope battling with her self-sufficient personality as she prepared to say no.

"I can do light housekeeping, too, and prepare meals. I enjoy cooking, and I don't get to do much of it anymore since I live by myself. I see it as a win-win. Unless you already have someone?"

"We did. But my mother told her to leave, or Patricia left on her own because she hadn't been paid—who knows. I've tried to call a couple of times, and I'll keep trying, but it doesn't seem as if she wants to talk to us."

"Well, then, see? It would help out everyone."

"Really, Celeste—there has to be a reason beyond needing something to do. Most people would have run screaming into the hills as soon as they walked through our front door."

I considered lying, but I liked and respected Phoebe too much. "Everything I've already told you is the truth. I do get lonely without Will here. Liam is wonderful, but he has his practice and his own life. And I actually miss working in my kitchen and putting delicious food on the table for friends and family. But you're right. There's more."

"Julie."

Her response didn't surprise me. "I miss her more each day. Being around you and your sister and knowing she would be about the same age makes my heart hurt. I have prayed every single day since she went away that I would find her and bring her home. Even though everyone I know has begged me to move on, I couldn't. I won't rest until I know what happened to her. Even if she's no longer alive, I need to know. When I ran into you and Ophelia at the bakery, I couldn't help but think that you were the answer to my prayers."

Phoebe studied her hands with their gnawed fingernails. "I told you. I don't have those dreams anymore." She didn't look at me while she spoke.

"Is it because you've taught yourself how not to dream, or did you just outgrow them?"

"Both, I think. But moving away stopped them completely." She picked up her mug and stood. "We need to get going. Addie's probably showing Mother how to make a bottle rocket and her hair's already on fire."

The mental image made me burst out laughing. "Sorry. I shouldn't be laughing."

"Why? Because it might be true?"

I grinned. "Yes. Also because it's a good sign that you've managed to retain your sense of humor. That will get you through a lot."

"Good to know." She held the door open for me and we entered the kitchen, where we found Will and Ophelia back inside raiding the cookie jar of the homemade cookies we'd made the night before.

"Kids!" I cried. "You just had breakfast. You can't possibly still be hungry!"

Ophelia shoved the remainder of a cookie in her mouth and tried to close it with a crumbly smile. "Sorry," she mumbled.

Will swallowed quickly. "Ophelia said she'd never made cookies before, and they were the best she'd ever tasted. She just wanted one more before she left."

"Understandable," I said, already reaching for the drawer where I kept my storage baggies. "And what's your excuse, young man?" I asked as I placed four cookies in the clear bag and sealed it at the top before handing it to Ophelia.

"Thank you," she said blowing crumbs at me and onto the floor.

I looked at Will, waiting for his answer.

"You always say that it's impolite to eat without offering others something to eat, too. And I didn't want Ophelia to think she was being rude."

"Nice try," Phoebe said, attempting to hide her own smile. To Ophelia she said, "We need to go."

"Can Will come with us?"

Phoebe's eyes met mine, and I knew she was envisioning what might be going on at her house at that moment. She said, "I have some things I need to take care of first, and then why don't we see how we feel?" At Ophelia's devastated expression, she added, "I can teach you both how to catch crabs from the dock. If my old pots aren't in the garage, I can show you how to make one. I saw a fishing rod on Miss Celeste's porch, so I'm assuming someone in this house has a valid fishing license we can use."

Ophelia's face brightened. "Okay," she said, then surprised me with a running hug that nearly toppled me over. Not that I minded. Not since Julie's last goodbye had I been hugged with such enthusiasm.

"Thank you, Miss Celeste," Ophelia said. I didn't care about the crumbs or smears of melted chocolate chips. They were a small price to pay for the sweet innocence of a child's love.

"You're more than welcome." I headed toward the front door, Phoebe and the children following. As Phoebe and Ophelia stood on the doorstep, I said, "You'll let me know? I'm available to start anytime. And I think whatever hourly rate you paid your previous housekeeper would work." I grinned at her look of surprise. "I know you'd feel better paying me, even though I would do it for free."

She didn't smile. "I don't control my dreams. Even if I wanted to dream about Julie, I couldn't force it." She stepped off the porch. "And there's no guarantee that what I see is something you want to know."

"I understand."

"Good." She gave me a brief smile. "I'll call you later."

I watched as they walked away, feeling hopeful yet scared at the same time, and realizing that it was impossible to be one without the other.

# 14

~

"Molting is a part of life for all birds. It's a shedding of
old feathers to make room for new ones. It's a required
renewal, crucial for the bird's survival as it gives them
a chance to get rid of old or damaged feathers.

"I think that people must go through similar molting periods,
although not as regularly as birds, yet still just as important
for our physical and mental well-being. Fortunately, we remain
mostly recognizable to our friends and families, but—if we're
lucky—we become unrecognizable to the person in the mirror."

**Excerpt from the blog *The Thing with Feathers***

## *Phoebe*

I TURNED OFF my mother's laptop and closed the lid. I'd just
finished my spreadsheet listing all her accounts and paid all her
outstanding balances. The electric company was still offline,
and I hadn't yet reached Patricia to make amends, but for the
first time since my return I felt as if I was managing to keep my
head above water.

I'd done a cursory check of Mother's inbox and had seen
several emails from her book club as well as meeting times and
locations for her garden club. None of these appeared to have
been answered.

As I stood, I made a mental note to ask Addie if she'd spoken
to any of Mother's friends or club members to let them know
what was going on. Mother would have been mortified if she'd
missed a single RSVP. I probably knew the answer already, but
in the midst of so much disappointment in my sister, I chose to

be optimistic. It was a lot easier than carrying around a sack of anger and resentment.

"What are you doing?"

My mother's acrimonious voice deflated my contentment, replacing it with dread. I turned to see her in the doorway of her bedroom. "I needed to borrow your computer. My battery is dead."

She stalked across the room toward me, her eyes narrowed. "You're lying. Tell me what you're doing in my room going through my drawers."

I wasn't going to take offense. I tried to think of what the booklets from Liam's office said about deflecting accusations. "I found your rings." I picked up the small Herend china dish from the top of the desk where her rings had been all along. "Would you like to wear them?"

She looked down at her bare fingers, looking surprised to find them empty. "Whatever were they doing there?" She narrowed her eyes at me again.

"Here. Put this one on first." I gave her the plain gold wedding band that I had never seen anywhere except on her left hand. She slipped it on, struggling just a little to get it over her knuckle. "Now this one." The second ring was a beautiful emerald-cut sapphire flanked by two smaller diamonds set in platinum. My father had given it to her for their twentieth wedding anniversary, and back in the days when I used to care about such things and didn't realize how morbid it was, Addie and I would argue over who would inherit it. Mother had stopped the arguing by explaining that it would go to Addie since she was the eldest.

When she looked at me again, it was clear she no longer remembered why she'd come up to her bedroom. I gently slid her arm through mine. "Why don't we go downstairs and fix you some lunch. Addie said you didn't eat much at breakfast."

She pasted her social smile on her face—something I was beginning to recognize in situations where she knew there was a memory lapse—and nodded regally. "That would be nice."

I had just cut her peanut butter and jelly sandwich when the doorbell rang. Addie had disappeared with the car shortly after I'd returned home, and Ophelia was sitting in the shade by the dock reading, so I wiped my hands on a dish towel and prepared to answer it.

"Coming!" I called out then settled Mother at the table with a glass of her powdered lemonade. The centerpiece bowl was filled with a bunch of overripe bananas.

"I'll be right back," I said, quickly walking toward the door and opening it without bothering to look through the sidelights first. Liam Fitch stood on the porch holding two fishing rods, with Will behind him holding a tackle box. "I know you were only expecting Will, but I thought it would be easier to get him and all of the fishing gear here if I drove my truck."

He was dressed casually in a T-shirt and cargo shorts, and I mentally ran through my morning routine, trying to recall if I'd washed my face or brushed my hair at any point, grateful that I had. But Mother would have been appalled that I hadn't even thought to apply lipstick before opening the door.

I smiled, hoping I didn't have peanut butter on my chin from licking the knife after making Mother's sandwich. "Of course." I pulled the door open as he turned to Will.

"Go ahead and take the tackle box down to the dock. I'll put the rods on the porch for now."

Will jumped down the steps, the box banging against his leg as he ran. I waited for Liam to head back to his truck, but instead he stood looking at me as if waiting for an invitation.

"Would you like to come in? I was just giving Mother an early lunch."

"Thank you," he said, following me inside and closing the door behind him.

We stood awkwardly facing each other, he no doubt recalling our conversation from the previous night. "Would you like something to drink or eat? I can make a mean peanut butter sandwich, and I've got warm lemonade."

He grinned, revealing a small dimple in his left cheek I hadn't noticed before. "Tempting, but no thanks. I just wanted to check on you and see how you're doing." He glanced down at my feet where socks covered the bandages I'd placed on the soles. I'd had to replace both after my walk to Celeste's and back since they were soaked with blood. "You might need stitches if any of the cuts are deep. And you'll want someone to have a good look to make sure you got all the glass out."

"I'm fine," I said. "I'm not your patient. My mother is."

He held up his hands. "I understand. I'll try not to take it personally."

The sound of the kitchen door slamming jerked my attention toward the back of the house. "Hang on." I started running, ignoring the pain in my foot. I caught sight of my mother heading down to the dock toward Will and Ophelia. She was barefoot, something I'd never seen her do before unless we were at the beach. I quickly crossed the screened-in porch and called out the door.

"Ophelia, Mimi is coming out. Can you and Will keep an eye on her for a few minutes? I'll come and get her shortly."

I reentered the kitchen, keeping the door open so I could hear them if they needed me. When I turned my attention back to Liam, he was focused on the kitchen table where my mother's plate held only crumbs, the lemonade appeared untouched, and five empty banana peels sat next to the empty bowl.

"Don't worry, they can't hurt her," Liam said. "Try to get her to drink as much water as you can to keep her digestive tract moving or she could get very uncomfortable."

I busied myself cleaning up the table, trying to avoid eye contact with him.

"You don't need to be embarrassed, Phoebe. I deal with this every day."

"But I don't." I let the lid of the garbage can slam shut.

"Is this her car key?" He lifted something from the counter.

I recognized the black Lincoln key fob. "Yes. It's the spare key that's supposed to be in the drawer. Addie must have taken it out because Mother kept on asking for her keys."

"Probably not a good idea. Your mother is at the stage where she can easily get lost and confused behind the wheel and might cause an accident."

"I know that." I took the fob from his hand and shoved it into my pocket. "And so does Addie because I keep telling her, but she won't listen. It's like she's in denial about Mother's condition."

"That's not unusual." He considered me closely. "Have you considered my grandmother's proposal?"

"I have."

"It doesn't have to be her, but I seriously recommend you get someone. Call Stephanie at my office for a list of vetted caregivers if you're dead set against my grandmother. Because I get the feeling that your reluctance has more to do with my family than any hesitation you might have about getting help."

I met his eyes but didn't say anything. Because then I'd have to tell him that the dream I'd first had since he'd saved my life loomed more imminent whenever he was near. He was like a lightning rod, except instead of defusing the bolt of electricity, he brought it close enough that I could feel the heat.

My eyes drifted to the shark's tooth around his neck as I recalled what he'd told me. *I haven't taken it off since my sister gave
it to me. After she left, I told myself that if I kept wearing it she'd come
back.* I doubted my sister or I would display that kind of loyalty
if either one of us disappeared, and his dogged devotion to his
only sibling softened my resolve. "I'll think about it."

The front door opened and closed followed by footsteps and
the sound of paper rustling. Addie entered the kitchen, holding
three white CVS pharmacy bags. Looking at Liam, she said, "I
was wondering whose truck was blocking my parking spot in
the driveway." She dumped the bags onto the table. "I picked
up Mother's prescriptions," she announced. "They had her insurance card on file, but on a wild guess, I looked under the
seat of the car and there it was, along with a bunch of change
and stray bills. Remember how she used to always throw stuff
there if she was in a hurry, then send one of us out to collect it
and put it back in her wallet?"

"Great job." I winced at how condescending I sounded, since
I really was grateful.

"What are you doing here?" she asked Liam.

"You're being rude, Addie. Ophelia and Will wanted to go
fishing, so Liam brought over two fishing rods."

"Yes, well, mission accomplished. Don't let the door hit you
on the way out."

"Addie," I hissed. To Liam I said, "Could you go check on
the kids? I'll be right there."

"No problem," he said, showing no indication that Addie
had offended him.

As soon as he left, I turned on my sister. "What is wrong with
you? He's only trying to help."

She closed her eyes and shook her head. "I don't trust him or
his grandmother. There's something not right about them suddenly reappearing in our lives and wanting to take over."

"Nobody is wanting to take over anything. Don't forget it was me who called and made the appointment for Mother with Liam on the recommendation from her GP. So just tell me— what have they done to make you so suspicious?"

She shrugged. "Nothing. Yet. It just seems . . . odd."

"The only thing odd here is your attitude. And just so you know, I'm hiring Celeste to help with Mother and the house."

"Are you out of your mind? She just wants to get into your head and bring back your dreams. Is that really what you want?"

"You can find someone else if she doesn't work out. But I like her, and she's wonderful with Ophelia, too. Just give her a chance, all right? It's for your benefit, too. You can't rely on Mother anymore for Ophelia's care."

"But what if Mother—"

"Stop," I said. "Mother is not getting better. We both need to accept it so we can move forward and make sure she's taken care of."

"Right. Like you even care. You come home once a year and make it so obvious that every second spent in our company is distasteful and that you can't wait to leave. And don't say it's because I'm Mother's favorite and we wanted it this way. Did you ever consider that the reason she chose to do things with me was because of your constant rejection? Maybe if just once you'd gone to the ballet with her when she invited you or showed any kind of interest in the things she loves. Do you remember how excited she was to have been given the honor to name two new rose hybrids, and she named them after us? Yours died because you never watered it. How do you think that made her feel?"

She slung her purse strap over her shoulder, pulling at the sleeve of her T-shirt and revealing a large bruise on her upper arm.

"What happened?" I asked, pointing at it.

She yanked up her sleeve. As if I hadn't said anything, she said, "Do what you want. You always have, no matter what anyone has ever said or thought. Mother cried just about every night when you moved to Oregon, not that you cared. So, hire Celeste. And when you start having your dreams again, I can't promise not to say *I told you so.*"

She left the kitchen, her footsteps heavy on the stairs.

I was still processing the bruise and everything she'd said when the doorbell rang again. This time I did look through the sidelights and threw open the door with a mix of surprise and embarrassment.

Mary-Simms McSwain, my best friend since kindergarten, didn't wait to be invited in but instead stepped past me into the foyer, holding the hand of a toddler boy wearing a knit shirt and matching shorts with dump trucks printed all over them.

"I had to come see for myself," she announced. "Rumor has it that you've been home for *days* and haven't picked up the phone to let me know. So *of course* I had to rush right over and see for myself, and sure as I'm standing here, there you are!"

She hadn't paused for a single breath, and the little boy wore an expression of confused worry, as if afraid she might run out of air and pass out.

"Let me squeeze your shoulders," she said then enveloped me in a hug, leaving behind the scent of Happy, Mary-Simms's favorite perfume from high school. I was immediately taken back to our graduation and our plans to celebrate at her parents' beach house in the Florida Panhandle. I knew I wouldn't have been allowed to go despite both Mr. and Mrs. McSwain acting as chaperones, so I'd lied, telling my parents that I would be staying with Mary-Simms at her family home on Queen Street in downtown Charleston and taking day trips to Folly Beach to get a head start on our summer tans.

I hadn't expected my mother to call and offer to send food since I'd be staying for the week, nor had I expected the punishment to be so brutal in my eighteen-year-old eyes. I had committed the cardinal sin of lying to my mother. It didn't matter that I had graduated with honors or that I had never been in any trouble. I was forbidden from leaving the house for a week while my closest friends went to Florida, creating memories from which I would be excluded.

I had already begun planning my escape from South Carolina, and this was the first thread to fray, making it easier to separate myself. Our friendship had never recovered after that trip, since I used the perceived estrangement as a reason to continue to turn down invitations and remove myself from my close circle of friends.

By the time Mary-Simms married, I wasn't a part of the bridal party despite pinky-swearing as girls that we would be each other's maid of honor. I didn't even attend the wedding, citing distance and work commitments. My visits home after I started college were sparse, and as the years went on, it became easier and easier not to pick up the phone.

My sporadic responses to her letters and emails didn't dissuade her from trying to maintain our bond. It was as if she knew me better than I knew myself and felt confident that our friendship was too important to both of us to disregard on a technicality and that one day I'd come around. Her persistent optimism was just one of the many things I loved about Mary-Simms.

She stepped back. "You're still as pretty as ever. Obviously, you don't have children or you'd look a little more worse for wear." Leaning down, she picked up the little boy. "This is Andrew Jackson Mobley III, but we call him Drew. He is the apple of my eye, and I wouldn't change a thing. Except for the sticky fingers and occasional whininess, but who doesn't need a good whine every once in a while?"

"Mary-Simms. It is so good to see you." And it was. We'd always joked that Happy had been made for her because she was perpetually in a good mood and had the annoying habit of always seeing the bright side of any situation. Even her dark hair, bobbed in the same hairstyle she'd worn since kindergarten, bounced with joy with her every step. Drew was her spitting image, and even he was grinning at me as if he'd just found his long-lost best friend, too.

The little boy surprised me by reaching for me, and I took him from his mother and hoisted him on my hip, feeling the crinkle of a diaper under my arm. He continued to grin at me, and I couldn't resist poking his button nose, which made him laugh.

"Look at you two. You're already best friends."

I smiled at her, surprisingly close to tears. "It's so good to see you. I'm so sorry I've been such a stranger. It's just . . ."

She put her finger to her lips. "You don't need to explain anything to me of all people, so shush. I'm just so happy to see you, and I hope you'll be here long enough so we can spend some time together. And no worries—I knew you would be a bit shy about reaching out if you needed a friend, so I decided to save you the trouble." She closed the door behind us. "I was about to say how hot it is outside, but I think it might be hotter in here."

"Yes. Long story, but the electricity was turned off."

"Let me guess. Addie had something to do with that." She flashed me a smile so I didn't have to answer. "I need to refill Drew's sippy cup with water. I know where to go." She brushed past us and headed to the kitchen as if no time had elapsed since she'd last been in my mother's house. Which, I calculated as I followed her into the kitchen, had been at my father's funeral.

She pulled out a blue plastic tumbler from her enormous purse and snapped off the lid before turning on the tap. "Are you throwing a party or something? There are so many vehicles in the driveway that I started to think my invitation got lost in the mail."

"Hardly." I felt something wet on my forearm and turned to see Drew drooling as he sucked hard on his thumb while closely regarding me from close range. His mouth opened in a smile around his thumb when he caught me looking. "Addie's here, and the dad of one of Ophelia's friends stopped by to drop off a couple of fishing rods."

She turned off the tap and leaned forward to get a better look at the people down by the dock. "Is that Ophelia? She's gotten so big. She was a baby the last time I saw her. My, how time flies. And is that your mama? I can't believe she'd be in the sun without her sunhat. I know how particular she is about her skin." She took Drew from my arms and handed him his sippy cup. "So, Phoebe. How *are* you?"

I gave her a genuine smile, wondering why I'd cut all ties when I'd fled across the country. In my desperation to leave, I must have thought that I needed a clean slate. "Much better now that you're here."

"Mama calls that a dose of vitamin Mary-Simms. Works like a charm, or so I've been told. How's your mother? Mama says she hasn't seen her at book club for a while. She called a bunch of times, but her cell might be turned off. And when she called the house and Addie answered, she was just told that Miss Elizabeth wasn't feeling up to it. Is everything okay?"

I opened my mouth to respond but instead felt another overwhelming need to cry. Mary-Simms gave my arm a sympathetic rub. "Is it Addie, your mama, or both?"

There was something to be said for knowing someone as long as Mary-Simms and I had known each other. We used to tell people we were sisters, which worked since she and I looked more alike than Addie and I did.

"We have so much catching up to do," I said. "Maybe we could meet in the back corner booth at Carolina's for lunch, just like old times?"

Her face fell. "I wish. Carolina's closed a while back, and I miss it every day. But *yes* to lunch."

Addie entered the kitchen, her hair wet from a shower, her face already starting to sweat, something that gave me more satisfaction than it should have. She stood at the kitchen sink and peered out the window toward the backyard. "Why is Mother outside without a hat?" She turned her head, spotting my friend for the first time. "Mary-Simms. It's been a while."

"It has been. Delia told me to say *hey* if I ran into you."

Delia was Mary-Simms's older sister who'd been on the same beauty pageant circuit as Addie but was now the morning anchor on the local television newscast. They'd been more competitors than friends, and this was the first time I'd wondered how Addie felt about Delia's success. The realization left me feeling gut-punched on Addie's behalf.

"Well, tell her I said *hey* back." Addie headed toward the screen porch where she snatched Mother's wide-brimmed hat from the hat rack. She let the porch door snap shut behind her as we turned to watch her go.

Liam was on his way back from the dock to the porch. He said something to her in greeting, but she waltzed past him as if she hadn't heard.

"Oh, my." Mary-Simms smacked her lips. "Is that Ophelia's friend's daddy? Good heavens, he's good-looking. I've never met him, but I've already decided I like him because he didn't turn his head to watch Addie's backside. Too bad he's married."

"Divorced. But you're married."

"Very true. But I wasn't thinking about me."

Liam came through the screen porch to the kitchen before I could question her. She walked straight to him, holding out her hand in greeting. "I'm Mary-Simms Mobley, formerly McSwain, and I'm Phoebe's best friend from when we were practically still in diapers."

Liam smiled back. "Nice to meet you," he said, shaking her hand. "Liam Fitch. My son, Will, is the boy down on the dock teaching Ophelia how to hook a worm."

"That's a story they can tell their grandchildren, isn't it?" Mary-Simms burst out laughing. "Sorry. I can't help myself. I missed my true calling as a matchmaker." She gave him a second look. "Did you say *Liam*? Are you the same Liam who saved Phoebe when she got hit by lightning?"

"The very same," he said, pretending not to see Mary-Simms's eyebrow wriggling directed at me. She knew the history of the lawsuit and would no doubt want to hear how Liam had come back into our lives.

Liam turned to me. "It looks like everything is under control. Give me a call on my cell when you're ready for me to come pick Will up."

"Sure." I began walking Liam toward the front door, eager to get him out of the house before Mary-Simms's matchmaking mind whirred into overdrive.

Following behind us, she said, "Hang on a sec. Are you by any chance a fan of the Backstreet Boys? Not that I'm saying you're old enough to remember them, but I'm suspecting that you are. And you don't really have to be a fan to go. It's more like an excuse to go out with a bunch of people your age who remember how cool it used to be to like the Backstreet Boys and won't judge you for singing along to the lyrics. Or you can pretend that you don't know them." She laughed. "Anyway, they're playing at the outdoor amphitheater on Daniel Island on Friday night, and I'd like to get a group together to go. I'm also desperate for a date night with my husband and a reason to wear heels and jewelry again. Please say you'll both come."

184 ||| Karen White

She bent down to scoop up Drew and his sippy cup. "I'll let you think about it—just let me know by tomorrow. And because I'm feeling hopeful, I'm going to go ahead and reserve enough seats to include you two."

I held the door open for her, seeing her bright red minivan parked behind Liam's truck, a painted logo of an *S* and a magnolia blossom surrounded by the words *Mary-Simms Designs* plastered on the side-door panel. "I know, I'm such a sellout. But a van really helps with storing all my design samples for my business as well as Drew's *accoutrements*." She said this last word with a mixed Southern and French accent.

I smiled and nodded as if I'd known she had her own design company. She'd studied business at Clemson, but our paths had diverged completely by the time I fled to the West Coast. She was the diamond ring I'd accidentally rolled up with the garbage and thrown away, and I was overcome with a wave of shame and regret. I'd always thought that once I'd reached my thirties, I would have the wisdom to close the book on my past, accept all the losses and gains, and move on. I was still working on that.

As Mary-Simms buckled Drew into his car seat, Liam turned to me. "You should go to the concert. You need a break. Maybe Addie might want to go with you."

"That would be more of a punishment. Even worse than going with you."

When he didn't say anything, I realized what I'd just said. "That's not what I meant. I'm sure there are a million things you'd rather do than go see the Backstreet Boys with or without me."

"Don't be so quick to judge. I happen to like the Backstreet Boys, and I'm free Friday night. I could also make up an excuse not to go if that would make you feel better."

I wanted to tell him then about the dream, and his part in its inception, and how terrified I was to have it again. It had taken me by surprise when I'd fallen asleep on Celeste's porch, and despite all my efforts to keep busy, a new detail from the dream kept prodding me like an apparition seen from the corner of my eye. The bobbing object in the water that I'd seen the last time was there, glinting in the ambient light but still unidentifiable.

But this time, before it was sucked down into the dark depths, I'd seen something new, something I did recognize. It was the bumper of the car. A white license place with dark letters, disappearing slowly, the palmetto tree and crescent visible for a second before vanishing. I was sure I'd seen the last three digits of the number, but when I tried to go back and remember, all I could see was the pale glow of the plate as the car was sucked to the bottom.

"I'll let you know." I moved back, opening the door wider so he could step out onto the porch.

"I'll drive," he said, his grin so much like Will's that I almost smiled back.

"I didn't say—"

"Not yet, but I know you'd like to go so, I'm saving you the trouble. I'll let you know what time I'll pick you up."

"But . . ."

"I'm looking forward to it," he said, smiling as he headed down the porch steps to his truck.

I wanted to call after him and let him know that I wasn't going, but the words got stuck in my mouth. Instead, I closed the door before he could see the silly grin on my face.

# 15

~

"When a killdeer mother spots a predator close to her nest, she will pretend she has a broken wing, calling loudly and limping along as she stretches out one wing and fans her tail to redirect attention. But the cuckoo bird will lay her egg in another bird's nest and eject one of the legitimate eggs from the nest. When the cuckoo returns later to see if her trick worked but discovers her chick has been discovered and ejected, she will peck to death the other baby birds. Too little, too late, I think, for a mother to demonstrate her love for her offspring."

**Excerpt from the blog *The Thing with Feathers***

## Celeste

I UNWRAPPED ANOTHER pink foam roller from Elizabeth's fine blond hair before tossing it in the sink. I used the comb to tease the hair and add volume at the top before uncapping the large can of Aqua Net and spraying it into the roots. I smiled at her in the mirror. "Is that enough? Or would you like more?"

She smiled back. "More, please."

I did as asked, referring to the photo of her as Miss South Carolina that Phoebe had taped to the vanity mirror to help me get it right. Sometimes, Elizabeth would point to it to let me know that was her back in the day when she was comfortable showing her legs. The day before, she'd asked me who the beautiful girl was. Addie had been in the bathroom with us and had started to cry.

Even after almost five full days of working as her paid companion and housekeeper, Elizabeth asked me my name each morning when I showed up with Will and Annie in tow.

If circumstances had been different, I might have relished the opportunity to erase any missteps from the previous day such as offering her oatmeal instead of grits with her breakfast or helping her dress, both mistakes I wouldn't make twice. Elizabeth was very particular about her appearance, a relief to both Phoebe and Addie since it assured them that their mother was still somewhere inside.

"There," I said, patting her hair and removing the towel from around her shoulders. "You ready to go downstairs?"

My first order of business had been getting everybody on a schedule. It seemed that it not only created more lucid moments for Elizabeth, but also seemed appreciated by Phoebe and Ophelia. Addie, not so much. I wondered if it was the routine she balked at, or just the fact that I was the one creating it.

We walked into the hallway where the bedroom doors were open to reveal beds made and the floors relatively clear of clutter and dirty clothes. I'd helped Phoebe clear off the guest room bed so she'd have her own room, and she, Ophelia, Elizabeth, and I had taken a field trip to Target to purchase closet-organizing options.

Addie's door was still closed. She'd worked another late shift the night before, so I let her sleep and didn't knock. But I would be up at eleven to drag her out of bed to join in whatever activity I had planned for Ophelia and Will. The way Ophelia looked up to her mother broke my heart. Not just because she was so overlooked by Addie but because one day in the not-so-distant future she would stop looking for Addie at all.

Phoebe glanced up from where she sat at the kitchen table, where Ophelia and Will were in the middle of a heated game of gin rummy. Will was keeping track of who won each game, which determined who had to get up and get their snacks. Annie sat in her new favorite spot of Ophelia's lap. Ophelia threw up her hands. "How does he win every time? I give up!"

"Phoebe," Elizabeth said, "when did you get here?"

Just as I'd rehearsed with her, Phoebe said, "I'm here for a long visit. Let me get you some coffee."

Elizabeth sat down at the table while Phoebe poured her mother a cup of coffee. She glanced at the clock on the stove. "It's almost eleven. Should I get Addie out of bed?"

"Yes, please. I thought that today would be a good day to set up easels in the shade and have fun with watercolors. I had Liam bring over enough for each of us."

Will groaned loudly, but at least Ophelia seemed more enthusiastic. "Okay, but can I finish reading my chapter first? And you don't need to wake Mama. She's already down on the dock."

Phoebe stood to look outside the screened porch toward the dock. "Unbelievable. She's been promising to meet with Dale at Daddy's law office since Monday."

She threw open the door to the porch, but I called her back. "She hasn't forgotten. My guess is she'll get it done a lot faster if you stop asking her."

Phoebe closed the door. "I've asked her to do one thing. One thing! I should just do it myself, but I refuse."

"Because that would mean she's not doing her fair share?"

"Of course not. This isn't a competition."

"Exactly. So don't make it one. You are more than capable of doing everything by yourself, and Addie knows it. She probably feels inadequate standing in the breeze you leave behind. Give her a chance to shine."

"Addie doesn't need me to help her shine. All she has to do is stand in the middle of the room."

"And how do you think that makes her feel?"

"I . . ." Phoebe closed her mouth, struggling to find an answer to a question she'd never heard asked before.

Elizabeth turned her attention away from the children's card game. "Phoebe! When did you get here?"

Phoebe grimaced. "I'm here for a long visit." Her face was like the sky darkening with intent. She was a tightrope walker, balancing her emotions between love, duty, and resentment, all liberally coated with a heavy layer of guilt.

I stood behind Elizabeth's chair. "I've placed some of the family photo albums on the dining room table for you to look through. I found a box of loose photographs, too. Maybe I can help you put them in one of the new albums we found at the store."

Elizabeth stood, wearing an expression I now knew meant that she recognized me but needed prompting with my name.

"I'm Celeste," I said, "and I'm dying to see pictures of Charles."

Elizabeth nodded regally. "He was very handsome. He graduated from the Citadel. He looked so nice in his uniform. He says that I fell in love with the uniform before I fell in love with him."

I led Elizabeth to the dining room, aware that Phoebe was still watching her sister through the kitchen window. "Why don't you join us, Phoebe, and bring her coffee? You can help write down the names of people and places on the backs of the photographs."

"Oh, I don't need her to do that," Elizabeth said with a scowl. I could sense Phoebe bristling behind me.

"I know. That's why I bought two archival-safe pens, one for each of you."

That seemed to satisfy them both as we settled at the dining room table with Elizabeth situated in a seat between us. Phoebe randomly selected an album with a dark green linen cover and placed it in front of her mother.

"I bought this one for you for Mother's Day, with all the colored pens and stickers, remember?" Phoebe opened it up to the first page revealing a full-length photo of Addie wearing a flowing pink gown with a sash and crown. The page had been decorated with colorful stickers and carefully penned words. *Miss Lowcountry Teen.*

Elizabeth stared at the photo, nodding as if she approved, and then turned the page where more photos of Addie at various events and costumes danced across both pages.

I felt Phoebe holding her breath when Elizabeth reached the fourth page. Small, torn flaps of paper indicated where photographs had once been attached with an adhesive. The only remnants of what had been there were the lines of stickered text going across the top border. *Spelling Bee First Place* stretched across the top of the page along with a picture of a petite, middle-aged woman wearing a loose blouse, white capris, Birkenstocks, and large glasses that were too big for her face. The picture had been cut in half, only the leg and foot of a girl remaining.

"I've never liked having my picture taken," Phoebe said. "But I thought Aunt Sassy looked adorable in this picture, so I kept her part of it."

Elizabeth tapped the photo with her index finger. "That's Sassy," she said. "I haven't seen her today."

"That's Charles's sister?" I prompted.

She nodded. "Yes. She is a saint."

"Because she took me off your hands?" Phoebe tried for a light tone, but there was an edge to it.

"No. Because she helped me get out of your way. Always so busy . . ." She made stabbing motions with her hand.

"Digging?" I asked.

"Yes. In the marsh. And climbing trees to look at birds. She was different." Her mouth worked silently as her brain struggled to recall the right words. "Different doesn't mean less beautiful. Just different."

Elizabeth flicked one of the torn flaps on the page with her fingernail, as if she hadn't just offered an emotional bombshell. The words had come so easily to her because it must have been something she'd often said. She wouldn't remember it in five minutes, but I was glad Phoebe had heard it.

To feign disinterest, Phoebe slid the box of loose photos closer to her. "At some point, I should have these digitized and put into an album. Our parents were slow to embrace technology. They still used real cameras and film even after they got their first smartphones."

She grabbed a handful of photos and began going through them, sorting a few into piles on the table while I continued to look through the album with Elizabeth, prompting her to comment on the photos that were almost exclusively of Addie or Charles.

I did my best to be objective when it came to pictures of Charles—to not imagine evil intent in his eyes. In my capacity as caregiver for Elizabeth, I had to force myself to see him as her beloved husband, provider, and protector. The father of her children.

"Is that Bailey?" I pointed to the largest of Phoebe's pile, with the picture of a beagle resting on top of the stack.

Her eyes glistened as if surprised to find herself in the present. "Yes." She held up a picture. "Mother—remember this? It was Halloween when Bailey was a puppy, and you and Aunt Sassy made her a pumpkin costume." She pulled out another of Bailey wearing stuffed red reindeer antlers with jingle bells. "I had no idea you had so many pictures of her."

Elizabeth's face softened. "Such a sweet dog. She loves her fried chicken. Just don't tell Phoebe, or she'll be mad."

"Mother, I'm Phoebe. I'm right here."

Elizabeth didn't like being corrected, but she returned to the album without comment, refocusing on the pages and pretty stickers.

I was about to turn another page when Phoebe laughed. "Oh, my gosh—I'd totally forgotten about this!" She held up a photograph of what looked like a lime-green new edition Volkswagen Beetle—or what had once been one. Its distinctive hood and logo were all that was recognizable in the crushed metal heap on top of a wrecker.

Elizabeth squinted at the picture, but I knew better than to suggest that she put on her glasses.

"It's Addie's car—the one Daddy bought her for high school graduation. She named it Kermit, remember? She got it way early, around Christmas, because she wouldn't stop begging." She looked hard at her mother, as if she could force her to remember by sheer will, but Elizabeth turned away.

Phoebe lowered the photograph to the table, then dug into the box again before pulling out two more pictures showing the same subject but from different angles. "I think Daddy must have taken these since he's the one who went to the accident scene and waited for the wrecker. Addie had that car for exactly two weeks and then totaled it. She was lucky to have walked away with only a few cuts and scrapes. Daddy put the insurance money into Addie's college fund, saying he wasn't going to waste any more of his money buying her another car."

"Ouch," I said. "I hate to say this, but he was right."

"Addie didn't think so," Phoebe said. "Even after all this time, I still think she'd disagree with him about it. I was supposed to get the car after Addie, so she let me pick the color. I stayed mad at her for a long time."

"Understandable." I imagined that she carried that grudge around like a pebble in her shoe, an irritation that grew into a large and painful sore over time. Not just because she most likely stewed on it in silence, but because nobody thought to ask her how she felt about it. "Did you get a car when you graduated?"

Phoebe flicked through photos inside the box. "Nope. I went out of state for college, so the tuition was higher, plus they paid for my room and board. Daddy said that was a fair trade-off."

"Did you think so?"

"Of course not. I thought it was a little mercenary, to be honest. It's not like he didn't have the money, and I graduated with honors. You'd think I'd get a pass."

"What did your mother say about it?"

Phoebe looked at her mother, who remained focused on the torn paper flaps under missing photos. "Nothing, of course. Whatever Daddy said became the law. She just went along with whatever he said."

I bit my tongue on all the things I wanted to say about her father and instead tried to change the subject. "Well, now you're an independent woman so you can get your own. Is that what you drive now?"

"I wish. They stopped making that model in 2011, and the newer ones weren't the same. I drive a Toyota Corolla now in boring gray. Not as exciting, but it gets me where I need to be."

I helped Elizabeth turn another album page. The borders surrounding the two-page layout were decorated with musical-note stickers and the stenciled letters *Wando Winter Concert*. There were more photographs of Addie wearing a long black dress and a strand of pearls, some while standing on the risers with other members of the choir, and a few in the auditorium chatting with identically attired girls, and boys wearing tuxedos.

Somewhere in my own albums, I had similar photographs showing the same group of singers, yet none of Addie, of course. The photos I had taken were of my granddaughter Julie, who'd sung in the Wando choir since freshman year. And who had sung at this very concert.

My gaze strayed to the front row of the soprano section, third from the left. There she was, my beautiful Julie, her face glowing with the joy that was as much a part of her as light is to the moon. She seemed to be scanning the crowd, no doubt looking for Liam and me.

Phoebe must have heard my intake of breath. "What's wrong?"

"Nothing." I turned the album for her to see and pointed at my granddaughter's face. "This is Julie. She and Addie were in the choir at Wando High School together. So they must have known each other, right?"

She leaned closer to get a better look. "I recognize her from the frames in your house, but I never saw her hanging around with Addie. Addie sang alto, so she'd be on the other side of the group, but I'm sure they at least knew who the other was."

Trying not to show my disappointment, I slid the album back in front of Elizabeth. "I thought you and Addie attended Ashley Hall."

"We did, but Addie got kicked out for bringing cocktails to school in her water bottle. Our father was so mad at the school that he wanted to pull me out, too, but I wanted to stay. My best friend, Mary-Simms, and I had started school together, and we wanted to finish together, too. Fortunately for me, Mother agreed. That might have been the only time she ever had a different opinion than my father." She regarded Elizabeth, who seemed oblivious to the conversation as she studied the photographs on the page.

"And Addie didn't walk at graduation. She had to take summer classes to make up a few failing grades before she got her diploma. She was too humiliated to show her face at the ceremony."

"My Phoebe sings like a bird," Elizabeth said softly.

"That's Addie, Mother."

Elizabeth frowned. "Addie sings, but you have the voice of an angel."

Phoebe shook her head. "That's the first time I've ever heard you say that. But Addie was the one who made the All State choir. I didn't try out because Addie would have been mad if I'd made it, too."

"Everything came so easily to you. Addie needed something of her own." Elizabeth's fingers fluttered like butterflies over the open pages as if summoning the memories before the momentary clarity deserted her again.

"This . . ." she began, patting one of the photos ". . . is Addie. She sings."

I turned to the next page. "Well," I said. "What happened here?"

Despite removable bindings, this page had been ripped out of the album, the jagged tear like a scar close to the spine.

Phoebe shrugged, keeping her focus on sorting a handful of photos from the box. "I'd forgotten I did that. These were taken at my middle school science fair, and I looked like one of the science experiments. They were embarrassing, so I took them out and shredded them. It was like Mother was always looking for the most unflattering photos of me to put in the albums."

Ophelia and Will ran into the dining room, Annie on their heels. "We're bored. Can we go outside now, please?" Ophelia asked. "Mama's still down there."

"Sure," Phoebe said. "I'll come with you."

As she stood to leave, I called after her. "Phoebe?"

She turned to face me.

"Would you ask Addie if she knew Julie?"

"I could, but why don't you?"

"Because I don't think she likes me very much, and you have a better chance of getting an answer."

She nodded. "What if she did?"

"When Julie disappeared, I made a promise to myself to leave no stone unturned. Maybe Addie heard something or saw something. She might have some piece of information that she doesn't even know is important. It's a stab in the dark, I know, but it can't hurt, right?"

"Right," she said, unconvinced.

She paused behind her mother's chair, watching as Elizabeth tapped her nail against each photograph like a magician with a card trick. Phoebe turned to go but instead leaned down to kiss her mother's cheek. "I'll see you later."

Elizabeth jerked her head away, rubbing at the spot with the back of her hand before returning to the scrapbook.

Phoebe stepped back as if she'd been stung.

"She didn't mean that, Phoebe. You know that."

"Do I?"

"Yes. I think you do."

She stared back at me, as if preparing to argue. But then she turned and left, the sound of her slow footsteps marking her way through the silent house to the back door.

# 16

~

"People tend to think of a nest as a home, but to the birds a nest is simply a cradle to hold the eggs and chicks until they are old enough to fly. The farther away from home baby birds fly after leaving the nest, the safer they are. I think this is true of humans, too, but not because of the danger from predators. Rather, it is the danger of having our wings clipped so that eventually we lose the will and the ability to fly away."

**Excerpt from the blog *The Thing with Feathers***

# *Phoebe*

THE SNAKELIKE HEAD of an anhinga bird slipped stealthily through the dark water near the dock, unseen by Addie, who remained by her easel, her jaw jutting forward in an inadvertent impression of the bird. Anhingas are rarely found outside of their freshwater habitat except when building a nest, yet I wasn't surprised to see one here. Nothing in my world was behaving as it should.

The heady smells of the star jasmine clusters that lay draped over the side fence like lazy cats tangled with that of the wax myrtles, sending a stab of nostalgia straight into my heart. Even the heavy shroud of humidity added to the allure of my memories of this place that was as much a member of my family as the people were. And just as complicated.

Two dragonflies hovered around me, seeming to dance to the rhythm of the Carolina wren's chirping from Ophelia's new bird feeder hanging from the cedar tree. I walked down to the dock, slipping in the mud from the recent rain.

Addie, wearing a wide-brimmed straw hat, had moved her easel out from the shade of the tall red cedar to the far end of the dock, protected from the heat of the sun by the cloud cover. It had been so long since I'd seen Addie paint that I'd forgotten about her fleeting passion when she was in high school, fueled by winning first place in a local store's art contest. Mother had tolerated it until Addie started talking about going to art school and becoming an artist. By the time Addie was a senior in high school, her paintbrushes and easels had been packed away and stored in the attic alongside the high chair and other relics from our childhoods.

I stopped in front of her, but she didn't look up, her eyes focused on the easel. Her movements were nearly frantic, her brush like a weapon punishing the painting. Celeste painted with thoughtful, gentle strokes, as she created the delicate feathers of birds or showed my mother how to paint the sky. But Addie's strokes were different, almost violent, the brush an extension of her unspoken emotions.

I waited for her to notice me, my ire growing as she continued to ignore me.

Without glancing up, she said, "You look like Mr. Morton when I didn't turn in my math homework. And it's no more flattering on you than it was on him."

"Since he was probably also expressing intense disappointment, then I suppose you're right. I've been waiting patiently all week for you to go see Dale. Mother has a follow-up appointment with Liam coming up, and I also need to take her to the eye doctor. Whoever is her POA will need to take her, since legally they can't talk to either one of us about Mother without it."

Addie dipped her brush into a plastic cup of ochre-colored water. "You weren't really all that patient, Phoebe. I heard your little snorts of fury every time I walked into a room."

"I don't snort."

"Right." Addie picked up another brush and continued dabbing paint on her picture while my anger grew.

I was getting ready to yank the brush from her hand when she said, "You can stop glowering." She lifted her eyes to meet my gaze. "I met with Dale on Wednesday."

A flush of pink stained her cheek, and I was sure it wasn't from the heat. "And you're just mentioning this to me now? What did he say?"

"You're the POA for both financial and health care for Mother. Apparently, Daddy had you sign the forms at some point, but it was years ago so I'm guessing you don't remember."

I stared at her, stunned. "Are you sure? I don't remember any of that."

She rolled her eyes. "Yeah. I'm sure. Go see for yourself."

"But why? You're the eldest."

"Because you're the smartest, remember?" Addie swirled gray and green paint together on her palette, creating the color of a dusk sky over the marsh. I stepped behind the easel to see what she was painting. She tried to block me, but I was quicker.

Darkness crept from the corners of the painting, an ominous reminder of an approaching storm. It was incomplete, but the intensity of the colors and movement of the brush sent shivers through me. It was evocative and mysterious, and beautiful in the way of a rose with hidden thorns.

"It's not done," she said, sounding defensive.

"I didn't know you still painted," I said.

"Neither did I. But having the easels and paints here . . . I figured why not."

She returned to the dusky paint, creating furious whorls of color on the paper, stopping only when the brush ran dry. Then she dropped her brush and abruptly sat down on the dock. Not knowing what else to do, I sat down next to her.

After a moment, I said, "Do you remember Celeste's grand-daughter, Julie Fitch? She was the girl in your year at Wando who went missing your senior year. I think you were in choir with her."

She shrugged. "I knew who she was, but we weren't friends. Did Celeste ask you to ask me?"

"Yes. She thinks you don't like her."

Addie grunted in response.

We sat without speaking, our breaths settling into the same rhythm. After a while, she said, "I read something interesting on Reddit today. Grandparents who are actively involved in their grandchildren's lives were parents who loved parenting so much that they relish doing it again."

I frowned. "Maybe you should be getting your information from a more reliable source. I think Mother spends so much time with Ophelia because she doesn't have a choice. You're not around much."

"Ouch. Thanks for that, Phoebe. The truth really does hurt. But, yeah. You're probably right. In any case, it's better this way. I don't think I'd be a very good mother."

"Why on earth would you say that? Ophelia is . . . wonderful and so eager to please. She looks up to you, you know. She just wants some of your attention."

"But Mother is doing such a good job of it. I don't want to mess it up."

Our eyes met, and I wondered if the devastation I saw in her eyes mirrored my own. "Addie . . ."

"I know. I know Mother isn't going to get better. I just don't want to think about it."

"But you have to. You're going to have to take over when I leave, regardless of whether you and Celeste come to an agree-ment. Ophelia needs you."

Addie shook her head. "I don't think I have the motherhood gene. Sometimes I wonder . . ." She stopped, her attention drifting as a soft breeze blew across the marsh, bending the smooth cordgrass in alternating swaths like the sweep of a divine hand.

"Wonder about what?"

"Maybe I'm being punished."

I turned to look at her. "Punished? For what?"

It took Addie a long time to respond, leaving me to wonder if she was searching for an alternate answer from the first one she thought of. "I don't know. For not meeting expectations, I guess. For allowing stupid mistakes to take over."

"Ophelia isn't a stupid mistake, Addie."

Her eyes widened with shock. "Of course not. My daughter is the best thing I've ever accomplished in my life. I'm trying my best not to ruin her." She put her head in her hands while I waited for her to explain what mistakes she thought deserved punishment.

Our gazes met briefly. "Maybe it's payback time for throwing away all my opportunities." She dipped her head so I could no longer see her eyes beneath the brim of her hat.

"I don't think that's how it works, Addie. Besides, if your idea of swift reward and retribution for our actions were true, I'd be a weather girl on TV and you'd be a troll living under the Ravenel Bridge—according to my childhood fantasies, anyway. But we're not birds, born with the genetics to know how to build a nest and care for our offspring. It's honestly a surprise to me that we survive at all."

Addie frowned. "Why is it always about the birds for you?"

"Because bird behavior, when it's not mimicking human behavior, makes a lot more sense to me."

A sticky breeze blew the scent of jasmine around us, and I was little again, having a tea party on the dock with Addie, our mother allowing us to use her good Limoges because I had asked politely, bringing it down from the house herself on a prized silver tray.

"I think you managed to steal all the good mother genes," she said.

"You know, Addie, to be a good mother you have to show up. I know that from being a teacher. Even Mother showed up, except when I asked her not to because I knew she'd be bored or disappointed when I didn't win. But at least she tried."

Addie watched the long rivulets of water searching finger-like through the marsh toward Jeannette Creek in the distance. "Right. So that's all I have to do, huh? Show up?"

"That's a start. But I'm not an expert, either. It's not like we got the best parenting instructions."

She stood and brushed off the dust from her white jeans now dotted with splashes of paint. "Yeah, well, you're the brilliant sister. Of course you could figure everything out on your own."

I stood, too. "Actually, I think I've figured out very little. I'm lost, too."

Just for a moment, our eyes met, and our pain and loss min-gled, lessening the weight each of us carried like a basket full of tarnished memories. And then it was gone, and Addie was a stranger again. She shoved her hands into her back pockets. "*Lost.* Yeah, that's a good word for it."

Her gaze took in what I was wearing. "Aren't you going out tonight?"

"Yeah. So, I won't be here for Ophelia."

"That's not why I'm asking. Are you planning on going like that?" She indicated my stretched-out Ashley Hall T-shirt and old gym shorts.

"I have a clean T-shirt, and I'll probably put on a pair of jeans. It's outdoors, so it doesn't matter."

"Seriously, Phoebe. I wish that just once you'd have gone with Mother and me to a pageant so you'd have a clue about how to present yourself. It wasn't just about looking good in a bathing suit and smiling pretty, you know. Wait, no you wouldn't know because you always refused to go with us."

I crossed my arms. "I always had better things to do. It wasn't personal."

"Yeah, it was. And that's a shame because you might have learned something important. Right now, the impression you're giving is of a young woman with a lot of natural potential who is afraid to let people see her feminine side at the risk of not being taken seriously. So instead, you look like a young woman who's either given up or is totally fine with people overlooking her instead of sitting up and paying attention."

"I don't need to impress anyone tonight," I said, bristling.

"Good. The last person on earth you should be trying to impress is Liam Fitch. But there will be other people there, and you should at least try to make a good impression. If you don't want to do it for yourself, do it for Mother. She'd be mortified to know you went out in public looking like something the cat dragged in."

Despite myself, I felt the corner of my mouth lifting. It was something our mother had said a lot and always directed at me. My smile fell as I realized that I'd never hear her say that again, and I felt suddenly adrift.

"Well, if you're going to do something with your hair, you'd better get busy. Although I don't think there's enough time left in the day to fix . . ." She waved her hand in front of me. "This. Come on," she said. "Let me at least do something to your hair."

"What's wrong with my hair?"

She was walking in front of me so I couldn't see her face, but I could picture her rolling her eyes. "Nothing that a curling iron can't fix."

We'd almost reached the house when I said, "Thank you for talking with Dale about the power of attorney stuff. It's a big help. Although I think that meeting with Dale wasn't as much of a hardship as you'd like me to think."

"He's just a friend—nothing more. It was nice to reconnect."

"You consider him just a friend?"

"Really. He's a nice guy and a welcome change from the usual jerks I meet at work."

"Like the guy in the Camaro?"

She stopped walking and turned to face me. "Joe?" She shrugged. "He sort of fits my life right now, you know?"

"Not really." I recalled the bruise I'd seen on her shoulder and the long-sleeved sweater, the two belatedly connecting in my thoughts. "Does he hurt you?"

Her face darkened. "We like to play rough, that's all. And why the twenty questions? He's just a guy."

I stared at her, not recognizing my sister. "*Play rough?* If he hits you, Addie, it's never okay. The Addie I used to know would never allow that."

She turned and continued walking toward the house. "Yeah, well, I'm not the same Addie I used to be."

"What about Dale?"

"What about him? Why don't you save your questions for tonight? He's coming over later to chat and catch up, and we're going to order takeout."

"Maybe his niceness will win you over and you can drop the jerk. You're too good for him."

She gave me a doubtful look, then turned around and led us back to the house. "Hurry up. We don't have a lot of time, and those dark circles under your eyes are going to take a while to cover up."

She stopped again when we'd reached the porch steps. "Are you having those dreams again? Is that why you're not sleeping?"

I considered lying again, as if speaking of them out loud would make them more real. But maybe, like a secret, sharing them might take away their strength. "Yes. But not every night. If I drink enough, I don't remember them. Sometimes, a flash of one will hit me and bring it back to me during the day when I'm going about my business, but that's rare. Last week, I dreamed about Liam's receptionist falling off her bike before it happened."

"So, it's like before?" Addie asked. "It's something that hasn't happened yet?"

"Pretty much." I thought of the car on the bridge, and how I still wasn't sure if the event was in the past or the future, or who the woman swimming to the surface was or the identity of the driver. I needed to tell someone, but the fear it evoked crept up my throat like an invasive ivy to strangle me. To remember it was to relive it.

Addie waited for me to say more, her uncanny ability to read me like that of a twin from a shared womb. It's why I never played hide-and-go-seek when she was a participant: she always knew where I was hiding.

When I didn't say anything else, she pulled open the screen door. "Well, then. We need to make sure we keep the fridge stocked with beer."

I followed her into the house, feeling the heavy nudge of the dream settling into my head like a storm cloud, waiting for lightning to strike.

# 17

"As soon as swifts free themselves from the nest, they start flying and won't stop for two to three years. They mate on the wing and feed on flying insects as they swoop low over lakes and rivers to scoop mouthfuls of water before returning to the air. I wonder what it is that makes them decide they've had enough of exploring the world, to realize how tired their wings are from constant movement. To yearn for a home they barely remember."

**Excerpt from the blog *The Thing with Feathers***

## *Phoebe*

AN HOUR LATER, the doorbell rang. Addie had put waves in my hair and color on my face, transforming me into someone she wasn't embarrassed to call her sister. The process had reminded me of when we'd played dress-up with Mother's clothes and makeup. As uncomfortable as I felt, I didn't stop her, willing to pretend, at least for a little while, that nothing had changed and we were the same girls growing up together in this old house.

"Are our guests here already?" Mother asked. She stood from where she sat at the table nursing a cup of coffee that had long since grown cold. Her hair was newly colored and neatly styled, and she wore a dress and jewelry that made her look like herself again. Anyone who didn't know her would say she was fine. But to Addie and me, it took only one look in her eyes to see the stranger inside.

"I'll go with you, Mimi!" Ophelia announced as she jumped down from the kitchen stool where she'd been watching my transformation with fascination mixed with boredom and had made it clear that she'd rather be fishing.

"Make sure you know who it is before you open the door," I called after her.

Addie paused with a mascara wand held aloft. "I was about to say that," she said.

"Then you should have."

She jammed the wand back into the tube. "Well, maybe you should have given me a chance."

"You're right. I'm sorry."

Mollified, Addie stepped back, admiring her handiwork and the pretty yellow knit top with the scooped neckline she'd let me borrow along with the short denim skirt, surprising us both that they fit. "You need jewelry. Do you have a necklace?"

I smirked. "Do you have a fishing pole?"

"Fair point."

I thought of my bluebird necklace that Ophelia wore, and then my eyes settled on the black pearl pendant hanging from the gold chain around Addie's slender neck, the replacement gift from our parents after she'd lost the original. She'd been wearing it ever since she'd picked me up at the airport. "Could I borrow yours?"

She seemed startled by the request. "No," she said, her vehemence startling us both.

"Fine. I don't need jewelry anyway."

"Here. Borrow these." She reached up to her ears where delicate gold hoops dangled. "You need earrings that can show through your hair since you're wearing it down. Just make sure you don't lose them."

The sound of voices came from the front foyer, and Addie's eyes widened. "Dale's early."

I slid a tube of lipstick in her direction. "Put some color on," I said, mimicking our mother.

As Addie lifted the lipstick to her mouth, I had a flash of a dream I'd had the night before. I stood in a hospital, holding a bouquet of pink balloons. A person wearing dark green scrubs hovered over a bed where a lone occupant lay. It was a woman, her voice familiar. A dark-haired man stood by the side of the bed, his hands entwined with those of the patient. I could hear his soothing voice but not the words. My point of view peered around the balloons toward the woman in the bed. She looked directly at me and said, "It's a girl." I studied the face and recognized the signature red lipstick of my old friend, Mary-Simms.

I glanced up at the sound of the approaching voices, trying to clear the dream from my head. Addie stood, her fingers plucking awkwardly at her white linen pants. My sister had the confidence to walk in front of an auditorium filled with people wearing only a bikini, high heels, and a sash, so this bout of nervousness surprised me.

"Hello, Dale," she said in greeting to the young man in the khakis and green knit polo shirt. He was a slightly older version of the man I'd seen sporadically at various law firm picnics and family-friendly functions while I was growing up. His curly strawberry-blond hair was thinner now, and he had the look of someone who spent a lot of time indoors judging by his pale skin and soft muscles. He wore wire-rimmed glasses and loafers without socks, but what made him memorable was his kind smile. He'd always made a point of speaking to me about birds and other things my adolescent self considered important, and he would bring me a second serving of dessert without me having to ask. His good nature did nothing to endear him to Addie, who would ignore him and continue texting on her phone whenever he spoke to her.

"Addie," he said, with the smile I recognized. Despite all the changes in my life, it was gratifying to see that Dale Prioleau hadn't been one of them. "It's good to see you again. I'm sorry I'm early. I anticipated more traffic on the Ravenel Bridge."

"It's fine," she said as she tucked her hair behind one ear, and I noticed that she was wearing flats, something I'd never seen when there was a male involved. Even when she went to work in her cutoff jeans and T-shirt, she wore high wedged espadrilles that exaggerated her height.

Ophelia danced around the newcomer as if they were old friends. "Dale said I could pick what kind of food we get for tonight, and then we're going for ice cream."

"Wow. That sounds like a lot more fun than my plans. Maybe I should stay here with you."

Dale turned to me, his light brown eyes enormous behind his glasses. "Hello, Phoebe. You're looking well."

"Thank you. It's amazing what a little spackle and paint can do."

"Nah," he said, stepping forward to kiss my cheek in greeting. "It's your natural beauty shining through. Are you still into birds?"

I was touched that he remembered, but before I could respond, my sister intervened.

"She is," Addie said, drawing his attention back to her, and for a moment, it occurred to me that my sister might be feeling jealous—a thought too surreal to unpack. "Ophelia, could you please bring me your iPad? We can go online and look for our dinner options. If that's all right with you, Dale?"

She smiled at him, and his cheeks pinkened, his old infatuation resurrecting itself. Or maybe it had never gone away. And the reason for the flats became clear when I noticed that they were the same height.

Dale's response was drowned out by my mother shouting from the foyer. Addie and I exchanged guilty looks, both having assumed that she was in the kitchen with Ophelia. We hurried to the front door in time to see Liam escorting her back inside, while she continued to protest, insisting that she needed to greet her guests.

"She was in the middle of the street," Liam said without judgment. "Let's add that to the list of things to discuss at her next appointment."

"Come on, Mother," Addie said, taking her hand. "Let me get you something to drink."

"She probably shouldn't be drinking," I said. "Because of her meds."

Addie sent me a dismissive look. "I know how to take care of her. I've been doing it without you for a while now."

I opened my mouth to argue, but Liam squeezed my arm, stopping me and leaving me feeling as if I were twelve years old again and vying for our mother's goodwill.

I introduced Dale and Liam, who, it turned out, had several acquaintances in common. Not completely unexpected since Mount Pleasant and the entire Charleston metro area was really just a small town disguised as a city.

"We should go," I said, eager to leave and get the evening over with. I was happy to spend time with Mary-Simms again, even though it meant being in close proximity to Liam Fitch for an extended period of time. I was glad he'd offered to drive because I would be drinking enough tonight to erase the dark dream his presence seemed to have triggered. It pressed against the periphery of my consciousness with growing urgency.

As I said goodbye to my mother, she pointed at my mouth.

"Do I need some color?" I opened the small purse I'd borrowed from Addie and pulled out a tube of lipstick and Mother smiled. It was a silly thing, and I shouldn't have felt such immense satisfaction that she'd approved of something I'd done.

Liam held open the passenger door of his truck and helped me inside. As he came around to the driver's side, I searched my phone for the Backstreet Boys playlist I'd compiled earlier.

As soon as he sat down and started the ignition, I connected my phone with his CarPlay and the opening lines of "Quit Playing Games with My Heart" started playing through the truck's speakers.

"Does that mean you'd rather listen to music than talk?" Liam asked.

It was almost embarrassing how easily he read me. "It's all Backstreet Boys music," I said, pretending I'd misunderstood.

He put the truck in Drive and backed out of the driveway. "It's not working, you know."

"What isn't?"

"Keeping your distance."

"I don't know what you're talking about," I said, trying to sound indignant.

"I think you do. So, what am I missing? Are you dating someone back in Oregon?"

"No. I'm not."

When I didn't elaborate, he said, "Is it because I'm your mother's doctor?"

"It's not personal. It's just that I'm going back in less than two months, and I don't need any complications."

"I think it's too late for that, don't you? I mean, your mother, sister, and niece are here in South Carolina. You probably don't want to hear this, but they all need you."

"And I'm doing all that I can while I'm here to make things smoother when I return to the life I've worked very hard to establish. I know how that sounds, and I'm not trying to run from my responsibilities, but everyone is better off without me being here."

"I don't think that's true. And I'm not even sure it's possible to leave for good. I had a great job offer in Atlanta when I graduated from med school, but my grandmother is here along with all my memories of Julie. And this place. It's like the pluff mud clings to your heart. It's like an anchor."

I turned away, staring out my window, the passing traffic only a blur. "You're wrong. Leaving gets easier the more I do it."

We were silent until he turned onto I-526 toward Daniel Island. "So, what did you do before going to a concert when you were a kid?" he asked.

Relieved to have the subject changed, I faced him. "I didn't go to concerts. My mother didn't allow it because I was too young, and when I was old enough, I was too worried about all the dangers my parents warned me about, so I didn't want to go."

"That's tough," he said.

"Not really. Aunt Sassy and I would watch old films together and eat homemade caramel popcorn, so I didn't suffer too much."

"I'd say you got the better end of the deal. I wasn't a big concertgoer as a kid, either. I was more into being outside and on the water than into music."

"Same. But I knew a lot of the popular music because Addie always had something blasting on the speakers in her bedroom, and I must have absorbed it by osmosis." I briefly turned to look at him. Liam Fitch was even better-looking up close, his relaxed hold on the steering wheel and tanned forearms that hinted of his time outside making him even more attractive. And that was something I couldn't explore. Being around Liam increased my chances of having that one dream. The longer I stayed in South Carolina, the more persistent the dream became, with newer details revealed each time, like watching an artist paint. Each detail intensified my terror, amplifying it through my waking hours until I dreaded going to sleep each night.

I cleared my throat. "You probably absorbed your love of the Backstreet Boys from your older sister, too."

"Actually, I couldn't tell you the name of a single one of their songs."

"What? I thought you said you liked them and wanted to go to the concert."

"Well, I half lied. I do want to go to the concert, but not because of the music."

I stared at my hands in my lap with their chewed-up nails that Addie had said were beyond her scope.

"You look nice tonight, by the way."

I crossed my arms. "That's Addie's fault. She didn't want to be embarrassed if anybody recognized me as her sister."

He made an odd sound in the back of his throat as we exited the interstate onto Seven Farms Drive toward the amphitheater. We drove the rest of the short trip without speaking, the strains of "I Want It That Way" flooding the inside of his truck and drowning out the chance for more talking.

After parking, we headed to where Mary-Simms said she and her party would be. I recognized my name being squealed, and then suddenly I was being embraced tightly by my best friend, who was holding a large cup with a straw. Something cold and wet dripped down my arm.

I laughed as Mary-Simms nearly toppled us both over. "Well, hello to you, too. How much have you had to drink already?"

"Not a drop! This is ice water because I'm not drinking tonight. I'm just drunk on happiness because you're here." She tugged on my arm. "Come on and meet everyone—you, too, Liam."

She introduced us to her husband, Andrew, and two of her former sorority sisters and their husbands. She said their names so quickly that I knew I wouldn't remember them.

We headed to the concessions, where Liam ordered beer and cheeseburgers for both of us and a large pretzel to share. I tried to pay for half to make it clear this wasn't a date, but he handed over his credit card and told me I could get the next round.

Our row was centered in front of the stage, our seats still warm from the sun, although we were closing in on sunset. It was seven in the evening, and the day's heat radiated off every surface. We were packed in tightly, our legs touching those of our neighbors on either side. I had tried to sit next to Mary-Simms so we could catch up and sing along to the songs we'd once sung together into our hairbrushes during morning carpool, but she had deftly maneuvered the seating arrangement to ensure that Liam was between us.

As we waited for the concert to start, I leaned across Liam, trying not to touch him although it was impossible considering how my bare leg was already pressed against the thigh of his jeans. "Mary-Simms, I enjoyed meeting your little boy, Drew, the other day. He's adorable. I can't wait to meet his sister. What's her name?"

In spite of the growing crowd in the amphitheater, it seemed as if the volume had suddenly been turned down. She stared at me and blinked several times as if trying to process what I'd just said.

"What makes you think I have a daughter?" she finally managed. "Drew is my only child."

"I . . ." I realized that I didn't have an answer other than I'd had a dream of my friend in a hospital room with her bright lipstick and pink balloons. "I don't remember. Maybe I thought you mentioned a daughter when I saw you?"

Mary-Simms shook the ice in the bottom of her cup, and I remembered her saying that she wasn't drinking tonight. "Nope. I definitely didn't." She looked at me expectantly. She'd known about my dreams, and it was foolish of me to think she might have forgotten. I knew that she would look for an excuse to drag me to the ladies' room and interrogate me at the first opportunity.

"Sorry," I said. "My mistake." I offered a small laugh. "I have no idea where I got that from."

I felt Liam looking at me, but I turned to my left and began chatting idly with one of the other couples until the warm-up band appeared and began to play.

Despite enjoying the high-energy dancing and music by the boys—now men—during the fourth song I said I was feeling sick and asked Liam to take me home. As we squeezed past Mary-Simms, she took my hand and pressed it between hers. "I'm sorry. I hope you feel better. I'll call you tomorrow."

We said our goodbyes and walked silently back to Liam's truck, the song "Larger than Life" escorting us out of the stadium.

We were almost back to the interstate before Liam spoke. "If you're really not feeling well, I can play doctor and ask for a list of your symptoms."

"I'm fine. It was just . . ." I searched for something that might sound plausible ". . . too loud."

He laughed. "That's a sign of growing older, you know. The music is suddenly too loud, and you'd rather stay home than go out. I get it. But I don't think that's why you wanted to leave."

I turned my head away and closed my eyes. The rumbling of the truck lulled me to sleep, and I was soon on that deserted road in the marsh, watching the car weaving over the wet road, hearing the sound of the car hitting the water and the lonely call of a nightjar. This time I knew to look at the spot where I'd seen an object floating before being consumed by the marsh. The brief reflection from the ambient light winked at me, as if we were both in on a secret, and then disappeared. I watched the back end of the car as it sank, once again spotting the South Carolina license plate, but the digits on the plate remained elusive. I slid my gaze back to the object in the water, needing to see it again, but it had already sunk beneath the surface. I realized with a sickening feeling that there was something about it this time. Something I thought I recognized.

I woke up screaming, and strong arms were holding me, and a voice was saying my name. I opened my eyes, my face pressed into a solid chest. The rumbling from the voice was as comforting as the lingering scent of soap. As soon as I realized it was Liam, I pulled away and threw open the side door of the truck, recognizing my driveway and the familiar sight of my front porch. I climbed out then leaned against the truck's hood as I dug the heels of my hands into my eyes, trying to erase the last remnants of the dream.

"Are you okay?" Liam stood in front of me, his voice full of concern.

"Yes. I'm so sorry." I was too embarrassed to meet his gaze. "It was just a bad dream."

He nodded. "If you're not ready to go inside, we can stay outside and talk for a bit. Unless you're still not feeling well."

I was glad for the darkness to hide the color creeping up my cheeks. "I'm feeling better, thanks." I met his gaze. His eyes were laughing but not mocking, and his invitation to talk for a while sounded a lot better than going inside and making pleasant conversation with Dale and Addie or trying to get to sleep with the dream fresh in my brain.

When he saw me hesitating, he said, "I think you need to talk, and I'm a good listener."

A warm breeze tugged at my hair and my heart, bringing with it the scent of the marsh and reminding me of the summers of my childhood before I'd had to leave it behind.

I glanced back at the house then turned back to Liam. "Can I get you a beer?"

"I thought you'd never ask. Just one since I have to drive."

"Go ahead and set up a couple of chairs on the end of the dock, and I'll meet you there."

He gave me a salute and headed toward the backyard while I crept into the kitchen, aware of the sound of the TV from the living room, and grabbed a six-pack and a bag of Doritos.

"Where are the chairs?" I asked as I reached the dock.

"I brought towels instead to watch the stars. And I grabbed a couple of cushions from the back porch so we have something for our heads."

I placed the beer between the towels. It usually took at least three to make me slip into a dreamless sleep, and I would do everything I could to make sure I wouldn't have the dream twice in one night. I handed him a bottle then took a long swig from mine before sitting down on one of the towels. In the distance, a nightjar cried.

"That's that ugly bird with the squished head, isn't it?" Liam said as he joined me on the adjacent towel.

I hid my grin with another long swig from the bottle. "If you mean a chuck-will's-widow, then yes."

"I knew that. I was just checking to make sure you remembered."

"Uh-huh." I opened the Doritos and took one before placing the bag on the dock between us. I drained my bottle and opened another to have it ready before lying down on the towel.

I felt him watching me as he set down his bottle and lay down next to me. "If you tell me what you're trying to forget, I might be able to help."

Without answering, I stared up at the night sky, feeling the beer relax my bones and soften the edges of the nightmare. I closed my eyes, listening to the rippling water and nocturnal creatures under the dock. The sound was as comforting as a childhood lullaby, made even more soothing by Liam's presence beside me. I didn't need to explain this world to him or share the feeling of the pull of the tides or the heady aroma of the pluff mud that tethered me to the Lowcountry: this place where the land and water intermingled, the stars above sprinkling the sky like pixie dust. He already knew.

With my index finger, I pointed out the three stars of the summer triangle. "That's Deneb in Cygnus, Vega in Lyra, and Altair in Aquila. The summer humidity will cloud the atmosphere so you can't see them as clearly, but they're there. My aunt Sassy taught me everything I know about the sky and the birds who inhabit it. She said as long as I kept looking up, I would only ever see endless possibilities."

"She sounds like a really smart lady."

"She was. I miss her every day. Addie had my mother's devotion, but Aunt Sassy was all mine."

"Maybe that's why your mother thought she could give Addie more attention."

I looked at him, the side of his face touched by a glow from the crescent moon above us. "Why would you say that?"

"It's not that unusual for a mother to shower more attention on the child she believes needs it the most. I see that a lot in my practice as adult children try on their new roles in relation to a parent with dementia-related diseases."

I lay silent, ruminating over his words, wanting to tell him that he was wrong. But I couldn't. Instead, I watched the pinpoints of light flickering overhead, listening to the tide creep in around us. High tide was a cloak that covered the marsh and all its secrets, leaving them exposed again as the moon pulled back the water six hours later. I never thought that was long enough to hide anything until I had the dream the first time and learned that a secret was still a secret if it was kept for half a day or for twenty years.

Liam moved closer, his head on my cushion, and raised his arm to point at a bright light near the moon. "What's that?"

His face was so close I knew that if I turned, our noses would touch. "That's the planet Jupiter. Did you know that it's so big that you could fit one thousand Earths inside of it?"

"I don't know why we'd want to, but good to know." I could hear the smile in his voice. "You talk like a teacher, you know. And that's a compliment. If I didn't know otherwise, I'd think that you were always meant to be one."

I shrugged. "I really love what I do. But I'm not going to lie. If somebody called me tomorrow and asked me to take over as the local weather girl, I think I'd jump on it in a heartbeat. Childhood dreams don't go away just because we're doing something else."

"And Addie? What did she dream of becoming?"

"For a while, she wanted to be an artist, but that was short-lived. Then she and our mother wanted her to become a news anchor. She got pretty close but then sort of checked out. I don't think it was because of Ophelia. I think Ophelia was just an excuse. I've always wondered about it, though. It's like she'd figured out her life and then suddenly forgot what she was supposed to do next. And now, trying to manage our mother, she's at a total loss. I mean, I am, too, but at least I'm trying to figure it out."

I felt Liam's warm breath on my cheek as he spoke. "Something else I've learned while working with my patients and their families is that we're all doing the best we can. It's like an escape room, where we can only figure out the clues from what we find hidden in plain sight. Sometimes we miss the obvious, but it's not because we're not looking."

"Sounds like something Celeste would say."

Liam laughed softly. "Yeah, well, that's because she did. My mother self-medicated herself to death after my father's accident. She didn't do it to hurt Julie or me or my grandmother. She did it because she didn't see any other option, and it was the only thing that gave her any peace. It took me a long time to realize that and to forgive her."

"I'm sorry you went through that. I'm glad that Celeste was there for you. I see situations like that all the time as a teacher, and they don't always work out so well." I felt the heat from his body against my side, but I didn't move away. "I don't know if I'll ever get to a place where I can forgive my mother. I don't think she ever intended to hurt me, but the scars are there anyway. Not that it matters. It's too late to reconcile."

"Is it?" he asked softly.

I sat up on my elbow, the beer settling in as the edges of the night softened and curled around my head. I lay back down, and my tongue felt heavy when I spoke again. "Aunt Sassy called the time when a daughter finally sees her mother without the stain of her childhood a *transfer of grace*. I'm not even sure what that means, but I'm definitely not there yet. Mother still seems prickly around me and even now continues to favor Addie. Maybe I'm just not mature enough."

He was silent for a while, as if waiting for me to digest what I'd just said instead of inserting his opinion, and I decided that I liked that about him.

"A *transfer of grace*," Liam said. "Sounds like a country song. Did the Backlit Boys sing that tonight?"

I grinned, which I felt had been his goal. "First off, it's the *Backstreet Boys*, which I'm sure you know. And they're not a country band."

I stole a glance at him and saw that he was also grinning. "Yeah, I knew that. Just wanted to make sure that you knew it, too."

A shooting star streaked across the night sky, disappearing almost before I registered that it had been there at all. "Did you see that?" I asked.

"Was that a meteor?"

"Uh-huh. Also called a *shooting star,* even though they're not stars. Just bits of rocks and dust hitting the Earth's atmosphere so fast that they glow with heat before burning out." I squinted into the darkness, hopelessly looking for some remnant of light. "It's good luck to see one, you know."

"I've heard that. I've also heard that they could represent love and connection between two people."

"Funny, I don't think I've ever heard that." I looked up again. "Some people live their lives like a shooting star—burning fast and bright. I'm not so brave. I'm more like a chimney swift, flitting through the sky without landing and never going fast enough to burn."

"I believe you're doing everything just right."

His voice was close, and when I turned my head, our noses touched. I didn't pull back. "Yeah?"

He touched his lips to mine, gently at first, like a question. I pulled his head toward mine, deepening the kiss, tasting beer and skin, and deciding I liked it very much. I closed my eyes and leaned back, welcoming the weight of him as he moved over me, each of us tasting and exploring while the watery world around us seemed to move in tandem.

The nightjar called out again in the distance, awakening my mind's eye. I saw the car on the bridge, heard the splash and the nightbird's cry as if it were telling me to pay attention. I pulled away and sat up, knocking over my beer and feeling it seep into the towel.

Liam sat up, his eyes fixed on mine. "I'm sorry. I didn't mean to—"

"It's not you. I just . . . I can't. Not with you."

I stood, swaying slightly. Liam stood, too, and tried to steady me, but I pushed him away. "I'm fine," I lied. "I'm fine," I said again as I made my way to the end of the dock, keeping my head down so I wouldn't see another shooting star telling me to go back.

# 18

## Celeste

I PEERED OUT the kitchen window to check on Will. I'd asked him to clean out the bird feeders and then refill them with fresh seed, knowing the entire process was painstakingly slow and laborious. The feeders didn't even need cleaning—I did it regularly and actually enjoyed doing it—but if I had to listen to another electronic boing or bing from his game console, I couldn't be blamed for tossing it into the creek. Forcing him outside had seemed like a better choice.

I watched as Will dropped a large bag of birdseed, his shoulders sagging. He'd been out of sorts all day because Ophelia was busy running errands with her mother. I was cautiously optimistic that Addie might finally be showing Ophelia some kind of maternal affection.

The timer on the oven rang. I removed the chocolate chip cookies and set them on cooling racks by the sink. I'd planned to bring them over to the Manigaults as soon as they were cooled.

Will had wanted to take the jonboat and do some fishing, but I didn't like the look of the clouds in the near distance, hovering over the harbor like a vulture. Storms in the Lowcountry could be as sudden as they were ferocious, and I didn't want him out on the water in a metal boat if one should decide to trouble the waters.

I heard the front door open and then Liam entered the kitchen, still in his work clothes. He usually went home first to change before collecting Will so they could go fishing before supper. It was also an hour earlier than he was normally finished with his office hours.

"What's wrong?" I asked.

"My last appointment of the day was canceled. It was for Elizabeth Manigault, and Stephanie said that Addie was the one who called." He frowned. "She didn't reschedule."

"That's odd. Elizabeth seemed fine to me yesterday. Did you call Phoebe to make sure everything's all right?"

"No," he said. "I don't think that would be a good idea."

I raised my eyebrows. "Why not? She would probably want to know." I studied him closely. "Did something happen at that concert?" He'd been avoiding any mention of Phoebe since the concert a week and a half ago. I might not have noticed if Phoebe hadn't also been avoiding any mention of Liam.

Instead of answering, he slid off his jacket and removed his tie before grabbing a beer from the refrigerator.

"Why aren't you answering my question?" I asked.

He took a long swig. "Because I thought it was rhetorical."

I shook my head then took out a small Tupperware container and began sliding cookies into it. "Will and I are bringing these over to the Manigaults, and you're welcome to come with us. Someone needs to make sure that Elizabeth is all right. Even if her doctor gets googly-eyed at the mention of her daughter."

"*Googly-eyed*? Seriously? Are we back in third grade?"

"Only if you continue to act like you are." I handed him the Tupperware. "Fill this up to the top, please. I'm going to call to let them know we're on our way."

The phone rang eight times before Ophelia picked up. I smiled at the sound of her voice repeating something I imagined Elizabeth must have taught her.

"Hello. Manigault residence. This is Ophelia speaking."

"Hello, Ophelia. This is Miss Celeste. May I speak with your mother, please?" I held the receiver away from my ear so that Liam could hear the other side of the conversation.

"She's not here. She dropped me off after we got our nails painted at the beauty parlor. We both got Shocking Pink. Even Mimi."

I looked at Liam, and our eyes met. That might explain why Elizabeth had missed her appointment.

"That sounds lovely. I can't wait to see them. Is your Aunt Phoebe available?"

"Nuh-uh. She left to go find Mimi on her bike."

A spark of worry pinched the back of my neck. "She did?" I kept my voice calm. "Why did she take her bike instead of the car?"

"Because Mimi has the car."

I jerked my gaze to Liam, who appeared to be as alarmed as I was. "I see. Did Phoebe have any idea where Mimi might have gone?"

"No. Mimi took a nap when Mama and I got back from the beauty parlor. Aunt Phoebe's friend Mary-Simms stopped by and they went for a walk, and while they were gone Mama's boyfriend showed up and she left with him and told me to keep an eye on Mimi. Aunt Phoebe was really mad when she got back and Mimi was gone."

"She wasn't mad at you, sweetheart, because you didn't do anything wrong. Have you called your mother to let her know?"

"Aunt Phoebe and I tried, but Mama didn't answer."

"Okay, sweetheart. Will and I and Will's dad are coming over. We're going to drive so we can help your aunt find Mimi, all right? We're bringing a mess of homemade chocolate chip cookies, too. We'll be there in a couple of minutes, but if your mother, aunt, or grandmother shows up, could you please call Will's cell phone to let us know?"

She agreed, and then the phone clicked in my ear, replaced by a dial tone.

Liam was already grabbing his keys and heading to the backyard to collect Will.

I snapped the lid over the cookies then followed Liam out to the driveway. "And that's why it's important to have a landline," I called after him as I locked the front door behind us.

It was an old argument between us, my stubbornness to get a cell phone. I continued to cling to my conviction that if satellites fell from the sky, I would still be able to communicate with friends and emergency personnel. But Liam, with the best of intentions, told me that as soon as I got one, he would get rid of the landline. Which was the wrong thing to say because, in the very slim chance that Julie was out there somewhere, that would be the number she'd call.

Once we were on our way, Liam tried to call Phoebe again from his truck, but it went straight to voice mail. He shook his head and hit the end button. "I think she's having her dreams again. At the concert, she told her friend that she was going to have a baby girl when I don't think the friend had yet announced that she was even pregnant. I think she knew about it because she'd had a dream. We left shortly afterward because Phoebe said she was feeling ill, but I'm pretty sure that wasn't the case. And then she fell asleep in the truck on our way back, and she had another one. One that shook her up pretty badly. She wouldn't talk about it."

"What a horrible burden. She must be afraid to fall asleep, poor girl." Even as I said it, a glimmer of hope sparked inside me, fighting with the shame of even feeling it. I wanted Phoebe to have peace from her affliction. Almost as much as I needed to know what happened to my granddaughter.

The driveway at the Manigault house was empty as Liam pulled in with his truck. Ophelia looked up from where she sat in a rocking chair on the front porch, reading a book. She ran down the steps to greet us.

"Nobody came home," Ophelia reported as she eyed the Tupperware in Will's hands.

"Why don't you two go into the kitchen and grab a couple of Cokes from the fridge to have with your cookies?" I suggested.

They didn't need to be asked twice.

Liam headed back to his truck. "I'm going to drive around and look for Phoebe and Elizabeth. Please stay here with the kids, and let me know if anyone returns. I'll try to get Dale's number from a mutual friend and see if he was the one who picked up Addie, but I doubt it. From what I know about him, he's a real Boy Scout. He wouldn't have left Mimi and Ophelia here alone. Even if Addie would." He pulled his phone from his pocket and slid behind the steering wheel.

I opened the front and back doors of the house, allowing a cross breeze through the screen doors. If anyone approached by foot or car, I had a better chance of hearing them.

I joined the kids in the kitchen and grabbed a Coke for myself while keeping my eye trained on the dock. A strong wind blew the bird feeders against the tree trunks as the marsh grasses bent low as if in prayer beneath the darkening sky. I kept looking for a flash of color bobbing in the water, but the approaching storm had erased even the shorebirds, who were smart enough to know to come inside in the rain.

I found the board game Clue in the family room and set it up on the kitchen table. Will made a face to show me he was too old for it, but I gave him a look he understood to keep it to himself. Childish handwriting covering the box made it clear that the game belonged to Addie Manigault and that no one else—especially someone whose name started with *P* and ended with an *E*—was allowed to touch it.

After explaining the rules of the game to Will and Ophelia, I went upstairs to Elizabeth's room, looking for any clue to where she might have gone. Finding nothing out of place, I headed toward the door, stopping in the threshold. The photograph of Charles, in its replacement frame, was missing from its spot on Elizabeth's bedside table. It might be a clue, but I had no idea as to what it might mean, and the two people who might know were currently unreachable.

On the way back to the kitchen, I peered into the dining room where I'd been keeping the scrapbooks in neat stacks along with the loose photographs to make them accessible to Elizabeth. Except now they were all strewn across the polished wood surface, books left open with photographs ripped off the pages and left in small heaps.

It almost seemed as if she'd been looking for something. I stepped closer, wondering if somewhere in the mess I might find an answer to her whereabouts. I sighed with dismay at the photographs of Charles she had once lovingly placed within the album but had now been brutally removed, some with tears and folds from being yanked from the page.

There didn't appear to be any rhyme or reason for the destruction. But there was also little logic behind the actions of a mind with dementia. While listening to the children in the kitchen and keeping an ear out for the arrival of a car or bike outside, I began to loosely sort the photographs into categories to assist me later when it was time to reconstruct the albums.

An album with a pink quilted cover had been pulled to the edge of the table. According to Phoebe, it was a chronicle of the girls' yearly school photos from kindergarten through high school graduation.

Two large photos had been removed from the album, one placed on top of it and the other on the edge of the table. A breeze blew in from the open door, sliding the second photo onto a chair. I picked up the photo on the table, smiling at the serious and younger face of Phoebe. She wore the white dress and red sash from her Ashley Hall graduation, clutching a long-stem red rose. I brought it closer to my face to get a better look at the necklace she wore. It was the enamel bluebird of happiness that Ophelia now wore that Phoebe said had been a gift to her from her aunt Sassy.

I picked up the photo from the chair, recognizing Addie's face immediately. This would have been her yearbook photo, and she wore a black drape around her shoulders and sat in front of a blue background. It was clear that she knew how to smile for a picture, how to angle her face and lift her lips for the perfect expression.

I had kept both the formal and informal senior portraits of Julie along with her yearbook, which had been distributed to the students long after she disappeared. The pictures had been taken at the beginning of senior year, which Julie had been excited about because she still had her summer tan. I kept it all, including the dress she'd worn in the informal photographs. I'd framed the portraits and hung them on her bedroom wall and placed her yearbook in a box in her closet for safekeeping. I'd moved it all when I'd left South Carolina, then returned with it when I came back to the same house, placing everything back in her room because I didn't know what else to do with it.

My eyes were drawn to the necklace around Addie's neck, noticing deep scratches in the photograph's matte finish. I held up the photograph. A small hole had been scratched through where the diamond had been, allowing a pinprick of light to shine through.

I recalled something Phoebe had told me, how the necklace had been a gift from their parents on Addie's sixteenth birthday and then replaced soon afterward when Addie had lost it. But they'd been unable to get a complete replica of the original so the one she wore now was without the small diamond. I smoothed my finger over the scratches. They could have been made by a single fingernail, digging into the picture over and over. Just like someone trying to pluck the necklace from the photograph.

The crunching of tires announced Liam's arrival. I met him at the front door. "Anything?" I asked, although his grim expression had answered my question.

Liam shook his head. "I talked with Dale. He hasn't seen Addie, although they're supposed to have dinner tonight. So we're back at square one." He rubbed his hands over his face. "How did Elizabeth find the car keys?"

"Since Addie uses the car, she leaves them on the kitchen counter. Phoebe and I are constantly putting them out of sight in the drawer, but Addie doesn't seem to appreciate the importance of hiding them."

He shook his head. "I think we should call the police."

"Hang on," I said, looking toward the street behind him. "Phoebe's here."

I watched as she jumped off her bike and dropped it in the grass beside the driveway before running up the steps to the porch. She stopped in surprise when she spotted Liam through the screen door. I opened it while they stared awkwardly at each other.

"Ophelia told us that Elizabeth took the car," I said. "Liam just drove around looking, but no luck."

Phoebe's face was red with exertion, her hair, face, and body wet with perspiration, her eyes fierce. I'd never seen her look more beautiful.

Liam's voice was calm when he spoke. "I was just saying that it might be time to call the police."

"Not yet," I said, turning to Phoebe. "I don't know if this means anything, but when I was up in your mother's room, I noticed that the framed photograph of your father was missing. Is there a place where she might go that reminds her of him?"

Phoebe clenched her eyes and squeezed her head between her hands. "I can hardly think . . ."

"You need water," Liam said with his doctor's voice. "You'll be able to think better once you're no longer dehydrated." He gently took her arm and led her back to the kitchen.

He pulled out a chair at the table where Ophelia and Will were playing their game. They looked at Phoebe with worried expressions, but she waved them away, assuring them that she was fine. I grabbed a glass from the cabinet then filled it with ice water.

"Drink it slowly," Liam said as I handed it to her.

Phoebe did as instructed, sipping slowly as I took a cookie from the container and handed it to her. "This might help, too."

Phoebe took a nibble then leaned back in her chair, her eyes closed. After taking another sip of water, her eyes sprung open. "Wait." She sat up. "I think I might know where she went. Christ Church Cemetery on Highway 17 where Daddy is buried. She used to visit him every week. She hasn't gone since I've been back, but maybe she remembered that's what she used to do."

Liam pulled out his keys. "I'll drive. Gran, could you keep an eye on Will and Ophelia?"

"Of course. Call Will's phone if you have any updates."

To Phoebe, he asked, "Do you have your phone?"

She didn't look at him but responded, "Yes. And I keep checking it in case I've missed a call from Addie or Ophelia."

To me, he said, "Call me if either one of them returns. We'll be back as soon as we can."

Liam motioned for Phoebe to go ahead of him then held the door for her as they exited. I stood in the doorway and watched as the truck pulled out into the street before walking back inside, returning to the dining room.

I slid the quilted scrapbook closer to me and flipped through the pages that chronicled Phoebe's and Addie's school history to see if any of their other photos had been disturbed. They hadn't. Except the senior photos of each sister that had been removed and placed on the table.

I held up Addie's photograph, my eyes drawn to the marred area around the necklace. I'd ask Phoebe and Addie if either one of them had done something to the picture, but I already knew they hadn't. What I didn't know was why Elizabeth might have felt compelled to damage the photo. Maybe in her confusion she thought she could remove the necklace from the picture.

The sound of music thumping from a car stereo approached the house. I walked to the front door in time to see Addie leaning into the open window of an old Camaro, the hem of her shorts rising so indecently high that I had to look away. I was grateful that Ophelia was in the back of the house and couldn't see it.

A hand reached out and grabbed her arm as she pulled away, yanking her back through the window before abruptly letting her go. She stumbled backward, rubbing her arm as she watched the car back up and pull away with a squeal of the tires.

Addie seemed surprised to see me standing in the doorway to the dining room.

"You again," she said as she headed straight for the stairs, leaving behind the scent of stale beer and cigarette smoke and the sickly sweet smell of cheap cologne.

"Why do you let that guy treat you like that?" I asked.

"Please mind your own business. I thought today was your day off."

"It is. But someone needed to be here to watch Ophelia while Liam and your sister went looking for your missing mother and her car. You must have left the car keys on the counter again when you came back from work last night." I didn't bother to hide my disappointment. I'd stopped trying when it became clear that most of Addie's problems stemmed from the fact that no matter what she did, no one ever claimed to be disappointed by her actions.

Her eyes widened like a remorseful child before quickly switching to belligerent innocence as she glanced behind me toward the dining room table. Her mouth tightened. "She was taking a nap when I left. Phoebe was supposed to be watching her."

I didn't argue with her skewed timing of the events, knowing my words would fall on deaf ears. "They've gone to the cemetery where your father is buried, in case you're interested. Phoebe thinks your mother may have gone there."

Her face hardened at the mention of her father. Lifting one shoulder in a half shrug, she said, "Yeah. That would be my guess, too." She pulled her phone out of her tote bag and turned on the ringer before reading something on her screen. "They found mother's car parked at the chapel five minutes ago, and she'll let me know once she's found her. See? Phoebe saves the day again. And it's not like I could do anything to help without a car, anyway."

I struggled to keep my voice low and even. "Regardless of what happened today with your mother, you need to keep in mind that you have a daughter, Addie. That means you should always have your phone on when she isn't with you. What if she were hurt and there was an emergency?"

"But she isn't, and St. Phoebe is here to make sure Mother gets home. So, see? It's all good." She brushed past me, but not before I'd seen her mask crack, her wounded eyes like that of a caged bird.

"It's not, though," I said, and she stopped. My training as a nurse meant that when I saw pain, I was meant to fix it, or at least try. "I know you care. Just as much as I know you love your daughter and your sister and your mother. But there's something going on inside your head. I might be able to help you if you'd let me."

Her eyes were empty. "You can't help me. No one can. Least of all you."

Her gaze slid past my face, taking in the mess on top of the table before settling on the two senior portraits. She approached the table and picked up hers, brushing the bare space on her neck where the pendant usually hung.

Addie stared at the hole in the photo. "What happened to my picture?"

"I was going to ask you or Phoebe. This picture wasn't like this yesterday."

"Did my mother do this?" Her pale green eyes met mine.

"That would be my guess. But I have no idea why. Could she still be angry that you lost the original necklace?"

Addie tucked the picture into the back of the album. "Anything's possible, isn't it? With her mind the way it is, who knows? I wonder how long it will be before she starts walking outside naked."

Her tone was flippant, but her pain oozed behind the words.

"While we wait to hear from Phoebe, I can whip up something for the kids to eat. Would you like to join us?"

She shook her head. "No, thanks. I'm going to go shower before Dale comes over." She headed toward the stairs, teetering on her platform sandals, then paused on the bottom step. "If you're still here when he arrives, I'd appreciate it if you wouldn't mention where I've been."

She didn't wait for a reply before continuing up the steps.

I returned to the kitchen to see what was in the refrigerator that I could turn into a nice meal for Ophelia and Liam. But my mind remained on the damaged photograph and the unspoken question of why.

# 19

～

"There's a meaningful quote from one of my favorite poets that compares a bird opening its wings so it can fly with our need to expose our hearts so we can love. It's impossible to have one without the other. Birds are born with the instinct to fly. I think that humans are also born with the instinct to love, but so many of us hit a snag along the way and struggle to remember what it was that we are supposed to do until the moment comes to step off the ledge and discover our own wings."

**Excerpt from the blog *The Thing with Feathers***

## *Phoebe*

THE SKY WAS a charcoal smudge of gray and black as we headed past the strip malls on Highway 17 toward the eighteenth-century church and cemetery where my family had been buried for three generations.

"Are you okay?" Liam asked. They were the first words spoken since we'd left the house.

I shook my head. "No. I'm not. I'm worried sick about my mother and angry enough that I might do physical harm to my sister when I get back. The only thing stopping me is Ophelia."

I dialed the number for Christ Church again and got the voice mail, telling me that the office was closed. But I tried again just in case.

"We'll be there in a minute," Liam said. "Maybe if you tell me why you've been avoiding me since the night of the concert, it'll distract you until we get there."

I glared at him. "That's pretty insensitive."

As if I hadn't said anything, he said, "I enjoyed our kiss, and I would have sworn that you did, too. So when you didn't return my texts or phone calls, I thought I'd misread things."

I turned to face him, the straps of my seat belt cutting into my chest. "My mother is missing! How can you talk about anything else except finding her?"

"So you're saying you didn't enjoy our kiss?"

"I didn't say any such thing. I'm just saying that—"

"We're here," he said, cutting me off as he pulled the truck off the highway and into a parking lot. "And there's your mother's car." He turned to face me. "See? It worked."

Too relieved to feel angry, I slid out of my seat and ran to my mother's Lincoln parked in the sandy grass with the back end of her car protruding into the road that encircled the cemetery.

The driver's-side door was unlocked and partially open. I pulled it the rest of the way to see inside, alarmed to find her purse and the key fob lying next to it on the passenger-side floor. The frame with my father's photo lay faceup on the driver's-side floor where it rested against the brake pedal as if it had slipped from my mother's lap forgotten.

I straightened to find Liam standing next to me as panic bloomed. I grabbed on to the open door to steady myself. "What if she couldn't remember where his grave is and is just wandering? She could step out onto the highway . . ."

"She made it all the way here, so that's a good sign," Liam said gently. "He's been gone for over a decade, right? Her long-term memory is still pretty good, and if she came here every week, my guess is that's where we'll find her."

"But if she's not?"

He gently took my elbow and closed the car door. "Then we'll cross that bridge when we get to it. I'll follow you since you know where you're going."

I led the way through the iron gate past the historic chapel and into the old graveyard.

A lone mockingbird trilled from a high branch of a magnolia tree then flew away as a hot, humid wind scattered dead leaves across the sparse grass. Older headstones with names and dates lost to time rested comfortably near more modern gravesites, all reposing beneath the towering trees and ancient azalea bushes.

I had only been here on the occasions of my grandparents' and my father's burials. But I remembered where he'd been laid to rest, recalled the sweltering heat of an August morning that made the black silk of my dress and nylon of the requisite dark pantyhose stick to my skin. Addie and I had flanked our mother, all of us dry-eyed because it would have been unseemly to be otherwise. Not that it mattered. Our makeup mixed with sweat slipped down our cheeks, leaving trails of unshed tears.

A fat blob of rain fell from the sky and stained the packed dirt of the path in front of us. I quickened my pace, with Liam following closely behind. We heard her before we saw her, listened to the strung-together words that weren't a song but weren't conversational, either. It was a repetition, like the rote memorization of a spelling test. Or the long-remembered words of a prayer.

She wore her dark blue housecoat, its sides dusty with dirt, and her feet were bare. Her bright pink toenails were visible in the short grass over his grave, almost like a desecration in this solemn place.

"Mother?"

She turned, her face composed and her eyes clear. "What are you doing here?"

"Looking for you. You didn't tell anyone where you were going." I stood next to her but didn't touch her. More rain dotted the granite headstone and my mother's face. I should have thought to bring the umbrella from the car since she'd just had her hair done, and it would upset her to have it ruined.

She turned back to the headstone. "I need to talk to Charles." She looked down at my father's name etched into the granite. "I think it's time for a reckoning." Her brows creased over her nose in an expression she'd always admonished Addie and me would give us wrinkles. I'd once had my leg pinched while sitting next to her in church for doing the same thing.

Liam glanced up at the low growl of thunder. My blood raced as it always did at the first signs of a storm.

"There's a bad storm coming." I made a mental calculation of how long it would take to get my mother to her car before the clouds opened and the sky erupted with flashes of heat and light. "Let's talk about it in the car, all right?"

Her lucid eyes met mine as she pressed her cool palm against my cheek. "You have good reason to be afraid of lightning. I'm so sorry. If I'd been home, that never would have happened. And all that came afterward." She blinked as harder rain began to hit her face, and she turned toward the darkening sky.

I placed my arm around her shoulders, huddling close to protect her from the onslaught of the pelting rain, and began to lead her back to the car. An arc of lightning lit up the cemetery, followed by a roll of thunder that bellowed from the sky making me scream. In that brief flash of light, I saw a reflection of something lying on the ground in front of my father's headstone. Liam must have seen it, too, and bent to pick it up.

He caught up to us and joined us on my mother's other side, helping to shelter her from the wind and rain. My jaw hurt from clenching it. Liam helped settle Mother into the passenger seat of her car while I crawled behind the wheel, tossing my father's picture into the back seat as my panic grew despite my resolution to stay calm. As Liam buckled my mother's seat belt he said, "You're safe in the car, Phoebe. Your tires are rubber, and it's a short drive. You got this."

I gave him a stiff nod, feeling the phantom pain on my shoulder following the crooked path of my scar. It was as if the nerve endings could communicate with the burnt ions lingering in the air, a reminder to always look up to prepare for what's coming.

Liam returned to his truck and flashed his headlights to let me know he was right behind me and ready to go when I was.

My mother's cold fingers grabbed the bare skin on my arm, making me jump. "I love you, Phoebe. Everything I've ever done for my girls was because I love you both. I only meant to protect you."

I put my hand over hers and squeezed. "I love you, too." It was a rare affirmation. Something had happened in her mind today, something that had brought her to the cemetery and my father's grave. Something that had worked its way through the clouds in her mind to clarify that she loved me. That she wanted to protect me.

"Protect me from what?" I asked, hoping she could hear me over the sound of the rain pounding the roof of the car.

She peered out her window at the water darkening the headstones and the puddles forming on the path. "Where are you taking me?"

My stomach tightened at the shrillness in her voice, already mourning the shared moment, realizing that it would probably be one of the last. "We're going home." I hit the gas pedal hard, jerking the car forward as I pulled out onto the highway. I glanced in the rearview mirror, comforted by the beams from Liam's headlights.

"Home?" She clutched at the seat belt across her chest.

"Yes. We were at the cemetery visiting Daddy's grave. You said it was time for a reckoning." I held my breath, having learned that asking questions she couldn't answer would make her lash out. But an uneasiness had settled inside me, an imbalance that made me think of stepping on a stationary escalator.

We stopped at a red light, the thump-thump of the wipers magnifying my anxiety as I waited for her to answer.

"I love Charles. From the first moment I saw him. He always knows the right thing to do. Except for that one time." She clasped then unclasped her fingers, spinning her wedding ring around and around. "I need to find him so he can make it right. I don't know how." She squeezed my arm, her nails cutting into my skin. "There's something wrong, but I can't . . . I can't . . ."

She began twisting in her seat as if trying to escape more than just her seat belt. The light turned green, and I floored the gas pedal, needing to get home before she decided to open her car door.

"I can't remember!" she screamed, slamming her palms against the dashboard again and again. "I can't remember!" she screamed again, and my eyes stung from the anguish in her voice and my inability to fix what was wrong. The threat to my family wasn't a known predator that I could peck at or feign an injury to distract it away from my home. This was a thief whose destruction was guaranteed and permanent, and there wasn't a damn thing I could do about it.

"It's okay, Mother. It's okay. I'm here. Everything is all right." I had no idea what I was saying. It wasn't okay. Nothing would ever be okay again.

She let go of her breath with a sob, her chin dropping toward her chest while I blew through a yellow light, unwilling to extend the drive for even thirty seconds.

"Where are we going?" My mother's voice was hoarse from screaming. My own throat felt raw from swallowing all the pent-up emotions I couldn't yet name, much less express.

"Home," I managed.

"No, we're not." With agitated movements, she turned her head to look out the side and front windows. "Where are you taking me?"

"I'm taking you home. Addie and Ophelia will be there."

"Liar," she roared at me, and I let the word settle on my skin. I wasn't the liar. The universe was. It had led her to believe that she would grow old gracefully, enjoying reading and gardening and all the things she loved until one night when she'd go to sleep and wouldn't wake up. Somewhere in the dark corners of her mind she was allowed to see the life she'd planned, outlined in stark relief against the life she lived now. And it terrified her. It also terrified me.

I wished I could call back all the terrible things I'd said to her when I was a teenager, when I knew even less about relationships and my mother than I did now. I wished I could tell her I was sorry. But as my mother was discovering, the universe can be an unforgiving place with rules that didn't always seem to apply to everyone.

She was silent for the final few blocks until we'd reached our driveway. Liam appeared at her door and lifted her from her seat, carrying her inside so she wouldn't have to walk barefoot.

Celeste immediately came from the kitchen wiping her hands on a dish towel and took charge as we came through the front door. Addie hung back, as if expecting a scolding. There was a lot more I wanted to do, but I had to remind myself that we were both grown women.

Celeste must have felt the brewing tension since she moved to stand between us like a referee. "Addie, would you please take Elizabeth upstairs and get her changed into some dry clothes? I'll heat up some of that chicken soup that I made yesterday and have it ready for her when you come back down."

Addie nodded and took hold of our now-docile mother's arm and began leading her up the stairs, Mother's head resting gently on Addie's shoulder, no longer resembling the woman who'd just been screaming at me in the car.

"Hang on a minute," Liam said, pulling something out of his pocket. He held up Addie's necklace. "I found this at the cemetery. I think your mother left it there."

Addie's eyes widened in recognition while something unnamable flickered behind them. "I wondered what happened to it. I was sure I left it on my dresser, but it wasn't there when I went to put it on." She plucked the necklace from Liam's hand without making eye contact then pocketed it. "I'll be more careful next time."

She moved to continue up the stairs, but Mother held back, her gaze focused on the empty spot on Addie's neck as she pointed at it. "Your father wants you to wear it." She dropped her hand but continued nodding her head as if to accentuate her point.

"Yes, Mother," Addie said with studied patience. "I'll put it on as soon as we get upstairs."

"Good." My mother turned to look at Liam and Celeste and gave them a gracious smile. "Welcome to our home. Please make yourselves comfortable." Then she turned and walked upstairs wearing a rain-soaked housecoat as if it were couture and she a queen.

"You left the key fob on the counter, Addie," I called to her departing back. "And Mother found it. She could have been killed or she could have killed someone else. You need to be more responsible."

She continued up the stairs without a word.

"The storm's moving out," Celeste said. "I hate to ask since you just got here, but the kids are asking for pizza from Coastal Crust, and they don't deliver. My treat." She smiled hopefully at Liam.

"I'll go," I said, already heading for the door. "I'm afraid I might kill my sister if I'm stuck in the same house with her right now—and I am not a violent person. She just brings out the worst in me."

"I'll drive," Liam said, following me out the door. "Please tell Will to phone in the order," he called over his shoulder to Celeste.

I stopped on the porch and crossed my arms. "I didn't ask for company."

"You didn't have to. I just thought I would stick close to you in case I'm forced to slap a blood pressure cuff on your arm."

"You're not my doctor."

"I know. That doesn't make me exempt from caring about you."

My eyes drifted to his lips, the memory of how they tasted still on my tongue. I stepped off the porch, walking in puddles because I was too distracted to avoid them. I slid into the passenger side of his truck just as an orange shard of early evening sunshine scuttled the storm clouds.

Liam started the car and turned on the AC but didn't take the truck out of Park.

"Is there a problem?" I kept my gaze focused on the windshield, watching the sun create prisms of light through raindrops on the glass.

"Are you still angry about me breaking your ribs?"

I jerked around. "What?" His smile told me he was joking, and I sank back down in my seat, fighting a reluctant smile. "That's not funny."

"Sure, it is. Not about me breaking your ribs but that you might be still holding a grudge."

I laughed despite myself, risking a glance at him. He was smiling, but when he spoke, his tone was serious. "Do you want to tell me what all that was about with your sister's necklace? Your mother was upset enough to take it to the cemetery with her. If you'd like, I can refer her to a psychologist who specializes in patients with memory loss. She might have unresolved issues she's trying to untangle. Sometimes they can be small things to the rest of us, but to someone like your mother, who's aware of her slipping memory, it becomes a sticking point."

"Could it lead her to believe that there needs to be a reckoning? That's what she said at the cemetery."

"Sure. Like I said, it could be a small thing, but it's something she remembers at least a part of. She might feel as if she needs to resolve it before she forgets it completely. She's at the difficult stage where her memory fluctuates between clarity and sometimes something as extreme as hallucinations. The medications I prescribed should help. It might take a while to get them adjusted, but that's my job. And Gran is the right person to help smooth the transitions and to make your mother's lucid periods longer and more meaningful for both you and your sister."

"Except I'm running out of time. I'm leaving in August, and I'd feel better knowing that Mother is content and not so agitated and upset all the time. I guess *content* is the right word, isn't it? Because it's not a matter of her getting better." My voice caught, but I fought the tears. I wasn't going to cry. Not here, not now. Tears hadn't saved Bailey or cured Aunt Sassy or made my mother understand that I wasn't ever going to be like her and Addie no matter how hard she tried to change me.

He shifted in his seat to look at me. "That might not be enough time, Phoebe. You might need to consider staying a while longer. I don't know if your mother or Addie will be ready by August."

"I can't." I felt the heavy presence of the dream. "I can't stay longer."

"Because of your job? Can you not take a leave of absence?"

"It's not that. It's . . . something else." I pressed my head against the leather headrest, feeling the icy cold blast from the AC, even colder because my hair and clothes were still soaking wet. "I was really hoping that with Dale reappearing in our lives and Addie seeming happy to see him, that was a sign she was growing up. And then she pulled that stunt today, skipping Mother's appointment and then disappearing with some dirtbag and leaving Ophelia alone with Mother and the car keys. It's like she thinks she's still sixteen and responsible for nothing and no one except for herself—and even there I have my doubts."

"I don't think she's doing it on purpose, Phoebe. If she believes she's not worthy of something, or if she believes she's being punished for something she did or didn't do, she could be self-sabotaging. Intentionally or not. She might not have any control over her actions if there's something she can't face."

His use of the word *punished* reminded me of my conversation with Addie on the dock, where she told me that she felt she was being punished. But I was still too angry at what could have happened to feel much sympathy.

"Why are you taking Addie's side?"

"I'm not taking sides, although for the record, I'm always Team Phoebe."

"It's a very small team," I said. Uncomfortable with his scrutiny, I said, "Can we go get pizza now? I'm starving."

He put the truck in Reverse and backed out of the driveway. "So is Mary-Simms pregnant or not?"

"She is. I suppose we all have a lucky guess every once in a while."

He was silent for a couple of blocks as we drove. "Okay. Let's say it's a lucky guess. But can I ask you something?"

A pinprick of fear brushed the base of my neck. "Can I stop you?"

He didn't smile as he flipped on his blinker. "If you had a dream about Julie, you'd tell Gran wouldn't you?"

"Of course. I'm not a monster. I just don't like being the object of derision and speculation. It's one of the reasons why I left."

"And the dreams didn't follow you?"

I studied the puddles on the road, blocking out the mental image of the lone car on the bridge. And the dreams I'd had about Stephanie and Mary-Simms. "Mostly."

He pulled into a gravel lot and parked the car before shutting off the engine. "Mostly?"

"If I had a dream about Julie, I would tell Celeste. But after spending all this time with her—and you—and I haven't had a single dream about Julie, then my guess is that I never will. I was with Mary-Simms for less than an hour and I dreamed about her baby."

"So if you haven't had a dream about Julie, then you probably won't."

"Maybe. There's still time before I leave. But when I'm across the country, they go away."

He nodded silently, thinking. After a while, he said, "So your dreams are always premonitions. And then they happen."

*Except for one.* "Yeah. I actually had a dream about Stephanie before she fell off her bike. I'm sorry I didn't warn her. I could tell she wasn't seriously hurt, and besides, how does one call a virtual stranger on the phone and tell them that you've had a dream that they're going to get hurt? At least Mary-Simms knows me so she didn't freak out. She also forgave me for spilling the beans to her friends. She was planning a huge gender-reveal party, and I guess I ruined that."

"Is that really a bad thing, though? I'm sure her friends are all grateful."

I smirked. "Probably. But I feel terrible for ruining her surprise. I'll be glad to put it all behind me again."

"That's a shame."

I turned to look at him. "What is?"

"That you can't reconcile yourself to this unexpected gift and find a way to live with it here. Unless Oregon really does have the kind of allure to pull you away."

I gave him a sidelong glance, and he laughed.

"Yeah, I didn't think so," he said. "So I'm thinking there's something else."

I closed my eyes and saw the image of the car slipping off the side of the bridge. I snapped my eyes open and shook my head. "I can't talk about it, because then I'll see it again." I glanced at him and quickly looked away. "There's a recurring dream that started soon after I was hit by lightning."

"A premonition?"

"I don't know. I can't see the faces in the dream and have yet to discover who it's about or what's really happening. I've always thought that it's something in the future that hasn't happened yet and that's why I keep having it."

"Could be. Although it seems your dreams and the actual events happen close together. I'm sure you've already considered that your recurrent dream might have been a premonition when you first had it, but now it's something that's already occurred. And the reason you keep having it might be because your mind needs some kind of reconciliation or acknowledgment before it will allow you to move on."

I pressed the heels of my hands into my eyes, wanting to obliterate the image of the two people in the front seat of the car, their identities unknown no matter how many times I tried to see who they are. And when the passenger climbs out of the water, I still can't see the face. I couldn't tell him that I thought the dream was about me or that something terrible was going to happen in which I'm destined to be involved.

Bile rose alongside my panic as I grappled for the door handle.

"No," I said, scraping a gnawed fingernail against the leather and chrome of the inside door panel. "No," I said again, slapping my hands against the door and pushing. Liam reached across and unlatched the door so I could open it, my seat belt the only thing keeping me from tumbling onto the sidewalk. I unsnapped it and slid from my seat then walked to the end of the gravel parking lot, oblivious to the stares of other people.

Liam waited by the side of the truck. "I'm sorry. I didn't mean to upset you."

"Let's not talk about it, all right?"

"Fine, if that's what you really want. But it looks like you're dealing with this all on your own, and it might help to have an ally."

"You're not—" I began.

"I know. I'm not your doctor. I would still like to help you. As a friend."

"I don't need you to fix me, okay? I'm used to handling things on my own."

"That doesn't mean you have to."

I remembered feeling the solidness of his chest and the strength of his arms around me, and I was tempted to shift the awful burden from my shoulders to his. I dismissed the thought almost as soon as I'd had it. I had more urgent things to deal with before I left.

"I know. And thank you for the offer. I'm sure as a doctor, trying to help is in your DNA."

"True. But that's not why I want to help you."

I turned and headed toward the door of the pizza shop, the image of a rainy night on a dark bridge and two people whose faces I couldn't see obliterating all other thoughts.

# 20

~

"A wise man once said that we should use what talents we have
because that is the road to our success and the way we will give
joy to the world. Because the world would be a silent place if
only the birds with the best voices sang. I think of this every time
I hear a nuthatch grating out its nasally notes as it shimmies
upside down on a tree trunk. It doesn't care that it's not the
best singer in my backyard. It just sings for the joy of it. Which
is a good-enough lesson for the rest of us to do what we love."

**Excerpt from the blog *The Thing with Feathers***

## *Phoebe*

MY HEAD THROBBED the following morning when I awoke with
the sun streaming into the window and the strobelike chirping
of a cardinal. I'd purchased wine during our pizza run and had
excused myself from dinner so I could retire to the privacy of
my bedroom and drink an entire bottle before passing out. I'd
never been a big drinker, and I hated being hungover, but it was
a small price to pay to avoid the terror that waited for me at the
edge of consciousness.

I rolled over and dug my face into the pillow to hide from
the sun and promptly fell back asleep. I was awakened an hour
later by Ophelia jumping on the side of my bed. I pried my eyes
open, running my tongue over teeth that felt as if they'd been
covered in cotton.

"Can you take Will and me to the beach? Celeste says it's
okay."

"Did you ask your mother?"

"Nuh-uh. She's down on the dock, and she left her phone in the kitchen."

That made me sit up. "Yeah?" A glimmer of a dream floated timidly to the surface of my awareness. It had been the mention of Addie. I closed my eyes and saw my sister as she'd been in my dream. I couldn't see her face, but I knew it was her because she wore a rhinestone pageant crown on her blond head. She was sitting in front of an open box ripping through layers and layers of tissue paper, flooding the room until the box disappeared along with the paper. Then the front door opened, and although the man was tall and slender, I knew it was Dale. He wore the same shirt and pants he'd had on the last time I'd seen him, except they were covered with large splats of paint the color of ochre.

"So can we?"

The image floated away as I looked at Ophelia, whose hands were folded in a praying position as she batted her eyelashes.

I held up a finger. "Hang on." I took two Tylenol tablets from the bottle on my nightstand and swallowed them dry. I breathed in deeply, willing the medicine to stop the hammering in my head. "I'll go talk to your mom. But first I need you to brush your hair and then check if we have any bottles of sunscreen in the bathroom."

"Thank you!" she shouted then jumped down with a thump as her feet hit the hardwood floor.

I pulled on my shorts under my sleep shirt and headed downstairs. I heard Celeste and my mother talking in the dining room. I wanted to stop and say hello, but even in my mother's current mental state, I knew she'd probably notice what I was wearing—and what I wasn't, since I hadn't put on a bra—and I wasn't in the mood to be scolded.

I crept past the doorway, avoiding creaking floorboards, and headed to the back door, grabbing Addie's cell phone from the counter on my way. She sat in one of two folding lawn chairs at the end of the dock, wearing a red string bikini top with polka dots and the cutoff shorts she wore to work. Large dark sunglasses hid her eyes, and her sleeked-back strawberry-blond hair had been tucked beneath the wide rim of a straw hat. Her easel lay facedown, pinning the paper pad onto the wood planks. She didn't turn to look at me as I took the seat next to her.

Morning on the marsh was a sacred time, the sky cleansed of the night's darkness, the air redolent with the heady scent of pluff mud and cordgrass warming in the sun. The sound of shorebirds mixed with snapping shrimp and the intermittent splashes of unseen fish as they hunted for breakfast while they, too, were hunted.

As a child, I'd cried whenever I'd seen a heron with a fish in its mouth, until Aunt Sassy had explained that death in the marsh was as much a part of it as life. That one was dependent on the other in the endless cycle of birth, death, and regeneration. Her ashes had been spread deep in the marsh, and even now I could feel her presence in the nurturing suck of the tides and the solemn glide of an osprey.

Only then did I realize that Addie was holding the painting she'd been working on. Ochre-colored streams of water ran down the paper like tear stains, the softened paper rippled throughout and missing an entire corner.

"Oh no, Addie—your picture! Is it ruined?"

"What do you think?" She thrust it at me, and I held up the wrinkled mess.

"I'm so sorry. What happened? Did you forget you'd left it out here?"

She pulled a cigarette and lighter from her bikini top and lit it before inhaling slowly. Shrugging, she said, "I guess I forgot it was out here. I was planning on taking a few art classes at a place downtown that Celeste told me about. She recommended that I reach out to a teacher who only accepts a limited number of students, so he's pretty selective. Just don't tell her that I was listening when she told me. I was going to use that piece as my audition." She gave a little laugh before taking another drag on her cigarette. "I guess that won't be happening now. At least with that painting. And I doubt I'll have time now to make another one."

She pulled up her long legs onto the chair and rested her chin on her knees. Addie was so effortlessly elegant. If I'd tried to do that I would have fallen out of my chair and then rolled into the water, and we would have both laughed. It had been such a long time since we'd laughed together that I was tempted to try.

"Maybe you did it on purpose."

"Don't be an idiot. Why would I do that?"

A cumulous cloud passed over the sun, momentarily darkening the endless stretch of marsh grass that seemed to touch the bottom of the sky on the horizon. "I don't know, Addie. I was hoping you could tell me."

Ignoring me, she took another drag from her cigarette and blew it out in slow rings. "Assuming you're here to bug me, I already rescheduled Mother's neurology appointment, so save your breath. I missed the original one because Mother was in such a good mood yesterday, and Ophelia wanted to get her nails done, so I made a day out of it, and we all had a good time. So sue me."

"Thank you. I would take her except—"

"Except you're leaving and I need to figure this out." She took a long drag on the cigarette then leaned back against her chair and closed her eyes to let me know she was done with the conversation.

"Fine, then." I stood, remembering why I'd come down to the dock. "Can I take Ophelia to the beach with Will? I'll have the car back before you need it."

"Sure." She lowered the sunglasses on her nose to look over them. "Do you have a bathing suit?"

"I didn't bring one. I thought I'd just wear shorts and a T-shirt."

"You can borrow one of mine. Bottom left drawer of my dresser."

"Thanks," I said, even though I doubted one would fit me. But I would try, just to show my sister that I was grateful.

When Ophelia, Will, and I returned from Isle of Palms later that afternoon hot, sweaty, and a little sunburned, I was dismayed to find Liam's truck in the driveway. I'd been too hot to throw on my T-shirt over the bikini top I'd borrowed from Addie, and I scrambled to find it now in one of the many bags in the trunk.

"Can I help you with anything?" Liam's familiar voice came from the porch.

I kept my head in the trunk. "No, thanks. I think we got it." I handed Will and Ophelia each a bag to bring inside.

"Let me help," he said, his voice closer. "Otherwise, I'll hear about it later from my grandmother."

Resigned, I stepped back. "Fine, if you insist. If you could please bring the large cooler into the kitchen, I'd appreciate it."

He took the cooler while I grabbed the last beach tote and closed the trunk before leading the way back to the kitchen. He set the cooler down by the fridge. "Would you like me to empty it?"

I felt exposed standing in the kitchen wearing nothing more than a bikini top and gym shorts. "No, but thank you. I thought Will was spending the night tonight."

"He is. Gran called and asked me to bring his stuff over. His duffel bag is in the hallway."

"Thank you," I said. I crossed my arms, wondering why he wasn't leaving.

"It looks good," he said.

I reached up to touch the bathing suit's halter strap. "It's my sister's."

He smiled. "I wasn't talking about the bathing suit. I was talking about your scar. It looks like lightning in the sky."

I blushed, embarrassed at having misunderstood. "Mother thought that the scar would fade over time, but it hasn't."

He stepped closer, his eyes moving from my face to my shoulder. Gently, he touched my arm, turning me around. "I think scars are good for us. They remind us of what we can survive." I sucked in my breath as his finger traced the smooth purple lines that circled my shoulder and scattered down my back like cracked ice.

"Does it hurt?"

I shook my head. "Not really. Sometimes when it gets really cold, I feel it. Mostly I don't even think about it."

"I'm sorry."

"It's not your fault. A scar is a small price to pay for my life." He leaned closer, his warm breath blowing against my bare back. "And I'm sure after my father sued your family, you wished you hadn't been there."

"Never," he said. "Because then we wouldn't have met."

I turned in his arms, my nose brushing his chin, my gaze on the shark's tooth necklace. I wanted to reach up and press my lips against his, to forget all the reasons that I couldn't. The terror was skirting too close to my waking hours. It was only a matter of time before I could see all the details in the dream. The faces of the car's occupants. And each time the dream came, it brought the conviction that one of them was me. The one thing I knew for sure was that as soon as I fled to the West Coast, the tableau would be frozen in warped dream space, and I would be safe.

I stepped back, my skin cold in his absence. "I need to shower. Thanks for bringing in the cooler."

I ignored the hurt in his eyes as I began walking toward the stairs before being redirected by the ringing doorbell. I opened the door to find a large beautifully wrapped box sitting on the porch. A plain white delivery truck was already driving away.

I bent down to pick up the box, not seeing a note to indicate who the box was for, although I was sure I already knew.

Celeste and Mother emerged from the dining room just as Addie ran down the stairs reeking of cigarette smoke. She must have been smoking in her bedroom with her head hanging out the window like she'd done when she was a teenager.

I held the package out to her. "It's from Dale."

A soft blush brushed her cheeks before she frowned. "I wonder what it could be. I'll take it up to my room to open it."

"Take a pair of scissors," I called after her.

"I've got some," she said, hugging the box to her chest and climbing the stairs.

"How did you know it was from Dale?" Liam asked.

"I smell cigarettes," Mother announced. "Who's smoking?"

"Not me, Mother. I'm headed to Target. Would you like to come with me?" I was sweaty and needed a shower, but not as much as I needed to remove myself from Liam's scrutiny.

Mother wrinkled her nose to show her displeasure. "I don't shop at Target."

I refrained from pointing out that the lipstick she wore had been purchased during our last trip to Target. "Why don't you think about it while I go take a quick shower, okay? I'll be right back."

I paused at Addie's open door as a feeling of déjà vu swept over me. Torn wrapping paper littered the floor as Addie lifted a small item from inside the larger box.

"Art supplies?" I asked, wanting her to tell me *no*.

"Yeah. A whole new set of brushes since my old ones were brittle from being stored in the attic for so long. I mentioned to

Dale that I needed new ones if I was going to take that art class."
Her face fell. "I wonder if I should even keep these."

"Of course you should. You have time to paint when you're
not at the restaurant. I can hang out with Ophelia while you
work on a new piece."

She was looking at me with solemn eyes, and I could tell that
she wasn't really listening to what I was saying. "How did you
know the package was from Dale? There wasn't a card."

"Who else would be sending you art supplies?"

"How did you know that's what was in the box?"

"A lucky guess." I cringed at how lame I sounded.

"Okay. Right. I thought you weren't having your dreams
anymore."

"Does it matter? I'm happy that you're rediscovering your
artistic talent, almost as happy as I am to see that Dale still has a
thing for you and that his interest might be reciprocated."

"Stay in your own lane, Phoebe, all right? I can manage my
own life."

"Can you, though? You left your nine-year-old daughter
home alone with her grandmother who has dementia along
with a set of car keys. That doesn't seem like managing to me.
It sounds like a disaster."

She picked up an empty water glass. "Get out."

"I'm only trying to help. That's why you asked me to come
home, remember?"

"Get out!" she screamed, waving the glass.

"Grow up," I said, quickly shutting the door and narrowly
missing the glass that clunked against the other side before shat-
tering onto the wood floor.

I stared at the closed door for a long time, unable to move
as a wave of emotions pulsed through me that felt like love and
hate or a combination of both.

# 21

~

"Some male birds, like northern cardinals, will fight their own
image in any reflective surface. They see their reflection as
a competitor and will attack to drive it off. I've seen people
exhibit similar behavior as self-flagellation over a perceived
failure. I think this world beats us up enough that we shouldn't
have to see ourselves as the enemy. We should be more
like the mockingbird, singing only because it wants to."

**Excerpt from the blog *The Thing with Feathers***

## Celeste

IN THE WEEK following Elizabeth's escape to the cemetery,
a tangible chill had formed between Addie and Phoebe. Not
that there hadn't been a decided frostiness between the sisters
before the incident, but it now seemed much more intractable.

I almost wished that they would take to verbal arguments so
I could understand better what their estrangement was about,
but Addie was spending even less time at the house than before,
coming home just to shower and change before heading out
again. We hadn't seen Dale since the gift from the art store, and
I wondered about his sudden absence. I'd tried asking Addie, but
she seemed to be avoiding me even more than she was avoiding Phoebe.

She had at least taken her mother for her appointment with
Liam, and she'd gone with Ophelia and Annie to a picnic at
Alhambra Park, which reassured me that she was aware of her
responsibilities even though she didn't always show it.

As an independent observer, it seemed to me that she acted aloof only to aggravate her sister, which wasn't unusual between siblings. Julie and Liam had had a similar dynamic because they were so close in age. But their squabbles had been short-lived and directly related to an actual incident like forgetting to put gas in the tank of the car they shared.

This thing between Addie and Phoebe was different. Something simmered beneath the surface. There was a piece to this puzzle that I couldn't find, and I needed to stop looking so I could focus on Elizabeth and not ancient family history. "I'm bored," Will said yet again from his position on the porch hammock next to Ophelia. It was her turn to pick their morning activity, and she'd selected reading. Phoebe had taken them both to the library the day before, and it was too soon to be bored. I blamed his lack of enthusiasm for reading on his mother, whose literary pursuits seemed to consist of fashion and celebrity-gossip magazines. We just needed to find the right books for him, and I was determined to keep trying while I still had influence. He was already ten, so I knew my time was limited.

I peered at the children through the porch screen from where I stood in front of the camellia bushes. They sat on opposite ends of the swing with Annie in between them, her head on Ophelia's lap. "If you're really bored, Will, I'll be happy to give you something to do," I offered. "Like scraping chipped paint off the front fence. It needs to be repainted, too."

"I thought child labor was illegal in this country."

"A jury of my peers would never convict, dear, so tread carefully. Now, what'll it be? Reading or scraping?"

Ophelia elbowed him. "I told you to pick a different book. Here—read with me. Mine's really good, and I can catch you up on what's already happened. And you can let me know if you get stuck on any of the words."

"Funny." Will moved closer to Ophelia and held on to the other half of the book. I smiled to myself when I read the title: *The Lion, the Witch and the Wardrobe.* If I owned a cell phone, I'd have snapped a picture because Liam would never have believed it otherwise.

I turned to Elizabeth, who sat on an Adirondack chair in front of the unruly camellias. Judging by their tangled and dark interiors, it was clear they had been neglected for some time. I'd taken it upon myself to ensure that Elizabeth's prized camellias were in top form for the fall blooming season. I'd wielded the pruning shears while she held open the garbage bag. She kept on dropping it and then forgetting what we were doing so that I eventually began to drop the clippings on the ground. It was another chore I could ask Will to do in exchange for ice cream at the Pitt Street Pharmacy.

Despite keeping us both hydrated and in the shade as much as possible, I was about ready to succumb to heatstroke if I had to stay outside much longer. "Elizabeth, are you ready for a quick lie-down before lunch?" I asked as I reached out to straighten her straw bonnet. She belonged on the cover of *Southern Living* magazine with the glossy leaves of the camellias as the backdrop and her still-glowing complexion evident beneath her hat.

I brought Elizabeth to her room and heard Phoebe arrive as I was closing the bedroom door. I went to meet her in the kitchen. "How did it go?" I asked.

She'd had a meeting that morning with the estate attorney, partly to reassure herself that she did have the authority to act on their mother's behalf in financial and health care matters and partly to get a better idea of her mother's finances.

She dropped her purse on the counter. "Very well. Daddy took care of everything, so we won't have to worry about our mother's ability to pay her bills or for home maintenance or health care.

She'll be fine. I just needed to make sure everything is in place before I leave. I also set up automatic payments for Ophelia's tuition, since there was money set aside for her education." She took a deep breath and smiled. "I can't tell you what a relief it is."

"I'm sure. And I know Addie will be relieved, too."

"I don't think any of it has even crossed her mind, so I hope so."

"Aren't you being a little harsh?" I asked. "I'm sure it hasn't been easy for Addie, living here and witnessing your mother's decline."

"Really? And here I was thinking you were Team Phoebe."

*"Team Phoebe?"*

She gave a small laugh. "Just something Liam said. To show that he was on my side."

I studied her closely, saw the insecurity she worked so hard to hide. "There are no sides here, Phoebe. If there were, I'd say we were all on Team Elizabeth."

She flushed. "I know. You're right. This animosity between Addie and me, it's like a bad habit. How old do we have to be to get over it?"

"As your mother becomes more and more dependent on you and your sister, and the parent–child role reverses, hopefully you and Addie will see each other in a new light. Watching a parent decline is one of the hardest things we face in life. Count yourself fortunate that you have a sibling to share the burden. Dementia has been called the longest goodbye for a reason, and it can be a long, lonely road."

Phoebe blinked several times, and I thought she might cry. "That's the hardest part, I think. It's like watching my childhood being erased, you know?"

"I do." I hugged her, and after her initial surprise, she hugged me back. After a long moment, I pulled back. "Your mother will be out for the count for at least an hour, and there's nothing better than decluttering to clear the mind. Would you like to help me clean out the large wardrobe in the upstairs hall? I've noticed that the door can barely latch, and yesterday when I went to pull out a blanket for your mother, there was a small landslide. I managed to shove everything back in, but I think it would be helpful to take it all out and only put back in things that should be in there. Right now it looks like there might be some overflow from Addie's closet."

Phoebe grinned. "I can't believe that I'm excited about this. It's been driving me crazy since I got here and was looking for clean sheets for the guest room. My mother used to keep everything so nice and organized."

I led the way up the stairs, and Phoebe grabbed a desk chair from her room and put it in front of the wardrobe. "You are not sitting on the floor, Celeste. I'll hand you things for the Keep pile for you to fold and stack. The rest I'm just throwing in a Toss or Giveaway pile. Sound good?"

"Sounds good," I said with a mock salute.

Most of what was in the wardrobe were old bedsheets and frayed bath towels. Those ended up in the Toss pile along with dozens of mismatched socks that apparently belonged to Addie. Also found, shoved in a back corner, were large Ziploc bags filled with costume jewelry with broken clasps and missing pieces.

Phoebe held up a pillowcase with torn lace edging, its sides bulging with old makeup and hair ribbons. "Mother used to give Addie an ultimatum that if her room wasn't picked up and her bed made, she wasn't allowed to go out. This is where she shoved everything. I can't believe Mother never suspected."

"Oh, I'm sure she did. She just knew which battles were worth fighting." I pointed at what looked like a book spine behind a balled-up beach towel. "What's that?"

Phoebe got down on her hands and knees and reached into the

back of the bottom shelf. She pulled out the beach towel—wrapped around a salt-crusted bathing suit—before pulling out a stack of paperback novels. "Ha! Eloisa James and Julia Quinn." She held up two books with clinch covers. "I begged Addie to let me read these when she was done, but she hid them because she said I was too young. Like I hadn't already read Mother's Judith Krantz and Rosemary Rogers novels she'd hidden in her cedar chest. Everything I knew about sex I learned from those romance books."

"That's alarming," I said with a smile. "So your mother never gave you The Talk."

Phoebe snorted and reached under a pile of sorority T-shirts to pull out a large hardbound book and placed it in her lap. "I think my mother would have self-combusted if the words *penis* or *sex* ever crossed her lips. Addie and I are convinced that our parents had sex exactly two times."

"You might be surprised. Just because some people find it difficult to talk about sex doesn't mean they are incapable of passion."

"Ew. Please. Now I have a mental image that will be hard to erase."

I looked at the book in her lap, recognizing the scrapbook-style photographs on the cover and the text on the top left. *Everyone has a story.* I recited the words in my head from memory before my eyes settled on them. *I'll tell you right now. Legend 2008.* "Is that Addie's yearbook? Julie had the same one, which makes sense, since they were the same year."

I held out my hands and stared at it for a long moment as I thought. Julie's yearbook had been taken by the police hoping to find some clue or cryptic notes within its pages or inside the covers where dozens of her friends and classmates had written little messages in colored ink with matching hearts and smiley faces. I felt an urgent need to hold it in my hands, to read the things her classmates had written to her. To hold a piece of her again.

I opened the cover, not surprised to find most of the white spaces taken over by words and hand-drawn pictures. One talented friend had drawn the South Carolina Gamecock, the mascot of USC.

"Did Addie graduate from USC?" I asked.

Phoebe nodded. "With a major in broadcast journalism. Her minor was in partying, but she managed to get a good job in her field right after graduation anyway. I'm still not sure how she did that, but whatever."

"Julie was planning on attending USC in the fall, too. She wanted to be a nurse. Like me." I scanned the signatures inside the front and back covers, and then, on a whim, I found the pages dedicated to the choir with Julie's picture spotlighted during a solo performance. It showed her doing what she loved best, her face transformed into something even more beautiful. I didn't display this picture in a frame. It was too hard to see it and remember what could have been.

Scattered in the margins and between photographs, there were lots of autographs and greetings with arrows drawn to faces, mostly in the alto section, since that was the part Addie sang. But there was one heart balloon hovering over the soprano section, tethered to a singer in the front row. My Julie. Inside the balloon were the words *Go, Cocks!* Julie had found it highly amusing that she could shout out two words that to the rest of the country might be construed as more than slightly off-color but to USC fans were a point of pride.

"Isn't that your granddaughter?" Phoebe asked.

"It is. Addie did say they might have known each other in passing from choir. They sang different parts so they would have stood in different sections, so that makes sense, I suppose."

"True," she said. "I don't think I could name half of the girls I graduated with."

I flipped through a few more pages then skipped to Julie's

senior page but saw no more notes from Julie. I handed the book back to Phoebe. "What pile does this go in?"

She indicated a towering stack of items whose fate had to be determined by Addie. "Put it on top there. I'm tempted to leave this pile in the middle of the hallway so she sees it, but I'm afraid it might stay there indefinitely." She stood. "Wait here a minute. I'm going to dump it all on her bed so she has to deal with it."

"She could just move it all on her floor," I said.

Phoebe leaned down and picked up a pile of clothing, the yearbook squeezed between her chin and the pile. "Not my problem. As long as I don't have to look at it and we have a functioning hall wardrobe, it's all good."

"Fair point." I stood and began replacing the neatly folded sheets and towels on the shelves.

"What are you doing?"

Addie stood at the top of the stairs. She wore cutoff shorts and a torn tank top, her face and hair splattered with paint. I'd been happy to see her on the dock again, painting with the new brushes Dale had given her.

Phoebe emerged from Addie's bedroom after tossing her last load onto the bed. "We were just cleaning out the wardrobe and found a lot of your junk that you've been shoving in there for at least the last decade. I've put it on your bed so you can decide what you want to do with it."

Addie's face flushed with anger. "You had no right to touch my things."

"Technically I did because this isn't your wardrobe. You just sort of appropriated it."

Trying to defuse the situation, I turned to Addie with a smile. "I would be happy to help you clean out your closet, too. It's sometimes easier with an unbiased participant to help you determine what stays and what goes. It can be very—"

She slammed her bedroom door, cutting me off.

"Well, that went better than I expected." Phoebe gently closed the wardrobe door just as Elizabeth awoke and began calling out her husband's name.

When Liam arrived home, he found me in front of the open refrigerator where I'd been standing for much longer than I should have been. I had intended to see what I might fix for supper, but my thoughts had been hijacked by memories of the afternoon, going through the hallway wardrobe with Phoebe.

I took out a partially thawed package of chicken breasts and tossed them in the sink. "Sorry, I forgot to finish defrosting these. Supper won't be ready for a while."

He kissed me on the cheek. "I had a late lunch, so I'm good. And you don't have to cook for us every night, you know. Will and I would be fine living on pizza."

"I'd have to turn in my grandmother card if I allowed that to happen."

He laughed and kissed me again. "We could always send Will to the dock to catch our supper."

"As tempting as that sounds, I'd rather not disturb him."

As if noticing the absence of electronic sounds for the first time, Liam said, "Where's Will? Don't tell me you've got him whitewashing fences in the neighborhood."

"Not yet, but I'll keep that on the list. He's actually on the back porch, reading."

"Reading? As in reading a book?" He peered out the door leading out to the porch where Will was oblivious to the world outside Narnia. "Who is that boy, and what have you done to my son?"

I laughed. "I know. It's refreshing to see him doing something besides video games, isn't it? It's the first book in the Narnia series. Ophelia lent it to him on the strict instruction that he take very good care of it and return it when he's done. She's already read it about two hundred times—her estimation, not mine—so he can keep it as long as he needs, but she expects him to come back for the second book within the week."

"Great. Is there anything I can do to help?"

I considered him for a moment. "You know, since we have time, can I ask you to do something for me?"

"For you, anything. What do you need?"

I led the way up the narrow stairs that opened up onto a short hallway that contained two bedrooms and a bath. I paused briefly outside Julie's room before opening the door. I hadn't been inside since the previous Christmas. I always decorated her room with tinsel and a small tree just as I'd always done before she'd left, just because it was too sad not to. I'd spend the first of January boxing it all up again, storing it under her bed until the next year.

The room smelled of dust and stagnant air, but I always liked to imagine I could smell the perfume she used to wear, too. The bottle still sat on her dressing table, the liquid changing color inside the glass, each darker shade like the rings on a tree marking another year gone.

I opened the door to her closet and stepped back. Pointing to a corrugated box on the top shelf, I said, "Could you please bring that down and set it on the bed?"

"What's this all about?" Liam asked as he placed the box in the middle of Julie's bed.

"I helped Phoebe clean out a wardrobe at her mother's house today, and we found Addie's senior yearbook. I just had a sudden need to see Julie's."

I sat down on the bed next to the box and pulled out the last item I'd placed inside: her diploma. Julie had been missing at the time of graduation, and Liam had walked up onstage to collect it for her.

"What's this?" Liam pulled out a small trophy, a brass-colored treble clef set on top of a wooden pedestal. The glued-on plate read *Most Musical*. It had been an informal award, bestowed by her fellow choir members, but one that she had cherished the most.

"She was so proud of that." I glanced behind him to her nightstand. "It shouldn't be hidden in a box. Put it on the table next to her bed."

He didn't argue as he did as I instructed.

We pulled out a handful of long strands of Mardi Gras beads that had been draped on her bedpost. Instead of the purple, green, and gold of Mardi Gras, these were all crimson, black, and white as a nod to Wando High School's colors. Next, I pulled out her final essay for AP history, and a frayed red-and-black pom-pom. We'd neared the bottom of the box before I found the yearbook. I pulled it out and held it to my chest. "Thank you for humoring an old woman."

"I'm not sure what old woman you're referring to, but you're welcome."

I laughed, and as I began replacing items back in the box, my gaze caught on a familiar red folder. "Look, Liam," I said as I pulled it out. "It's Julie's choir music from when she made All State her senior year." Her name had been written across the cover in purple glitter glue, most of it long since flaked off.

I opened the folder, seeing the sheet music for *Jubilate Deo* on top. I could almost hear her sweet soprano voice practicing the descant in her bedroom over and over with a recorded piano accompaniment. She'd have me sing the alto part so she could practice harmonizing but quickly found an alto friend to rehearse with at school since I had trouble staying in the right key.

I pulled out the music and opened the cover, wanting to see Julie's meticulous notes in the margins where she'd jot down the director's instructions. It was all so clear in my head, as if she'd just left to go to school, the rooms still echoing with her voice.

"What's that say?" Liam asked, pointing to writing in the margin.

I squinted, but I couldn't see the small letters. I handed the music to him. "Here—you try."

He raised the page close to his face. "Only part of it is in Julie's handwriting." He tilted the page to read it from a different angle. "Looks like another person is begging Julie for a ride somewhere. It's not mentioned where, so it must be from an ongoing conversation. Lots of question marks after the word *please*, and the periods beneath the marks are diamond-shaped instead of just dots." He turned the music the other way. "This looks like Julie's handwriting, but it's only one word—*maybe*."

I continued replacing items into the box. "Sounds like they were passing notes in class."

"Something like that." He flipped to the next page. "Here the other person says *I promise to be careful*. And there's a little drawing next to it that looks like a *V*, but it's hard to tell." His eyes met mine over the music. "Any idea what she meant or who *V* is?"

"No idea," I said. "What did Julie say to that?"

Liam shook his head. "Not a thing. Not here anyway. It's blank." He thumbed his way through the rest of the pages then closed it. "You want me to keep this out?"

"No. That's all right. You can put it back."

We replaced the rest of the box's contents and tucked in the top flaps. He put his hand gently on mine. "It's been seventeen years, Gran. When will it be long enough before you can let us grieve?"

"I know, and I'm sorry. I know there's only a small glimmer of hope that she's still alive. But if I don't have hope, what's left?" I stood and placed the yearbook on the shelf with Julie's other books then left the room.

# 22
~

"When birds feel the time to migrate is approaching, they
become restless. They begin to feed heavily to build up
fat stores for the trip. When roosting at night, they will
orient themselves on branches or other perches facing
in the direction in which they will be heading. Of all the
wonderful, magnificent, and magical things I know about
birds, this is the one skill I wish I had been born with."

**Excerpt from the blog *The Thing with Feathers***

## Phoebe

I STOOD NEXT to my mother at her dressing table, spraying yet
another layer of Aqua Net at the crown of her head for extra
volume, just like she'd taught me when I was in high school and
she still had hopes that I might evolve into someone who considered a hair out of place as bad as a visible bra strap.

It was Celeste's day off, and after a fractious day spent trying
to entertain and involve my mother in her daily tasks, I'd made
a last-minute plan to take another trip to Target. Despite claim-
ing that she didn't shop there, it was a place I could take her
where she would be purposefully engaged and almost content
for the duration.

I held up two different earrings for her to choose from, a
gold hoop and a small pearl stud. "Which one would you like
to wear?"

She twisted her mouth and made a dismissive wave with her
hand. "No, thank you," she said.

I knew better than to argue. Even with her medications, her moods and outbursts could be unpredictable. I placed the earrings on her dresser and then selected two tubes of lipstick, one pink and the other coral. "Which color would you like? I think the pink would match your scarf."

She barely glanced at the tubes before making her selection.

"Coral it is," I said with false cheerfulness. My nerves were already so close to the surface I wasn't sure how I could get through the rest of the day. I handed her the tube, confident that she would do a much better job of applying it than I ever could.

As we headed to the stairs, I heard the sound of movement inside Addie's room. Her door was open a crack, and I knocked lightly. She looked up in surprise, caught in the act of shoving loose socks into a plastic garbage bag. The mess on her floor had been there for almost a week, and I had to keep reminding myself that it wasn't my responsibility as long as it wasn't a tripping hazard for our mother.

"Just so you know," she said, shoving a faded yellow sock inside the bag, "you're taking the giveaway bags to Goodwill since this was your idea."

I leaned against the doorframe. "Okay, I don't mind. I need to clean out some of the dresser drawers in my old bedroom and can take it all over together."

She seemed mollified by my answer, as if she'd been expecting an argument. Her phone rang, and she glanced at the screen, hesitating a moment before rejecting the call.

"Was that Dale?" I asked.

"Why do you want to know?"

"Because I like him, and I thought you two were enjoying each other's company. I'm just curious why I've been seeing a lot of Camaro Joe and not a lot of Dale."

She placed her phone facedown on the rug. "Like I said before, Dale's a nice guy. Just too nice for me."

"What about Joe? Is he a nice guy?"

"Nope. He's what I call *karma*."

"What's that supposed to mean?"

She shrugged then hastily touched her sleeve as if to make sure it still covered her shoulder. "Nothing. Joe's just more my speed. He doesn't expect me to be any better than I am."

"I have no idea what you're talking about. Any guy would be thrilled to be with you. Could you please translate?"

"Never mind. It's just that Joe and I are a better fit than Dale and I ever could be. Leave it at that, okay?"

"Don't say that, Addie. Dale's known you forever, so he knows what he's getting. And if he keeps coming back for more, then I say he's a keeper."

Addie barked out a laugh. "Maybe I'm not looking for a keeper."

I watched as our mother wandered toward Addie's closet door where she still had a pageant sash and photos from various events tacked to the wood. "Seems to me if you're going to be wasting your time with Mr. Camaro, you might as well be wasting it with someone who cares about you and wouldn't dream of dropping you off in the morning so you can do the walk of shame up to your front porch."

"That's enough, St. Phoebe. Maybe you should hang out with Mr. Camaro. Then maybe you wouldn't be so uptight."

"Stop arguing, girls. It's not ladylike."

We both turned. "Sorry, Mother," we said in unison.

"Why do you keep pushing Dale?" Addie asked. "Is there something I should know? Something else you saw in a dream?"

She looked so intent on hearing my answer that I considered making something up. But the truth was that Addie didn't need a dream to tell her what she needed to do.

"No, sorry." Indicating the almost-cleared floor, I said, "If you're done here and don't have plans until you have to be at work, why don't you come to Tar-jay with us? Ophelia's been asking for her own copy of the Narnia books so she can let Will have the ones they got at the library. Target has a pretty decent book section, so we can look."

"I don't shop at Target," Mother said, looking at the photographs tucked into the frame of the cheval mirror.

Addie and I shared a look. I remembered something Celeste had said about being lucky to have a sibling to share this journey, and in that moment, I knew what she'd meant. Nobody who hadn't been raised by Elizabeth Manigault could ever appreciate the combined humor and grief of watching her slowly battle this unseen assailant, losing her armor piece by piece.

"Might as well. Ophelia is at Will's house, and I don't have to be at work until five." She stood, smoothing the linen of her jumpsuit before casually swinging her hair into a messy bun and still managing to look like a cover model.

Addie drove so that she was the object of Mother's repetitive question from the passenger seat about where we were going. My sister didn't seem to mind and answered with patience and redirection to get a conversation going. She was terrible with schedules and following the rules and controlling her impulses, but even I had to admit that she was much better with our mother than I was.

We headed toward the cosmetics aisle. During the previous visit, Addie had made me buy an eye shadow quad—the first I'd purchased since college—and a pencil eyeliner. She'd even taken the effort to show me how to apply them so I wouldn't look like I was for sale, should I take my look out on the street.

Addie and I took turns pulling items from the shelf and showing them to our mother, being careful to wait for her to respond instead of overwhelming her by asking. We were halfway down the aisle when Mother announced, "I need to use the ladies' room."

I turned to Addie. "I thought you took her before we left."

"I asked her if she needed to go, and she said *no*."

"Addie!"

"I'm sorry. You're right. I should have taken her."

"I need to use the ladies' room," Mother announced, louder this time.

I shoved the handbasket at my sister. "Hold this. I'll take her."

One of the stalls was roped off with an Out of Service sign, and a line of four women stood waiting outside the only other one. I plastered on a fake smile I usually saved for meeting the parents of my most behavior-challenged students during parent–teacher conferences.

"I'm so sorry, I don't want to cut in line, but my mother here really needs to use the bathroom . . ."

My mother looked at me as if I'd struck her. "I do not!"

"Mother, you just said that you had to go to the ladies' room . . ."

"You lying bitch!" she spat out. "I said no such thing!"

The breath left my lungs as I felt the eyes of each woman staring at me. I recognized mixed expressions of surprise, embarrassment, and understanding, none of which made me feel any better. Before I could think of something to say, the door to the bathroom flew open, and Addie walked in.

"I thought that was Mother I heard shouting. I've got this, Pheebs." She pressed the key fob into my hand. "You go wait in the car." Mother allowed her to take her arm and lead her into the now-vacant stall while Addie nodded her thanks to the women waiting in line.

Everything was a blur as I stumbled out of the bathroom and into the parking lot. It took me a while to clear my eyes and remember where we'd left the car, but instead of getting inside I did ever-widening laps around the Lincoln in a vain attempt to calm down.

I was sitting in the back seat when they returned to the car. My mother smiled when she saw me. "Phoebe! What a nice surprise. What are you doing here?"

I grimaced so that I wouldn't cry. "I've joined the circus, and I wanted to come back to say goodbye."

She smiled at me then sat down in the passenger seat. "That's nice."

Addie started the car and turned on Mother's favorite Sirius station, *70s on 7*, and began to sing along to Simon and Garfunkel's "Bridge over Troubled Water." Her strong alto voice picked out the harmony as I tentatively sang the melody. Both of us mangled the lyrics to nearly every song until she turned the car into the driveway.

The dream came to me that night, an unwelcome surprise. I'd been so exhausted when I'd finally fallen into bed that I'd forgotten to prepare myself.

It was different this time. My view now seemed to come from a wide-angle lens, taking in more of the bridge and the water and the surrounding nocturnal landscape. I was able to see more of the road, too, including a small yellow warning sign. The white letters undulated like rivulets of water, making them illegible.

The dream floated back in time, showing more of the car's approach and the two occupants through the front window. Their mouths were open as if in the middle of what appeared to be a conversation, although that would have meant they were talking at the same time. Maybe arguing, then. But that wasn't it, either. Their faceless expressions were calm—joyful, even.

My dream self looked closely at the front window of the slow-moving car, trying to make out more of the facial features to determine if they were male or female. If one of them could be me. Something moved against the glass of the windshield, catching the ambient light of the still night. It slithered in slow motion with the car, swaying with the rhythm of the bumps in the road. Like a necklace, a long necklace with heavy, chunky beads.

The dream was a tableau painted in shades of gray: the car, necklace, and even the clothes of the passenger were hidden from view, their colors muted. I felt something pulling on me, plucking at my sleeve, trying to make me see something my brain kept hidden from me. I watched the car approach the bridge, willing it to stay in its lane as the terror expanded into a physical thing inside me.

The necklace swayed as the car hit the side of the bridge before careening over the edge. I heard the splash and saw the South Carolina license plate, the reflection of an object that I thought I recognized sinking slowly into the dark water near the car. A nightjar screamed somewhere close to my ear. The tugging continued on my arm, insistent and unrelenting until I opened my eyes.

Ophelia knelt on the edge of my bed staring down at me, and she was sobbing as she pulled on my arm. "Aunt Phoebe. Please wake up. Please."

I jerked upright, fully alert, and switched on my bedside lamp. I gently took her face in my hands and smoothed her hair from her face, while using my thumbs to wipe the tears that spilled down her cheeks. She wasn't wearing her glasses, and she looked like a small child. "Ophelia, sweetheart. What's wrong?"

"It's Mama. She's outside in the front yard because she doesn't want me to hear her, but I was going downstairs to get a drink of water so I did, and she's crying real hard and I can't make her stop."

I hugged her to me, rubbing her back until her sobs subsided. Then I slid from bed and patted the spot where I'd been. "Lie down here and wait for me until I come back, okay? It'll be all right."

"Miss Celeste says everyone has sad moments sometimes and that it's okay to cry because the tears take away the sadness to make room for happiness."

I pressed her nose with my index finger. "Well, that must be true because Miss Celeste is one of the smartest people I've ever met." I stood and tucked the covers around her. "Do you want the light on or off?"

"On, please."

"You got it. I'll be back soon."

I had trouble finding my bearings in the dark, the dream still vivid in my mind. I grabbed hold of the banister with both hands as I descended the stairs.

The front door was partially open. My bare feet felt the humidity-damp wood of the porch and grass as I followed the sound of racking sobs to the barren corner of the yard opposite the giant oak tree where Addie and I had played as children. Only a stump remained to mark the oak's twin that had been hit by lightning long before I was born. The sap inside the tree had conducted the heat so that the tree burned from the inside, leaving the outside bark intact so it appeared that the tree was whole. The oak had been cut down, but the stump had been allowed to stay. Throughout my childhood, my father would occasionally make noise about having the stump removed, but I would protest saying it was as much a part of our house's history as the red roof, and he'd always relent. It was the only time I could recall any of us winning an argument with our father.

I don't know why I'd decided to be the dead tree's advocate. Maybe because I was fascinated by a living thing that could remain so beautiful while its heart and soul turned to ash.

I found my sister sitting on the ground next to the stump, her head bent forward with her forehead resting on her knees as her shoulders shook with choking sobs. I sat down next to her, feeling the scratchiness of dead leaves and knobby roots against my bare legs.

I waited quietly, sitting in the empty yard with the burned-out stump, listening to my sister cry and the screeching of a nightjar in the distance while lightning bugs dotted the dark with their signatures of light.

"I hate that damn bird," Addie finally managed through softening sobs.

"I'll let him know next time I see him." I waited for a reaction, and when she didn't say anything else, I said, "Thanks for rescuing me at Target. I was praying for a hole to open up in the floor of the restroom and swallow me, but you were the next best thing."

Addie sniffed loudly then scrubbed her palms over her face. "You're welcome." I heard the hint of a smile in her voice. "She doesn't mean it, you know."

"Then why doesn't she say those things to you?"

Her laugh sounded brittle, the edges hoarse from crying. "If I knew the answer, I'd be a billionaire on the lecture circuit. Instead, I'm here in the trenches trying to figure things out a day at a time."

"Welcome to the club," I said. "I just don't remember getting the invitation to join this particular club or I would have thrown it away."

"Same," she said, turning her head so I couldn't see her starting to cry again.

"What's wrong, Addie? Is there anything I can do to help?"

She stuck her legs out in front of her next to mine, then surprised me by resting her head on my shoulder. "Mother's dying, Phoebe. Maybe not today or tomorrow, but this is the beginning of her end, and there's not a damn thing I can do

278 ||| Karen White

about it. I've never known a world without her in it, and I can't . . ." A deep sob convulsed throughout her body, transferring her pain to me.

I put my arms around her, and she clung to me like I had all the answers. Somehow the hierarchy of responsibility that had once been captained by our father had skipped everyone in between to land on me, and I was wholly unprepared.

I couldn't tell Addie that the answer didn't exist and that we were embarking on a journey where the path disappeared for long distances and that the destination stayed the same no matter what we did. It wasn't about fairness or birth order. We were sisters, and we needed to find a way to navigate together.

"I know. It feels like half of our lives is being erased. When Mother dies we'll be orphans, and I don't think it matters how old a person is, facing that certainty scares me more than anything."

"Maybe they'll find a cure in time to save her?" Her voice was so hopeful that I wanted to lie to her, to give us both more time before we had to face reality. Instead, I tried to pretend that I had everything under control, and that even if I didn't have the answers I at least understood the nature of the beast lurking in the woods.

"I don't know if this will help you, but I've found it a little easier to consider Mother as a person separate from this disease by seeing it as a physical thing. A monster called dementia. It's an insidious burglar who steals one thing at a time so that no one notices until the safe where you stored all your memories is empty."

She was silent for a moment and then barked out a laugh.

I pulled away. "What's so funny?"

"I was trying to picture the monster, and I keep seeing Barney the purple dinosaur."

"You're weird," I said, even though I was smiling. "I loved that show even though you hated it." I started humming the theme song under my breath before we both fell into a long silence.

"Please don't leave." Her voice was so quiet that it took a moment for me to register her words.

"I have to, Addie. I have a house and a job in Oregon. A whole new life I've built all by myself. I'm happy there."

"No, you're not." She said it with such conviction that I wondered how she knew.

"Am I so awful that you can't stand the thought of living near me again?" she asked, her voice heavy with unshed tears.

I hugged her tighter. "No, Addie. Of course not. Even during our roughest spots, I always knew you were my ally. I knew you were the one who chose my Christmas presents because Mother didn't have a clue and you knew me better than anyone. You taught me how to ride a bike because Daddy wouldn't since he thought I didn't have good-enough coordination to avoid getting hit by a car. And for the short time you had your VW Bug, you taught me how to drive a stick shift, even though I scared you to death when I got behind the wheel. You told me I could do it, so I did."

She was silent while we both remembered the times when we were good together, small snippets that often got overlooked in the large sweep of our childhoods, but they were the parts that shone the brightest.

"Please, Phoebe. I can't do this on my own."

I pulled away, wishing she could see my face in the darkness. "I'll never leave you on your own, Addie. I'll never be further away than a phone call or a plane ride. We'll always be sisters."

I felt her looking at me. "Will we? Because I think there's something else that's keeping you away. Something you're not telling me. And sisters should tell each other everything."

I studied the pale shapes of my fingers against the skin on my leg and listened to the sounds of the night marsh. "There is. I'm just not sure you want to hear it."

"Try me."

I began to speak before I could stop myself, telling her about my dream of the car and the bridge and the water. The lone survivor. And all the reasons why I thought the person climbing up the bank had to be me.

When I was done Addie didn't say anything, and for a moment I thought she'd fallen asleep. Finally, she said, "Why do you think it's you? Can you see your face?"

"No. That's the thing. It's like there's some sort of protective filter that only allows me to see what I can handle. The faces of the two people in the front seat are completely obscured. So is the license plate. It's as if my subconscious is trying to protect me from the truth."

"And it's always been that way—just a snippet?"

"Yeah. Except since I've been home this time, I'm starting to see more detail. Like I'm being teased. Or warned."

"Warned?" she asked.

"Yes, because all the other dreams I've had before and since have showed me outcomes. Not always in time to do anything about them, but enough to know when they happened that what I'd seen was a premonition of something that *would* happen. And I always recognized the players inside the dream, and the actual event always happens shortly after I had the dream—no more than a week usually."

"Except this time."

"Right."

She was silent, the blinking of the lightning bugs like a marquee around her thoughts. "So maybe it's not a premonition at all."

"That's what I thought, too. But Liam thinks that when I first had the dream, it was a premonition at the time I first had it, and then the event occurred without me being aware of it. My mind keeps showing it to me until I can figure it out so that I can have some kind of closure. Otherwise, I might never stop having the dream."

She turned to me in the darkness. "And that's why you don't want to move back here? Do you not have the dreams when you're in Oregon?"

"No—only the night before I flew to Charleston. And I've been having that dream along with a few others ever since I've been back."

"So you told Liam. Anybody else?"

I stood. "No reason to. I only told Liam because . . ." I tried to remember. "Because he's a good listener, and I needed to tell someone. You didn't seem available." I reached out my hand, and after a pause she took it, and I hauled her up so she stood next to me.

"I'm sorry," she said softly.

"Me, too."

We stood facing each other in the darkness as the shrill call of the chuck-will's-widow continued its nocturnal litany of soulful angst.

"You should call Dale," I said.

"Why do you say that?"

"Because from what I've seen, he makes you happy, and I think you do the same for him. He's a nice guy, which is something I don't think you have a lot of experience with. Let something good come out of all of this, Addie. And maybe my dreams will stop, and we can both move on."

"Do you really think that?"

"Mostly." I didn't specify which part. "Come on, it's late. Let's go back to sleep."

"You go on ahead," she said. "I need a little more time to think."

We said good-night then I made my way back to my room where Ophelia was still in my bed, spread out on her back like a starfish, the bluebird of happiness charm glinting from the light of the bedside lamp. I pulled the covers over her before kissing her forehead and turning off the lamp. "Good night," I whispered before curling up at the foot of the bed and closing my eyes, too tired to dream at all.

# 23

*~*

"In Druidic fables, three blackbirds perching in the World
Tree sing a magical lullaby that can put the listener to sleep,
enabling the sleeper to travel to the Otherworld in their
dreams. I find this to be a sweet sentiment, but horrifying,
too. What if we don't wish to travel in our sleep? What is
wrong with being satisfied with a comfortable bed in a still,
dark room that remains stationary throughout the night?"

**Excerpt from the blog *The Thing with Feathers***

## *Celeste*

ELIZABETH AND I sat in lawn chairs at the end of the dock,
each chair with an attached umbrella—something Phoebe had
picked up on one of her frequent trips to Target. We wore wide-
brimmed hats and long sleeves, drowsily watching Phoebe teach
Ophelia how to check the crab pots without getting pinched and
the best way to hold a fishing rod. So far, Ophelia had caught
two redfish and a speckled trout, and I was already thinking
how I'd prepare them for supper.

Will lay on his back, reading the second book in the Narnia
series, holding it above his head as a shade from the sun. Every
once in a while the silence was broken by Elizabeth asking me
to go get her hat because she didn't want any sun on her face.
I'd reassure her and help settle her back in her chair, then wait
for her to ask again.

Addie's easel sat in the middle of the dock where she'd left
it earlier that afternoon before heading to work. She'd been

painting out here every morning for the last week, her comings and goings on a predictable schedule. She'd make breakfast for Ophelia before Phoebe or Elizabeth got up, and the two of them would sit on the screen porch to eat and talk. We didn't see the man in the rust-colored Camaro anymore, and Dale was a more frequent visitor on evenings when Addie wasn't working. They'd gone on a few dates, but most of the time he included Ophelia in whatever plans he and Addie made. When I'd asked Phoebe, she'd told me that Dale had never spent the night.

I didn't want to analyze the sea change in Addie, choosing to believe that it was directly related to the approaching date of Phoebe's departure. But there was something else, too. A wariness I hadn't noticed before, and an almost fierce sense of protection over Elizabeth. She paid more attention now to everything Elizabeth did and ate. Everything she said. Phoebe had noticed and commented how relieved she was about Addie's new attitude. I was more reserved in my opinion, knowing from experience that drastic changes never occurred simply because of a change of heart.

"Phoebe," I called out, "would you please take Addie's painting inside when you go in? I don't want it to get ruined. It's not supposed to rain tonight, but she's been working so hard I don't want to take any chances."

"Got it. I might actually do it now, since all the fish seem more interested in Ophelia's worms than mine." She smirked at her niece, making the young girl laugh. Phoebe stood, brushing off the bottom of her shorts.

Will sat up, lowering his book. "How much longer before I have to go back to Nevada?"

"You have about two weeks left of your summer vacation."

He made a face. "But it feels like I just got here," he protested.

"It feels that way for me, too. Every summer seems to get shorter and shorter."

"My mother used to say the same thing when Addie and I were growing up," Phoebe said. "She used to say she wished she could bottle time and open it at the end of summer so it wouldn't end so fast."

Phoebe cleared her throat and glanced over the edge of the dock where the tips of the spiky cordgrass emerged from the dark water like swimmers searching for air. Placing her fists on her hips in a pose I'm sure she used a lot in the front of the classroom, she turned her attention back to Will and Ophelia. "Extra credit question, kids—why is today special?"

"Do we get a prize?" Will asked.

I laughed. "Learning something new should be a prize in itself."

Will rolled his eyes.

"It's July twentieth," Ophelia said.

"That's right. Anything else?"

"It's a full moon," I offered. "Or am I disqualified because I'm not a kid?"

"I should have clarified *kids of all ages*," Phoebe said. "But what else is today?"

I heard footsteps approaching on the dock and turned to see Liam. "The day after July nineteenth?" he asked, bending down to kiss my cheek.

I smacked him playfully on the arm. Liam had become a frequent visitor to the Manigault house, no longer bothering with an excuse to explain his presence, but no one, including Addie, had complained. I wasn't sure what was going on between him and Phoebe, but there was a tension there, a taut wire that soundlessly vibrated whenever they were in the same room together. But that didn't stop me from hoping that Phoebe would realize that whatever was keeping her away from this beautiful place would never be stronger than what brought her back.

"It's International Moon Day," Elizabeth said.

"That's right, Mother." Phoebe's voice showed her surprise. She gave Elizabeth an assessing look. "And a full moon in July is known as the Buck Moon since that's when male deer will start growing new antlers. Anything else we should know about July twentieth?"

Elizabeth frowned, seemingly annoyed to be asked such an easy question. "It's my daughter's birthday."

"Which daughter?" Phoebe asked.

Elizabeth thought for a moment. "My youngest."

"Right again. It's my birthday today."

"Oh, Phoebe," I said. "Happy birthday! I would have baked you a cake and put out balloons so we could celebrate properly if I'd known."

"That's all right. I almost forgot myself. Mother usually calls first thing so that she can wish me happy birthday before anyone else, and that's been my reminder since I left home." Her smile dipped. "This is the first year I didn't get that call."

"I'm so sorry, Phoebe," I said. To forget someone's birthday was as much of a sin as not having fresh baked goods in the house for drop-in visitors. "I'll make sure to put it on my calendar for next year so this won't happen again."

Phoebe's brittle smile reminded me that her stay here was temporary and that there were no plans for a return visit the following summer.

"No worries," she said. "I'm getting too old for birthdays, anyway."

I barked out a laugh. "Trust me, birthdays are a blessing, and they certainly beat the alternative. I think each time we can celebrate something by eating cake is a good day."

Her laugh was cut short by Liam's approach. I wondered if special glasses were required to see the sparks flying from both of them because I definitely felt them.

"Happy birthday, Phoebe." He leaned closer and kissed her gently on the cheek, his lips lingering slightly longer than Will and Ophelia thought was necessary.

"Ew!" Ophelia threw her hands over her face to cover her eyes.

"Get a room!" Will shouted, using his book as a shield.

"Will!" I shouted. "I don't know where you heard that, but it's not appropriate."

Phoebe stepped back in embarrassment but was saved from responding by a text from her phone. The sound of fireworks exploded as she swiped to answer it. "It's from Mary-Simms wishing me a happy birthday." She grimaced. "She wants to know if I can join her and Andrew for dinner, and she says to bring Liam."

"I'm available, if you're asking," Liam said.

She glanced at her mother. "I don't know if I can. Addie's working until nine o'clock tonight, so I need to be here."

"Don't be silly," I said. "I'm happy to stay until Addie gets home, and I know Will won't mind sleeping over, so there's no need to rush back. I'll make popcorn, and Elizabeth and I can watch a movie. So, see? Problem solved. Tell your friend that you and Liam would love to join her for dinner."

Liam shrugged and forced a straight face when he turned to Phoebe. "I guess it's settled, then. Where are we going and what time should I pick you up?"

"Fine," she said. "Let me find out." She tapped something on her phone, and when the reply binged, she smiled then quickly hid her screen by shoving it into her back pocket. "She's made dinner reservations for four at Fig for seven o'clock."

"How did she get a reservation at such short notice?" I asked. "I heard that you need to make them weeks in advance."

"Mary-Simms is an enigma," Phoebe said. "She doesn't take no for an answer and will sweet-talk and charm you until you say yes, and she leaves you thinking that it was your idea in the first place. It's just her nature. She also knows everyone in the state of South Carolina, including the governor, which helps."

"Well, then," Liam said. "Let me take Will home, get him showered and changed, and I'll bring him back when I pick you up."

"I don't need a shower," Will insisted. "I can just jump off the dock here."

"What about soap?" I asked.

"Ophelia can toss me a bottle of shampoo."

Liam tried not to smile. "Good try, but no. Get in the car, please. I'll have you back in a couple of hours."

After Liam and Will left, Phoebe said, "I guess I'll need to make myself presentable, although I have no idea what I'm going to wear."

"I'm sure Addie won't mind you borrowing something from her closet. Assuming she owns clothing that isn't too short or low-cut?"

Phoebe smirked. "I won't tell her you said that. For the record, Addie has excellent taste in clothes—something she got from our mother and the pageant scene, I guess. I've always wondered if that's the reason she tried so hard to get kicked out of Ashley Hall, so she wouldn't have to wear a uniform anymore. So, yeah, I'm sure the back of her closet is full of nice things."

I winked. "Go look in the back of her closet, then. I'm sure you'll find something."

She shook her head. "I highly doubt any of it will fit me."

"You won't know unless you try. And if you know where I can find a needle and thread, I can fix any shoulder strap or shorten a hem in less time than it will take for you to shower. So you go on ahead and put any possibilities on the bed. I'll be up shortly."

"You coming, Ophelia?" Phoebe asked.

Ophelia wrinkled her nose. "Do I have to?"

Phoebe looked at me, and I nodded.

"No, you can stay here," Phoebe said. "Just don't forget to bring the cooler and fishing rods inside when you're done.

"Yep." Ophelia gave her a thumbs-up.

*"Yes, ma'am,"* Elizabeth said sternly. "Please mind your manners."

It never failed to surprise me what the mind chose to hold on to and what it let go. Maybe it wasn't a choice at all.

"Yes, ma'am," Ophelia repeated.

A short while later, I told Ophelia to start packing up and stood to take Elizabeth back to the house and into the air-conditioning. My gaze caught sight of Addie's easel, and I realized that Phoebe had forgotten to take it inside. I couldn't bring the easel, but I could at least bring in the paper pad so it wasn't left out in the elements. I moved to the front of the easel to make the pad easier to remove but froze with my hands held aloft as my gaze fell on the scene before me.

It was awful and terrible and frighteningly beautiful all at the same time. The harsh brush strokes and congealed color framed the scene of what could have been a night view of the marsh, but my eyes couldn't focus on any part without being pulled away by separate swirls of dark colors. I slid off my glasses trying to get a closer look.

It was indisputably a close-up rendering of the marsh at night shown in a wide arc of light as if from a car's headlights. But it didn't appear to be the view from behind the Manigaults' house with Sullivan's Island and the lighthouse visible in the distance. There was no way of telling exactly where it was, but the waterways of the Lowcountry were like close family relatives, interconnected by so many branches that it was hard to tell where they began or where they ended.

A dark shadow cut across the painting, leading to a hint of light on the edge of the paper. This wasn't an omniscient point of view, but one of first person where the narrator was the art-ist and not a silent bystander. The tall grass bent away, as if the viewer were stepping on it to move forward, revealing a small, glittering object in the water. I leaned closer, trying to identify it, realizing only that it wasn't a fish or something that belonged in the marsh. There were no lightning bugs to relieve the solid night, and I wondered what Addie was trying to show except for a forward movement in a dark space where there was no light. Like being inside a person's head who'd taken a wrong turn and found themselves hopelessly lost.

I stepped back, thinking I understood. The angry, muted blobs of circular brush strokes showing the thoughts of some-one truly and irrevocably lost with no hope of turning around. I leaned closer toward a cluster of dark paint in the foreground at what I thought might be a dead tree, and perched on top was a thick brown bird with a flattened head and pointed wings, its dull eyes perusing the viewer, its large mouth open midscream.

"Miss Celeste? Can we go in now?"

I turned to Ophelia, although it took me a moment to re-member where I was and what I was doing.

"Yes, dear. Of course." I picked up the paper pad before col-lecting Elizabeth and heading back to the house, Ophelia fol-lowing with the fishing rods clanging against the cooler.

It was close to nine thirty when Addie returned from work. Elizabeth was asleep upstairs, and Will and Ophelia were sprawled out on the floor in Ophelia's room reading with bowls of pretzels and popcorn to keep them happy. Annie as usual was curled up against Ophelia's side, occasionally smiling in her sleep to show her utter contentment. If Ophelia weren't such a perfect target for my dog's devotion and adoration, I might have been jealous.

I was tidying up the kitchen in preparation for leaving when Addie entered. She remained standoffish with me despite doing everything I could to reassure her that I wasn't there to stir up trouble. After discovering that she loved oatmeal peanut butter cookies, I made sure there were always freshly baked ones in the cookie jar.

I'd come to care about Elizabeth and the rest of the Manigaults. Since Will had moved away with his mother, I'd missed the daily business of taking care of another human. Liam didn't count because he was a fully functioning adult—according to him—but I hoped our frequent meals spent together in the house where I'd raised him and Julie made him feel grounded. I could only hope that Phoebe's imminent departure wouldn't knock him off his perch.

"How was work?" I asked, drying my hands on a dish towel.

"Fine." She lifted the lid to the jar on the counter and pulled out a cookie. She closed the lid without offering me one and took a small nibble.

"Busy?" I asked.

"Very." She took another bite of the cookie.

"Your mother's asleep, but Will and Ophelia are in her room reading. At least they were when I last checked. I told them if they got tired of reading, they could watch a movie on Ophelia's iPad."

"Great," she said, slowly chewing on another bite.

I picked up my purse and keys. "I guess I'll leave you in charge now."

She'd stopped chewing, her gaze focused on the kitchen table behind me where I'd left her art pad.

"You left your painting out on the dock, and I didn't want it to get ruined so I brought it inside."

Addie approached the table and touched the edge of the pad delicately.

"It's different from your other work, but it's very good. There's a depth of emotion in it that few artists are capable of conveying with any medium."

Very softly, she said, "It's Phoebe's dream. The only one she's had where she's not sure if it was a premonition for something that has already happened or is yet to happen."

I frowned. "Still? I thought she wasn't having dreams anymore."

She turned to look at me. "She wasn't. But now that she's back . . ."

I moved closer, studying the painting, trying to see more than before. I gently touched the bird with my index finger, then slid down to the wide, dark shadow I'd seen before. Except this time I thought I knew what it was. "Is this a road?"

She nodded.

"And I think I recognize a chuck-will's-widow in this tree." I pointed to the same brown spot I'd noticed before.

"Yeah. I don't remember if Phoebe told me there was one in her dream, but I wanted it to be there."

"Why is that?"

Her eyes were distant. "Because I hate them. Since I was a little girl they were always out there in the summertime. Mocking me."

"Mocking you? But why, Addie? I've seen the photographs from your childhood. You were loved by your parents and given every advantage. And you had a sister who adored you." I tilted my head, examining her perfect face. "You were also born with a rare beauty that no doubt opened a lot of doors for you."

She grunted. "Right. And closed just as many. Don't get me wrong. Being pretty did have its advantages. To a point. I think I was twelve when I realized that people took one look at me and immediately assumed I was an airhead. I loved math—can you believe that? And I was good at it, almost as good as Phoebe.

Phoebe has a much better singing voice, too, but Mother encouraged me to join the choir but not Phoebe. She was left alone to look at birds and bugs with Aunt Sassy because that was her passion."

Addie shrugged and turned back to the table. "I thought my passion was painting, but Mother wanted me to focus on the beauty pageants—her way of telling me to stay in my lane."

"I'm sorry. I know that must have been hard. Did your mother have a sister?"

She shook her head. "No. Just a brother. He went to Harvard Law School and stayed in Boston, so we didn't really ever see him." She let out a bitter laugh. "He practiced for a couple of years before quitting and joining a band where he was the lead vocalist. He and his partner live in Beacon Hill and own a beach cottage on St. Simons. I only know this because I overheard my parents talking one night."

"Eavesdropping is truly one of the best ways to find out what's really going on, isn't it?"

Addie gave me the first genuine smile I'd seen since we'd met. "Mother once admitted to me that she was the one who'd wanted to be a lawyer, but she married young and then had three babies. I guess marrying a lawyer was the closest she could get without losing the approval of her parents."

"That would explain a lot." I leaned closer to the painting, noticing again the bright spot submerged just beneath the surface of the water. A small object, sinking into the dark water. I squinted trying to make it come into focus. "Is that why you got pregnant with Ophelia? To jump off the path your mother had designed for you?"

"I love my daughter. I had her because I wanted her."

"I never said that you didn't. But maybe having your daughter solved two problems at once—you got your mother's attention, and you had the child you wanted. And you stayed here while Phoebe moved to the West Coast."

Addie nodded. "She was always the brave one." Her lips twisted. "I was jealous of that. If she wanted to do something, she found a way and did it. Including moving across the country to a place she'd never been before to start a new life. It's the one thing she had that I didn't. It made me hate her and love her at the same time. There's something so wonderful about a girl who believes in herself and goes out and creates her own adventures."

"And if Ophelia did something courageous, you'd approve?"

"Are you asking me if it would make me love her more?"

"Would it?"

She didn't answer, and I knew I'd pushed too far. I was usually good at getting people to open up, while at the same time never knowing when to quit. Addie was an enigma to me, her relationships with her mother and sister complicated enough that I felt the need to untangle them to be a better caretaker for Elizabeth. But I felt Addie chafing under my words and quickly changed the topic. I turned back to the painting, at the heavily pigmented swirls and slight divots on the paper, imagining the force exerted to create them. "There's so much anger in this painting. Or maybe *anguish* might be more accurate. Is this a translation of Phoebe's emotions related to the dream? Or something that's very specific to you?"

I saw the shadow fall on her face, the previous openness between us disappearing as if a door had been shut. My question about the object in the water would have to wait. "It's none of your business," she said, flipping the cover over the painting and lifting the pad of paper. "Weren't you just leaving?"

Without waiting for a reply, she headed for the doorway. "I think you know your way out," she called without a glance back.

# 24

~

"Globally, it is usually the male bird who begins the
intricate and fascinating courtship display to give females
a way to assess who is the fittest and most vigorous
mate. Admittedly, after not too much research, I've come
to the conclusion that this is not that different from the
human mating process, although the courtship displays
seem to be more prevalent from the female camp."

**Excerpt from the blog *The Thing with Feathers***

# *Phoebe*

I HEADED DOWN the stairs, wearing a red sundress with a high-low hem and a matching pair of espadrilles, both from Addie's closet. Addie and I had always worn the same size shoe, but the dress fit, too, with just a stitch here and there to take in the bust and tighten the straps so they wouldn't slip off my shoulders. I'd considered using concealer to cover my scar, but decided against it when I recalled Liam's words. *I think scars are good for us. They remind us of what we can survive.* His finger had traced its lines as if it were a beautiful piece of jewelry and I knew he wouldn't want me to hide it.

Without Addie there to assist with my hair and makeup, I did the best I could, helping myself to Addie's supply of cosmetics on her dressing table. She'd left the chain with the black pearl charm on her nightstand, and I knew it would look perfect with the neckline of the dress. I hesitated before justifying that if she'd wanted to wear it tonight, she'd have it on now. I clasped it around my neck, making sure it was securely fastened, then took a dab from one of her perfume bottles on my way out.

I returned briefly to borrow a clutch purse I'd seen on her closet shelf. I'd apologize when I saw her in the morning, even though I was fairly certain she'd be more amused than annoyed. Growing up, she'd always offered to lend me clothes, and I'd always feigned disgust, imagining the damage I'd cause by wearing them to go fishing or bird-watching deep in the marsh.

Liam and Will were in the foyer with Celeste when I came down the stairs, and Will let out a wolf whistle when he saw me.

Celeste closed her eyes and sighed heavily. "Will! I don't know where you learned that, but I never want to hear it again. Is there something you'd like to say to Phoebe?"

Liam nudged him in the back. "I'm sorry, Miss Phoebe. I meant to say that you look very intelligent tonight."

"Thank you, Will," I said trying very hard not to laugh.

"We'll have a talk later, son," Liam said with a stern look before turning to me. "You ready?"

"Sure. I just hope Celeste's sewing skills are as good as she claims, or this dress will fall off if I make any sudden moves."

"And that would be a shame," he said with a strangled voice.

My mother walked in from the dining room where she'd been going through the albums. "Phoebe? What are you doing here?"

I pushed my feeling of disappointment aside, not willing to let it ruin the evening. "I'm here for a short visit."

She nodded slowly, a rare smile lifting her face. "You look pretty."

"Thank you," I said, feeling suddenly awkward. I didn't remember my mother ever saying that to me. "It's Addie's dress." I wasn't sure why I thought I needed to clarify.

Her gaze drifted to the necklace, and her smile disappeared. She walked to stand directly in front of me, then jabbed her finger at the dangling pearl charm. "No." Her lips moved as if trying to remember the correct shape of words. "No," she repeated with growing agitation.

"Okay. I'll take it off." I reached behind my neck and unclasped the chain.

Celeste held out her hand. "I'll put it back in Addie's room."

"Thank you," I said as I placed the necklace in her palm.

My mother's fingers patted her own neck, and I noticed the frailness of her hands, the spidery web of veins that reminded me of the marsh, the parchmentlike skin like the briny water.

I leaned down to kiss her soft cheek, smelling the soft scent of her fragranced bath powder that brought back years of memories of my mother when she was whole and our relationship fractured. But the scent reminded me, too, of times when I'd sat on her lap while she read a book to me, or as she bent down to tie the sneakers she would sometimes allow me to wear to church instead of the patent-leather Mary Janes that matched my sister's.

I wanted to grasp it, to hold it in my hands as a reminder that our relationships evolve over time like the colored feathers of a bird, constantly shifting to accommodate the changing seasons.

We said our goodbyes before Liam led me outside to a vintage red Mustang convertible. "Where's your truck?"

He held open the passenger door. "On the off chance that you might be wearing a dress and heels, I thought this would be easier for you to get in and out of. I can put the roof up, too, if you don't want to mess up your hair."

Having no skills with a curling iron or hot rollers, I'd opted for a high ponytail that I'd coated with several layers of Aqua Net. "Definitely down. I don't think a hurricane could move my hair."

"Good to know. I'll be careful not to light a match too close to your head."

After sliding behind the wheel, he started the car and put it in gear. "You look beautiful, by the way." His cheek creased in a smile. "And intelligent."

I laughed, suddenly glad I'd said yes to tonight. I wouldn't think about the dream that would inevitably creep into my sleep. I was going to pretend, at least for one night, that I was just a girl going out to dinner. I would deal with the fallout later. "Thanks," I said.

The wind blowing through the car was too loud to talk over, so I relaxed in my seat for the short ride to downtown Charleston. Heavy clouds had moved in, pushed along with a growing offshore breeze. A storm was coming, but I wouldn't let it dampen my mood. Things at home were far from perfect, but they were so much better now than they had been when I'd arrived. I could almost begin to think about returning to Oregon without a sense of dread.

I embraced the timeless view of the iconic Charleston skyline with its church steeples marking the highest points as we traveled across the Ravenel Bridge. It reminded me of Addie's ill-fated VW Bug, lime green with a cream-colored convertible roof. By the time Addie got her license, the bridge was still new and exciting enough for her to make any excuse to drive across it. When she couldn't find a friend to go with her, she'd bring me for company, and so I could be the DJ, constantly digging through the CDs on the passenger-side floor to find the one song she wanted to blare out of the car stereo.

We exited onto East Bay, our journey slowed enough that we could feel the strong breeze on our faces that smelled of rain.

"It's not far, but I can still put the roof back up if you'd like," Liam suggested.

I leaned back in the seat, turning my face up toward the sky. "Nope. I'd forgotten how nice it feels to be warm all the time and not need a sweater in June. It will be hard to go back."

"Then don't."

I didn't respond. Instead, I closed my eyes, drinking in the heat and the warmth of the air and the scent of salt that I could still smell no matter how far I went.

After parking in a nearby garage, we walked the two blocks on Meeting Street to Fig where Mary-Simms and Andrew waited for us in the crowded bar.

"Phoebe," she called out, her voice carrying over the hubbub of conversation. I spotted her immediately, despite her being at least a head shorter than everybody else. Maybe it was the bright red lipstick or just the force of her personality that turned all heads, making it easy to pinpoint her location.

She hugged me tightly and then hugged Liam, too. Andrew, a slightly less gregarious personality than his wife, grinned broadly and offered his hand to Liam but hugged me. Mary-Simms held up her highball glass filled with a clear bubbly liquid and lime wedge and an umbrella stuck in the top. "I'm pretending there's gin in here. Just promise me that you'll drink enough for both of us, because it's your birthday!"

Before I could say anything, she reached into her handbag and pulled out an elaborately wrapped gift. Handing it to me, she said, "It's just a little something to mark the occasion. I had to get you something—I mean, we were at each other's birthday parties from age five to eighteen. We've got a lot of making up to do!"

"I'd love to see those pictures," Liam said.

"I'm sure I could find them if you're serious," Andrew said with a wink. "I bet we could come to some kind of arrangement."

The men laughed while Mary-Simms and I shared horrified glances, no doubt remembering the awkward hairstyles and gap-toothed smiles of our shared schoolgirl years.

As we were led to our white cloth-covered table, Liam placed his hand gently on my back, his thumb grazing bare skin and sending heated flares throughout my body. I found him watching me, and I wondered if he'd felt the same thing.

After placing our drink orders, Mary-Simms pointed at the gift. "Go ahead—open it now." She looked at me with anticipation.

I ripped into the paper, being careful not to ruin the bow, then slid out a small leatherlike box with a hinged lid. "It's just a little something I saw at a shop on King Street and immediately thought of you."

I pulled out the slim silver chain with the enameled bluebird charm dangling from it. I glanced up with surprise. "It's identical, I think."

"I thought so, too, when I saw it. I was at your tenth birthday party when your aunt Sassy gave you the first one, and you never took it off after that. And the day I came over and we went for our walk, I remember Ophelia wearing it, and that's what reminded me. I hope you like it."

"I love it," I said, giving her another hug. "It's perfect."

"Hold your ponytail out of the way," Liam said as he took the necklace from me. I did as he asked and waited for him to place it around my neck.

"How does it look?" I asked.

"Like it was made for you." Mary-Simms reached over and straightened the charm. "I was hoping that every time you saw it in the mirror, you'd think of home and want to come back."

"We have bluebirds in Oregon, too, you know. But they're called western bluebirds instead of eastern bluebirds. And yes, they have other differences than just their names, mostly in coloring variations."

"And of course you'd know that," said Mary-Simms, and I laughed as I stroked the smooth enamel of the bird like a talisman of home.

When the waiter appeared at the end of the meal with the dessert list, I was the first to raise my hand. Growing up with my mother and sister meant that I'd been taught that dessert was nice to offer friends and visitors but not something in which I should indulge. Liam and I split an order of sticky sorghum pudding, and I made sure there wasn't a crumb left.

As we stood outside the restaurant, saying goodbye, Mary-Simms gave me another hug. "It's been so good to see you, Phoebe. I've missed having you in my life. I wish you could stay longer. Think of all the trouble we could get into! Just like old times."

"If you're referring to the peeled bananas we taped to the bottom of Mrs. Dorgan's desk over spring break, I plead the Fifth." I giggled, the memory made more hilarious by the wine I'd consumed over the course of our dinner.

"And I'd love to hear more of that," Andrew said, "but Drew is an early riser, and we both need our sleep. Let's do it again soon, though, okay?"

I hugged him and Mary-Simms again, and as Liam and I walked back to the garage, it was hard to remember why I'd ever left.

As we got back into the car, Liam's phone pinged with a text. I watched him frown as he read and then tapped in a long response before looking at me. "Will wants to know if the jonboat in your shed is still waterworthy."

I sat up. "What? I mean, I have no idea, but why is he even asking right now? It's dark out."

"Don't worry. I told him that under no circumstances is he allowed to take it out tonight, and he said he and Ophelia were thinking about taking it out tomorrow."

I pulled out my phone. "I should call Addie since she's in charge. Just to be sure."

He put his hand over mine. "Let Addie handle it, Phoebe. I think being responsible is something she needs right now."

I relaxed back in my seat. "You're right. We'll let them work it out."

"So," he said. "Where to?"

"I thought you were taking me home."

"I could. If that's what you want."

"Is there another option?"

"My place? Will is at your house, and Celeste is at hers so . . ."

He let the question fade away. When I didn't say anything, he turned on the ignition. "Never mind. I get it. I'll take you home."

I turned to face him. "Who said I wanted to go home?"

He leaned toward me, wine on his breath, and kissed me softly. He lifted his head, the air between us like a promise.

I closed my eyes, my body lulled into a stupor by the delicious food and wine and the warm air that slipped over my skin and the promise of what was to come. I tried to stay awake, remembering too clearly what happened before when Liam drove me back from the concert, but I fell asleep before we'd exited the garage, feeling the weight of Liam's hand on mine.

The dream came quickly this time, a sense of urgency I didn't remember now nipping at my back. My skin prickled, and the hair on my arms stood up as the nightjar screamed closer and closer to my ear. It seemed to be screaming *at* me. Wanting me to pay attention. To see what it wanted me to see.

I wanted to back away from the scene, but I was immersed in it, like being inside a painting, imprisoned within the four edges of the canvas. The bird screamed again, but it wasn't the bird, it was a woman crying, the sound coming from the woman emerging from the edge of the water. *A woman.* The first clue I'd had about the identities of the car's occupants. I wanted to look closer at the woman's face, but the bird shrieked in my ear, urging me to look at something else. To *pay attention.*

Panic reached around my throat, squeezing out my breath as my gaze darted from one spot to another, searching for what I was supposed to *see.* The car seemed to move slower this time, its inevitable progress toward the edge of the bridge even harder to watch. I should be able to stop it, yet it remained just out of reach. And then I was on the road leading to the bridge, and I was running toward the car, my feet heavy. I looked down and saw that pluff mud was sucking at my feet.

The sobbing filled my ears, saturating the night, flooding the sticky air with an unholy agony. I forced my gaze toward the woman, trying to see her face, knowing it had to be me. The nightjar called out again, and I turned to see that it was on the bridge, its dull eye focused on something in the water. I followed its gaze, seeing again the small shiny object. My dream self knew it was about to go under any second, but I needed to see it. I *had* to see it. It was important. But as much as I knew that I needed to see it, the more my conscious brain blocked it. Because I *recognized it.* I just wasn't ready to accept it.

The bird lifted from its perch, its wings spread in an ominous arc as it swooped toward me with its feathers bowed. It shouted as it came near, but its voice had suddenly become my father's.

I screamed as the feathers brushed my face, its wings folding around my body, and then there was Liam's voice, whispering soothing words in my ear, and it was his arms around me as he lifted me, carrying me away from the dream. I kept my eyes closed, aware only of the beat of his heart beneath my ear and the sound of wind whistling through sailboat rigging. Then a door opened, taking me out of the dream, and I knew that I was safe.

I opened my eyes. I was lying on a soft couch, and Liam's face was in front of mine, and it was quiet except for a howling wind outside. My gaze shifted to the shark's tooth around his neck. An image from the dream flashed through my head, gone almost as soon as it had arrived. I reached out and touched the dangling charm at his neck, trying to grasp at the wisp of memory.

"You had the dream again."

"Yes." My voice sounded raw.

He was silent, watching me closely. "Will you be okay here by yourself while I get you a glass of water?"

I shook my head. "Don't leave." I reached for him and brought my mouth to his, needing the sanctuary he had offered me the first time our lives had collided all those years ago. It felt as if he were saving my life again.

He pulled away, leaving my skin suddenly bereft. "Are you sure?"

I nodded and reached for him again, pulling him toward me, erasing the bridge and the car and the woman and the lonely call of the nightjar. All that remained was Liam and his marsh-green eyes and the sound of the sailboats pulling on their moorings in a growing wind, caught inside a storm we hadn't seen coming.

# 25

~

"When environmental changes predict an incoming storm,
birds are able to take early action to stay safe. Some
will feed frantically, fueling up for energy to leave the
area. For those who remain, they will seek shelter until the
storm passes. To a certain extent, humans share this trait
of preparing for storms. Unfortunately for us, we lack the
keen sense of awareness that birds have that warns them
of impending danger. If we did, maybe we could avoid
life's pitfalls that we can't see coming until it's too late."

**Excerpt from the blog *The Thing with Feathers***

# *Phoebe*

AN UNFAMILIAR RINGTONE jarred me awake. The room was
pitch-dark, the bed beside me warm but empty. Despite my
abrupt awakening, I knew where I was. Liam's scent was still on
my skin, my limbs heavy with an unfamiliar satiety.

I sat up, realizing that the phone had stopped ringing and that
Liam was speaking quietly from the other side of the bed, his
voice barely audible over the slashing sound of rain against the
windows. I could barely see him, which meant it was still in
the middle of the night or the electricity had gone out. Or both.

I was only half-awake when Liam's warm fingers touched my
bare shoulder, and I became aware of the urgency in his voice
as he spoke into the phone.

"She's here. We'll leave right now. Stay where you are, and
we'll be there as soon as we can."

The word *we'll* had erased any thought that the call had been
about a patient, and I was immediately thrust back in time to

another late-night call letting me know my father was dying. Nothing good ever came in a late-night phone call.

I was already scrambling off the side of the bed, fumbling for the lamp switch in the dark. "Was that Addie? Is Mother all right?"

"No. That was Will." I listened as he searched for discarded clothing while I turned the knob on the lamp to no effect. "He woke up and discovered that he's alone in the house."

I turned toward him. Blinked at the darkness. "But he can't be. Ophelia and Mother are there. And Addie. She would have called me."

"Will said an old Camaro came and picked up Addie around midnight. She's not there. But he doesn't know where Ophelia and your mother are, just that they're not inside the house."

"No," I said. "Addie wouldn't do that. She's so much better now." I knew I was rambling, trying to make sense of the nonsensical, and Liam let me. "I'm sure she called me. I just need to find my phone."

I reached toward the nightstand but only felt cold, smooth wood. "Where's my phone?" I could hear the rising panic in my voice.

I felt Liam's hands on my shoulders. "It's in your purse, which I think I left on the sofa. I'll go get it while you get dressed. Here." He turned on his phone's flashlight and put it in my hand. "Use this. I know my way around."

I nodded even though he'd already turned to leave, my body beginning to shake despite the rising temperature inside the house. I found my clothes on the floor and threw them on. I was struggling to reach the zipper in the back when Liam returned.

"I'll get that," he said as he handed me my purse.

I pulled out my phone, letting the purse drop on the floor, and I stared at my incoming texts. "No," I said, scrolling up and down, searching for a text that should be there.

"Check your voice mail," Liam suggested. His voice remained calm despite my rising panic.

Even though I knew that Addie would never leave a voice mail, I clicked on the icon anyway, desperate for an explanation or a reason as to why Will would have awakened in the house all by himself in the middle of the night.

"No," I said again, embarrassed at the sob in the back of my throat. I quickly dialed her number, and when it went to voice mail, I dialed the landline, which rang and rang with no answer. "Why isn't Will picking up?"

"He probably doesn't recognize the sound, or he stepped outside to wait for us."

"But—"

"Phoebe." He turned me around to face him, his fingers lifting my chin. "I'm here with you. It's going to be okay."

I wanted to argue, to tell him that there was no way he could know that, but my jaw was clenched tight to keep my teeth from chattering.

Another thought sent my panic into overdrive. "Did you ask him if my mother's car is in the driveway?"

"It is, so at least that means your mother didn't drive off with Ophelia."

Our eyes met, the implication of where they could be too horrible to say out loud.

He grabbed his phone from the bed where I'd left it and shone the light toward the doorway. "Let's go," he said, gently taking my hand. "We'll take my truck."

I followed barefoot, not having had the time to find Addie's shoes. I barely comprehended his words but was reassured by his voice. He led me through a kitchen before opening a door to a garage where his truck was parked. He manually lifted the heavy door, the opening bringing in a rush of rain and wind.

Liam turned to me. "You ready?"

"Yes," I said, before kissing him on the lips and running with him toward the truck.

The relentless rain pounded the windshield as the wipers futilely whipped across the glass. I kept dialing Addie's cell number over and over, hanging up at the sound of her voice mail picking up and dialing again. I didn't allow my thoughts to go where they shouldn't and instead tried to focus on the here and now.

I jumped as lightning arced across the sky like divine fingers, illuminating the rainswept streets scattered with blowing debris. I shut my eyes then forced them open again. I had a good reason to be terrified of summer storms, but that didn't stop me from being embarrassed to show my fear. I'd chosen to restart my life in the Pacific Northwest because they receive the least number of thunderstorms per year. But grown women weren't supposed to be afraid of thunder and lightning. Except now as we raced across town toward the house and family I had so carelessly discarded, I understood that there were much bigger things of which to be afraid.

Liam's headlights fanned over the house as he pulled into our street. Will ran out onto the front porch just as I spotted my mother's car parked in the driveway. As soon as Liam stopped the truck, I slid out of the passenger seat, my bare feet hitting the pebbled driveway as rain pelted my face. I ran in the direction of the shed, cutting my foot on something sharp. Despite the pain I kept running until I'd reached the shed. Another flash of light illuminated the side yard and the open door of the small structure. I stepped inside and held up my phone to shine light into the dark space inside. I immediately saw the empty spot on the wall where we'd always kept the jonboat.

"Phoebe!" Liam's voice came from outside somewhere, his voice snatched away by the wind.

I ran back toward the driveway, nearly colliding with him. "The jonboat's gone," I shouted. I watched as his eyes widened.

"Come on." He grabbed my hand, and we sprinted up the porch steps.

"I didn't know what to do," Will said, his voice showing the strain of trying to be brave and not cry.

I hugged him despite my sodden hair and clothes. "You did the right thing by calling your dad, okay?"

He nodded, his lips trembling as he struggled to hold in the tears. "Addie came home. Right before you got here. I told her about Mrs. Manigault and Ophelia not being here, and she ran outside without telling me where she was going."

Liam put his hand on Will's shoulder. "You did everything right, Will. Right now, I need you to help by staying here, and keep your phone handy in case I need you, okay? If your phone service goes out, use the landline in the kitchen. And if you see anyone, call me immediately. We're counting on you. Got it?"

Will gave his father a solid nod. "Yes, sir."

I ran into the dining room and pulled out a box of matches and a handful of tapered candles and brought them back for Will. "If you lose phone service, we will, too. Use a candle to communicate with us from the back porch. We'll be able to spot it from anywhere in the back of the house. Wave it side to side if you see someone."

"Yes, ma'am."

To me, Liam said, "Go around the side of the house where the camellias are, and I'll check out the other side. We'll meet up at the back porch."

"Okay," I said before following him back out the front door just as another flash of lightning lit up the sky like a celestial light bulb. *One Mississippi, two Mississippi, three Miss—*

A crash of thunder rattled my teeth before I'd finished the third *Mississippi*. The storm was close and getting closer.

Moving quickly down the side of the house, I kept my phone sheltered from the driving rain with the folds of my dress as I used the flashlight to guide my way and to search the ground. If Ophelia and my mother were in the yard, we would have found them by now. The thought raised my anxiety even higher. *Calm down, calm down, calm down* became my litany, occupying my mind so I couldn't dwell on all the reasons why I wasn't.

I met up with Liam at the screened-in porch, and I shone my light into the space to be sure, finding only empty chairs and a dog-eared book lying facedown on the swing. After a similarly futile sweep of the empty backyard, the hope that they hadn't taken the boat into the water evaporated. As if he could read my mind, Liam took my elbow and began leading me down the slippery slope toward the dock.

While Liam moved toward the end of the dock, I stayed behind, training my eyes on the water, looking for the glint of reflection off the side of the aluminum jonboat and saw none. I moved the light to the other side, refusing to consider the alternative if I didn't see it in the water.

I turned toward the end of the dock, shining my light to avoid slipping off the edge as I followed the beam from Liam's iPhone. He was squatting over the supine figure of my mother lying on the dock while another figure knelt next to him. I recognized Addie huddled at our mother's feet, oblivious to the rain continuing its merciless assault and ran toward them.

"Mother!" I knelt by my mother's head, only vaguely aware of Liam's discarded shirt. I leaned over her face, trying to shield her from the rain, just like I remembered Liam doing when I was the one lying on this same dock. There was a sense of déjà vu, and something else, too: something that made me think I'd been here before.

"I think her leg is broken," Liam said. "I just tried to reach Will to have him call 9-1-1, but I can't get service anymore. I called the landline, but he isn't picking up. Can you run up to the house and make the call? I'm going to stabilize the leg with

an oar and my shirt and bring her up to meet the ambulance."
His eyes met mine. "And ask for a search-and-rescue team down
at the dock. Ophelia's missing. She's in the jonboat, but Addie
said there's no gas in the motor, and she only has one oar."

Bile rose in my throat. *What was Ophelia doing out on the water
at night?* She was safe in her room when I had left. I couldn't
imagine how scared she must be to be adrift during a storm in
the dark. Addie was supposed to have been at home watching
her. Fueled by anger and sick with worry, I ran up the grassy incline, slipping twice and crawling on my hands and knees until
I reached enough grass to hold on to. I let the back door slam
behind me, dripping water through the kitchen as I made my
way to the phone. Will stood next to it, staring at it as if it were
an alien creature.

"What are you doing?"

"I was trying to figure out how to answer it if anyone called."

I knew looking back I'd find this funny, but right now I
needed to get help. I picked up the receiver, beyond relieved to
hear the dial tone before punching in the three numbers and
explaining the emergency.

After briefly letting Will know what was going on and telling him to wait for the ambulance to direct them where to go,
I returned to the dock through the back door, nearly running
into Liam and Addie carrying my mother back toward the house.

"Is she going to be okay?"

Liam's eyes briefly met mine. "Her pulse is thready. I need to
monitor her until the ambulance gets here, but I'll send Addie
back to help find Ophelia."

Ignoring my sister, I ran toward the end of the now-empty
dock, shining my light out into the storm-tossed marsh, watching for any sign of the boat or Ophelia. I called her name, even
though I knew there was little chance of her hearing me over
the wind and the rain. But I had to do *something*.

Stuttering flashes lit the sky. I squatted down, making myself as small as possible and less of a target for the wild lightning. My scar burned as if it were on fire, reminding me that I should seek shelter. But Ophelia was out in the marsh all alone, and I couldn't leave her there. I waved my phone, hoping that it might guide her back. "Ophelia!" I continued to yell her name until my voice was hoarse, unwilling to give up.

I felt the percussion of running feet on the dock but didn't turn around. Addie stopped to stand next to me, and I grabbed her hand, pulling her down. Her hair bled down her face, the pale strands darkened by the rain, her face crumpled with anguish.

"Where the hell were you?" I screamed, unleashing all the fear and anxiety I'd felt since I first learned Ophelia was out in the boat.

"Don't, Phoebe. Please don't! She's my daughter."

"Then start acting like her mother!"

She drew back as if I'd struck her. "Why is she out there all alone?" I shouted.

"I don't know! Mother asked me to take her far out in the boat, and I told her to wait until tomorrow." She shook her head. "She must have asked Ophelia after I left. She tried to call me, but I had my phone turned off."

I wanted to shake her or throw her in the water. "You don't deserve her! If something happens to her, it will be all your fault!"

"Do you think I don't know that?"

We were both screaming at each other, wasting energy when we should have been focused on finding Ophelia.

I brought my face close to Addie's so she could hear me and pointed to the other front corner of the dock. "Go there and wave the flashlight on your phone in the opposite direction from me. Hopefully she'll see it, or you'll get a reflection from the boat. Do you understand?"

She meekly nodded and crawled toward her corner while I headed to the opposite side and began waving my phone. We continued calling out Ophelia's name, but it was like attempting to empty the ocean one teaspoon at a time. The howl of the wind and the rain overpowered the sound of our voices, but we kept calling.

Brilliant forks of lightning shot through the sky, and before I could say the first *Mississippi* the earth shook with thunder. The storm was directly on top of us now, the lightning touching an unlucky tree in the near distance with a loud explosion. Cold sweat prickled between my breasts, mixing with the rain.

"Look!" Addie screamed as she stood, pointing out into the darkened marsh not far from the hapless tree. "There—do you see it?" She held up her phone again and turned it to where she was pointing. I saw the unmistakable reflection off something that might have been metal. Or the aluminum side of a jonboat. On a good day, it would be an easy swim. But storm or not, I knew we couldn't wait for help. If the storm didn't capsize the boat, then the tide would pull her out into the open ocean.

Addie slid out of one of her sneakers. "I'm going to swim to her and pull her back."

I grabbed her arm. "Don't be stupid. I'm a much better swimmer."

"But I'm her mother!" she shouted, angrily swiping the relentless rain from her face.

"Then wait here where you can actually help. She'll need you to grab her from the boat."

I stripped out of my dress and handed her my phone. "Keep your flashlight on the boat so I know where I'm going." The sky flashed again, making me flinch. The incoming tide had flooded the marsh, the water now reaching the underside of the dock as the storm shoved waves over the top. But I wouldn't think about that now. *One thing at a time.* It was as if Aunt Sassy had spoken directly into my ear. "And keep your head down." Then, before I could talk myself out of it, I stepped off the dock and into the dark water.

The saltmarsh surrounding my home was as familiar to me as my own skin, yet it was a different place at night, a strange city with darkened corners hiding unseen dangers. I tried not to think about anything except reaching Ophelia as I let myself sink beneath the surface of the water to see how deep it was, allowing my toes to touch the sticky mud at the bottom. The water closed over my head, the storm barely a soft drumming in the odd quiet. I pushed off with my feet, my hand grasping onto a dock piling. I'd have to swim through the churning water knowing that the farther out I swam, the deeper the water would get. I wouldn't have a chance to stop and rest. With one last look at Addie, I took a deep breath and pushed off the dock with both feet, propelling myself toward the small square of light.

I had done little to no swimming in Oregon, but adrenaline forced the muscle memory in my arms and legs into action. I'd only reached the halfway point when my strength began to falter. I tried to float on my back to catch my breath, but the turbulence flipped me over, exhausting me further as I righted myself and began a slow crawl toward the boat and Ophelia.

Time and space ceased as I focused on a rhythm: *stroke, kick, kick, breathe.* After several repetitions, I'd allow myself to look and gauge how much closer I was, fighting the discouragement each time I realized I'd hardly made any progress at all.

Something skimmed the bare skin of my leg and I kicked hard at whatever it had been, wasting energy and throwing me slightly off course. I tried not to think of the black maw past the jonboat, of the vastness that was the open sea and all the dangers it contained.

I opened my mouth, desperate to fill my lungs with air, and instead inhaled saltwater as a wave washed over my head, swamping me and pushing me under. A sound echoed inside my head. Something familiar. A nightjar. I opened my eyes under the water, the salt stinging. I couldn't close them, trying to see the bird, knowing it had to be nearby. My feet touched bottom, and the nightjar screamed again. Except it was coming from the surface, and I was in the dream again and it was telling me something. Telling me to *pay attention.* To look at the object floating in the water just seconds before it descended into oblivion.

I allowed my feet to sink into the soft familiarity of the mud as my mind's eye followed the bird's direction and focused on the small object in the water. It drifted in slow motion, imprinting it into my memory. Except it was already there. Because I'd seen it too many times to forget.

The nightjar screamed again, or maybe it was my brain screaming for me to come up for air. Bending my knees, I pushed off the bottom. I shot up from the surface, almost crying with joy when I realized that the storm had pushed the boat closer and it was now only about ten yards away, close enough that I could hear Ophelia crying.

"Ophelia!" I screamed, choking on another mouthful of saltwater. I began sidestroking toward her as a chain of lightning electrified the sky and the marsh trembled with thunder. *Lightning never strikes twice* took over as my new chant, Aunt Sassy's voice in my ear with each stroke.

I bumped into the boat, making Ophelia scream. I met her terrified gaze as she peered over the side. I reached up with both hands and clung to the wide front edge of the boat, trying not to think about the metal I held on to or the science experiments I'd led in class using aluminum foil to showcase what an excellent conductor of electricity it was.

The waves tossed the shallow boat up and down, making it almost impossible to keep my grip. When the front dipped to its lowest point, I pulled myself up and over the front end, catching my knee on the metal cleat as I threw my leg over the edge.

I gave Ophelia a brief hug then began frantically looking around for the oar.

"Where's the oar?" I shouted. The words were barely out of my mouth before the boat reared up then slapped the water as it landed, splashing more water inside.

She pointed toward the churning water. "I dropped it!" she wailed.

"It's okay," I said, even though everything was far from okay. I looked back toward the dock where Addie remained with her phone light shining like a beacon in the dark.

I carefully crawled back to where I'd climbed in, found the cleat again, and reached for the dark rope tied around it.

Getting closer to Ophelia to make sure she could hear me, I shouted, "I'm going to get in the water and pull us back to the dock. If I get tired, I'll hold on to the rope, so don't get scared if we're not moving and you don't see me. Keep your eye on the light, okay? That's your mama, and she's waiting for you."

She nodded, her eyes wide with fear. "Do you want me to sing to you to keep you company?"

She looked so hopeful that I couldn't say no. "Sure, sweetie. That would be nice."

I then told her to get as low as she could, keeping her feet together as close as possible, and put her hands on her head. That's what you're supposed to do if you get caught outside in a field during a lightning storm. I had no idea if it would also work in an aluminum boat in the middle of the marsh. With dread pulling on my heels, I jumped back into the churning water, the saltwater stinging the gash in my knee and reminding me of the cut on my foot.

The sweet notes of Ophelia's singing cut through the storm, surrounding me as I began towing the boat, my fatigue making me rest more than I wanted to. I'm not sure how I managed to bring the boat back to the dock or how long it took. Maybe it was Ophelia's endless repetition of the verses to "Jesus Loves Me" that pushed me forward. Or the vision of the object in the water from my dream, and the growing understanding of what it meant. And what I needed to do.

I almost cried when we reached a place where my feet could touch the bottom, giving me a burst of adrenaline I didn't know I possessed as I pressed my toes into the sticky mud and bounced up with renewed energy. When we reached the dock, I threw the rope to Addie, who tied it around a cleat before reaching for Ophelia.

Red flashing lit the yard as I swam my way down the length of the dock to the place where the water met earth and climbed up the bank just as Liam rounded the side of the house. I stepped up onto the dock as static electricity plucked at the hair on my arms, standing it on end. The air seemed to pulsate, and I turned toward Addie and Ophelia in horror.

Addie began running toward me and I shouted "Get down!" just as a bolt of lightning reached down from the sky and touched the giant cedar tree at the edge of the dock, and the world exploded into a million pieces of light.

# 26

~

"If a hurricane happens during migrations, some birds
will take a detour to avoid the storm. Others will use the
prevailing tailwinds for a boost. Others will become trapped
in the storm, some in the eye of the hurricane, unable to
escape. The ones who survive can be blown miles off course
and end up in unlikely places where they will need to learn
to adapt. We all experience storms in our lives, despite
our best efforts to take a detour. Landfall can sometimes
find us in a new and unexpected place, and sometimes to
our surprise it's the place we were always meant to be."

**Excerpt from the blog *The Thing with Feathers***

## Celeste

A LOUD CRACK of thunder awakened me. I sat up and fumbled for my glasses before looking at my alarm clock. Eight minutes after three o'clock. No light came from outside, telling me that the power had gone out. Fortunately, it wasn't anything I needed to worry about. Liam had added a backup generator that would automatically switch on at a power interruption, something that happened frequently in coastal South Carolina. Liam had yet to add one to his own house, which surprised everyone except me. The house he currently lived in was the house he'd shared with his ex-wife. It was temporary, like his marriage had been, and not something he wanted to sink any more money into, only hanging on to it because it was the house Will knew.

I thought about checking on Will, just as I'd done when he was little and afraid of storms, then remembered that he'd stayed at Ophelia's. I left Annie sleeping in her bed and went into the kitchen to make myself a cup of tea. As I waited for the kettle to boil, I stood at the window and glanced out into the yard, picturing the birds sheltering from the wind and rain. I thought of the phoebe bird that perched on my windowsill each morning, waiting for me to open my curtains and greet her. Will insisted that it was just coincidence that the bird would wait to fly off until I'd appeared at the window. But he was wrong. Birds were much smarter than most people thought and a lot smarter than many humans I'd met.

Knowing I'd never get back to sleep, I took the cup up to Julie's room. It was located at the front of the house and had a large double window, which was why I sometimes brought small projects up here to work on. Presently I was attempting to repair the albums that Elizabeth had damaged and add blank pages so she and I could add more of the loose photos to the existing album.

My plan had been to bring them back in the morning before Elizabeth might notice. Despite her memory lapses, her mind was still sharp enough to detect when things were out of place or didn't look right. Like when she observed that Phoebe was wearing Addie's necklace and made her take it off.

After turning on the small television to the Weather Channel, I sat down at the desk and pulled a handful of photos from a baggie. These were more pictures of Addie and Phoebe as schoolgirls and had already been sorted by Phoebe with names and dates on the reverse side. I opened a box of adhesive squares and got to work, soon losing myself in the sound of the rhythm of the rain hitting the window glass.

It took almost an hour to finish filling up three pages, front and back. Drawing the family album toward me, I flipped it over to insert the new pages. I opened the back cover and paused. A concert program had been placed between the last page and the cover, as if an afterthought.

I ran my finger over the front, recognizing it. It was from the last holiday program Julie had sung with the choir her senior year. The last concert before she disappeared. Somewhere in Julie's box of mementos there was an identical program. Except this one had Addie's name written across the top. *Adeline Waring Manigault.* Each capital letter was elaborately drawn with loops and swirls as if she'd been practicing calligraphy. There was something about the *A* that drew my attention. Something that made it seem familiar.

I stood and turned on the overhead light to see better, holding the program up near the window where the growing light of day had begun to touch the glass. I stared at it until I remembered where I'd seen it.

I opened the closet door and peered up at the box Liam had brought down for me before. I should wait and call him to get it down again. But I couldn't. I had to know. I dragged the desk chair over to the closet and very carefully climbed onto the seat. I knew better than to try and lift the box off the shelf so instead I nudged it little by little with my fingertips. When it had cleared about four inches or so, I leaned away from it and nudged it just a bit farther so that it toppled over, landing upside down on the floor.

Lowering myself to sit next to it, I righted the box and unfolded the top. I dug through the layer of mementos before I reached what I was looking for. The sheet music for *Jubilate Deo* was there, with Julie's name written on top with purple glitter. I opened the music and saw the cryptic words written between Julie and someone else whose name started with the letter *V.* Except it wasn't a *V.* I turned the music upside down. It was a decorative capital *A*, just like the *A* in *Adeline* written on the program.

I continued to sit on the floor, listening as the rain and wind softened their assault on the roof and windows and dawn lit the sky. My head spun with possibilities and a growing fear I could not name.

I was still sitting on the floor when the phone rang downstairs. The ringing stopped and then started again as I made my way down the steps, taking longer than usual because my legs were shaking. I finally reached the phone when it began ringing for the third time. It was Liam. And even as he told me to stay home because the roads were wet and littered with debris, I knew I had to go to the hospital. I needed to speak to Addie, to ask her why she'd lied about her and Julie just being acquaintances. And I knew it was a lie. I had proof in the handwritten notes from two young girls on the edges of a piece of choral music. Addie begging a reluctant Julie for a ride because Addie had wrecked her own car and wanted to get somewhere. Somewhere Julie didn't want to go. Julie and her car had disappeared at the same time, leading me to thoughts about what might have happened that I didn't want to contemplate.

I shut my eyes, trying not to see what my mind insisted on showing me. But there, behind my lids, was Addie's disturbed painting of Phoebe's dream with the small object in the water that I hadn't recognized. Until now.

I drove slowly, my limbs still shaky, my head filled with rotating images of Julie as a child and teenager, along with ones of her as a young woman as I had imagined her to be as she grew older. But she'd never been given the chance. Despite telling Liam that there would always be a glimmer of hope that Julie was still alive, I had always known this wasn't the truth. I just hadn't had the courage to face it because it hurt too much. That's the thing with lying to yourself. It's a temporary bandage that becomes harder to remove the longer you wait, until you reach the point where you'd rather live with a lie than face the inevitable.

As I drove to the hospital, avoiding palmetto fronds and tree limbs scattered on the road, I still tried to tell myself that I was wrong. That just because Addie had lied didn't mean anything. Except for those cryptic notes between Julie and Addie that hinted of Addie coercing Julie to go somewhere with her. Even that wouldn't have meant anything if Addie hadn't said they weren't more than just acquaintances. There had to be a reason for her to lie, and since Julie was missing, the reason had to be very important.

My anger made my hands shake on the steering wheel. Anger at Addie, but mostly anger at myself for deliberately looking the other way despite all the signs that Addie knew something about Julie's disappearance. Her unexplained antagonism toward Liam and me should have been the first sign that I should look more closely. We both knew about Phoebe's premonitions and how people in close proximity to her were the usual subjects. She must have been terrified that Phoebe would have a dream about Julie and expose Addie's connection if Phoebe spent enough time with either me or Liam.

But Phoebe did have a dream about Julie, except she didn't know it. And she must have told her sister because Addie had painted it. I remember the unsettled feeling I'd had when I'd looked at the painting, seeing the angry strokes and the haunting quality of the marsh at night. I wondered if I'd known then its connection to my missing granddaughter and if I'd simply become so accustomed to lying to myself that I ignored my heart and head telling me to look closer.

There were so many pieces to this puzzle. And there, slotted somewhere near the middle, was Elizabeth. There was no doubt that Elizabeth loved her daughters. She loved them enough to protect them any way she could. And in that, I wouldn't judge her. Because I knew that if the tables were turned, I would do the same. There is no fiercer love than that of a mother. There is also nothing more blind.

Whatever Addie's secret, her mother knew. And so had her father. I recalled how Elizabeth had gone to the cemetery to visit Charles because, as Phoebe had told me, she'd said that there needed to be a reckoning. She'd taken Addie's necklace to the cemetery for a reason. And when Phoebe and Liam had brought Elizabeth back to the house, she'd pointed to Addie's empty neck and told her that her father wanted her to wear it. What did that mean? *Why was the necklace so important?*

I closed my eyes as anger and hatred exploded inside of me. A car honked, shaking me out of my stupor and forcing me to pull to the side of the road. I couldn't let those emotions consume me. Charles Manigault was dead, no doubt facing the consequences of his actions in the next life. If there was ever a reason to believe in heaven and hell, he alone would be reason enough.

I rested my head against the steering wheel, breathing deeply. If I had a heart attack now, Charles Manigault would have another win on his side, and I was not willing to give him one more victory over me and my family.

After putting on my turn signal, I eased back out onto the highway, my thoughts on Elizabeth and my certainty that whatever Addie had done Elizabeth knew. She clung to her memories with an admirable tenacity. I had no doubt that Charles was behind any decision to remain silent, just as much as I knew Elizabeth wouldn't have gone against her husband. But now that she was losing her memory, she craved atonement before it was too late.

I thought about the damage Elizabeth had done to Addie's yearbook photo, obliterating the pearl charm necklace. And why she'd brought the replacement necklace to the cemetery. It was important, somehow. Important enough that Phoebe had dreamed about it. And Addie had put it in her painting. I realized now that the object I'd seen glittering in the painting was undoubtedly the necklace. It held the key to unlocking the past. I just couldn't quite figure out how.

There were plenty of available parking spots, and I took up two spaces because I couldn't manage otherwise. I made my way up to the hospital entrance, my head down to avoid the glare of the sun. It was time for an overdue reckoning.

# 27

~

"When a crow dies, other crows will raise an alarm call to alert the other members of the murder—the name for a congregation of crows. The group then observes the corpse, eventually breaking into intense cawing, as if in grieving. It's remarkably human. I hate to see a dead bird, but there is something especially ominous about seeing a dead crow. They're seen as messengers announcing the coming of a new era in one's life. I suppose if a crow had to die, I wouldn't mind seeing it, if only to reassure myself that I was on the right path."

**Excerpt from the blog *The Thing with Feathers***

# Phoebe

AS I LAY in the back of the ambulance, I kept insisting that I was fine and that I didn't need the sedatives they were intent on administering. I was alone except for the EMTs. I'd heard Liam saying he was going in the ambulance with my mother, but my memory kept clouding over, obscuring my vision. I wanted to ask where Ophelia and Addie were, but I couldn't get the words to form.

The last thing I remembered for sure was standing beneath the cedar tree and shouting for Addie and Ophelia to get down. I vaguely remembered Ophelia squatting down with her hands over her ears, but Addie . . . I winced as something cold and stinging was poured over my knee. I needed to remember. There was something about Addie I needed to remember. Something important.

And there it was. Addie. Running toward me, her hands colliding with my chest as she shoved me onto the dock just as the tree exploded with fire.

My head hurt from where I must have hit it when I fell, and my knee and foot stung, the pain made worse by whatever the EMT was doing. I wanted him to stop, but the dark curtain of oblivion had already begun to close. I opened my mouth to scream, needing to tell them not to let me fall asleep, but it was too late.

I heard the nightjar first, telling me I was back in the dream. I stood on the bridge watching the car approach. It was heading right at me, but I didn't step back. I was transfixed by the two occupants of the front seat. My emotions cycled between relief and horror when I realized that I wasn't one of them. But my sister was.

Addie sat in the driver's seat, and I could hear her singing. I even recognized the song, "Before He Cheats." She'd played it nonstop her senior year. Before she'd stopped listening to music at all.

I stared at the passenger, recognizing her even though I'd only seen her photograph. That's how I knew that the girl in the passenger seat was Julie Fitch. They were both singing, neither one paying attention to the sign on the side of the bridge. I could read it now: *Slippery When Wet*. Mardi Gras beads hanging over the rearview mirror shimmied side to side as the car moved forward.

I tried to hold up my hand, to get Addie to stop, to reverse this story before it reached a foregone conclusion. But I was paralyzed, unable to wave my hands or do anything that might change the outcome. The logo on the hood stood out as the car made its slow progress toward me. It wasn't Addie's Volkswagen. It was light blue, not the lime green of Addie's car, and for a brief moment I allowed myself to feel relief that this dream wasn't about Addie at all.

But it was. She was in the driver's seat as the car veered, hitting one side of the bridge before swerving across both lanes. The singing stopped as the car hit the opposite side, breaking through damaged wooden slats. Leaving the road and plunging into the dark water below.

The acrid scent of exhaust fumes filled the air. Skid marks on the empty bridge curved toward the edge, ending abruptly. I peered over the side of the bridge, seeing only a small funnel of water. Right there, in the spot the nightjar had been showing me over and over, was something I recognized. Something that filled me with horror and sadness and grief. And I finally understood why my mind had blocked the image for so long.

Addie's head emerged from the water beneath the bridge, then disappeared as she dove under again and again before finally stopping. She half crawled, half swam to the edge of the water. Her agonizing moan echoed in the quiet of the marsh, and in my head as she collapsed into the pluff mud. I watched as she eventually stood, gave one final look at the spot where the car had disappeared, then headed back in the same direction from where they'd come.

I opened my eyes to bright fluorescent hospital lights and the sound of Liam's voice saying my name. I turned my head and found him sitting in a chair next to my bed, and I smiled. But then the dream came back like an angry ghost reminding me of who Liam was and why I shouldn't be smiling.

I started to sit up, desperate to find my sister. To have her tell me to my face that my dream wasn't real. That she'd never been in a car with Julie Fitch.

"Whoa, slow down." Liam placed his hands on my shoulders and eased me back against my pillow. "What do you need?"

I glanced behind him to the door, unable to look in his eyes. They were too much like his sister's.

"Where's . . . ?" I couldn't settle on just one name. They were all precious to me.

"Ophelia is fine. She's in the waiting room with my grand-mother and Will." He paused. "Addie suffered a cardiac arrest from the lightning strike. It's too early to tell if there will be any permanent neurological damage, but the doctors are hopeful. She's young."

I thought of my beautiful sister and failed to reconcile the version I knew with the one from my dream. "She saved my life."

"I know. I watched it happen. And you saved Ophelia. You're both heroes."

He was only saying that because he didn't know the truth. "And my mother?"

"Her leg is broken, right below the knee. It's a clean break, which is good. She'll need rehab, but I can help you find the best facility for her." He took my hand, and his warmth spread through me. "I've never been so scared in my life. I thought . . ." His voice broke, unable to finish.

I wanted to tell him that I'd seen him running toward me and that I knew that with him there I would survive. That he was the reason I wanted to survive. But I couldn't. I pulled my hand away, knowing I had no right to his comfort. Then I turned my head and closed my eyes.

He stayed there for a long time before leaving, his footsteps slow as he headed out the door. I waited until I was sure he was gone before I allowed myself to cry. Eventually, a nurse came in to check my vitals. She announced that I was good to go but that I needed to wait for the doctor to make his rounds and sign off on my release paperwork.

I stared at the ceiling as I waited, my mind flipping through scenes from the last twenty-four hours like an old silent-film reel. I mentally sorted through each frame, rewinding and for-warding just in case I missed anything. Liam, Celeste, Addie, Ophelia, my mother. Julie.

A low-pitched *tu-a-wee* from the window made me turn my head. A bluebird stood on the sill looking at me as if waiting for me to make a decision. I couldn't see a bluebird without thinking about Aunt Sassy and the wisdom she had poured into me in the short time we'd had together. I closed my eyes, listening to the cheerful chirps, and tried to remember what my aunt had told me about the significance of seeing a bluebird.

She had been dying at the time, her hospice nurse telling us that she didn't have much longer. Aunt Sassy remained cheerful, doing her best to help me cope. *Even during harsh winters when food is scarce, bluebirds will continue to cheerfully sing because they know better days are ahead. They remind us to never lose faith, even in our darkest hours, and to hold on to our belief that in the end everything will be all right.*

When I opened my eyes, the bird had gone, but its brief appearance had left me with the strength and knowledge I would need to decide what path I'd take when I left the hospital. I allowed my eyes to close again, and when I fell asleep, I didn't dream at all.

Ophelia sat beside the bed when I awoke an hour later. Someone had tried to tame her hair into a ponytail, and she wore an oversize Clemson sweatshirt that had to have been borrowed. Her eyes were red from crying, but she smiled when she saw me open my eyes. "Aunt Phoebe!" she whispered loudly.

I smiled back. "Hey, Ophelia. Why are you whispering?"

"Because Miss Celeste told me to stay in the waiting room while she went to get us something to eat." As if anticipating my next questions, she said, "Dr. Fitch left to take Will to a friend's house but said he'd be back soon. They were going to stop at our house first so Will could pick up his book."

"Yay, you. You might have converted a new reader."

She nodded, her smile fading.

"Are you okay?"

She shrugged. "I guess."

"Oh, Ophelia. I'm so sorry. You've been through a lot. But I think we're all going to be okay."

"No, we won't. You're leaving, and Mama and Mimi are both sick, and nobody will be here to take care of me."

I shook my head. "I couldn't do that to you or anyone else. And I'll stick around and help Mimi and your mama get better, all right? I'll be here to take care of you, too, so you don't have to worry."

"I'm glad," she said. "I've been praying that you would stay here longer, but . . ."

I opened my hand, and she put hers in it, the once-bright fingernail polish now chipped and dull. "Hey. None of this is your fault. Do you understand? None of it."

After a moment, she nodded. "I have something for you, but I think it's supposed to be a secret." She showed me her other hand, the fingers closed over her palm, and placed it in her lap.

"Does it have something to do with what happened last night?"

She nodded once. "Mimi wanted to take the boat into the water, so Will dragged it out to the dock for her. He called his daddy to ask if it was okay and he said no, so we told Mimi it would have to wait until the next day."

"What did Mimi do then?" I kept my voice calm, trying to keep out any conjecture or accusation in my tone.

"Will and I brought her back to her room. Will fell asleep, but I couldn't because Mama had left, and somebody needed to make sure that Mimi was okay."

I squeezed her hand. "Thank you for doing that." I wanted to add that it wasn't her job, that Addie was supposed to have been in charge and to put the responsibility on a nine-year-old was the worst kind of neglect. "And then what happened?"

"I heard Mimi go downstairs, so I got up and followed her. She went down to the dock and tried to get the boat in the water, but she couldn't. I told her that we needed to wait until the morning, but she yelled something awful at me." Her face crumpled, and I squeezed her hand.

"I'm so sorry. But you need to know that Mimi loves you so much, and the real Mimi would never yell at you or say anything mean. She's sick, and it's the disease saying those things. But deep, deep down, where the real Mimi is, she loves you and would never say or do anything to hurt you." My own voice cracked, surprising me. How long had I known that to be true? Maybe I hadn't until just now, while trying to explain dementia to a nine-year-old.

Ophelia nodded as she tightened her left hand, still closed into a fist.

"And then what happened?" I gently prompted.

"She yelled at me to help her, so I did. And then I got inside the boat so I could help her get in, but that's when she slipped and fell. I saw her throw something in the water. I'd seen her holding it before, so I knew what it was. Mama would be mad if she found out what Mimi had done, so I jumped in to get it before it sank too far. By the time I came up for air, the boat had drifted away, so I swam after it to bring it back." She shook her head as fat tears rolled down her cheeks. "I climbed inside, but when I tried to row back, I only had the one oar, and I accidentally dropped it in the water." She began crying in earnest now, and I kept squeezing her hand to let her know that everything was okay.

I struggled to sit up, cursing the IV line. I untaped it and slid the needle out, impervious to the pain, then reached over and hugged her. "Ophelia, you're a great kid. You're smart, and kind and compassionate, and you love your grandmother. When she asked you to do something, even though you didn't know why, you did it. Everything that happened afterward wasn't your fault. None of it, okay?"

She nodded once, just enough to let me know that she'd heard me, then continued crying.

I waited for Ophelia's sobs to subside while I carefully considered my next words, though I realized that no matter how I asked it, the answer would be just as devastating.

"You were very brave, Ophelia. You did what you thought was right, and nobody can blame you for that." I let go of her hand and cupped her sweet face, using my thumb to wipe away her tears just like my mother had done for me years ago when I'd allow her to see me cry. "What did Mimi throw in the water?"

She opened the fingers of her hand one finger at a time. In her palm lay Addie's necklace with the black pearl. The almost-identical replacement necklace for the one she'd lost. Almost. The one in my dream, the small object floating briefly on the surface of the water, had the small diamond perched on top, its reflection of the ambient light winking at me. Addie had been wearing it the night she drove Julie Fitch somewhere in Julie's car. She'd lost the necklace in the accident, and it had sunk to the creek bottom where it would never be found. And its absence wouldn't be noticed because our parents had bought her another one to wear instead.

I took it from her, allowing my fingers to close over it. "Thank you, Ophelia. I'll give this to your mama when she wakes up."

"You're not mad at me?"

I hugged her again. "Never. I promise to never be mad at you."

She pulled away to look me in the eye. "Really?"

"Okay. Maybe not never. How about never without explaining why I'm angry, and then working it out together? How does that sound?"

She lay her head on my shoulder, and I kissed her hair, which still smelled like saltwater. And then I remembered something Aunt Sassy used to say to me. "It's you and me, kid. We're in this together for the long haul. Got it?"

Ophelia nodded. "Got it."

After Ophelia returned to the waiting room, I changed into a pair of clean scrubs that had been left on a chair in my room then went to find my sister. When I located her room, Addie was alone with the sound of the beeping monitors. Her face was blanched of color, and she seemed smaller, almost childlike, as if she were disappearing into the hospital bed. A large bouquet of red roses sat on the bedside table. The small card that had been delivered with it sat faceup next to the vase. *Get better soon. Love, Dale.* I wondered how much he knew. Or what he would do when Addie told him the whole story. A rush of sympathy for my sister surprised me. I found myself hoping that Dale truly did love her and would stay by her side for what would come, whatever that might be. She'd need more than one ally.

Her eyes were open, and she watched me as I sat down next to her bed. "How are you feeling?" I asked.

Her voice was slow and deep. "Like I was hit by a train. You?"

"I'm fine. They're letting me go home today, so I'll be there for Ophelia."

"Thank you." Her voice was barely louder than a whisper.

"I should be thanking you. You saved my life."

She shrugged her narrow shoulders. "What are sisters for?"

I reached for her hand and placed the necklace in her palm. She didn't have to look at it to know what it was.

"Mother was trying to throw this in the marsh," I said. "That's why she and Ophelia were out on the dock."

Addie closed her eyes. I watched her throat move as she swallowed. "I need to tell you about Julie Fitch."

"I already know, Addie. Maybe not all the little details, but I know that she's dead and that you were driving when her car went off a bridge with her in the passenger seat."

Tears leaked out of the corner of her eye, creating a dark stain on her pillowcase. "I wanted to go to a party in Awendaw, but I didn't have a car because I'd wrecked mine, and all my friends had already left." Her voice sounded weak, and I wanted to tell her that it could wait, that I knew enough to put the story together. I also understood that she needed to tell me. Not for exoneration but to free herself of the burden of carrying the secret. She'd once shared it with our mother but had unexpectedly found herself struggling to bear it alone. "Julie and I had stayed late after choir practice to work on our parts, so when I saw her in the parking lot, I convinced her to go to the party. I'd been asking her all week, and she'd kept saying no, but . . ." Her eyes closed briefly. "I finally wore her down. Except it had started to rain, and she said she didn't like to drive at night when it was raining, so I told her that I would." She shook her head as tears fell down her face. "I didn't mean for her to get hurt. And I tried to save her. I did. But I couldn't get her out of the car."

"I know."

She didn't seem surprised. "You saw it in a dream, didn't you?"

I nodded.

"I've been wanting to tell you for so long, but I'm such a coward. I was always afraid you'd dream about it, especially after Celeste and Liam became involved in your life." She paused to take a breath, as if the memories were pressing all the air from her chest. "I wanted to go to the police right after it happened, but Daddy said no. Nobody saw Julie leave with me, and he said it was best just to let her family think she'd run away, and I could forget it ever happened. But that wasn't true. I should have known. I should have told him no."

"You were eighteen years old, Addie, and we'd been conditioned to never say no to Daddy. He was a bully to all of us, including Mother. Mother just wanted to protect us."

More tears slid down her face. "What am I going to do now?"

Even though Addie was the older sister, she'd always looked to me for direction. Birth order had little to do with the parceling out of talents. I'd always been able to look at a problem and find its weakest point to know where to attack it. That was the one good thing I'd inherited from our father.

"You need to tell Celeste. She has to know where to find her granddaughter so she can bury her and finally have closure."

"I don't think I can do that."

"Yes, you can. You have to."

Her eyes didn't leave my face. "I'm in a lot of trouble, aren't I?"

I considered lying, but there had already been too many lies. "Even if you didn't mean to cause harm, your actions led to the death of another person. And then you hid the fact so that a family was kept in the dark for decades. It might help your case if you tell your side of the story to the authorities as soon as possible."

"Will you be there with me?"

"Of course."

She pressed her lips together and gave me a brief nod. "So what do I do now?"

"First, I'm going to talk with Dale. I'm sure he knows a good defense attorney. Then we'll go to the police, and you can tell them the whole story."

She stared at me with wide eyes. "We?"

"Yes, Addie. *We.* No matter what. We're sisters, and I'll always be here for you. And for Mother and Ophelia." Saying it out loud made it seem more real. A passing shadow of grief for the life I'd be leaving behind flitted through me. But there was also an unexpected hopefulness for the life I hadn't planned but was still ripe with possibilities.

"Thank you," she whispered, her voice hoarse.

My gaze drifted to her arm lying on top of the bedsheets. Beneath the fresh scratches and abrasions from the previous night, a fading bruise glared from the crook of her elbow. Her eyes met mine when I lifted my head. "That's why you thought Dale was too good for you, isn't it? Because of what you'd done."

Fresh tears filled her eyes before she turned away.

"For the record," I said, "if I ever see that Joe creep, I'm going to kick him where it counts. You didn't deserve any of what he did to you, no matter what you might have thought. You are way too good for the likes of him."

She faced me again, her expression hopeful. "You really believe that?"

"Really." Addie closed her eyes, and I stood to leave. "Try to get some rest now." I bent to kiss her forehead. "I love you," I said.

"Me, too." Her words were mumbled, and despite everything they made me smile. Since we were little, she'd always insisted on having the last word.

When I turned to leave, Dale was waiting in the doorway. "How much of that did you hear?" I asked.

"Enough."

"I hope the fact that you haven't run away is a good sign."

"Meaning will I help Addie through this? Absolutely." He shrugged. "I don't really have a choice. I love her, Phoebe. I think I always have."

Some of the tightness in the pit of my stomach loosened. "Thank you." I reached up and surprised him by hugging him.

He returned the hug then headed into Addie's room.

I spotted Celeste in the hallway. I started to speak, but she shook her head. "You can give me the details later, but I figured out most of it on my drive over. It was Addie's painting that told me most of the story."

"And you're still speaking to me?"

"Oh, Phoebe. Do you really think so little of me? You had nothing to do with it. But I'd be lying if I denied that in my heart I'm struggling with exonerating you completely. Guilt by association, I suppose. It's going to take some time."

"I get it," I said, feeling an immense wave of relief. My friendship with Celeste had come to mean a great deal to me, and her departure from my life would have been almost like another death. "I know that anything I say won't really help, but I'm so sorry. About Julie. I really was hoping that one day . . ." I couldn't finish.

"Me, too. But now we know."

I glanced toward Addie's room where I could see Dale sitting by her bed, her hand in his. Drawing a deep breath, I said, "I think my mother knew. All of it."

"I think she did, too."

I studied Celeste's face, trying to read her expression. "Then why aren't you angry? After all we've done to your family?"

A soft smile settled on her face. "I am angry. But most of all I'm sad. Sad for Julie and for the life she wasn't allowed to live and the children she wasn't allowed to have. I'm working on pushing that anger aside. I've discovered in my seventy-five years that feeding anger only robs me of peace. I'd rather spend my last years without looking back at what might have been and instead enjoy what I have in the present. I can grieve for Julie now, and for that I'm grateful. And I'm choosing to replace my anger with compassion. It's just something else that's going to take time."

"Of course," I said. "Just know that I'll be waiting for you with open arms when you're ready."

She surprised me by hugging me, and I hugged her back. Pulling away, I said, "How can you be so strong?"

"I learned the same way you did. We become strong when the only other choice is to quit. And you and I are not quitters."

I stepped back. "I need to ask you for one more favor. Can you wait until Addie is strong enough to talk to the police? It will go better for her if she's the one who approaches them first."

Celeste hesitated for a moment. "I'll do it for you. Because you're my friend, and you didn't ask for any of this, either."

"Thank you." I forced the next words out of my mouth. "Does Liam know?"

She nodded. "I couldn't keep him in the dark, Phoebe. I'm sure you understand."

"You both must think I'm so stupid. How did I not realize that the dream I've been having all these years was about your missing granddaughter? I'd seen her die at least a hundred times, and I never stopped to think it might be Julie."

"You're not stupid, Phoebe. Our minds will only allow us to see what it thinks we can handle. You weren't ready. Neither was I. There were so many clues once I got to know Addie, and my mind also let me keep blinders on. I think it's called self-preservation."

"Thanks for saying that. Although, I won't blame Liam for disagreeing with you." I exhaled, suddenly aware of how exhausted I was. "I need to get back to my room so they can discharge me."

Celeste nodded. "And don't worry about Ophelia. She's in the waiting room, and I'll keep her with me as long as you need."

I smiled my thanks then headed down the hall to the nurses' station, feeling her watching me. It would be a while before the doctor would come to my room, so I decided to go find my mother.

I'd been warned that she'd been given pain medication and would be sleeping, but I wanted to see her. Whether or not she could hear me, I needed to talk to her.

Like Addie, her face was devoid of color, and I made a mental note to bring lipstick when I returned in the morning. Even if she wouldn't know or care, I would. I pulled up a chair next to her bed and sat in silence for a while, listening to the bustle of the hospital from the hallway and the steady beeping of her monitors.

Despite what I'd prepared myself to see, my mother appeared even frailer than my worst imaginings. Maybe because the image of her that I carried with me was of the indomitable woman who'd raised my sister and me while keeping the peace with our father. Until now, I hadn't realized how much she'd protected us from his influence. She might not have been able to stop him from hiding Addie's complicity in Julie's death, but I couldn't help but wonder if it had been her who'd convinced him to drop the lawsuit against a young Liam. She kept her victories private, but that didn't make them any less meaningful.

I took her limp hand in mine, remembering these same hands holding mine before crossing a street or pressed against my chest when she braked the car even though I wore a seat belt. An overwhelming sense of absence spread through me like a choking vine. Maybe this was the destiny of all adult children, to mourn for the end of our childhoods when faced with the fragilities of our aging parents.

"Hello, Mother. It's me. Phoebe." I stared down at our clasped hands, almost expecting her to squeeze my fingers in response.

"I don't know if you can hear me, but I don't think it matters. I just need to say a few things." I'd already decided that I wasn't going to mention Julie or Addie. Whatever Addie's story would be, I would make sure that our mother wasn't part of it. She'd done what she did to protect her daughter. And she'd been punishing herself for years.

"I'm sorry for not seeing you as a person for all those years growing up. Maybe children aren't supposed to, but I was so busy trying to force you into the mold I wanted that I don't think it would have mattered. I hope you can forgive me. And I forgive you for letting me see your disappointment that I wasn't the daughter you wanted me to be. I can see now that you just wanted to make my life easier. But you gave me Aunt Sassy to fill the gap between our expectations. So thank you."

I used the hem of my shirt to wipe my eyes. "I think you didn't know how to mother a child like me, and I didn't know how to be your daughter. We should have stopped trying so hard and just let things work themselves out. But we're both so hardheaded. I guess I got that from you. It's not a bad quality, you know. So I guess I should thank you for that, too."

I cleared my throat. "I do love you, Mother. Even though at times I found it hard to show you. But you also sometimes made it hard for me to love you. That never meant I didn't."

I gently placed her hand on the bed then stood. "I don't want you to worry about anything, okay? I'm going to take care of you and Addie and Ophelia. Just don't expect perfection. I'm sure I'll make mistakes along the way, but that just means I'm trying. We'll get through this. All of us." Leaning over her, I kissed her forehead and left the room, feeling the cold hospital floor on my bare feet.

# 28

~

"A bird sitting on a tree is never afraid of the branch breaking,
because her trust is not on the branch but on her own wings."

**—Anonymous**

"I had an aunt whose wisdom surpassed her inability to hear
or speak. She shared this quote with me a long time ago, and
I have referred to it again and again over the years when
I needed guidance. My aunt also imparted to me her love
of birds and taught me how avian behavior can guide us
on our own journeys, especially during those times when we
feel lost and need help to point us onto the correct path."

**Excerpt from the blog *The Thing with Feathers***

## *Phoebe*

IT ALWAYS SEEMED that the most beautiful days in the Lowcountry were those following the worst storms. As soon as Ophelia
and I returned from the hospital, we went out to the backyard
to survey the damage, only to find the blackened tree and shards
of wood made eerily picturesque by a spectacular sunset of deep
purple and magenta.

"The poor tree," Ophelia said.

I leaned down to pick up a large chunk of bark. "Yes. The
poor tree. We'll plant another, I think. Maybe two. It did a beautiful job of giving us shade, didn't it?"

Ophelia nodded. "Mimi said it was her favorite."

"Well, then. We definitely need to plant two more."

She smiled up at me. "Can we have pizza for dinner?" she
asked hopefully. "And have Will come over?"

I felt a sharp stab somewhere near my heart. "I'm sure Will's
father has other plans, but I'll be happy to get pizza. I just need

to shower and wash my hair first, and I think you should do the same."

"I don't—"

I gave her a look that would have made my mother proud.

"Okay. But I don't have to dry it, right? I can just put it in a ponytail."

"As long as it's clean, you can do whatever you like."

"I'll be fast," she said, sprinting up the steps to the back porch.

Before following her up to the house, I made my way down to the dock, stepping around the muddy footprints of the first responders and the sooty boards that were closest to the tree. I felt compelled to walk to the end of the dock, as if to reassure myself that we had all managed to survive. The boat was gone, no doubt floating out to sea. Which was for the best as I had no intention of ever getting in one again. Or at least for a while. My life to this point had been full of *nevers*. But I was beginning to learn that life wasn't a zero-sum game. Things changed. People changed. I had changed. If I'd been asked only two days before if I would remain in South Carolina to take care of my mother, sister, and niece I would have said *Never.*

I sat down cross-legged, touching the bluebird pendant that had managed to remain around my neck, and listened to the melodic warble of an invisible marsh wren. These birds were more often heard than seen, nature's camouflage helping their feathers blend in to the swaths of needlerush. It made me think of Julie, shy and quiet according to her grandmother, but whose timidness disappeared when she sang. It was a poignant way to remember someone, her existence made even more memorable because of it. I would never hear a marsh wren again without thinking of Julie and her voice, but not the circumstances that had silenced it forever. Or my sister's part in it.

There was no doubt that Addie was in a lot of trouble. An innocent girl had died, and Addie had hidden the truth for almost two decades. Her second mistake had been to confide in our father. That one miscalculation had compounded the first, and it had haunted my sister through her young adult years, compelling her to punish herself again and again, thinking it was too late to admit to the crime. The time of reckoning had come, and I knew that despite what it might mean, Addie's relief was a palpable thing.

Footfalls sounded on the dock behind me, too heavy to be Ophelia's. I was surprised when Liam sat down next to me.

I didn't look at him when I spoke. "I didn't expect to see you. Celeste said that she told you what Addie did and what happened to Julie."

"She did."

"If this is about my mother and you remaining as her doctor—"

"Phoebe."

I stopped talking.

"Did you really think that I wouldn't want to see you again?"

"I wouldn't have blamed you. My family has done awful things to yours."

He gently touched my chin and turned my face toward him. "They have. And there's a lot I've got to work through. But that doesn't mean I never want to see you again. It wasn't your fault."

"Just because I was oblivious doesn't exonerate me. You have every reason to hate me."

He stroked my cheek with the backs of his fingers. "I could never hate you, Phoebe. I wish I could. Because then saying goodbye would be a whole lot easier."

I looked away, unsure of what I'd see in his face. "About that. I heard there were schools here with teachers, so . . ."

"Yeah?"

I turned to look into his eyes that matched the color of the marsh, and I wondered if I'd loved him since the first time I'd seen them all those years ago. "I've decided to stay here. Addie needs me. And so does Mother and Ophelia. It scares the crap out of me, but your grandmother is under the impression that I'm strong and can figure it out."

"For the record, my grandmother is never wrong."

"Yes, well, we'll see. But I'm not just doing it for them, either. I want to come back. I've missed all of this." I waved my arm to encompass the marsh and the ocean and all the teeming life in this watery world I'd been lucky enough to be born into. It was stamped on my heart in indelible ink, and I'd been foolish to believe I could belong anywhere else. It was like a member of my family: unpredictable, complicated, and indescribably beautiful.

"So, you're not going to try to be a weather girl?"

I laughed. "I wish I hadn't told you that. But no. I really love being a teacher. I never realized how much because I spent so much time wishing everything had been different." My gaze drifted to the shark's tooth hanging from his neck. I reached up and touched it. "Are you going to keep wearing this?"

He put his hand over mine. "I think so. At least for now."

"Good. It suits you. It'll always remind me of the first time we met."

"Not that I could ever forget." He leaned forward to kiss me, his lips warm and sweet.

The wren resumed her song to mark the closing of the day, reminding me that everything is a cycle. The ebb and flow of the tides, the seamless turn of the seasons, the migration of birds. The relationship between a parent and a child and the inevitability of growing older. The intractable connection to our siblings. I had wasted too many years telescoping myself into my future, envisioning a better place and a less complicated life than what I'd been given. When all I'd ever needed to feed my soul was right here in this place where the water and earth bleed into each other, waiting for the moon to call us home again.

★★★★★

# Acknowledgments

I'd like to thank the lovely staff at my local Wild Birds Unlimited store for not only helping me feed the wide variety of birds in my backyard, but also teaching me so much about birds and bird behavior. I also thank them for not acting judgy when I admit to having fifteen feeders.

I'd also like to thank the birds who populate those feeders and whose habits, mannerisms, and joyful songs are a constant source of wonder and happiness when I need it the most. They made the research for this book an immersive and fun experience.

I'd like to thank fellow authors Wendy Wax and Susan Crandall for being my first readers and constructive critiquers—I couldn't do this without you! And thank you to my husband, Tim, for not blinking an eye when I come home with yet another bird feeder and a trunk full of seed bags, or when discovering live worms in the refrigerator.

Last but not least, I'd like to thank my editor, Erika Imranyi, and my agent, Amy Berkower, for your insight and guidance while embarking on this new journey with Park Row Books. I can't wait to see what the future holds!